JIDDY VARDY
Full Sail

Praise for *Jiddy Vardy – Full Sail*

"You'll fall in love all over again with Jiddy and her Baytown world in this skilful, deeply layered final instalment.

"Ruth Estevez has provided her readers with a nuanced, exquisitely expressed, vivid conclusion to Jiddy's story. The tone of the novel is at times elegiac, at times joyous, always brimming with life and feeling as the writer draws together the threads of Jiddy's past, her new present and the turning point she has to confront in an extraordinary and moving novel.

"Just brilliant!"

– Jennifer Burkinshaw (*Igloo* and *Happiness Seeker*)

"As a trilogy, Jiddy Vardy is a remarkable work of fiction and one that deserves to be read widely. Jiddy herself is as good, well-rounded and just human a character as I've read and I love her. I'll never be able to forget her."

– Bob Stone (The Beat Trilogy, *Letting the Stars Go*; Owner of Write Blend Bookshop, Liverpool)

"...the descriptions are incredible. It's so obvious (Estevez) knows her characters and their world like the back of her hand and this writing is just fabulous."

– Louisa Reid (*Gloves Off, Wrecked, Activist, The Poet*)

JIDDY VARDY
Full Sail

Ruth Estevez

Beaten Track
www.beatentrackpublishing.com

Jiddy Vardy – Full Sail

Published 2023 by Beaten Track Publishing
Copyright © 2023 Ruth Estevez

The moral right of the author has been asserted.

Paperback ISBN: 978 1 78645 625 0
eBook ISBN: 978 1 78645 626 7

Cover Design: Debbie McGowan
Artwork: Enid Allen

Beaten Track Publishing,
Burscough, Lancashire.
www.beatentrackpublishing.com

PREVIOUSLY IN
THE JIDDY VARDY TRILOGY...

A summary of key events from the first two novels is included at the back of this book (p. 396). This contains significant spoilers for those who have not read those two books.

For maximum reading enjoying, we recommend you read the trilogy in order:

1. Jiddy Vardy
2. Jiddy Vardy – High Tide
3. Jiddy Vardy – Full Sail (this volume)

MAP OF
ROBIN HOOD'S BAY
AND SURROUNDS

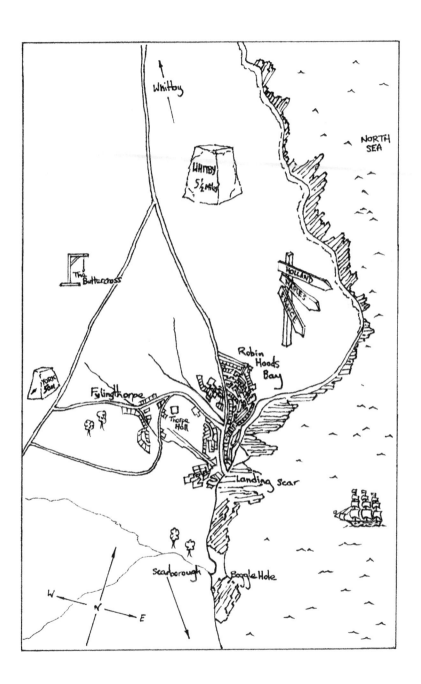

ACKNOWLEDGEMENTS

I'd like to go back to the beginning and remind myself and those who are interested that the Jiddy Vardy trilogy began by my finding a copy of Patricia Labistour's *A Rum Do!* on the shelves of the second-hand bookshop that once existed in the Old Chapel at the end of Chapel Street. Amongst the accounts of smuggling were a few pages about a real life, dark-haired female smuggler, Jiddy Vardy.

Thanks to Patricia and her books, which I'd highly recommend, how could I not bring this little-known but big personality to life and put her centre stage?

Place is very important in my novels. If coastal villages like Robin Hood's Bay hadn't been built into such remote gullies facing the North Sea, smuggling in this area might never have existed, and without smuggling, with all its repercussions, this trilogy would not exist.

Jiddy Vardy – Full Sail went through the in-depth story-editing skills of Manolya Oezbilen (Noly) at www.thEditors.com. I am so grateful I found this company on Twitter! I am honoured to now call Noly a friend as well as the editor that hauled my chapters into the story it has become. We will be working together again if all goes to plan!

Without the dynamo that is Debbie McGowan, MD of Beaten Track Publishing, books 2 & 3 in the trilogy would not be here. She tweaks, checks and hones. Thank you! Not only is Debbie an expert in all aspects of writing, she is also a creator of stunning book covers. I love her combination of a breathtaking painting by Enid Allen from the Robin Hood's Bay Art Group with an expressive close up of Jiddy's face. It is the perfect cover for the story's conclusion. With every book, Debbie astonishes me.

A little shout out here to the Robin Hood's Bay Art Group. Enid arranged our collaboration, and I am extremely grateful for her generosity. Enid, Pam, Trish and Sadie provided initial mock-ups, and Enid and Sadie, wonderfully finished covers which I will treasure always. Enid's landscape is incorporated into the final cover of *Full Sail*. Thank you to each of you – capturing the spirit of Robin Hood's Bay and Yorkshire in talent and open-heartedness.

Writers need early readers, and I thank Bob, Genevieve and Jennifer for freely giving their time and feedback, advice and suggestions. It has been ongoing and thoughtful.

Thanks to Noel for the maps in book 2 as well as 3. These act as a guide rather than offering historical and geographical accuracy so that visitors to Baytown today may feel they can walk in Jiddy's shoes. This is a work of fiction and not a historical document.

Books would not reach readers without bloggers, marketers and bookshops, so I want to thank in particular readers Erin (thepagesofmrsd) and Carole (The Reading Jackdaw) plus Joanna Pedley and the team from the Robin Hood's Bay Victorian Weekend committee. Also, Aberfeldy Watermill Bookshop, Book Corner, Saltburn, the Grove Bookshop, Ilkley, Helmsley Bookshop, The Higgledy Pig, RHB, The Stripey Badger, Grassington, Wave of Nostalgia, Haworth, Whitby Bookshop and Write Blend at Waterloo, Liverpool.

I also thank Elaine Bousfield, MD of ZunTold, who took a chance and published *Jiddy Vardy*, the first in the trilogy, and who arranged an audiobook of this title read by voice artist, Gill Mills.

This trilogy has been a journey, and along the way, I've forged many friendships. My publishers, editors, SCBWI writing group colleagues, booksellers and artists. And of course, my family, Noel, Genevieve and Miranda. Thank you.

Mum and Dad, I hope you're as proud as my dear sister Jane says you would be. x

CHAPTER ONE

London, England
1779

M aria Vardarelli sat cross-legged on the rug with a mound of jewellery in her lap. The weight of sparkling gems made her skirt sag. They'd weighed even heavier in the pockets of Gregory's jacket. She'd thought they'd drag her down to the bottom of the sea, but here she was. Even two weeks later, she could still see the bristle of the pirate's cheeks and smell the stale tobacco of his breath.

She wiped away a tear. The smell of brine and cold lingered. She looked down at the jewels and untangled a diamond bracelet. It glistened in sunbeams streaking through the window, making the bedroom dance with rainbows. Spreading an emerald necklace in front of her, she admired the intense green stones against the brown floorboards. As she raised a dazzling ruby brooch, she heard voices from the other side of the door. Footsteps halted in the corridor outside. Grabbing the necklace along with the rest of her treasure, she pushed them into the pockets of the officer's jacket she wore.

"Is she awake?"

Maria recognised John Ryethorpe's voice but not the strange lilt of a female who spoke next.

"I'm not keen to go in, sir," the woman said. "She doesn't like me."

A gentle tap made Maria scramble to her feet. She scurried to the window and stepped behind the drape. The door creaked open. The sound of one pair of heavy footsteps told her the woman had remained outside. Shoving her hands in her pockets and clutching the jewels tightly, she stepped into view. "What do you want?" Maria demanded, her words laden with her Neapolitan accent.

The door closed and John strolled towards her in his unhurried way. "We were worried," he said, plucking at the ripped shoulder of her jacket. "We need to get you out of this uniform." He rubbed his fingers, looking at them with disgust. "You may borrow some of my wife's clothes."

Maria glanced through the window at the blue sky. "When can I meet Gregory's parents?" she asked. "They are my family now he is dead, and they must meet me." John touched her shoulder, but shrugging him off, she reached the bed and held onto one of the corner posts. "You keep making excuses for them."

"Maria, they are grieving their son and they know nothing about you. Come downstairs. You must be hungry. It's past eleven o'clock."

"Tell them!" she shouted, making him flinch. "Tell them their son has a baby daughter!"

"Maria..."

"Tell them we planned to be married. Tell them I will marry their other son if that is what they want! Tell them I am here!" She pressed her face into the bed drapes. "Tell them," she mumbled into the thick cloth.

John strode to her side. "Let's get rid of this coat," he said. "Get you looking like a lady again. You want to look like a lady, don't you?"

Pushing him away and returning to the window, Maria shook her head, her dark hair tumbling in matted curls. John followed her and they stood side by side, looking at the velvet lawn and neat borders of clipped hedge.

Absentmindedly, John tapped the glass with one finger. "Catherine says you can stay here as long as you need before taking a ship home to Naples."

She turned sharply to face him. "I am never going back to Naples. I am going to find where the family of Gregory live."

John sighed. "Lord and Lady Hartshorn may not admit you."

Dragging a handful of jewels from her pocket, Maria held them out. "They will want to see these."

John's eyes widened. "Where did you get those?"

Shoving them back into her pocket, she faced the window again.

"Are they the old woman's? Did she give them to you? I thought she had family near Paris?"

The jewels dug their hard edges into Maria's palms. "They are mine now," she said.

"Maria, these are not any jewels. These are worth a great deal of money. You should return them to the lady's family." He paused, waiting for her to answer, but when she remained staring at the garden below, he shrugged. "We will talk about this later."

Maria swung around, jacket flaring, her grip on the gems tighter still. "They are all dead!" she shouted. "That pirate killed my baby. He killed Gregory and Madame Popineau—that's the old woman's, my *companion's* name. She died of fever as we set off from France. In the ship, leaving me alone! Everyone has gone and these jewels are all I have left!"

John reached out his hand. "I am here."

Her eyes sparkled dark. "Your wife does not want me in the house. She is worried you will fall in love with me. I see it in her face, and you have a son, and we are not the same blood." She pressed her lips together to hold in the upsurge of emotion. "Please ask Catherine if I may have one of her gowns. I want to look like a lady when I meet Lord and Lady Hartshorn."

John exhaled. "I am so sorry, Maria, but they can't meet you." He looked down, embarrassed to witness the pain on her face.

"How do you know?" she asked.

"I went to visit them, but they had already left the house for Yorkshire. They spend every summer in the north."

Her eyes brimmed with tears, and she blinked them away. "Then we must go back to Yorkshire."

John waited for a few moments. "Stay with us," he said. "You like little Samuel, and he likes you."

Dragging off Gregory's coat that she'd refused to discard ever since they'd emerged wet and battered from the North Sea, she threw it on the floor and, crouching, dragged diamonds, rubies, emeralds, and threads of pearls from the pockets. Glaring at him, her face a battleground of emotion, she fought to steady her voice. "If that is true, I cannot give these up," she said. "If these are as precious as you say, they are my fortune, and I need to know what they will buy me."

John knelt on the floor by her side. "Maria, they are not yours to sell. As I said, stay here, or if you really want, return home to your family."

"Gregory's family are not humane," she shouted, leaning on his arm as she struggled to her feet. "I am not a devil. I am me. I am a person. I have feelings. I have needs! Why do they shun me? It is not a crime to want to survive!" She sobbed, no longer able to hold in the surge of tears. "You will take me to meet his family," she said. "And they will see me!"

CHAPTER TWO

Robin Hood's Bay, England
Spring 1796 – Seventeen years later

Lines of rock reached their gnarled tentacles out to sea. Jiddy longed for the waves to cover them again yet feared the lick of water over the causeway and pounding depth of unbreathable grey.

She'd barely slept since clawing her way off the beach, wet and battered, and now she was back on the slipway, both hoping and dreading finding Samuel's corpse spewed onto the shingle. Either way, Deputy Staincliffe and the preventives would come searching for him when he didn't appear soon. And if, by some miracle, he was alive, what would Samuel do when he realised she was part of the smuggling ring that had left him for dead in the dock?

Baytowners would never understand why she'd even tried to save a captain of the Dragoons, and she couldn't bear the thought that her closest friend Annie might look at her in disbelief.

She shivered. One positive was people were staying away from the shore with its dangerous spring tides. She meandered over stones, jumping off the rocky, bladderwrack-strewn ledges onto sandy stretches, pacing to the water's edge and scrutinising the swell. She couldn't spy a jellyfish, never mind a dead body.

The tide had turned and already advanced, one surge at a time. She scuttled sideways as a wave reached further than the rest, soaking her boots and hem. Looking along the beach, she pulled her shawl tighter around her head before pressing along the shore, looking for the shape of a body, a piece of clothing, anything that might belong to Samuel.

She reassured herself there was little likelihood she would find him. After she, Betsie and Annie had removed their old friend Nellie from the gibbet, and Jiddy had taken the body out to sea, Nellie had never reappeared. Samuel had been swept away when that same sea had gushed up the causeway and swallowed his corpse, and in all likelihood, his body wouldn't reappear either. The difference was nobody cared about a dead Ashner lass's corpse, but plenty of people cared about the head of the Dragoons. Deputy Staincliffe was known for being tenacious. He needed a body to catch a culprit, and he would believe someone had done his leader in, and that culprit couldn't possibly be the high tide. As far as Jiddy was concerned, nobody, not Abe Storm nor Sandy Killock nor any other Baytowner must be punished.

She glanced towards the cave for storing contraband during a raid. She'd have to use all her strength to drag Captain Samuel Ryethorpe's corpse there if, by a hand of bad luck, he did wash up on the beach.

On top of that, and as pressing, Mrs. Farsyde would need to be told gently because the lady of Thorpe Hall wouldn't be able to hide her agony at Samuel having gone for good. Someone there was bound to guess this was the man she loved, whether it was from her outpouring of misplaced grief or when her baby was born blonde-haired and blue-eyed, the image of Samuel rather than Squire Farsyde.

Veering back along the beach, Jiddy shook her skirt. The damp folds clung together. In another hour or so, the light would begin to fade and she'd not see her own feet in the sand let alone a body.

The cliff loomed dark, topped by waving grass and bleating sheep. It was a lonely sound, and she couldn't get used to it, even though she'd heard it all her life. Turning again to take one last look at the sea, she almost wished she was on the other side of that huge expanse of water, warm, dry, and smelling the scents of a hot climate rather than having the cold weight of Samuel's death on her shoulders. If a ship had been anchored offshore, she'd have swum out to it and not looked back.

It was what she'd yearned for as a child. Another place. A place to belong when the other Bay children said she was odd and different and even some of the grown-ups had been suspicious of her tanned skin and jet-black eyes. Samuel's father, Lord Ryethorpe, had said she belonged in a place called Naples, but Jiddy couldn't understand. If she belonged in such a distant city, why had her mother come to England? Why would her mother have rejected

9

her family and the paradise of home for these unknown shores? Arriving here to the brutality of Captain Pinkney ransacking the ship she travelled on, to a freezing sea, near death on being thrown overboard, and then what? The female companion she'd travelled with had died; her lover, the father of her child, had drowned; she'd been severed from her family. The emporium hadn't sprung up overnight, so the time until it did must have been difficult.

Why had she stayed? If it had been her, Jiddy would have caught the next ship back to France and returned to Naples and the bosom of her family without a second thought. Yet her mother had gone to London with Lord Ryethorpe and stayed there. And Jiddy had grown up, the adopted child of an aging couple, in Robin Hood's Bay. She'd loved Thomas and Mary, and even cantankerous Rebecca, who'd been more an aunt than a neighbour, but now they all were dead. She took a deep breath. *Don't think about it.*

Trudging over the shingle, she could still make out gulls swooping in the dusk, landing on rocks, and taking on human shapes in the dull light. An evening breeze nipped colder, and she quickened her pace. Shadows altered the crevices in the cliff face, and deepening lines began to spread across the sand.

"There's no-one here," she repeated over and over, heading for the causeway and trying not to think about the creeping waves. She'd almost reached the slipway when she looked up and gasped.

A figure, standing at the edge of the dock, forced her to stop. She hadn't anticipated anyone being there in the fading daylight. She narrowed her eyes. It couldn't be Silas, crouched and crabby, or Abe, taking double the space of any other man. He and Sandy would be in hiding if Big Isaac had anything to do with it. The dull light made it difficult to tell who it could be. It was a man, that was certain, and a shapely figure made apparent by the taut jacket, long boots, and breeches.

Jiddy couldn't bring herself to move.

"Oh, stop being silly! Andrew, you barnpot, is that you?"

It would be typical of Annie's brother to want to scare her. She took a few strides. A red jacket caught the fading light and she stopped again. It wasn't possible. It couldn't be. She waited. The scaurs lurked underwater now, and the sea crept up the promontory. She'd be cut off if she didn't hurry. The figure moved. She recognised the gait. She knew that turn of head.

"Samuel!" She broke into a run, holding her skirt so she didn't trip.

She couldn't think about the consequences, only that by a freak of luck, he hadn't drowned. Balancing on the rocks, alert to avoid slipping, she jumped onto the causeway.

Her heart pounded, and a prickle of fear furred her neck. He stood so silent. Ominous. Was he angry? Injured? She waited for him to approach.

It was almost dark. His breath sounded heavy. She'd called to him, but now she didn't know what to say. Why didn't he speak? Why didn't he yell out for an arrest? Something. Dripping sounds from wet clothes. Waves lapping against the rocks. She shivered and pressed her nails into her palms.

The sea rippled darker. The beach was lost in night. Her own breath now fretted the cold air. She tensed at Samuel's silence. Foaming brine. She clenched her hands tighter. Stepped forward. She'd no reason to be afraid of Samuel. It wasn't her fault the high tide had swept them away.

Waves splashed the causeway. Clouds billowed dark, and the sea, a swamp of black, seethed where the beach had been. She shivered again, pushing straggles of hair off her face.

"Samuel?" she whispered.

The officer stepped forward. "Good evening," he said. Jiddy immediately recognised Deputy Staincliffe. "Why are you calling out that name, Miss Vardy?"

CHAPTER THREE

The fire threw out heat, powdering ash as the wood bedded down. Annie sat quietly, waiting for Jiddy to finish the broth she'd brought. Jiddy spooned the thin potato soup into her mouth. A flavour of fish petered through. Annie's mam wasn't an inventive cook, never one to add flavour from nettles or docks gathered from the woods, but its seeping warmth was welcome. She swallowed.

"Everyone's worried about you," Annie said. "It's all over Bay Captain Ryethorpe drowned last night and you were last one to see him."

Jiddy took another mouthful. She scraped the spoon around the rim, licked it clean and placed both spoon and dish on the floor. "Thank your mam," she said.

Annie leaned forward and grasped Jiddy's hands. "You're so cold!" She rubbed them between her own.

"Fire's warming me."

"What happened?"

There it was. The question she didn't want to answer. How had she survived? She'd survived and Samuel had drowned. His greening body rotted at the bottom of the North Sea, but she'd mistaken Deputy Staincliffe for him. Heading down to the beach and on her return to Fisherhead, walking along ginnels, and turning corners—

everywhere—images rose of people who had died. The traitor, Gobbit, skin stretched thin over bone, twisted limbs, blood in the dust, battered to the ground by the villagers' anger. Rebecca, dear, sharp-tongued Rebecca, surrounded by scuffed boots and her face draining to grey as blood wept out of the bullet hole. Nellie, poor Nellie, who'd only wanted to escape Bay, blackened on a gibbet and eyes pecked dry by ravens. Worst of all, Thomas, bashed on the head in a ginnel at daybreak. Her precious bag of salt, vomited on the path, stained pink with his life. Skin like candle wax. A gull flapping its wings. They'd blamed preventives. It wasn't sodding preventives, it was them. Baytowners had done the killing, and it was smuggling that had been the cause. Captain Pinkney killing her da, her real da, not Thomas, and the life she could have had. And now she was responsible for another death.

"I bumped into Deputy Staincliffe on beach," she said, wiping her hair from her face.

"Was he looking for Captain Ryethorpe?"

Jiddy shook her head and turned to look at the fire. "What are people saying?"

Annie shrugged. "It's going about Sandy and Abe said they saw Captain Ryethorpe in dock as they were heading to their beds."

"Did anyone see them?"

"Silas Biddick's told Andrew how Captain Ryethorpe forced his way into his cottage and held a pistol to his head and made him open the secret door between his place and here. Andrew told me. Asked me to ask you if it were true." Annie's grey eyes flickered to the floor.

Jiddy glanced over her shoulder at the panelling beside the fireplace as if Samuel would reappear at any moment. It looked innocent enough, pans hanging from hooks and the ladle in its usual place.

"Did he threaten you with his pistol?" Annie asked. "You must have been frightened."

Jiddy didn't want to go over what had happened. She wanted it never to have happened. If there were no other option, she wanted to sit and listen to the fire crumble and not talk.

Annie leaned closer. "Did he hurt you?"

Had he hurt her? Waves crashing. Slipway smothered in foam. The cold grip of water.

"He didn't know about high tide."

That said it all, didn't it? Fully aware of the sea's treachery, she'd almost died. He didn't know and he'd drowned, dragged out to sea, swept back, to be battered against the rocks and mulched and pulverised, and all because he wanted to punish her out of lost pride.

Annie sat back. Jiddy couldn't think of what else to say. Annie picked up the empty bowl and stood. The spoon clattered to the floor. Jiddy jumped and Annie swooped to retrieve it.

"I'm sorry. I'm a clumsy pup."

"I don't feel too good," Jiddy said, hoping Annie would take the hint and leave with the bowl and spoon and all her questions.

The fire belched. Annie's noisy breath filled the room.

"Do you want me to stay with you tonight?"

Annie would tuck her in bed. Make her hot drinks. Bring supplies to prepare broth. Maybe add flavouring. She'd act as a shield against other visitors. Jiddy might never have to leave Fisherhead and walk along ginnels and climb steps and talk to anyone ever again.

"If you want."

"Are you saying yes?"

Tears beaded Jiddy's eyelashes and Annie fell to her knees, clasping her friend's hands. "Cry all you want," she said. "It's about time. It must have been frightening. You must have thought you'd drown and be dead. I wouldn't have survived. You're so strong, you're a giant. You're a—"

"No," Jiddy cut in. "I were lucky."

Words choked her. They crammed in her chest, and she couldn't let them. If she started crying, she'd never stop. She'd be like King's Beck in full flood. She bent her head, hair falling over her cheeks. Annie swept the thick curls back behind her neck and over her shoulders, leaving Jiddy's face exposed. Jiddy couldn't bear it. She stood, stumbling as her foot caught.

"Mam says a spot of brandy does wonders for shock," said Annie.

Jiddy laughed. An explosion. "So did Mary!" Relieved for the distraction, she looked at the fireside cupboard. "D'you think Captain Pinkney left a secret store behind?"

It didn't take long to find a stone flacon and fill two cups. They sat by the stoked fire with darkness blanketing the closed shutters. The flickering firelight and warming brandy lured them into a cocoon, far away from the twisted ginnels and dank flights of steps, from twitching curtains and cruel tongues. The two of them sipped more brandy than they'd ever tasted in their lives. They giggled over childhood mishaps and escapades. Annie even found the courage to ask about Jiddy's time in London and what had made Samuel so angry.

"Was he right mean to you?" she asked.

Jiddy took another gulp and shook her head. The brandy tasted sweet and bitter at the same time. The fire cast dancing shapes along the walls. The dishes of food remained on the table. Baytowners could be kind, though outsiders wouldn't find it. Gracie, Dottie, Annie, and even Helen Drake had been kind and brought food. Captain Pinkney, who she'd once tried to shoot, had given her the ultimate gift of a home. Now she drank his brandy by the hearth, *her* hearth, with her closest friend, deep in her own thoughts, mouth resting on the edge of her cup, her questions forgotten.

Samuel had been as kind as the others in the beginning. Kinder, because he'd had the time and the means to be so. Strange how saying 'no' brought about such anger and revenge. Jonas's bitter eyes and set mouth flashed in her head.

"Did I tell you me and Captain Ryethorpe kissed?"

The cup in Annie's hands tipped. "Captain Ryethorpe kissed you? I don't believe you!"

"Why wouldn't he kiss me? He's a man, isn't he?"

Annie flushed. "Oh, my goodness, you didn't? I mean, why did you let him?"

Jiddy took another sip. Annie clutched her cup.

"Did you like him?" Annie asked.

"I'm seventeen!" Jiddy burst out. "I'm supposed to have kissed a couple of lads by this age, aren't I? Couldn't go to my grave only kissing Jonas."

"But you love kissing Jonas!"

Samuel certainly hadn't kissed like Jonas. No-one kissed like Jonas.

"Don't you remember Mary telling us she had a choice between two sweethearts, and she had to kiss them both because the kiss would tell her who to spend her life with? If it isn't right, the lad isn't right. Don't you remember?"

"Yes, but you said Jonas's kisses were perfect. You said they made you want to do all sorts of things with him." Annie slid to the floor and sat close to Jiddy. Her pale eyes shone. "What were it like kissing a gentleman like Captain Ryethorpe?"

"Let's call him Samuel," Jiddy said, "I hate those formal names."

"Samuel." Annie tested saying his name. "No, I can't call him Samuel. Don't seem proper."

Jiddy slumped sideways. "Being a captain is only a title, you can be Captain Cuddler and I can be Captain Contraband. We can all have titles."

Annie giggled. "Captain Cuddler!" She wrapped her arms around herself and swayed before glancing up. "But he's not on same side as us. He's like, enemy?"

Jiddy lowered her cup. Under all the fancy clothes and rich food and attention he'd given her, she'd forgotten he was the enemy. Annie hadn't. Annie was a solid Baytowner. She didn't forget whose side you were on. "I flirt with Dragoons to get information, don't I? Nobody complains about my flirting."

Annie studied the fire's red caverns and charred woods. "Is that why Jonas went to France?"

Jonas had seen her in Samuel's arms in the chapel. It seemed a lifetime ago. She'd been to London and back and he'd never mentioned it. She and Jonas had kissed themselves raw plenty of times after, but he'd still gone to France. It made her question if Jonas suspected more had happened between her and Samuel that he couldn't forgive. Seemed men held grudges in silence.

"Jonas went to France because he wants to be a soldier," she said. "Or because he's a dullard and doesn't appreciate the way I kiss." She smiled, hoping Annie would think it genuine.

"Best not tell Betsie," Annie said. "She'll say you're no different from Nellie and only want to get away from Bay and all of us. Nellie were hung for trying to get away."

"Nellie informed on folk, and I'd never, ever do that."

"But you both kissed the enemy."

There it was again, the feeling she and Nellie were almost the same. And now Annie saw it too.

"It's different," Jiddy said.

"Betsie won't think so."

"It is different," she snapped. "I were on my own in London. Nellie were here, surrounded by family and friends and everyone who knew her. I didn't know anyone. It were like Robin Hood's Bay didn't exist and I were a lady and him a gentleman, and it were like a dream. He were kind, when no-one else were. Nellie'd turned everyone against me. You remember? Folk were going to stone me to death? Mary said to go. She understood. Why can't you?"

She rose to her feet. She'd not felt this agitated since she was a little girl stamping her feet up the front steps of Sunny Place after falling out with Nellie.

"I don't know why I'm explaining," she went on. "Men kiss lasses all time and no-one says a word, and I kiss one person other than Jonas and I'm made to feel like I've sold my soul to devil."

Tears welled in Annie's eyes. "I don't think you have. You've every right to do what you want…"

"You weren't there! You don't know."

"I only said don't tell Betsie."

Annie's face, flushed by brandy, her emotions, and the heat of the fire, made her look five years old. How could she understand when all she'd seen was the Bay? Annie didn't know anyone but Bay people. She'd never come across the temptation of wealth. That was it. The kindness of wealth, and Jiddy had grasped it with all her long, greedy fingers.

"I don't see what all fuss is about," Jiddy said. "I've all these feelings in here." She clutched her stomach. "Samuel were handsome and charming, and Jonas and I weren't married. It's natural I'll have my eye on more than one lad, and there's nowt wrong with that."

She looked at Annie again, who stood, twisting her hands.

"I guess there's nothing wrong," Annie said. "If you don't love Jonas."

Jiddy kicked the fire irons and they crashed over the hearth. "It's because I love him too much all this has happened."

Annie shuffled forward and put her arms around her taller friend.

"I didn't want to leave Bay, I were forced to!" Jiddy insisted. "And I kissed Samuel because, well, I am ashamed of it, but I kissed him to find out, and that's not wrong. It were best thing to do. Mary said so!"

Pushing back Jiddy's hair, Annie smiled. "'Course it were. You're right, it's what Mary told us all to do."

"My mistake were not realising how soft men are. You can't just kiss them. They think it means more, and they get all uppity if a lass says no to them."

"Especially captains."

"Especially them not used to hearing no from a lass, and that's most men from what I can make out."

Annie's eyes widened. "Not Jonas, though."

"Jonas is worst because he won't listen to me, and he knows I love him! He doesn't reason, never has. He tells you what to do and think, and he goes on and on about his ideas, but when it comes to listening to me and my ideas, oh no. I've worked it out, Annie. He's always been like that. Stubborn as a mule, and he'll never change! He's worst one of them all."

Annie's mouth fell open. Jiddy cuffed her arm.

"Don't look glum, it isn't so bad. We're both here. Lasses together." She couldn't bring herself to admit, either silently or aloud, that Jonas might hate her. That was the crux of it and the reason she didn't want to talk about him. Jiddy stroked Annie's head. "For all he is, Annie," she soothed, "I didn't want Captain Ryethorpe to die."

"I know."

"I didn't plan it, I ran…"

"And he followed."

She grabbed Annie's hands, squeezing tight. "I didn't mean to end up in dock."

"He didn't know about causeway."

"Or spring tides."

Annie's eyes filled with tears. "Or how high sea comes up street?"

"I tried. I caught his hand."

"You held his hand?"

"Until sea got me." Releasing Annie's grip, she pushed back her hair. "I never wanted him dead, Annie."

"I know you didn't."

"I hate sea."

They remained silent for a few moments.

"No, you don't," Annie said.

"Yes, I do. I hate North Sea and I don't care if I never see it again!"

Annie stared as she always did when she didn't know what to say. The fire made reassuring snaps. It broke the tension and they both laughed. When they stopped laughing, Jiddy wandered to the fireplace.

"I don't hate sea," she muttered, "and I'm going to make type of school I want to, so other lasses don't kiss wrong lad and mess up," she said. "I'm going to give lasses another choice to scrubbing fish and mending nets. Folks are heading to towns now. There's more to raw knuckles and slapping grease on your arms so your skin don't crack."

"Mills don't sound too grand," said Annie. "I've heard terrible tales."

"It's about having a skill," said Jiddy. "If I teach lasses a skill, they won't be going to no mill, but they'll be making gowns and stitching shirts and jackets and not be relying on anyone."

She crouched by the fire as if she'd noticed it needed her attention. Grasping the poker, she prodded hard. A lump of wood shifted, and ash powdered down.

"What about kissing and cuddling?" asked Annie.

"Only gets you into trouble." She watched the embers glow smaller and smaller.

"I still think girls'll be searching for a bit of romance wherever they are," Annie said, stretching her arms above her head and yawning.

"Why don't you go to bed? I have a spare room, you know."

Annie yawned again. "All right, but I'll not be dreaming of making dresses and stitching a man's jacket, and I know you won't either."

"What will we be dreaming of if not finding our own way, Miss Annie Briggs?"

Annie smiled and dragged herself up the stairs, leaving Jiddy by the fire where, closing her eyes, she immediately fell asleep and dreamt about being eight years old again and playing on the beach with Jonas.

CHAPTER FOUR

Jiddy woke during the night. She hauled herself to bed and, lying next to Annie, listened to her friend's heavy breaths. Every noise sounded louder than it usually did. Wood cracking, dogs barking, the scratch of a gull's feet on the roof, even ash crumbling in the fire downstairs. The next morning, nerves raw, she flinched at sounds that normally she'd treat as background babble, and she wrapped in on herself, shawl taut around her head, shoulders hunched.

She could find no sanctuary, even at Fisherhead. Annie and Betsie, bustled in and out as if they lived there, stoking the fire, filling a pan, chattering, laughing, noise, noise.

Out in the ginnels and lanes, buildings hemmed her in, bairns whined, dogs yelped, nets tangled, beating, slapping, the suffocating stench of fish and mould and the sight of pinched eyes and red, flaking knuckles. No sanctuary anywhere.

Straining up the bank, she half-wished the sea had taken her as well as Samuel. It would be quiet on the seabed. The weight of water would be her cocoon, her protection—a place where she could sleep.

Spring hid behind winter gloom, but even knowing lambs would soon be frolicking in the fields and chicks scrabbling in the yard, Meadow Bank Farm no longer offered friendship without Jonas's banter and embraces. She pushed the thought of him aside and pulled her shawl tighter still.

At the top of the hill, she took deep breaths and, turning around, looked back over the mizzle of rooftops. Smoke teased from chimneys. A general murmur of lives simmered. The air smelt cleaner than in the ginnels, but the silver sky shivered cold.

Heading towards the Buttercross, she didn't change her pace. If anyone had spoken to her, she wouldn't have been capable of responding. She couldn't even have looked them in the eye.

Trees replaced the network of houses, and the track spread wider for carts and carriages. Branches, marked by tiny green kisses, stood out mean and sharp against the sky.

She walked on, meandering over the moor, until she saw Thorpe Hall's chimneys standing out amongst the budding trees. Drab stone and an empty drive gave no welcome. Windows with no reflection sapped the light. Out of sight, horses' hooves clipped the ground and dogs grizzled while chains rattled. She knocked on the side door. Her knuckles stung. It didn't matter who opened it. When it swung open, she stepped inside.

"Is squire in?" she asked.

Voices from the kitchens. "Well, how do to you too, Jiddy! Want me to take you straight in?" said Violet Ashner with her head cocked to one side and arms folded across her skinny chest.

Jiddy clenched her jaw. "Sorry. It's all right, I know way," she said, leaving the younger girl to stare after her.

Standing on the rug, fire blazing, Jiddy shivered. The cold that gripped her body created a barrier to the heat and she couldn't shift it. The spit of damp wood. The crackle of flames, flickering, fluttering. The smell of tobacco and wet coal. She caught the squire observing her.

"Mrs. Farsyde is still in her chamber," he said. "Does she expect you?"

She couldn't help herself, what with the bright flames in the fireplace and the familiarity of the squire's voice and the sanctuary of his study. Her body gave way, and she sank, knees bending, skirt rumpling, hands touching the solid floor.

He strode to her side, shoe buckles cold against her fingers. If only she could sleep and wake the next day to find none of this had happened. *Let me stay here, let me sink further,* but instead, a hand grasped her arm and another hand, her elbow.

"Help!" he shouted. "Robert!" He heaved Jiddy to her feet. "Let's get you sitting in a chair. Robert!" She held his arm, pressing her feet hard into the floor to stand. "Do you feel faint?"

Stretching out a hand, she took several steps and reached a chair. Releasing her, Squire Farsyde hurried to the door and pulled it wide. She couldn't stop shaking, her whole body trembled, even her teeth chattered, and she closed her eyes, pressing in the tears swelling under her lids.

"Robert!"

Jiddy sat, hands clasped to stop them shaking while tea was brought and set on a table.

It could have been Robert who brought it, or Violet, or both. The silver grey of the sky pooled in her eyes, and she couldn't see the room in its true colours. She couldn't hear what people were saying. Maybe the sea had seeped into her body while she fought for her life in the waves, and she viewed the room through brine and heard noises through the gloop of an ocean's depths.

Someone wrapped her hands around a cup. A flounce of dress appeared. Noises became more distinct. Mrs. Farsyde spoke, and Squire Farsyde answered. Remembering why she'd come to the hall, Jiddy stood. The cup fell, making a dull thud on the rug. Faces turned to look. She'd come to the hall for a reason, and she had to deliver the news. She had to say the words out loud. She opened her mouth and a voice, *her* voice, came out. "Captain Ryethorpe's dead."

A scream brought the two figures into focus. Squire Farsyde, stern, shaking his head. Mrs. Farsyde, face white, hands clasped to her cheeks, her mouth wrenched in horror.

CHAPTER FIVE

Mrs. Farsyde sprawled on the settee, clutching her belly. Standing in the doorway, the squire shouted orders to anyone within earshot. Jiddy fell to her knees at her mistress's side and reached for her hand. "I didn't mean to give you shock," she said, holding back her tears.

"Where have you gone?!" Footsteps, fast-paced, the squire marched across the room and appeared beside the settee, breathing fast and heavy. So much noise. "We need to get Mrs. Farsyde back upstairs. Bed rest, doctor said, nothing but bed rest."

"Captain Ryethorpe cannot be dead!" Mrs. Farsyde sat, pulling her hand free from Jiddy's grasp.

Jiddy reached out for her again. "Yes, yes, it's a shock, I know. I'm sorry to break news of a death like this." She glanced at the doorway. "Maybe you'd be better upstairs?"

"He was here the day before yesterday..." Mrs. Farsyde's words petered out as she tried to remember. "What happened? Did this happen last night?"

"Night before," said Jiddy, panicking at the show of grief from her mistress. "I really feel you'd be best upstairs, ma'am. Let me help you?"

Tears rolled down Mrs. Farsyde's cheeks and she brushed Jiddy's hand away. "Why is he dead? How? Explain!"

"My dear," the squire soothed, "there is no need for you to be so distraught."

"He was our guest." She craned her neck to face her husband. "How could you let this happen? You're supposed to take good care of our guests."

"I can't be responsible for everyone. Lord Ryethorpe lodged at Musgrave's."

"He lodged with us first! He was one of us, not an ordinary soldier."

The squire recoiled at the masked accusation, and Jiddy, scrambling to her feet, stood between them. "It were high tide other night, and it came right into dock," she said. "It were no-one's fault. Tide swept him away."

Mrs. Farsyde grasped Jiddy's hand again, making her jump. "You were there when it took him?"

Caught in the glare of her mistress's eyes and vice-like fingers, she nodded.

The squire strode to the door again, pushing the bemused servants away. "Come back when I call." He slammed the door closed. "Quiet, quiet," he said. "If the captain died the night before last, why have you waited a whole day and another night to tell me? Is there more to this than you're saying?"

Mrs. Farsyde used Jiddy's shoulder to stand up, leaning on her, spoke before Jiddy had a chance to reply. "Maybe it wasn't him. He could ride up at any moment. He visits you most days, and I thought I heard horse's hooves..." She ambled to the window and looked out.

"I'm afraid it was Captain Ryethorpe," said Jiddy, addressing the squire more quietly. "Sea came and swept us off our feet. I barely survived myself, but I got to beach, and I were exhausted. I went home and passed out and slept right through. When I woke, Annie were round, and I were in shock I suppose. I didn't want to be out... I'm sorry I didn't come straight to let you know. Has no-one else been to see you?"

"No. Should they?"

She shook her head; she couldn't bring Sandy and Abe into it if Squire Farsyde hadn't been told of their presence during the night.

"But why were you there?" he asked equally quietly and with one eye on his wife's back, then, after a moment, "It doesn't matter. If no-one saw you, it can only be assumed what's happened to the captain."

"Silas knows." Jiddy sighed. "And Annie's brother Andrew suspects."

Squire Farsyde nodded, eyes still on his wife. "Well, the good news is, I've not heard anything from anyone else at present. Deputy Staincliffe hasn't called, none of the Bay men have been here, and there's been no tittle-tattle in the kitchen. You've not heard any gossip, have you?" He addressed his wife, who, clutching a handkerchief and turning to face them, shook her head.

"Seems we have luck on our side," the squire continued. "No-one has picked up on this yet. Shows no-one saw or has talked."

"I did go on beach to make sure he'd not been washed up, and there's no sign of him," Jiddy said, glancing in Mrs. Farsyde's direction; she appeared not to have heard. "He didn't realise how waves can sweep you off your feet. He must be far out by now, otherwise tide would have swept him back in."

With a cry of anguish, Mrs. Farsyde looked around. "What do you mean?"

The squire joined his wife by the window and took her arm. "Spring tides are dangerous, my dear. It seems the captain did not know how dangerous. Now, let's get you—"

"No, I won't go to my room!"

"This is serious," he said to Jiddy. "Deputy Staincliffe will be putting out an inquiry any time now if the captain has vanished. You really didn't need to be involved. I don't understand why you think you needed to be."

Jiddy shrugged. "As I said, Silas and Andrew know."

He nodded. "Best be prepared. Staincliffe will ask why you were there if he gets a single whiff of this."

Both the Farsydes looked expectantly at her.

"I were on my way home."

After a moment, the squire slid an arm around his wife to lead her away to her room. "It's time you were resting, my dear." Mrs. Farsyde shook her head, pulling back and twisting around, but the squire held her firm. "I'll make sure you're informed. Any news and I will send Jiddy or Violet to tell you."

"No, I want to know why Jiddy was with Captain Ryethorpe!"

Jiddy searched for a reason that would hurt neither of them, but the squire wasn't engaging with his wife's question. He opened the door and, still holding his wife, called out, "Violet?"

The girl appeared quickly, as though she'd been waiting nearby.

Mrs. Farsyde took Violet's arm and looked over her shoulder at Jiddy. "You will come straight away when you have news?"

Jiddy bobbed. "Of course, ma'am."

Once Squire Farsyde closed the door and they heard Mrs. Farsyde and Violet ascend the stairs, he returned to the fireplace. "You need to tell me everything."

Jiddy looked to the door before meeting the squire's gaze, considering how much he should be told. "I can't tell Deputy Staincliffe what really happened."

The squire let out a long breath. "Right. Well, I agree, but I need to know who to warn."

"It weren't quite an accident."

"I gather it wasn't," he said, resting one foot on the fender.

"I tried to save him, not kill him." Jiddy moved to the window, looking out as Mrs. Farsyde had done. "He didn't believe how sea can flood dock."

The squire raised his hand. "It's all right, I don't need details, but I do need to know why you and the captain were in the dock at the same time."

33

"I can't tell you."

He stepped forward, his face reddening. "This is me you're talking to. You came here for a reason, so out with it."

"It won't look good," she insisted.

"We'll find something else to tell Staincliffe."

Sinking into a chair, Jiddy clutched her hands together. "I saw Deputy Staincliffe yesterday when I were looking for Captain Ryethorpe's body on beach, in case it had washed up."

"And?"

"And I told him I were looking for Mrs. Grainger's lad, Samuel, but I wasn't looking for him."

"I didn't know she had a Samuel."

"She hasn't, but I were shouting Samuel so I had to think of some explanation! Luckily, three of Storm lads turned up, so I pretended that one of them were him. I made sure they didn't say anything."

Squire Farsyde clicked his tongue. "This isn't good."

"It's worse. Abe and Sandy were there other night as well. It's only a matter of time before that gets to Deputy Staincliffe's ears."

"The three of you did this?"

"No! Well, yes! It were all a muddle!" she said, raising her head. "Captain Ryethorpe had come to Fisherhead. He were still angry with me about inventing smugglers' names and making him look a fool, and he were on his way out door when Abe and Sandy showed. Abe, could have been Sandy, one of them knocked him out, and we all ended up in dock. I followed them. They didn't see me."

"What happened in the dock with Abe and Sandy?"

Jiddy avoided his eyes. "Causeway were completely underwater," she said in a low voice, "and waves were lapping higher. Captain were unconscious, and Abe and Sandy left him on ground and headed up King Street, and, well, I couldn't leave captain, could I? He did come round, and I got him on his feet, but he wouldn't understand we had to get out of dock and a massive whoosh of water swept in."

"I'm not going to ask exactly why the captain came to Fisherhead late in the evening rather than in daytime, but did anyone else see him there?"

She shook her head.

"Did anyone see Abe or Sandy?"

"There wasn't a soul out," she said. He scrutinised her face, and she held his gaze. "I'm telling truth."

"Right," he finally muttered after studying her for several moments. "I'll have to tell Deputy Staincliffe something feasible before they tear the Bay apart looking for the captain."

Jiddy nodded again. "I've seen soldiers about."

"Of course, they're bound to be. Fine then, he'll want to talk to you in more depth. I doubt he believed you were looking for a little lad. I thought you were cleverer than this." He studied her again, spreading his hands when she didn't respond. "Well? What reason did you give?"

Jiddy looked down at the rug. "I didn't need to say a word."

The fact that three of Abe Storm's grandchildren had appeared in the dock, shouting and chasing each other, and she'd run and grabbed the eldest, yanking him to her side and marching so fast his little brothers had had to follow must have convinced Staincliffe. She couldn't know for certain if he believed young John Storm was the Samuel she'd said she was looking for, but she'd never been so happy to see those little lads running round Bay when they should have been in bed.

"All right," the squire said. "If there is a problem, we'll soon know about it. He'll probably want to speak to you this afternoon, so stay in the house. And you were passing through the dock, nothing more. No mention of Ryethorpe being at Fisherhead or any nonsense of the sort. Not a peep about Abe and Sandy, I'll be talking to them myself."

"I wouldn't, I'd never—"

"I know, but we must check we all have the same story to tell. You were passing through the dock...why?"

Jiddy's mind drew a blank. Why on earth would she be walking through the dock after dark? Where could she have been and why?

"What time was it?" he asked.

"I can't involve anyone else and risk getting them in trouble," she said, folding her arms.

"How late was it?"

"I can't say I were visiting anyone. That would drop them right in it."

The squire walked to his desk and opened a drawer, rifling inside. "Have you seen anyone today?"

"Only Annie Briggs."

"In God's name! You haven't told her anything, have you?"

"She won't say a word."

He hit his hand on the desktop. "Can you trust her?"

"I've known Annie all my life!"

"But can you trust her?"

"There are only two people I trust completely, and Annie is one of them," Jiddy said, rising to her feet.

He slammed shut the drawer. "But she knows Captain Ryethorpe drowned?"

"Yes." Jiddy paused. "And I think Silas Biddick and Andrew Briggs know about captain being at Fisherhead as well."

The squire rubbed his chin. "It's getting messy. We'll have to say it as it is. You'd been—"

"It had gone dark," Jiddy interrupted. "Annie and Betsie had left, and Captain Ryethorpe came out of the hidden passage which comes from beach and links to next door. They didn't see him."

Again, the squire looked as if he was going to ask a question before he changed tack. "You were doing an errand for me," he said. "You were to ask the midwife to call to the hall in the morning to tend to Mrs. Farsyde, but on the way, you heard a shout from the dock."

"Mrs. Grainger lives off Sunnyside. I'd go straight there from Fisherhead."

"You came from the hall, so you went down Main Street."

"Betsie and Annie left me at Fisherhead," Jiddy corrected. "They'd wonder how I got a message from you, and saying I'd forgotten wouldn't wash."

He ran his hands through his greying hair.

"I know!" She raised her finger. "I were taking a pie for Grace! They're always short, and I'd been given so much by neighbours. I were on way when I heard a shout."

"Exactly! You drop the plate, the whole lot is washed out to sea!" He walked to the door and yanked it open. "Robert!" he shouted.

The lad rapidly appeared, but the squire continued to bellow. "Get my horse saddled and you..." He turned to Jiddy. "You go upstairs and tell my wife only about the pie, the sea and how nobody could have saved Captain Ryethorpe."

CHAPTER SIX

T he weather had both Baytowners and preventives in mind when it swept inland to coat the village in a fine mist. Relieved the sea fret meant people stayed indoors, Jiddy tramped back to Fisherhead, soon drenched by the light rain. She wished she'd known how to comfort the distraught Mrs. Farsyde, who had only ceased crying by falling, exhausted, asleep.

Once home, Jiddy knelt by the fire, rubbing her wet stockings with a dry cloth. When Annie and Betsie arrived, bustling noisily through the door, she didn't even raise her head.

"I hate this drizzle," declared Betsie, dragging off her hood, while Annie collapsed into the chair next to Jiddy.

"So, what did squire say?" asked Annie, leaning closer.

"'Bout what?" said Betsie, slumping into the opposite chair.

Jiddy swung the kettle over the fire. "I went to tell him about Captain Ryethorpe drowning, Betsie," she said, sinking into the chair, "so he's prepared when Deputy Staincliffe asks him what he knows."

"Not much to say if you ask me, if sea got him," said Betsie, holding out her hand. "Can I borrow your rag?"

Jiddy handed over the cloth without looking away from the fire.

"Did it go all right?" Annie pressed.

Jiddy shrugged, remembering how Mrs. Farsyde had cried when she told her the news. "I told squire I were taking a pie to Gracie when I saw Captain Ryethorpe in dock. Squire says Staincliffe will question me about it." She shrugged again, glancing at Betsie. "You're right. Not much to say. Sea swept in, and nothing could be done."

Betsie pulled a face and started telling Annie how she'd bumped into Annie's brother, Andrew, and what an idiot he could be. Relieved not to be questioned further, Jiddy gathered cups for their tea and jumped, as did the others, when a sudden gust of wind threw a battering of rain at the window.

"Good we're all here now," said Annie. "I never thought Captain Pinkney's cottage would be this cosy."

"You're daft in head," said Betsie. "Anywhere out of weather is cosy."

Betsie looked at Jiddy, expecting her to say something, but Jiddy had fetched a basket and was giving it all her attention as she placed it on the table.

"What'll we do all afternoon?" Annie said.

"Drink tea?" Betsie suggested.

Jiddy took out threads and a pin cushion spiked with needles from the open basket. "I thought we could start proper plans for school. I've worked it out."

"Ooh, yes!" exclaimed Annie.

Jiddy lifted a small cotton nightgown out of the basket.

"Where've you got that from?" asked Betsie.

"Mrs. Farsyde's baby needs clothes and I've been making them for months. That's something we could teach younger lasses. This one still needs a fastener."

Standing, Betsie picked up a pot warming on the fire shelf and spooned in loose leaves from a tin she took from the mantel top. "Thought there'd be stashes of baby clothes all perfect at hall," she said.

"Mrs. Farsyde gives them away," said Jiddy. "She can't bear to keep them after, well, when they're no longer needed."

"All right, if you've got money coming out of your pockets so you can give clothes away," muttered Betsie, ambling over to the table.

"Keeps me in employment, so I'm not complaining. Could keep more of us busy if we can find out if other ladies in area need baby clothes too."

"I liked them afternoons at Sunny Place, sitting around table, sewing," said Annie, joining them. "I miss it." She reached into the basket and took out a small sheet. "Shall I hem this?"

Jiddy nodded and pushed the pin cushion towards her.

"Nellie's not here, so it's not exactly sewing all nostalgic like, for Sunny Place," said Betsie.

"Mary's not here either," said Jiddy. "Or Rebecca."

This time, Annie and Betsie exchanged looks while Jiddy rummaged in the basket, throwing whatever came to hand onto the table.

"D'you remember when we had to hem all them squares and darn petticoats and embroider cloths to take to Thorpe Hall for Mrs. Farsyde to choose one of us to sew for her?" said Annie. "I thought I'd die of fright waiting for her to come into room and inspect our work."

"You snitched Jiddy's pile of sewing and managed to stay alive." Betsie laughed, nudging her arm.

"Oh why do you have to remember that?" Annie groaned, covering her face with both hands.

"It's all right, Annie," Jiddy said. "It sorted itself out."

"Yes, you got job," said Betsie, dragging the basket towards her and taking out a pinned garment.

"There's a shirt to mend," said Jiddy. "Would you mind darning it?"

They sat in silence, cups of tea within reach, pulling thread in and out. The fire spat as drops of rain fell down the chimney, and the wind gusted.

"So, school," began Jiddy.

"Ow!" Betsie sucked her finger.

"Least you pricked yourself," said Annie. "Nellie were always stabbing me with her needle."

"And Jiddy stabbed Nellie!" Betsie retaliated.

"So Nellie knew how much it hurt!" Annie said. "Nellie were mean."

"She had her reasons," argued Betsie. "You were lording it over us, Jiddy, if you remember right."

Jiddy looked up from the line of fine stiches she had made. "I don't remember. We were only at my house because Mary offered to teach us, and Nellie's ma didn't."

"There weren't space at Nellie's, and you pushed yourself in with Jonas. He were Nellie's friend first," said Betsie.

"If you're going to drag Jonas into it, that were up to him, not me." Aware she'd snapped, Jiddy looked back at the white cotton gown. "We could do same as we did at Sunny Place here, you know. I'd rather talk about sewing."

"Do what? Stab each other?" said Betsie, needle raised.

"Have a sewing group."

Annie shuffled in her seat. "I've told you. I'd do this every week."

"Us three hardly make a group. It were a group when Nellie were here." Betsie pushed the needle through the shirt cuff.

"I were thinking more a school. Annie's asking her sisters, and you could ask yours, Betsie, and their friends. We could fit a fair few along the bench, or we could do different days with different lasses. Any of the littlies in Bay want to come?"

"I'm sure they will." Annie nodded her chin for emphasis.

Betsie laughed. "They can sew at home. Don't need to sit here and learn. Their mammies teach them. You've got so up yourself since you've worked at hall, Jiddy Vardy."

"Stop it, Betsie!" Annie chided. "What's wrong with you today?"

Betsie bent her head and attended to pulling the needle through the cloth in her hand.

Jiddy sighed. "I got job at hall because Mary taught me to sew. I thought we could help other lasses get jobs instead of having to sort lobster pots or, heaven forbid, get a job in them dreadful alum mines."

Annie shrugged. "We can all darn and hem. It's all we need to do."

Betsie put down the shirt and folded her arms. "Or we could get married," she said.

Jiddy laughed. "Really, Betsie? You want to be wed?"

"I don't see what's so funny about that." Betsie pushed the shirt across the table and, gathering her shawl, headed for the door. "As I know all I need to know about sewing, I'm heading off. I'd rather talk to your brother, Annie, than you two right now."

"Betsie!" Jiddy called after her. "Sit back down and finish your tea!"

"You're needed here!" added Annie.

Betsie pulled her shawl tight around her head and stuck out her tongue at them. "Three old maids sewing dreams around a table? Not for me, thank you very much!"

A gust of wind wafted their skirts and sent the shirt tumbling over the table. Rain splattered across the stone flags.

Hurrying to the door, Jiddy looked out. The sound of Betsie's clogs clomping on the path faded amongst the lashings of rain.

"She's going to get soaked," said Annie.

Jiddy closed the door against the weather and peered out the window. "She's always going to think if I hadn't come to Bay, Nellie and Jonas would be together and probably James and she would be too, and everyone would be living happy as skylarks."

"She misses Nellie. She thinks we're closest and she's jealous."

Jiddy traced a finger over the windowpane. "I don't think Betsie realises even if Nellie were still alive, she probably wouldn't have stayed in Bay."

Annie nudged her friend so they could both look at the rain-streaked view.

"One thing Nellie and me had in common," said Jiddy, "we both wanted to know more about world out there."

"Do you still wonder about place your mam came from?" said Annie.

Jiddy splayed her palm on the cold glass. "Sometimes."

CHAPTER SEVEN

Deputy Staincliffe expected the squire to lead the conversation, but he quickly realised that wasn't going to happen. He also realised he had been rash. Interrogations should not occur anywhere but on Dragoon or preventive territory, and a local squire's study put him, the outsider, at a disadvantage.

Domestic sounds filtered in from the rest of the house along with smells and aromas, familiar to everyone but him. The squire, paper and pen in hand, suggested he should hurry and be gone. Jiddy Vardy, not a member of the Farsyde household, but obviously at home with her surroundings, stood unusually silent. He wondered if he would have the nerve to haul her away for more intense questioning.

Captain Ryethorpe had disappeared. In all possibility, someone in Baytown had murdered him. He needed clues. He needed to make an arrest, or he and his officers would lose any authority they had over the locals.

Jiddy Vardy was the only name that had been repeated often enough for him to believe she was involved. It didn't take him by surprise; she was bound to be involved with anything concerning the captain. It followed she would be after the trick he played on her in Whitby when he'd arrested that farmer, Jonas Chaplow. Deputy Staincliffe didn't have any liking for the captain or his ways, but justice had to be done.

Squire Farsyde sat at his desk waiting for instruction and raised his head at the sound. The girl refused to open her mouth. Staincliffe began to wish he'd brought two soldiers with him to make this interrogation more official.

"Is there anything else?" asked the squire, raising his pen. "Perhaps I can be getting back to the important tasks I have in hand and Miss Vardy to taking care of my wife?"

Deputy Staincliffe cleared his throat. "I need to ascertain why Miss Vardy was in the dock in the village when Captain Ryethorpe disappeared. It's hard to believe, Miss Vardy, that you were passing through at the late hour you say you were." The girl's eyes unnerved him, and he cleared his throat again. "Are you usually out of your home after the sun has set?"

"I told you. I were delivering an apple pie."

Every movement she made unsettled him. If they'd been on his territory, it would have been different. If they'd been in the jail, he'd have grabbed her arrogant chin and forced the type of answer he wanted to hear.

"Why so late?" he asked, steadying his voice.

Jiddy kept her eyes on the view through the window. "I'd been busy all day."

Yesterday's rain skulked in the trees and in the stone walls, darkening the crevices. Grizzled clouds shifted inland. Flames in the fireplace sparked off the damp wood. It may have been warm in the thickly draped room, but outside, walking back to Fisherhead, she had felt the chill of the northeasterly wind.

"I asked you why you and Captain Ryethorpe were in the dock. Did you follow him, or did you lead him there?"

"It were pure chance," she said. "I don't know why he were there. Maybe he had a pie to deliver too."

The squire made a loud kerfuffle in his throat; the deputy jingled his sword.

Jiddy kept her eyes on the billowing clouds outside. She was chancing it, but she couldn't help herself. The squire would be exasperated, but what could the deputy do when they were avoiding his questions?

Staincliffe stared at the squire, who continued to write, so the deputy made a show of walking over to the window.

"Why did you go to the dock and not straight home?"

"Baytowners know not to be in the dock at high tide, sir," the squire interrupted, rising from his chair. Had he not, Jiddy would have made an even more cheeky remark than her last. "Captain Ryethorpe was either ignorant or ignored advice. I liked the man, and I am saddened for his family and for you, but we have lost neighbours of our own to the sea. While we want to find blame in another person, just as you are trying to do, the truth is, the tide is to blame and unfortunately, we can't punish the sea as we would a man or a woman. You can ask all the questions you want, Deputy Staincliffe, but you won't find a murderer amongst our inhabitants, not unless you can harness the waves."

Jiddy stared directly at the deputy, whose eyes flickered with discomfort.

Though he tried not to show it, Staincliffe hated both the young woman and the place. To him, she smelt of dry grass and brine, but with her black hair and dark eyes, she had bewitched the captain long before he ended up in the sea, no doubt having tried to kiss her. He hated how she somehow always got the better of the preventives. He hated that the corpse of a young lass had disappeared from a gibbet, and that a farming lad they'd almost packed off on a ship for Australia had also vanished. Now the captain had mysteriously washed out to sea, no body to be found. How could anyone be certain he wasn't beaten and buried in the woods somewhere or under the stone flags in one of those rotten holes of a cottage? One thing was for sure: Jiddy Vardy was involved, no matter what she said about delivering a pie.

"It's a nasty business, but it's the sea for you," said Squire Farsyde, joining them at the window and breaking the tension between them.

"I may still need to question her," Staincliffe said, turning to the squire.

Jiddy caught a whiff of stale sweat and noticed the deputy's eyes sagged with dark circles.

"Have you told Lord Ryethorpe his son is missing?" she asked, her voice soft now. "I think the captain was his only son, and he'll want to know."

CHAPTER EIGHT

Mrs. Farsyde, gazed hopeful and alert, while Jiddy scrutinised the immediate shoreline with its scrabble of bladderwrack-strewn rocks. She was surprised but grateful Staincliffe hadn't positioned his soldiers along the beach, or at least in the dock. She'd been so sure she'd seen the captain the other night, until it turned out to be Staincliffe. She'd been overtired, she persuaded herself. You imagined all sorts when you were tired, but if Mrs. Farsyde saw a red jacket, she may assume it was Samuel and have hysterics.

Looking over her shoulder, Jiddy reassured herself no-one stood on the sloping promontory and, once convinced the scaurs hid no beached corpse, helped Mrs. Farsyde over the seaweed.

"I don't think we should stop long," Jiddy said, still astonished her mistress put finding Samuel's body above the well-being of her unborn child. "Squire didn't say what time he'd be home, and he'll not be happy to find us here."

Mrs. Farsyde gripped Jiddy's arm. "The squire has ridden to Whitby. He won't be home until this evening."

Although the squire might not find out about this escapade and staff at Thorpe Hall wouldn't say anything directly to him, Jiddy was aware that in Baytown, tongues would be wagging about the two women on the beach.

She concentrated on navigating the slime and slip of the rocks until they both stood on the dry, ashen sand where Mrs. Farsyde let go of her hold and took firmer strides.

Jiddy kept at her mistress's side, nervous she might trip or fall. After all the miscarriages her mistress had suffered, this baby had to be born alive.

"It's chilly," she said as they scrunched over pebbles to reach another spread of sand. "I can come by myself and look if you want."

"Nonsense." Mrs. Farsyde waved her hand. "I am the one who needs to find him. "What's that?" She pointed and set off again.

The anxious tremor in Jiddy's stomach grew. 'What's that?' had become Mrs. Farsyde's constant refrain, and Jiddy hurried again and again to the pointed spot, only to find a straggle of rope or a mound of shells and pebbles or a twist of driftwood. Some clusters even Jiddy, nerves now frayed, took for a body of sorts. This time, when she kicked a carefully structured pile apart, she cursed Bay's young ones for their playful structures and the sea's vengeful tides.

By rights, she should hate Samuel. She'd tried often enough, lying in her bed, unable to sleep, waiting for the creak of the secret door next to the kitchen stove and for him to appear as he had that fateful night. If only he'd not thought himself so clever in a place built for secrets and deception. If only he'd never come to Robin Hood's Bay.

Mrs. Farsyde had only known the kindly Samuel. She'd be devastated to find out his body rested on the seabed, nibbled and withered and unrecognisable.

Jiddy shuddered. "Mrs. Farsyde?"

Her mistress waddled some steps in front, her head turning from left to right, and Jiddy skipped over puddles to catch up. "We really should go back."

"What's that?" Mrs. Farsyde paddled through a sheen of water.

Jiddy stared at the frayed stub of rope protruding from behind a rock, startled when Mrs. Farsyde let out a long howl.

She hurried to her side. "Are you all right? Why don't we return now?"

Hands waved her away. "I thought it was him."

Jiddy encircled the distraught woman but was pushed roughly aside with a surprising amount of force.

"How can you make such a suggestion?" The anguished face contorted, and when Jiddy could not answer, Mrs. Farsyde wrenched herself away in disdain.

Jiddy followed, trying to decide what best to say to comfort the woman. Already slowing, Mrs. Farsyde nodded her head like a hungry bird, looking for scraps in the sand.

"Wait!" Jiddy called. "We'll come back. It's getting cold with the sun dropping, and the squire may return early. Think how worried he'll be if you're not there."

Weary, Mrs. Farsyde took Jiddy's arm. "We will find him, won't we?"

Jiddy stared at the shoreline rippling over the sand. Sometimes the beach was the loneliest place in the world, and a sadness filled the pit of her belly. Other times, it was the only place she wanted to be, eyes on the horizon, dreams in her eyes. It was different at Fisherhead, inside Captain Pinkney's old cottage. Alone in bed, in the dark, noises would stir in the house, and she'd see Jonas's face appear out of the gloom, his chestnut hair brushing her cheeks as he kissed her softly; kissed as if he loved her. Kissed her the way she'd seen Samuel kiss Mrs. Farsyde. And it would be as if he'd never gone away.

"We'll do our best," she said.

"Thank you." Mrs. Farsyde watched her. "Thank you for helping me. I couldn't do this without you."

Jiddy forced a reassuring smile, pushing away the image of Jonas.

"I hope I have a son," Mrs. Farsyde said, touching the mound of her stomach.

"I hope so too."

"I wish I could give him the name I'd like to give him."

"A family name might be best," Jiddy said, wishing she could think of a distraction.

She glanced at the cliff and thought of the times she and Jonas had spent telling each other their dreams, spilling their secret thoughts. The ache in her chest when she thought of Jonas made her wonder if she could bear never seeing him again.

"Would one of your family come to stay with you?" she asked. "I'm sure the squire would send for your sister or even your mother."

Releasing Jiddy's arm, Mrs. Farsyde tipped her head up to the sky. "I want him back," she said. "I can't go on without him. I don't want to. I want to lie right here and die if doing so will mean I will be with him again."

"He wouldn't want you to hurt yourself," Jiddy said, wrapping an arm around the woman's waist and turning towards the causeway. "I see Billy—he'll be waiting to take us back."

"I loved Samuel!" Mrs. Farsyde raised her voice. "I've never loved anyone, not a single soul, until him. I don't love my husband, and I can't go on without him…" Sobs overcame her words, and she bent her head.

Stunned, Jiddy looked at Mrs. Farsyde's curved shoulders and heavy frame. Her vulnerability took Jiddy by surprise, though Mrs. Farsyde surprised her more often than she ever had before she'd fallen in love with Samuel. Hearing her declare that love out loud made Jiddy's heart crack open after she'd held it tight for so long.

"You can help me," Mrs. Farsyde continued as they took a few unsteady steps. "You can suggest the name Samuel, say it's only right we name the baby after him because he died and Robin Hood's Bay owes it to him. You'll find a reason, make it sound the right thing to do. I want to say his name every day and have him with me. For me, you will. You have to. Say you will!"

Jiddy nodded, aware of the impossibility of such an idea but unable to find an argument to decline.

"Only we will know the real reason, and we'll talk about him when we're alone," Mrs. Farsyde continued conspiratorially. "I'll make sure we're often alone, and you'll listen, won't you? And say nice things about him and praise him and let me say aloud all I want to say about him? You will, Jiddy, promise me you will. Our secret. Our love for his baby."

Jiddy faced the incoming tide, ripples criss-crossing over the flat sand. What could she say? How could she possibly promise to spend all her time with Mrs. Farsyde and say nice things about the man who'd been responsible for Jonas leaving?

"What about Squire Farsyde?" she asked. "He loves you, and he is looking forward to raising his son. Maybe you'll be happy then too. At least you'll have the baby."

"It's a relief my husband doesn't know. He doesn't know, does he? No-one's said…you've not said?" Suddenly, Mrs. Farsyde gripped her arm. "You haven't told him, have you? You haven't sneaked behind my back and given away my secret? You have, you have! Who knows? Mrs. King? Violet? Have you told the entire village?"

"No, no." Jiddy hooked Mrs. Farsyde's arm and squeezed it to reassure. "No-one knows. They'd never suspect because you have always been so thoughtful and kind to the squire, and he loves you, and he already loves the child."

"Ha!" Mrs. Farsyde broke away and stood, rubbing her hands. "He doesn't love me. I am his wife. His property. What he loves—do you want to know what he truly loves?"

Confronted again, Jiddy could only stare. She didn't recognise the mistress of Thorpe Hall who alternated moods like a wild storm. Maybe this was what having a child inside did to you. Like the storm in her head before she bled. The body did strange things; she'd found that out years ago. Maybe if they left the beach and got out of this tugging wind, Mrs. Farsyde would calm herself again.

"I'll tell you what he loves!" She seized Jiddy's arm again. "What he loves, what he really loves, is his land and his horse and cleaning his wretched pistol! He's so busy galloping around his estates and heading off to market and Scarborough and pretending he knows more than he does, he's no time for loving me or talking to me or even noticing who I really am. He certainly never noticed how attentive Samuel was—never gave a second thought to why the captain really came to visit us so often!"

She stared at Jiddy as if willing her to understand what it was like being the wife of Squire Farsyde.

Jolted into a response, Jiddy nodded. "He must never know," she said, her heart beating fast. "Come, let's get back before he returns. We need you back in your bed. We shouldn't have left the house, never mind come here."

"Poring over maps with his so-called friends," Mrs. Farsyde continued, animated with her train of thought. "They're not really his friends. They only tolerate him. I've seen them. They laugh at him for his lack of style—I've heard them! But he tries so hard to make them like him he's not time for me, for his wife, and so I don't tell him. I let him carry on in his deluded way."

Jiddy kept her eyes on the causeway, hoping Billy would appear and come to meet them. The thought of anything happening now to Mrs. Farsyde or the baby had begun to terrify her even more, and if the squire found out, he'd blame her and Billy.

"It's all tedious debates about land and laws and taxes and prices and the gentry." Mrs. Farsyde wouldn't stop. "The real gentry aren't bothered, but my poor husband is convinced he must keep up with them, and so I'm hushed away. Who could blame me when someone like Captain Ryethorpe appears?" She stopped, tilting her head and listening to the gulls.

Waves frothed over the shingle. Oblivious, Mrs. Farsyde raised her chin higher, eyes staring upwards.

"Samuel?" she shouted. "Where are you?"

Astounded, Jiddy watched Mrs. Farsyde, a woman she'd thought unfeeling and too old for passion, stumbling in circles, crying out for the man she loved. Jiddy had always thought she was the more passionate, yet she could barely speak about Jonas and how the last words between them had been full of hatred.

"Samuel?" Mrs. Farsyde cried.

Tears welled in Jiddy's eyes. She had seen this love in the gentle kiss between her mistress and the captain, and she had felt what a soft touch of lips had done for her and Jonas when she'd called for restraint in their lustful feelings. She could understand Mrs. Farsyde's anguish. It bubbled in her own chest. They were not so very different if you took away all the money and privilege.

"Mrs. Farsyde?" She reached for the woman's hand. "Think of the baby and getting back home."

Thought of the baby did the trick, but it wasn't an easy walk and they lurched along the beach, Jiddy keeping the causeway in sight and praying Billy Hardcastle wouldn't have fallen asleep or been cajoled into the inn. If she could keep Mrs. Farsyde moving, she'd have done her duty for the day, and she could put the emotions she felt back in the box she'd made to contain them and have Mrs. Farsyde back in her bed and the squire none the wiser.

They'd reached the larger rocks where pools were already forming, and the scaurs, now underwater, made Jiddy uneasy. This was where you could turn an ankle, stumble and come to harm. Billy was nowhere in sight. She'd throttle him, she really would.

"Steady here." She pointed out a gap to avoid and bladderwrack to tread carefully over. They were almost there when Mrs. Farsyde clenched Jiddy's arm again and drew her close.

"Jonas Chaplow!" she said. "What about your young man? Does he love you like Samuel loves me?"

Horrified she might have to talk about Jonas when every thought of him made her heart ache, Jiddy shook her head. "Please," she said, "not now. Now's not the time."

"But I've been selfish, talking about my love when we must bring yours back. We can't both suffer. We must send for him. I heard he was in France? Not to worry. The squire will know. We'll speak to him."

"It's all right—there's Billy, thank goodness." Jiddy spied him and waved. "We're here!" She faced Mrs. Farsyde. "He has the carriage, and he's within hearing distance now. We'll get you home. You'll be fine."

She hoped Mrs. Farsyde would quieten and they could ride in silence, but her mistress's thoughts would not be stilled.

"I will find Samuel and you will find Jonas," she persisted.

Jiddy couldn't bear it and tugged forwards, not caring anymore if they caught a foot or twisted an ankle. "Right now, we must keep moving towards the slipway. Here's Billy coming to help."

Seeing the danger, Billy came running and reached out an arm to his mistress, which she readily grasped, clinging as they mounted the causeway. Following behind, Jiddy tried to make sense of what Mrs. Farsyde had said. Did it mean she didn't love Jonas as much as Mrs. Farsyde loved Samuel? Jiddy didn't rant as if she'd lost her mind. Did that mean she loved Jonas less? Shouldn't she give her heart and soul to get him back, even if it risked sobbing until her eyes shrank to slits and the wall she'd built around her emotions crumbled?

She couldn't bear the thought of talking to Squire and Mrs. Farsyde about Jonas, but what if they could bring him back from France? The sea ate people. It rarely spat them out alive again, and soldiers rarely came back from war. Jonas was most likely dead already. Dead on the ship or battlefield. The thought was too much to bear.

Now she had Jonas's mutilated body in her head, the thought made her days not only lonely but desolate.

CHAPTER NINE

Jiddy was determined to keep busy and not think about Jonas. None of that swooning around, lovesick, and forlorn weeping for her, she decided. Busy, busy, busy, barging through the days, filling every hour with activity. She put her plan into action straight away.

"Thanks for helping with the nettles, Betsie," she said, carrying the basket of nettle tops through the door.

"You're sure all insects have crawled off?" asked Annie, placing a pan on its hook and swinging to the side of the fire.

Jiddy peered at the bright leaves. "They'd better. Basket has been on step for long enough."

"It's too early to pick them, you should have waited," said Betsie, flopping into a chair at the table.

"Not at all. These are fresh, and they're always early in woods. We need to get on with cloth dying now." Jiddy placed the basket at Annie's feet and lifted nettle sprigs into the pan with a pair of tongs. "How are your hands, Betsie?"

"Easing," said Betsie, rubbing dock leaves between her palms. "But why've you been talking about Jonas all afternoon? I thought you didn't like talking about him?"

Jiddy glanced up, startled. Is that what she'd been doing without even noticing?

"Why shouldn't she? Jonas is always on your mind, isn't he?" interjected Annie, watching her friend press the nettles. "Should I pour water on?"

Jiddy nodded, nervous now of opening her mouth. "Just cover them," she mumbled.

Of all the fustylugs! Jiddy thought she'd been holding Jonas at bay when she was putting him out there for others to see. What an idiot because now Betsie mentioned it, she realised she'd done nothing but talk about him since trudging on the beach with Mrs. Farsyde. Who was she fooling?

"Why do you want Jonas back so much?" asked Betsie, throwing away a wrinkled dock leaf and picking another. "Thought you hated him for leaving."

"I'm glad you're talking about him," said Annie, swinging the pan over the fire. "And I never believed you when you said you hated him."

"Well, I believed you," Betsie said, "and I don't blame you. How dare he head off to France when he always said war with Frenchies were none of our business?"

Jiddy didn't answer but carried on compressing the leaves. Keep busy, keep busy.

"I still think he'll be working on a farm over Goathland way," said Annie, sitting in a nearby chair.

Jiddy shrugged. Every mention of his name brought his abrupt departure more starkly to mind again, and she couldn't bear to tell even Annie and Betsie the truth of why he'd left. If only Jonas would realise they weren't brother and sister. If he did, the numbness she'd sealed over her heart might melt.

"It were more to do with his cousin and his wife showing up," she said, peering into the pan.

"Well, I don't know why you're allowed to go on about him when you both kept mithering me to be quiet when I wanted to talk about James," Betsie mumbled.

"Oh, my word!" Jiddy shouted and marched over to the table, slamming the wooden spoon on the wood, making both Annie and Betsie jump. "James were a complete pudding head, Betsie. Why on earth would anyone want to talk about someone who were such a pox to them?"

"Oh, of course, slag off me and James because you're so miffed at Saint Jonas Chaplow. Saint my little finger!"

"Are you all right, Jiddy?" asked Annie, standing. "Did you catch a fever from all time in sea other night?"

Jiddy returned to the fire. "I'm fed up. It's nowt."

Annie sat again. Jiddy avoided eye contact by checking on the simmering water.

"We don't mind you talking about Jonas, do we, Betsie?" said Annie. "Jonas isn't like James."

Betsie kept her eyes on Jiddy. "I wanted James back because there were no-one else. Is it same reason you want Jonas back?"

Jiddy didn't move. She hadn't meant to explode and worried she'd throw the boiling pot of liquid if she exploded again.

Annie looked from one to the other. "There's loads of lads in Bay, Betsie," she eventually said. "You don't need James."

"Oh, really?" Betsie swung round to face Annie. "D'you see a lad by my side?" She made a mock glance to her right. "Ever seen even so much as a farmhand talk to me after Sunday service at chapel? Maybe a suitor's waiting outside door right now with a bunch of flowers? Oh, I can hear him coming!" She glanced at the door, and Annie followed the direction as if someone really did approach.

"Annie were only—" Jiddy began.

"Were what?" spat out Betsie. "I can't bear people already looking at me as if I'm an old maid, and you're no different from me, Jiddy Vardy, even though you think you're better than any of us."

"She doesn't—" Annie said, looking at Jiddy.

"Oh, come on, Jiddy, we're in same bag now!" said Betsie. "Lads round here don't want lasses like you any more than they want me or this wet limpet!"

"I am not a wet limpet!"

"Yes, you are, Annie. Best shut up."

"Don't tell Annie to shut up," said Jiddy, spoon raised and dripping grey-green water on the hearth where it sizzled.

"I've known Annie longer than you," said Betsie, blowing on her hands. "She knows I don't mean much by it."

"Stop it, Betsie," Jiddy warned.

"No, you stop it."

"Both of you, stop it!"

Both girls looked at Annie, who stood, hands clenched over the back of her chair.

"I don't want a lad when I've got you two. Why would you ever want a horror bag like James, Betsie, and if I'm honest, Jiddy, all I know is you love Jonas and he loves you, and I don't know why you're not trying harder to bring him home. Honestly, what's the matter with both of you?"

Boiling water hissed from the pan onto the coals, but Jiddy didn't take her eyes off Annie, who, flushing pink, slunk into her seat.

Betsie broke their silence first. "Jiddy needs Jonas to make her pop."

Annie and Jiddy shared the same wide-eyed surprise before Jiddy burst out laughing and went to take care of the overspilling pot while Annie gawped.

"I don't need Jonas or any lad," said Jiddy, joining the others at the table. "I don't need a lad for anything, thank you very much."

Slouching in her chair, she rested her chin in her hands and closed her eyes, unsure whether it was to recapture Jonas—his face, eyes, hair touching her cheeks, how they were together, his voice, their laughter, whatever she missed—or to shut out Betsie and Annie. Her heart ached. If she let herself think about him, he flooded in, sitting side by side in the foaming waves, pouring water into each other's mouth and the saltiness of it and the sand and grit and laughing. Running along the sand, wet skirt clinging to her bare legs, hilltops, sitting astride him, him smiling at her, reaching to hold her, and the kissing. The shining stars, what kissing.

The pot hissed and threw a spittle into her thoughts, but she clung on, squeezing her eyes tighter. She wanted their childhood back. She wanted to spend hours with him, showing each other shells and winkles, pots capturing salt, Jonas angry at the Government, soldiers, war, everything. And she, equally angry, but at Nellie and her own skin and dark hair and dark eyes.

"Well?" Betsie chipped her way through.

"I miss him," Jiddy finally said, eyes still closed. "I taught a farmer to swim, and he taught a fisher-girl to care for chicks and lambs. It were like we were so close, we knew each other's thoughts before we knew them ourselves."

"Thought you said you didn't need Jonas or any lad." Betsie's voice came in strong.

Jiddy couldn't hold Betsie out much longer. Jonas slipped from her head and tears weighed heavy in his place. She breathed out through pursed lips. She shouldn't have let herself remember. She shouldn't have stopped being busy to let him in because now the pain of his absence was too much to bear.

"Might not need him," she whispered, "but I miss him."

There was a reason he'd stormed away; anger at himself, at her, at the world, but she had to believe it was mainly anger because he loved her, wanted and needed her. Maybe Annie was right. She hadn't tried hard enough to bring him back, but Annie didn't know the reason he'd left. No-one had worked it out.

"Jiddy? Are you all right?" Annie's voice now. Tender, tugging.

"She don't know what to say," interjected Betsie. "She knows I'm right."

"You whispered something, what were it?" asked Annie.

"You can't block us out. We're here, you know. Even with your eyes shut, we're in front of you, and you can hear us," said Betsie.

They belonged to each other without belonging. It was a fact. She could swim, and he could build stone walls. She could sew, he could milk cows. They could kiss, they could both kiss. Ebb and flow, push and pull, seed and pod. How to explain they made each other brighter, shinier? And if he never came back, she'd still be Jiddy and he'd still be Jonas. But together? Ye gods, together, they shone like stars in a clear night's sky.

"Aren't we enough, Jiddy?" Annie's voice pleaded.

She opened her eyes and, reaching for their hands, looked easily at Annie and not so easily at Betsie. She smiled. "Only we three know each other well enough to run a school together," she said.

"What are you talking about?" said Annie.

Betsie withdrew her hand. "A few lasses round a table isn't a school."

"Do you mean teach them like Mary taught us?"

Betsie folded her arms. "We've been through this. Lasses in Bay know how to sew."

Jiddy painted images in the air with her hands. "I don't mean only patch and mend, Betsie, but embroider, cut out patterns, create beautiful dresses ladies over whole county will want to wear. Baby clothes, any type of garment we're asked to make."

"But we live in Bay, Jiddy," said Annie.

"We live a hundred miles from anywhere!" added Betsie.

"Is having a job you enjoy doing not worth travelling for?" asked Jiddy. "Is earning your own money not a good thing? If we teach lasses to be proper seamstresses, more than your basic mending and patching, we're doing them a service, aren't we?"

"I would love to embroider as good as you," said Annie.

Betsie threw a scornful look. "If everyone embroidered like Jiddy, all jobs'd soon be filled, and your sisters and mine would not only be back twisting twine and salting fish, they'd also be begrudging every second they do it! No local lad'd do for them because they'll be so uppity about themselves, no fish-smelling whaler would be good enough. They'll all be spinsters scrubbing other people's floors. They'll look back on your little sewing school and be overflowing with gratitude and be *so* glad they came and learned how to embroider silk when they must go back to potting lobsters and crabs and slapping whale grease on their chapped knuckles!"

Annie looked as if her world had been destroyed. Jiddy's head pounded. The fire threw out several spats.

"No need to be sarky, Betsie," said Jiddy. "Yorkshire is a big county, and not every lass will want to leave Bay. It's about giving them a choice. Don't you want a choice, Betsie?"

"I would," said Annie, squeezing Jiddy's hand. "I'd love to have choices."

Betsie let out a huge sigh. "I get it! I do. I'm not daft. But wanting to be Jiddy will upset lasses' everyday doings." She thrust back her chair. "You may want to do it, but is it best for others? That's all I'm asking."

Grabbing her shawl and sweeping it over her head, Betsie busied herself tucking in her hair. Annie remained quiet.

Jiddy couldn't find anything to say. Answers usually came so easily, but lately, she'd struggled as if she were no longer herself. She took a deep breath. "I want to teach Bay lasses to sew proper for their benefit, not mine, Betsie," she said. "There are jobs in cities as well as in big houses. No-one needs to stay in Bay because they were born here. Nellie didn't want to, and I bet Violet and many others don't want to either, but you don't want them to have that choice, do you? Because it'll mean you might be left behind here, all on your own?"

She sensed Annie tense, and Betsie paused, rigid in the doorway.

"Yes!" Jiddy answered her own question, louder than she'd intended, and walked to join Betsie in the doorway.

"Then why have you stayed in Bay if there are so many better opportunities on other side of moor?" said Betsie, recovering her composure.

"Jiddy, don't listen, don't go." Annie hurried to the doorway, where they all stood facing each other.

"It's all right, Annie," Jiddy said. "I'll not leave Bay without a good reason."

"You're a right nicky-ninny, Betsie." said Annie. "Of course Jiddy won't leave Bay when Jonas could be back at any time."

Betsie put her hands on her hips and squared up. "Jonas hasn't anything to come back for, though, has he? His cousin runs farm now." Catching Jiddy scanning the room, she dropped her voice. "And Jonas would never live in a place that wasn't his own." Her eyes showed she'd caught the idea. "He would never, ever live in the home of the biggest smuggler in Robin Hood's Bay. He'd never live in Bay. He's a farmer, not a fisherman. Even I know better than you, you…" she laughed, "nicky-ninny yourself, Annie Briggs!"

Annie grasped Jiddy's arm, but Jiddy didn't lash out as Annie had suspected she might. Instead, she stood, arms loose by her sides, like the dignified figurehead on a ship.

"Jonas is more broad-minded than you think," Jiddy said, her voice calm. "He stopped farming to be a soldier. Jonas can do whatever he turns his hands to. And it isn't a smuggler's home anymore. It's mine. And what's mine is Jonas's."

"Well said. Yes, yes, of course it is!" Annie clapped her hands.

Betsie fiddled again with her shawl, trying to appear nonchalant. "You'd be happy setting up home with Jonas, would you? You'd be happy watching for him coming home when you've a bairn in your belly?"

Jiddy reached out her hand and Betsie flinched. Calmly, Jiddy tucked a few strands of Betsie's hair under the shawl. "I know it's not all working out as we'd hoped when we were littlies, but worst thing is if we turn on each other, Betsie. We've known each other too long. We're friends, and we must look out for each other. And be kind." She looked from Betsie to Annie and took hold of Annie's hand while scooping up Betsie's. "Don't our friendship matter more than any lad?"

Betsie struggled to maintain her fixed stare as her face crumpled. Tears welled in Annie's eyes, and she looked at Jiddy.

"You're crying too!" Annie exclaimed.

Jiddy smeared her sleeve across her face. "It's like plague," she said, her voice muffled.

"Don't marry Jonas!" Betsie blurted out.

"She has to marry Jonas," said Annie.

"Even if Jonas comes back, don't leave us."

"I'm not going anywhere, Betsie," said Jiddy, smiling reassuringly. "Bay comes first. Always has."

"Do you promise?"

Jiddy looked around the room, taking in the little wooden ship and knick-knacks gathered from faraway places and left on the mantel shelf by Captain Pinkney. She took in her sewing basket and reels of thread. Betsie and Annie were watching her and waiting for her to promise.

She gazed from one pair of grey eyes to the other and smiled again. "I told you, Bay comes first, which means Baytowners do. They always will." Her voice sounded strong and insistent, but all she could think about were two stars shining brightly in a night sky, like the ones she and Jonas had stared up at from the doorstep at Sunny Place. She couldn't have explained why the thought of those two stars made her heart ache as painfully as it did.

CHAPTER TEN

Jiddy tramped down the hill to Main Street, where she stood for a moment.

"I won't see Jonas again anyway," she muttered. "I don't need to make a promise out loud."

She looked along the street and towards the dock, but there wasn't a soul to be seen. Ruts and shoe prints mangled the ground. A chicken, scrawny with age, pecked at the dust. She'd never studied the road like this, not since she was a child slouched on the front step at Sunny Place. The cottages had seemed huge, but now they huddled small.

Funny how much she didn't notice about the Bay. She'd forgotten, with the day-to-day doings, how she'd talked of other places and how she'd wanted to cross the sea and explore different lands and find where she belonged or come from at least. She'd constantly mithered Jonas with her thoughts. She smiled to herself. She'd believed she was the daughter of Romanies, of a King and Queen in some distant land, and she had their royal blood running through her veins. Jonas hadn't scoffed at the idea. He'd let her dream.

And, it had turned out, she had royal blood of sorts. Her mother was Signora Maria Vardarelli, and she had diamonds in her eyes and blood rubies on her fingers. All that wishing and dreaming, and the reality of beauty and riches had been greater than she could have imagined. The tragedy had been, when faced with reality, she and her mother hadn't understood each other. She wondered if Jonas despised her for not staying with the only family member that had appeared. Well, running off to France when you found out something you weren't happy with wasn't exactly admirable either, so his opinion didn't matter.

She walked straight past the Ashners' cottage and along Bloomswell and knocked on the end door. Hearing a clatter inside, she stood back. The door opened. "How do, Mrs. Fletcher?"

"What you want?" The woman stood, fists on hips.

"Is Sarah in?"

"She's not." Mrs. Fletcher's rolled-up sleeves and red knuckles did not give room for pleasantries.

"I'm teaching a few lasses sewing skills, pattern cutting, hemming, embroidery and such," Jiddy explained. Mrs. Fletcher shifted her feet. "Would Sarah want to come? Two mornings a week?"

Sarah's mother's eyes flickered. "So, what you saying? You'll pay Sarah to work for you? You are going up in world now you're living at Fisherhead, aren't you?"

Jiddy caught the meaning in the woman's voice. "No," she said, taking a step back. "It's like school. I'll be teaching Sarah a skill."

"A skill?"

"How to make a dress pattern and cut it out and pin it together, embroider a pouch, skills like that."

Mrs. Fletcher laughed. "Who round here wants an embroidered pouch?"

"Ladies. Like Mrs. Farsyde and ladies of county."

"I can't be doing with this," Mrs. Fletcher said, turning inside. "And Sarah's got a skill, by the way. It's called helping me out!"

The door slammed. Jiddy stared at the wood and, taking a deep breath, focused on the cracks. Did people really think she could pay others to sew for her? She looked back along Bloomswell before heading towards Silver Street where Gilly Baxter lived.

"How do, Mrs. Baxter. Would Gilly like to come to my sewing school?"

Mrs. Baxter, a fair-haired, wiry woman, couldn't hide her surprise. "Gilly's twelve!" she exclaimed. "Lass has been sewing since she were four!"

"Oh, I know," Jiddy said, clasping her hands together. "I'm only asking girls who are good with their fingers..."

Mrs. Baxter nodded, a proud expression on her face.

"I'll be teaching pattern cutting and how to make a dress and proper hemming and pleating. It's two mornings a week." Jiddy rushed out the words, but Mrs. Baxter still managed to interrupt.

"I'm sorry, Jiddy. Darning and mending are all what's needed in our house."

The door began to close.

"But this is to get work!"

"Get work? Aren't you doing all this fancy work for Mrs. Farsyde?"

"Well, yes…"

"You're not moving away, are you?"

"No—"

"Our Gilly is fine. Good of you to praise her, but she's busy enough with all we have to do here."

"But—"

"Got to be getting on. Some of us can't stand around gossiping all day."

The door closed. Jiddy waited a moment. Cally lived a couple of doors away, and Molly and Jane on King Street, Abby Baker and a couple more around Sunnyside. It had to be worth all the work they'd put in dying fabrics, unpicking clothes and drawing out thread to reuse. She couldn't go back and tell Annie and Betsie they had no pupils to teach.

"They'll be employed in one of the big houses," she said to Cally's ma.

"They've got employment here."

"It'll give them a regular wage."

"We get what we need between us all doing our bit."

She sighed. They had nettle dye already made. They were ready to start the school, but Cally wouldn't be joining them. Or Molly.

Another door slammed.

"It'll give Jane the opportunity to get out of Bay," Jiddy said, a note of desperation in her voice.

"What's wrong with Bay?"

Jiddy dragged her feet up Main Street.

"But what if Abby wants to?" she reasoned when Mrs. Baker shook her head.

"What's that got to do with anything?"

"It'll give her more choice."

"Will you feed her?" Abby's mum asked.

Exhausted, Jiddy headed back towards Fisherhead, anticipating a hot drink and a seat by the fire, only to slow her steps when she saw a tall figure outside the front door. The moment she had dreaded. Samuel's father, Lord Ryethorpe, must have been told the news of his son and had finally come back to the Bay.

As she approached, she noticed his stooped shoulders, creviced face and watery eyes brought on by more than a cold wind.

"D'you want to come in?" she asked, gesturing to the front door.

He stepped back. "Thank you, no. I wondered… It is the last time I shall ever be in this place, and we have unresolved business, do we not?" He faltered. Her heart sank. "I have a request."

Her mind raced. What could he want to ask? What could she tell him about Samuel? About the imaginary pie? About their conversation? About the surging water? Maybe Deputy Staincliffe had voiced his suspicions and Lord Ryethorpe wanted to know if Jiddy really led Samuel to his death. *That's guilt talking. Don't give anything away. Least said, best.*

She looked over his shoulder at the rooftops across the beck and the distinctive yard of Sunny Place leading to the Openings. She was used to tricking preventives, but she didn't know if she could lie to Samuel's father. "It's wet to be standing about," she said and clicked the door latch.

He hesitated again. "I thought it might be preferable…"

She had never known men like Lord Ryethorpe not be able to form a sentence. Men like him gave orders. They spoke decisively. They never groped for words.

"Please come inside," she said. "I will make a hot drink to warm you."

Lord Ryethorpe touched his hat. "Thank you, no," he said. "I am leaving within the hour, as I want to cross the moors before dark."

An hour. She'd only need to spend an hour with him—less if she answered him quickly.

"I don't know what I can tell you," she said, "but I'm sorry about what happened. I'm sorry you've lost your son."

He stared unblinking. She couldn't make out what thoughts flashed through his head. "I haven't come to speak to you about Captain Ryethorpe," he said.

She should have been grateful, but she unexpectedly felt cheated. It didn't make sense. She didn't want to talk about Samuel, yet now she didn't have to, she was disappointed. Another thought weighed heavy. What could he want to talk about?

"Will you walk with me?" He held out his hand. The glove was a good fit. Black hide. "The carriage is at the top of the hill."

Lord Ryethorpe walked in front. With his back to her, his cloak sweeping the ground and hat shrouding his head, he looked every part of someone in mourning. She closed the door and followed.

He didn't say a word as they headed across the field, and she tried to work out what he wanted. She couldn't produce Samuel's body. She couldn't tell him what had happened to his son. She dodged a cow pat and lifted her skirt. The long grass drooped with raindrops. Lord Ryethorpe waited for her when they reached the track. The carriage stood, driver aloft, as he had said. She noted from the spot he'd chosen, no-one from the village would have noticed the carriage or seen him approaching Fisherhead.

They stood by the open carriage door. Jiddy looked questioningly at the older man. He took off his hat and pushed back thinning grey hair.

"Your mother is living in York," he said. He gestured to the empty interior. "Consider what this could mean for you both. A new start. A new life. Together. Please, climb aboard."

CHAPTER ELEVEN

The rumble of carriage wheels still in her ears, Jiddy returned to the village, the look of astonishment on Lord Ryethorpe's face seared into her memory.

She tried to pin it down. Did she feel angry, upset or something else? Why, was the big question. Why would her mother want to see her after she'd called Jiddy a thief and everyone in Bay thieves, and murderers? And she'd left Jiddy behind when she went to London and had never come back to see if her daughter was alive. Being sixteen was no excuse. Jiddy would never leave a baby to fend for itself.

Anger. Yes, anger was the emotion raging in her blood. She strode out. She'd not be having anything to do with her mother and red and ochre dresses and diamond necklaces and stolen garnets.

A couple of little lads rolled pebbles down the hill before running after them, stumbling into each other, pushing and shrieking. Jiddy might not have family in Bay, as Lord Ryethorpe had pointed out, but she understood people in Bay better than she understood people elsewhere, even her own mother. What could Signora Vardarelli possibly offer that would be more important than the school she had decided to run for Baytown lasses?

She bounded up Jim Bell's Stile towards the slanted cottages of Fisherhead, desperate to be inside. Once she'd closed the door, she took a deep breath. The smell of warm nettles filled her nostrils. Sunlight slanted through the windows. Four chairs and a long bench stood around the table. Annie and Betsie had left the room neat and tidy. Even so, she would stick to her plan. Keep busy. She grabbed the broom and swept the floor.

On the table, she placed squares of calico alongside reels of different colours, pin cushions with needles of varying sizes. In the centre of the table, she laid a piece of cloth showing a range of embroidery stitches, and a pair of scissors took pride of place.

Surveying the table, she folded her arms. This was far more important than helping her mother run a fancy department store. She'd train Bay lasses to work there, though, and show Signora Vardarelli just because people were poor, it didn't mean they were thieves or they murdered people.

***

The next morning, Annie arrived early. "Are you all right?" she asked, touching Jiddy's hand. "I heard you didn't get a good result yesterday."

"I've got us ready," said Jiddy, gesturing to the table. "I caught a few of the older lasses who were walking up from beach last night."

"Aye, Andrew were right sarky when he told me you'd stopped by."

Jiddy smiled. "He's a wallop, is your brother, but at least he passed on message. It's good to see you and Betsie'll be along soon. Look, aren't I organised?"

"Betsie's helping her mam with baby," answered Annie, looking at the table. "She'll be here if she can drag herself away. Betsie's a beggar with us, but she's grand with bairns."

Jiddy laughed. "Her saving grace!"

Annie examined the dye in the pan while Jiddy straightened the rug and repositioned the two fireside chairs for the umpteenth time.

"Did your sisters say they'd come?" asked Jiddy, touching the cracked leather tankard on the mantel shelf Captain Pinkney had left behind and which she couldn't bear to throw out.

Annie stirred the mixture.

"Annie? Are they coming?"

"I'm not sure," Annie said, laying down the spoon. "Mam needs them today. There's a lot of haddock on top field to turn, what with it being a sunny day."

Jiddy strode to the table and adjusted a chair before righting a cotton reel that had fallen on its side. "D'you think we're ready?" she asked, walking around the table and touching each chair as she passed it. Determined not to lose confidence, she admired the layout. "Does it look all right? Maybe we should have started teaching how to dye cloth."

"It's perfect," Annie said. She sauntered to the door and looked out while Jiddy continued to straighten the neatly cut squares of calico, placed ready in front of each seat.

She had woken in the morning and cast away thoughts of Lord Ryethorpe, her mother, and York. Of Samuel, of Jonas, of everybody and everything except starting the school.

"I can see Betsie coming," announced Annie. "Let's hope she's in better mood today."

Betsie appeared in the doorway, out of breath. She looked from them to the room.

"I got your message. Hasn't anyone arrived yet?" she said ambling in and scraping out a chair.

Jiddy bounded past her and stepped out onto the path.

"Looks right professional," said Betsie, fiddling with a square of calico. "So, do you think any lasses will come?"

"Of course they will," said Annie. "All the lasses Jiddy asked direct and without their mams in earshot said they couldn't wait to get out of gutting fish and packing lobster and having to rub fat on their hands to stop them chafing."

"Lasses say one thing but do another when their mams do come back in earshot," said Betsie.

Annie looked towards the door where Jiddy stood, hands clasped like a real schoolteacher. Jiddy tried to block out her friends' voices, squinting at the houses across the way and searching for movement, straining to hear the girls chatter as they approached. Mary would be astonished at where she now lived and what she'd done. It had been a long time ago when Nellie, Betsie, Annie and she had sat around the table at Sunny Place, with Rebecca hunched by the fire and Mary darting forward to maintain peace. Nowhere near as much room as they had here around this big table, they'd been crowded together with petticoats and chemises, pillowcases and sheets piled for darning and embellishing, clothes to practise on because Mary didn't have cloth to spare. They'd shared needles, reels, even squeals at pricked fingers.

"We could go knocking," suggested Annie.

Betsie lifted another piece of cloth and examined it.

"Violet said she'd definitely come," said Jiddy.

"Her face is still bruised from her da's backhand," said Betsie. "I doubt she'll come. I'd strike her off list."

"Oh, my lord, what's this thing about men hitting their daughters?!" Jiddy exclaimed. "It's 1790s, not dark ages."

"You can't really blame him for being annoyed," said Annie. "Violet's earnings from Thorpe Hall helps support her whole family."

"Be annoyed but don't hit anyone!" Jiddy stamped her foot. "She'd earn more as a proper seamstress. How does he not understand?"

"Come inside to talk to us," said Annie. "Standing there won't make girls come any quicker."

Jiddy leaned against the doorframe. "I'm not asking Violet to be here all day every day. I did explain she'll continue at hall until she's ready to apply for sewing jobs. It's not like it'll be tomorrow."

"I don't think Mr. Ashner will understand even if she does speak to him," said Annie. "With shiner she's got, I doubt she's mentioned it again."

"Can't see him letting Violet step beyond Bay," said Betsie, "and there's nowhere round here that needs a seamstress like you are at hall, Jiddy. Where'd she work? Seems a lot of bother for nowt to me."

"Betsie, don't be unhelpful. It's not a waste of time," said Annie. "There's plenty of big houses hereabout."

"Ashners cling tighter than clams to their own, that's all I'm saying," said Betsie, throwing the piece of cloth.

"He's scared," said Jiddy. "When he sees how much Violet could earn at a place like Vardarelli's in York, he'll change his mind."

"York!" exclaimed Betsie. "Ha! Rather you tell him than me!"

Jiddy edged to face them. "We have to make people see this isn't only good for the girls. It's good for everyone if lasses learn new skills and get chance to choose what they want to do."

Annie and Betsie remained silent until, yawning, Bestie rose to her feet. "Well, this one's choosing to head off home. Some of us can't sit around idle all day."

"You've not given it no time at all!" said Jiddy, returning to the doorway.

"Don't tell me you haven't got chores to do back at your mam's, Annie?" said Betsie. "And don't tell me you're not thinking about them." She readjusted the knot holding her shawl around her waist. "You coming?"

Cocking her head on one side, Annie played with her skirt. "Jiddy, if they're not coming, would it be all right if I went with Betsie? I do have some things Mam needs me for. You know Sarah and May. They'll be squabbling like mad, and fish'll be left lying on same side until the blooming things are cooked!"

"Oh, fine!" Jiddy said, raising her hands. "Have no faith, leave me to do everything! Go! Why should I need any help? Go and help your mas!"

"I'm sorry," said Annie. "We'll be here next time. I'm sure some will come when they give it proper thought." She looked at Betsie for approval.

"Violet definitely won't, I can promise you," said Betsie. "And my mam does need me, I'll have you know."

"Go, Betsie," said Jiddy moving for her to pass outside. "Violet might not be coming today, but I'll see her at hall, and I'll talk to Mr. Ashner again. So, you can go, get your chores done. And you go too, Annie. I don't mind. It's not as if we'll have fifty lasses to check on!"

"I can help you clear up first," said Annie, lingering behind as Betsie went ahead.

Jiddy crossed her arms. "No. A few of them may still arrive. You catch up with Betsie. I'll be fine."

Annie stared at Jiddy for a moment. "I'm sorry," she said again.

Jiddy patted Annie's shoulder and smiled. "I'll bake some biscuits. Smell of sweet dough will bring them in!"

Hearing Betsie's voice, Annie gave a quick nod.

Closing the door, Jiddy leaned against it and hugged herself tightly. Her wool shawl felt rough with salt air, her skirt drab with wear. She stared at the table and chairs, neatly pushed under. The room did look perfect as Annie had said, but no wonder the girls couldn't imagine what it would be like to sew clothes like the ones Mrs. Farsyde wore when their clothes, darned and handed down from an elder sister, were all they had ever known.

A sneaky thought wound into her mind. She should have gone to York as Lord Ryethorpe had suggested. If the Vardarelli store there was anything like the one in London, it would be filled floor to ceiling with richly coloured fabrics and glittering sights. If she could show it to Violet Ashner, Nellie's sister would be desperate to learn to sew if it meant she could find work there. And where Violet led, others would surely follow.

CHAPTER TWELVE

Violet, cap pulled closer around her face than usual, didn't say a word to Jiddy about her absence from the sewing group.

Jiddy gently touched the younger girl's shoulder. "Don't worry, Violet. We'll find a way."

Violet glanced up, a tear rolling down her cheek. Brushing it away, she led the way to Squire Farsyde's study.

The squire sat at his desk near the window. Before him lay an open box and the paraphernalia of a firearm. He looked cheerfully content. "Ah, Jiddy," he said. "Grand day, grand day."

Jiddy turned to give Violet a smile of reassurance, but the younger girl had already gone, so she closed the door and approached the desk. The squire touched the thin ramrod, flints, ball and a small sack that contained the black powder catalyst. He picked up a grubby pouch and placed it next to the pistol.

Jiddy moved closer to see the items more clearly. Glancing at her, the squire tore a rag into small pieces. Perhaps this was what was needed to persuade Mr. Ashner to let his daughter go.

Pistols weighed heavy, heavier than she'd have thought when first holding one. They were hard to aim because of their weight. She'd practised many times under Captain Pinkney's piercing gaze but had used the pistol only once. And missed. The squire fired at trees and clouds all the time but never cared if he struck home or not.

She looked through the window at the bumbling sky then again at the squire. He took a pellet and wrapped a piece of cloth around it. "Am I interrupting you?" she asked. "Should I come back?"

He held the wrapped bullet on the desk and glanced towards the door. "Mrs. Farsyde is resting today. I want to give her some peace."

"With a pistol?"

She eyed the items on the desk, startled when the squire guffawed.

"With keeping out of her way!" He laughed. "I'm always doing wrong thing at the moment."

Jiddy watched him turning over the firearm. "I'm sure you not," she said, "and you'll have plenty to do when child is here."

Pride flushed his face. "Bairn won't be born until end of summer-tide, but my wife has all she needs. She's got a crib and nursing chair, all clothes a babe can wear and more besides. She's even got new gowns of her own! I've done all I can for now."

"Right," said Jiddy, looking at his hands clutching the rag-wrapped bullet.

As if given permission, he pulled forward his chair, untied the small sack and tapped black powder into the barrel.

"Go and see the cradle I've had made. My wife will be glad to see you. I'm not good at saying what she needs to hear right now, you womenfolk are much better at that." He laughed awkwardly. "The crib's big enough for triplets, but Doctor Newburn assures me there's only one heir going to appear." He laughed again as if he'd made another joke, peppering black ash on the desktop as his shoulders shook. "Dear me," he muttered, sweeping it into one palm and attempting to funnel it into the sack, but particles insisted on dusting the wood. He looked at the pistol as if unsure what to do next.

"The bullet?" Jiddy suggested. "With the ramrod?"

"It's not merely Mrs. Farsyde who's distracted," he said, grasping the narrow stick and wrapped ball. "Now, what can I do for you that's so important?"

He rammed too hard, and she winced. For all his size, Captain Pinkney had a delicate touch, and he'd taught it to Jiddy. The squire had the touch of a floundering trout.

"Cajole the bullet," the captain had said, *"never force."*

"Well?"

She jumped.

The squire studied her for a moment. "Do you remember how to use a gun?" he asked.

Nodding, she took it from him. Cold and as heavy as when she'd last held a weapon.

Squire Farsyde closed the pistol box before lifting the lid again. "I'll have to order my son one of these. And a pony. It's market day tomorrow. I'll set about purchasing a little cracker for the lad. Maybe a Shetland."

Jiddy imagined a chubby little boy, dressed exactly like the squire, legs astride a round-bellied little horse.

"Maybe a wooden sword before a pistol?" she said, brandishing the long-barrelled gun.

"Sword? Oh, yes, ha-ha. And a leather belt with a hilt. I'd best get along with sourcing one."

"Not too long, though. You don't want your son tripping over it."

"No, absolutely. Don't want the little chap falling over himself."

The squire wandered over to the window and gazed out as if imagining the little boy thrusting the air with a blade.

"He'll need more clothes by the time he's jousting," Jiddy said. She cocked the trigger and dribbled powder into the pan.

"How are you doing?" he asked, walking back to the desk. "Ah, good. Good."

She offered him the handle, but he held up his palms rather than take it.

"He who loads, fires," he said, gesturing to the window. "Open it wide and don't aim for the horse chestnuts."

He looked over her shoulder at the door, and she realised he didn't expect a refusal. *She who loads, shoots.* She'd tried to shoot Captain Pinkney with the last pistol she'd held. It probably lay at the bottom of the sea now, too heavy to float, too broken to be put back together. Nobody had ever found it after the cliff had collapsed.

The squire began folding the cloth and retying the bags of powder and pellets.

"Open the window wide," he reminded her.

"May I ask for your advice?" she said, unfastening the latch.

"Have you forgotten how to use it?" He paused, ramrod in one hand, sock of bullets in the other.

"No, I remember everything Captain Pinkney taught me. It's about Violet Ashner."

"Fire away."

It was easy to hold her hands steady without a strong wind to battle against and the absolute need to hit her target. The bullet fired into the silver sky, disappearing into black specks of crows, cawing into the blast.

"Please will you help me persuade Mr. Ashner to let Violet come to my sewing school, sir?" She watched the birds resettle in the treetops.

Taking back the pistol, he ambled to his desk. "Your sewing school could be a good idea, but Violet is a busy girl. She's a handy lass in the house. Why make such a fuss of her when there's plenty of others who would benefit?"

"I believe it'd be good for Violet, and she's already shown she has a knack. She's helped me a couple of times with house mending. Would you talk to Mr. Ashner and explain point of teaching her a proper skill?"

"Hmm. Mr. Ashner isn't an easy man to persuade, and I'm reluctant to take a heavy hand with him. He is Violet's father after all."

Jiddy followed to his desk. "I've heard lasses are heading to big towns to work in factories. Seems to me, it's better to have a skill few have rather than be one of many. Housemaids are easy to find, a good seamstress less so. If you've got a skill, you can earn more. Everyone, especially Mr. Ashner, will like sound of that."

"Are you thinking of leaving us?"

"No!" She laughed. "I heard there's a new store in York, and they'll be looking for seamstresses. They'll pay well. It's not only Violet, though she's a start. I'd like to get some of other girls I teach to work there." She looked him steadfastly in the eye. "It's a good plan, and you know as well as me, there's not enough work in Bay."

The squire made a ticking sound with his tongue. "All right," he said, closing the box, "but I won't promise he'll say yes."

She smiled. "Thank you. And I'll do anything you ask for Mrs. Farsyde, anything to help her with her baby."

The squire tapped his fingers on the desk. "I've been thinking..." He paused and looked at Jiddy. "Mrs. Farsyde needs a treat before the baby comes. I suggest a ball and inviting all our neighbours. If there is work for your girls at some of the big houses around here, they won't need to go as far as York. Families might prefer them closer."

She nodded. The squire surprised her. "Would ladies from Fylingthorpe and Egton and Whitby come?" she asked. "And from Pickering and Sleights and all the grand houses in Scarborough?"

"I'm sure Mrs. Farsyde will talk to them. She always speaks highly of the work you do for her."

Dancing and laughter and all the rich ladies of the county in one house. Placements could be found for all the girls.

"Mrs. Farsyde would love a ball," said Jiddy. "Thank you, sir. I feel a great weight has been lifted."

CHAPTER THIRTEEN

Scrubbing the gull droppings from the headstone,
Jiddy felt content. She had a ballgown to alter for Mrs.
Farsyde and the prospect of jobs to entice lasses to come
to her school. For the first time in ages, life was good. She
looked at the snatches of sky between the leafy branches
and smiled, wondering how the gulls aimed so precisely.
Did they practise? Maybe that was what success meant.
She wet the cloth and rubbed again. Maybe they did it
to give her something else to keep busy. It didn't matter.
She loved scrubbing the stone.

The damp earth curved around her knees, and she
shifted into a crouching position. Pouring water from the
canister, she watched it trickle over the grave's inscription
before tracing her fingers across the letters. Even though
she felt uplifted, tears still pricked her eyes as they always
did when she visited the cemetery. In the green and
cool, hearing the little wrens chirping, she couldn't help
but think about Thomas and Mary. God had been cruel
making her final memory of them both so painful. She
tried to focus on the laughter and the teasing and funny
moments, but images of salt, stained pink with Thomas's
blood and the spewing of black, coffee-like sludge staining
Mary's chest always came into her mind.

She concentrated on the stone. Poured more water. Scrubbed harder than she needed. Sometimes being busy worked, and sometimes her thoughts drifted whatever she did. Sometimes, you needed people.

If Jonas had been sat there, commenting she'd missed a bit or to put more elbow in, she'd not have these thoughts in her head. Typical it would be Jonas coming into her mind. Maybe it was because he'd always been there, knowing Thomas and Mary and all their neighbours. Jonas distracted her from anger by pointing out how lucky she was. He stopped her from crying by finding the right words to say. He told her about farmers he met when at market with his da and relayed the news merchants brought from the big cities. He told her about cottages left empty because weavers had abandoned them to find work in those cities. He helped her understand about the empty homes and why people left behind fields and lands to live in black stone rooms and streets where you couldn't move for crowds.

Jiddy shook herself and leaned back to look at the headstone. Small green and white rings of age spread over Thomas's and Mary's names, and no matter how she tried, she couldn't remove the creeping growth.

"It's the damp and shade," Annie had said.

"It's lack of elbow grease," Helen Drake had shouted when the older woman had been tidying some corner of the graveyard. That's what Jonas would have said too.

Being kind meant Mary hadn't been able to say no to Captain Pinkney when he'd trawled the Baytown ginnels looking for someone to take in a mewling outsider's baby.

"Sorry, Mary," Jiddy said, brushing her fingertips over the shell-shaped signs of fungus. At least she'd cleared away the missiles of bird poo. The stones that formed a border around the grave rested in neat lines. She cupped her hand for a moment around the sole white one at the top before turning to look around the graveyard. No-one there.

Pouring water into the chipped earthenware pot, she arranged the handful of wallflowers, taken from Thorpe Hall gardens with the squire's permission. There had always been a few of the deep-yellow blooms on the table at Sunny Place. Her eyes filled again, and she wiped them with the back of one hand. "Stop it right now," she said, dropping the empty canister into her basket along with the dirty cloth.

She looked around at the straggle of gravestones. So many familiar names. Directly ahead, up by the top wall and more like a boulder than a cut slab, stood a grave removed from the rest. After studying it for a few moments, she lifted one of the stems from the pot. Striding through the lengthening grass and a flurry of bluebells budding from the green, she approached. Her skirt, catching on a shoot of bramble, tugged her to a stop, and she untangled its sharp claws.

The lop-sided rock stood half-hidden in the undergrowth. The name had shrunk into the stone.

Hating to see it hidden, Jiddy pushed aside the grass. She'd not sought it out since Jonas had left.

She laid the stem of mustard-coloured flowers in the overgrown grass. After a moment, she took out the damp cloth and wiped it over the letters.

Hettie Chaplow
1776

The year Jonas was born. Jiddy wished she'd asked more about his mam. Hettie was the same age when she died as Jiddy was now, and it was hard to imagine old Mr. Chaplow with such a young bride. She wondered what Hettie had looked like.

Hearing a noise, she stood. A rabbit lolloped between graves and disappeared into bushes on the right. A flash of sun bouncing off the sea caught her eye, and she raised her chin to look.

Be kind, Mary always said. She'd head to Meadow Bank and pay Jonas's da a visit. She grasped the basket handle and, one hand on the top stone of the wall, began to climb.

"Where are you off to, Jiddy Vardy?"

The unexpected voice made her overbalance, and she tottered backwards on the rough grass. Catching herself, she steadied her feet. Helen Drake sat beside a grave barely a yard from where Jiddy stood. The bowed figure brushed her hand over the stone. Resigned to walk straight past rather than clamber over the wall as initially intended, she nodded to the older woman.

"See you were looking at Hettie Chaplow's grave," Helen said.

Jiddy swung her basket. "I were tending to Mary and Thomas's headstone," she replied, edging through a narrow gap between stones.

"I knew Hettie," Helen said. "By rights, she should be buried out near Goathland, but William Chaplow wanted her here because she loved sea."

Jiddy stopped, clutching her basket in both hands. Helen Drake never gave away information readily, yet she'd opened up about the dead woman and revealed an interesting detail about Jonas's mam. There must be a devious reason for her offering this information. Jiddy guessed Helen had been watching her, waiting, like the great big spider she was. Could she give her the satisfaction of asking a question?

She spun around. "I didn't think Mrs. Chaplow were here long enough to make any friends."

Helen pulled wilting flowers out of the chipped pot resting at an angle in the grass and placed them by her side. Taking a spray of buttercups and cow parsley, she made a fuss of arranging them. Jiddy waited, desperate to hear about Hettie but reluctant to show her interest. Helen Drake spat on a cloth and rubbed the lettering again.

Jiddy took a few paces and stood by the grave. "She were Jonas's mam," she said.

Helen Drake's sharp features looked less pointed in the green light of the graveyard. Jiddy read the headstone.

Joseph Drake, Helen's husband, followed by six names and dates, one year after another.

Helen patted the headstone. "Not one of my babes survived," she said.

Jiddy sat, wondering why she'd always thought Helen Drake was barren. "What were Hettie Chaplow like?"

"What were Hettie Chaplow like?" Helen repeated. "Lads didn't sweep lassies like Hettie Fletcher off their feet, that's what lass was like," Helen said. "Did you know her da called her runt of family?" Jiddy shook her head. Helen sucked her teeth. "Old man Fletcher weren't a pleasant man. William Chaplow knew all farmers in area were aware of his nature from their dealings with him at market. No-one went near Highlands Farm unless they had to."

"How did Mr. Chaplow meet her?" Jiddy asked.

"Hettie as youngest, weren't supposed to marry." Helen dropped her hands in her lap. "She were supposed to care for her da in his old age."

Jiddy waited for her to continue. She hated it when people drew out a story, and this is what Helen always did. "But she didn't?" Jiddy prompted eventually.

"She couldn't," corrected Helen. "Farmer Fletcher had to find Hettie a husband in a hurry."

Jiddy looked across the churchyard. She wasn't going to be the one to offer the name of Harvey Hartshorn as the most appropriate husband in the circumstances.

"I'm only going on what Hettie told me," Helen continued. "She were desperate to talk. It were as though she knew she'd not survive birth."

"But Jonas were a healthy baby!"

"Oh, yes," said Helen, "and it were an easy birth. He wasn't a big babe either, but she faded straight off." She rubbed the lettering again. "You never can tell."

Jiddy followed the names on the stone. Babies less than a year old. Every one of them. "You said Hettie liked the sea?"

Helen's gaze flickered. "Lasses used to go to market, hoping to meet a dashing farmer's son or a drayman or horseman, maybe a lad who worked in one of them big houses. Anyone but a fishing or whaling man from Robin Hood's Bay, Whitby or even Staithes." She paused. "No-one wants to be a widow left with a bunch of bairns. But Hettie Fletcher were different. She were an inlander who wanted to live by sea."

Helen rubbed the top of the stone and over its sides. Mary had never mentioned Helen's losses, and as a child, Jiddy had been oblivious. "D'you want me to leave you?" Jiddy asked, struggling to stand.

Helen gestured for her to remain seated. "Stay," she said. "I liked Hettie, but I don't like sea the way she did. Odd an inlander was so fascinated by tides, but I suppose it were its novelty."

"Jonas weren't keen on water," Jiddy said.

Helen nodded. "No, that were always you, weren't it?"

Jiddy smiled. "Jonas were more interested in what you could get from sea than enjoying it for what it were."

Helen stood awkwardly. A slip of slate grey glistened between the rooftops. "Sea gives us plenty," she said, "but it knows how to take as well."

"I'm sorry you lost your bairns," said Jiddy.

Helen folded her arms, and her face took on its usual knife-like quality. "Hettie wanted her baby."

"Mr. Chaplow must have been pleased, but he'd have been grieved as well."

"You daft ninny," said Helen, setting off. "Hettie wanted a baby resembling Hartshorn fellow she loved so much, or so she said. He broke her heart, seems obvious to me."

"But she married Mr. Chaplow."

"Weren't you listening?" Helen raised her voice. "If a lass gets in trouble, she must marry first man that'll take her. Fletcher were a clever bugger. He spotted William Chaplow across livestock pen, and there were no escaping for poor man."

Jiddy felt like a fly in a spider's web, but she couldn't stop her curiosity. "He could've said no, couldn't he?"

"Every farmer wants a son to help 'em out. William Chaplow's no different." Helen set off, but turned and eyed Jiddy. "Nice of you to tidy his wife's grave," she added before heading down to the gate.

Jiddy watched her go, wondering if Helen implied a meaning in that last statement. She held no animosity to

Hettie or Mr. Chaplow, but she'd shown an unusual lack of curiosity about Jonas's real father.

The Hartshorn lads were obviously not too bashful about coming forward with young lasses and leaving them with problems to sort. She thought back to when she'd met Harvey Hartshorn, sitting in a corner of the moorland inn, next to Lord Ryethorpe. He'd smelt of beef, wine and saddle wax. His chestnut hair had fallen over his eyes, exactly as Jonas's did.

Jiddy returned up the slope to stand in front of Hettie Fletcher's grave and wondered what Jonas's mum had really been like. It sounded like Hettie never had a say in what she wanted. She'd lain with Harvey Hartshorn as an unmarried woman, though. She'd chosen her fate, and she'd told Helen Drake she loved him, same story as Maria Vardarelli, only Jiddy's mother had never been forced to marry. It seemed both Jiddy and Jonas had been cursed in some way because their mothers had fallen for Hartshorns.

She swung her basket and clambered over the wall. Wrenching her skirt free from yet another bramble, she plodded through the long grass, passing beside silver birches and rowan until she reached the bottom sheep field and saw Meadow Bank Farm in the distance.

Jonas's cousin John leaned on the farm gate talking to two men. Even from behind, Jiddy recognised Sandy Kellock and Abe Storm, and she retraced her steps, not in the mood for banter or having to put on a sassy air for them. Too late. Abe had caught sight of her.

"What brings you here?" he shouted.

She sauntered back along the track. "Might have to ask same of you," she said, keeping eye contact. "Never took you for being much interested in sheep and cows."

Abe grinned. "They can be interesting from time to time."

She shrugged. "I'll leave you to it."

Sandy whistled and thumped Abe's arm, for which he received a punch in return. John stood apart, looking wiry and pinched beside the rough fishermen.

Sandy leaned over the gate. "We've finished here," he said. "Think on what we've talked about."

John nodded and ambled across the yard towards the farmhouse.

"We'll be in touch," said Abe, patting Jiddy's shoulder. "Something new to get our heads around."

She jerked away from him. "Don't drag me into any cock-brained scheme!"

Abe touched his cap and waved a hand, following Sandy striding towards the ridge. Left alone, Jiddy tapped her basket against her leg, wondering what they were plotting, only to jump at the sound of a voice.

"Hello?" Sarah Chaplow approached, rubbing her hands on her pinny.

Jiddy leaned on the gate. John must have sent his wife out to speak with her. "How do?" she said. "Saw your husband heading inside." She wasn't going to let him off the hook for not inviting her in.

"Have you come to buy some eggs?" Sarah asked, unfazed.

Jiddy took in the hens scratching in the mud; a new dog, rusty-coloured and matted, stretched by the kitchen door. "Is Mr. Chaplow about?"

Sarah straightened her back. "Thought you said you'd seen my husband."

"Old Mr. Chaplow," Jiddy corrected. "Jonas's da."

Sarah cocked her head. "He's busy. Can I pass on a message?"

Jiddy recalled what Helen Drake had said about making friends with Hettie Fletcher. "How's it going?" she asked. "Are you getting to know women in Bay?"

The muscles in Sarah's face twitched, telling Jiddy all she needed to know.

"Have you a cup of tea on go?" Jiddy asked. "I'm parched."

She wasn't sure whether she'd be invited in until Sara unlatched the gate and pulled it open.

The kitchen hadn't changed since Jonas had left. John was nowhere in sight. Sarah nodded to the table and Jiddy pulled out a chair, placing her basket on the floor. She really was thirsty and sipped eagerly at the proffered tea. Sarah watched, wary. It made Jiddy wonder if this was how Hettie had felt when Helen Drake came a calling, at first out of curiosity, hopefully later out of friendship.

CHAPTER FOURTEEN

T he first touch of stone made Jonas's heart swell. Feet sore from walking, muscles and bones aching from sleeping rough huddled close to barns, enclosures or whatever nook out of the wind he could find, for the first time in what felt like months, he'd found a place he wanted to belong.

The chief stonemason may not agree. Jonas would have to prove he had a place amongst the Minster workers if he wanted to remain, but he'd not spent years building and mending drystone walls for nothing. It had taught him to gauge a stone's weight while it rested in his palms; he could judge its size and whether it was sandstone or grit. He had an innate sense if it would break easily or hold like granite. He might not have sculpted angels or saints, but he knew beyond a shadow of doubt stone felt right in his hands.

He'd never seen a building more beautiful than the Minster or felt excited about using his hands to create something since making channels in the sand with Jiddy, and he wanted a new life to blot out the past. He clenched his jaw, glancing at the cluster of young men.

"You!"

Several heads twisted in the direction of the shout.

"You lot, up to the one with red hair."

Jonas glanced along the line before realising the man beckoning meant him. He touched his chest, and the man nodded. Rejigging his bag, he followed a dozen others. The man merely glanced at them, pointing a chalky finger to vacant places at the long table laden with blocks of stone looked over by a line of anxious faces.

"Right," the man said when they had discarded their bags. "You've each a chisel and a hammer and a clean stone. See if you can copy this."

He pointed to a stone figure of a man clothed in a long robe, with flowing hair and a beard.

"Christ," the lad next to Jonas mumbled.

Jonas stared at the perfectly proportioned figure. How could any of them copy such a statue?

"You've one hour."

The man addressed the remaining lads in the line. "You can wait or come back. Up to you."

No-one in the line moved.

Instinctively, Jonas grabbed the block of stone with both hands. Some stared at their chisels and hammers while others gathered their tools and began chipping straight away. A cracking sound filled the air.

If they'd asked Jonas to repair the Minster walls, he could have done it easily, but to find Christ in a piece of rock seemed impossible. Everyone around the table was whittling away now. He glanced at the figure they were meant to reproduce and shook his head. The lad next to him was hitting his stone with all the strength he could muster. The lad on the other side was almost kissing his block.

Jonas ran his thumbs on the edge of the facing side of his own stone before measuring again with his thumbs. He'd always been able to pick the right sized rock for a corresponding gap in a wall. He thought of his da, useless at the task. Knowing the shape of a stone was a start. He could do that without a second glance. Fixing all his attention on the task, he measured the height of the figure.

With shaking hands, he collected the tools set on the table. He'd used a hammer plenty of times but not this chisel contraption. After a moment, he struck. Wiping the surface, he saw he'd made his first mark. Sounds of tapping emanated around him. No-one spoke. What had he got to lose?

Jonas concentrated until he had created a profile, the outlines of a tunic and the start of bare feet. He formed the lump of one hand, but he was taking too long. All around the table stood stone men, and he had an unrecognisable blob, at best an imprint of a man.

"Enough!" The stonemason raised his hand, and they released their hammers and chisels.

Jonas stared at his hands clasped on the table. Dust settled everywhere, even in the grooves around his nails and in the lines of his skin. Droplets of sweat beaded his forehead, and he wiped his face. He'd started too late; he'd idled. He'd not done enough. He should leave straight away and avoid the humiliation of having his attempt criticised.

The stonemason and another man were examining the first stone. Jonas made out a robe, two arms and a head. He couldn't stay to hear them scoff at his attempt or even stay to bear the silence of their dismissal. It had been a stupid idea. Better a sword in the belly than the slow twist of scorn. The master mason and his assistant shifted down the line, pointing at a brilliantly captured Christ, commenting on a well-fashioned shoulder. These lads were better than him. What had he been thinking? The stonemasons stepped closer. He couldn't stand the shame of being rejected. He wouldn't be able to face the tapping of hammers and see others doing a job he'd hoped he could do if he stayed. He swung his leg over the bench and hopped to retrieve his bag, vowing he'd keep well away from York Minster in future.

He crossed the square under the shadow of the vast church. The emptiness in his belly brought on a clench of sickness, and he wondered if here, in the city, he'd find any form of employment. Strangers wouldn't notice how low he'd come. On the other hand, knowing no-one, he had no-one to ask for a meal or a bed. If he had something to eat and gather his strength, he could try the inns, see if they needed someone to tend to the horses or, if not, find work breaking stones or crushing bones to make fertiliser.

He wished he could return to Robin Hood's Bay. Why not? He readjusted the bag on his shoulder. Why not? There was always work on a farm. He'd find a way to be friends with Jiddy. He closed his eyes as the image of her face filled his head.

"Lad!" A voice cut into his reverie. "You there!"

A man nudged Jonas's arm. The stonemason beckoned from across the square. "Don't you want a job?"

CHAPTER FIFTEEN

In the mauve dusk, trying to keep quiet while tingling with excitement, Annie shifted from one foot to the other. Betsie clasped her hands together and crept towards the window. Jiddy, one palm on the window jamb, leaned into the glass, looking for Mrs. Farsyde's familiar figure inside. The room dazzled with light and movement. She had forgotten. She'd forgotten how magical a room, sparkling with candles, crystal and ladies in their best frocks and most treasured jewels, could be. Men, colourful too, frothed with lace at their necks and cuffs, shoe buckles and coat buttons, gleaming as they jumped and side-stepped and twirled in dance.

In a corner, a group of musicians, faces flushed with heat, swept bows across strings; one man, fingers curled, sat at a keyboard, and another blew into a flute. Even through the closed window, melodic notes petered through.

"Have you seen food?" squealed Annie.

"Makes your mouth water, don't it?" said Betsie, licking her lips.

Jiddy caught sight of the squire, standing by the fireplace with three or four other gentlemen, wigs puffed and white, the squire's wig askew, but no sign of the mistress of the house.

110

"Can either of you see Mrs. Farsyde?" she asked.

"Give us a minute," said Betsie. "I'm still eyeing food."

Annie pointed. "She's there, on sofa by wall."

Jiddy caught sight of the lady of the house and sighed. "What's she doing? She promised she'd talk to ladies tonight about employing Violet."

"She will," said Annie. "People are still arriving."

Three couples walked through the door and gazed around the room.

"Oh, my word, the squire!" laughed Betsie, and they watched Squire Farsyde hurry across the floor to greet the newcomers.

"Mrs. Farsyde should get up and greet them too," Jiddy grumbled. "Would be the perfect time to admire their gowns and mention she knows seamstresses who would make even better ones for them."

"She can't say that!" said Betsie, face so close to the glass she almost kissed it.

"Why not? She said she would when I asked her."

"Maybe she doesn't feel very well and doesn't want to move," suggested Annie.

"Must be torture having to sit and not dance," said Betsie.

Mrs. Farsyde remained seated with her hands in her lap and staring in the opposite direction to the latest arrivals. An older lady at her side sat equally still and silent. The sight made Jiddy uneasy.

"Who's sat next to her?" she asked.

"Magistrate's wife. They've come all way from Scarborough!" said Betsie.

"Why were you on beach with Mrs. Farsyde other week?" asked Annie. "I've never seen Mrs. Farsyde on beach before. It's odd with her in her condition."

"Maybe she wants to see what your life's like, Jiddy, hey?" said Betsie before Jiddy could reply. "She wants to know what it's like to go crabbing."

"Do you think she's happy?" asked Jiddy. "I thought she'd be happy."

Annie shuffled sideways to half hide behind the casement. "I hope nobody notices us."

A new dance began. Figures stepped left in unison and several paces to the right before marching forward and back again. Mrs. Farsyde wasn't watching the dancers; rather, her gaze was trained on a window to the left of the girls.

Betsie pressed her nose to the glass. "I wish I could be one of them instead of having to stand out here like a beggar asking for scraps."

"I'd be frightened," said Annie. "I don't know any of the steps."

"They're not born knowing how to dance," said Jiddy. "They practise all time, so it seems easy, but it isn't."

Betsie pushed herself away from the window again. "You told us it were easy when Mrs. Farsyde took to teaching you."

"Shhh!" Annie hushed them both. "I want to listen."

Undeterred, Betsie grabbed Jiddy's arm. "Teach us the dance. I want to dance like them."

"Betsie, stop pulling her," said Annie.

"I want to learn," insisted Betsie.

"But you hate it when Jiddy even breaks into a twirl. D'you remember them two preventives?"

Betsie scowled. "That were different. She were showing off. I'll enjoy it if you teach us to do what they're doing without being on show."

Jiddy glanced at the dancers inside, jumping and turning in lines, palms pressing, replicating each other as they side-stepped. The ladies' skirts swished; the men's jackets flared.

"Over here." She pointed, striding to the lawn. Light from the windows spilled across the path. Giggling, Annie followed with Betsie close behind. Reaching the grass, Jiddy pinched her skirt with her fingertips and jigged on the spot.

"Wait," said Annie. "You have to show us what to do."

Stepping to the right, Jiddy spun on her toes before returning to the left. Annie hoisted her skirt and attempted to follow.

"I said wait! Which way do we go?"

Jiddy spread her arms wide and twirled around and around.

"No! Stop! There are set steps! This isn't fair! You're too quick!" moaned Betsie.

"Listen to melody," said Jiddy, taking Betsie's hand and reaching for Annie's. "It's like we dance at midsummer."

They snaked together, alternating shoulders, holding and dropping hands faster and faster until they skipped around each other, turning and spinning, panting louder as the musicians led a steady, distant beat. Intermittently, one or another laughed aloud, their smiles growing, and when the music stopped, they slowed. Dropping hands, they caught their breath and looked at each other, until, suddenly self-conscious, they glanced away. Betsie wiped her face with her sleeve. Annie, hands on her hips, closed her eyes. Jiddy dropped back her head and gazed at the starry sky.

If this moment lasted forever, Jiddy thought, she could be happy. Happy to listen to Betsie and Annie breathing heavily and to the click of night air, feeling the cool darkness on her warm cheeks. She took a deep breath. Dancing had made her forget Jonas had left and Samuel had drowned in the high tide. Right in this moment, she could believe those things had never happened. She might even be standing on a ship with Captain Pinkney, the wind at their backs and the world rich to explore.

The sound of footsteps broke the spell. Betsie was meandering back over the flagstones towards the window with Annie strolling behind.

"Let's get off and comfort ourselves with some thin soup and pretend it's blancmange!" said Jiddy.

Groaning, Annie and Betsie reached the spillage of light on the path. Mrs. Farsyde hadn't moved. She still sat at the far side of the room, eyes fixed directly ahead. The lady who had been sitting next to her had moved across to the table and filled a dish with jelly while talking to someone in a maroon dress. Mrs. Farsyde, in pale grey and with a fine shawl around her shoulders, hands clasped in her lap, could have been a statue.

"Bet she wishes she weren't with bairn," said Betsie.

"Bet she wishes she could be dancing," said Annie.

"I wish she were on her feet talking to the other ladies," said Jiddy.

"Don't know why you bothered asking her to help," said Betsie. "Not worth the effort when she's gentry and don't really care about likes of Violet or other lasses."

"Squire should be sat with her," Jiddy said, ignoring Betsie's comment. "She can't be finding this easy. If he held her arm and supported her, she could be talking to lots of those ladies."

Annie pointed. "He's over there."

Surrounded by his usual companions, they could make out the squire. Shorter than those he stood near, but wider and with a glass in one hand and waving a handkerchief in the other, he guffawed. One or two of the other gentlemen smiled.

"Squire's got a new coat," said Jiddy. "He's trying his best to be smart."

"He looks like a right bumpkin," said Betsie.

"He's not comfortable, you can tell. He's best in his daily clothes. He's only done this for Mrs. Farsyde."

"Can't see him being any good at dancing."

"Ooh! They're eating!" said Annie.

She and Betsie scurried around the bushes to the next window for a better view of the long table. They whispered to each other about the candelabras illuminating rows of cakes decorated with sugared flowers standing next to bowls of jelly and blancmange and platters of biscuits and pies.

Jiddy could still hear them, though they were hidden by large evergreen shrubs.

"Maybe there'll be some left in morning and Mrs. King will give us some," said Annie.

"I can almost taste the frosting on them cakes," Betsie said.

"My mouth is watering. This is making me so hungry."

"Have you seen tall man's plate! He's got enough piled on there for six people!"

"Shhh!" Jiddy warned, and Betsie and Annie lowered their voices.

She continued to study Mrs. Farsyde; maybe she did wish she was able to dance. The music continued; the room glowed with an army of red jackets and swirling fabric, gowns like sailing ships. Despite what she said, Jiddy could have stayed all night. The ladies were so elegant and the men so smart with their bright jackets and epaulettes and gleaming buttons so perfect. Mrs. Farsyde didn't engage with anyone even though people nodded and tried to approach. "She doesn't see you," Jiddy whispered.

She wondered what would happen if Mrs. Farsyde caught sight of her through the glass. Would she scream? The squire kept mastiffs against interlopers. If anyone cried out or gave warning, he'd set them loose, and who could outrun vicious, hungry, sharp-fanged dogs?

Mrs. Farsyde must be wishing Samuel were one of the officers dancing in the room; she must be picturing him, imagining their palms touching, his hand on her back, turning and turning, eyes transfixed—the image had certainly entered Jiddy's mind. She remembered the touch of Samuel's jacket. She remembered how jealous Jonas had been.

Samuel coming to Mrs. Farsyde's aid on the stairway would give her pleasure. Leaning over and making her eyes shine. Jiddy shook herself to banish the thoughts. She didn't want to think about love when it proved time and again to be no good.

The squire wandered back to the small crowd by the fireplace, his face even redder and more animated. Betsie and Annie still chattered. Jiddy raised her shawl over her head. The thought of Samuel and Mrs. Farsyde made her think about Jonas. Time to go. She took one last look at the sofa. It was empty. There was no sign of the lady of the house. Where had she gone?

Jiddy gasped and stepped sideways, pushing into the prickle of leaves. Too late. Through the dancing figures, Mrs. Farsyde walked towards the window, eyes fixed and mouth open. Jiddy couldn't tear herself away. There was something about Mrs. Farsyde's expression, something about her eyes. Her features trembled. Jiddy glanced at the window to her left and, hand tracing the wall, crept towards it. A figure stood in the window, and Jiddy let out a sharp cry. Luckily, they didn't appear to hear. She peered closer. So that was what had been holding Mrs. Farsyde's attention. She couldn't see her mistress now, but the shoulders and back of an officer filled the glass, the rich red fabric of his tunic, the blonde sheen of his hatless head. After the revelation on the causeway, she'd not be taken in again. Jiddy raised her knuckles to the glass, then stopped herself. Whoever the officer was, they'd probably arrest her on grounds of trespass.

"It's not Samuel!" she wanted to shout, but Mrs. Farsyde wouldn't thank her. Let her have her moment of hope. Let her believe, if only for a few more seconds. Turning quickly, Jiddy stumbled towards the other girls.

"Annie, Betsie," she stuttered, rustling the bush as she blundered past. "We've got to go."

"What now? Why the sudden rush?" asked Betsie.

"Mrs. Farsyde..." Jiddy glanced at the window, at the lady with the jelly and Squire Farsyde, jolly and oblivious to his wife. "It's not worth chancing it further. Come on!"

"Ow!"

"Oy!"

"Annie! Stop shoving!" shouted Betsie.

Jiddy pushed them in the direction of the lawn, and not needing telling twice, Annie and Betsie scurried over the flags towards the wall at the far end of the garden.

They stopped running halfway across the adjacent field. Betsie bent over, hands on knees, her throat rasping. Annie crossed her arms over her stomach, eyes closed, face uptilted, panting loudly, while Jiddy looked back the way they had come. She half-expected to see the same figure she'd seen in the window, riding on horseback towards them.

Her chest ached. Her throat hurt. She took deep, painful breaths. They had left the lights of Thorpe Hall behind, and the glow of the moon and starry sky cast a white glow over the trees. Hands shaking, Jiddy touched Betsie and Annie on the shoulder. "You both all right?" she asked.

"Flaming hell," said Betsie, catching her breath. "I'm sweating cobs, aren't you?"

Annie grasped Jiddy's hand. "Can you hear dogs?"

"It's in your head," said Betsie. "I can't hear nowt."

"I'm not so sure..." said Jiddy, putting a finger to her lips.

The sound of barking drawing nearer made them all jump. Simultaneously breaking into a run, they headed for the trees.

"Make for beck!" Jiddy shouted.

A few fields away, dogs howled. Annie tripped and floundered, and catching her friend's arm, Jiddy stumbled in the tufts of grass and spires of brambles. Betsie, blundering amongst the trees, had almost disappeared. Heart pounding, Jiddy stayed with Annie as they pushed through the straggling undergrowth. The beck bubbled, and they slipped and slithered along its bank, clutching at the damp earth. Into the trees again, Jiddy glanced over her shoulder to check Annie followed. In the near dark, she made out Annie's moving shape.

119

At the first building, at the end of the Bolts, they stopped. Betsie hadn't even waited. Jiddy listened. No sound of the dogs. "What a night!" she said, bending over and squeezing her sides.

"It were horrible," said Annie, panting hard. "I thought we were going to be ripped apart and fed to pigs."

"Come on, we'd best keep moving," said Jiddy, taking Annie's hand.

Keeping close to walls, they made their way along the Bolts until they reached Annie's house. Jiddy hugged her before heading to Fisherhead with only the moon to light her way and an unsettling feeling in her belly.

CHAPTER SIXTEEN

Grey light filtered through the window, spreading a sombre dawn into the bedroom belying the previous night's clear sky. Jiddy pulled the covers to her chin. Gulls scrambled on the roof, and she listened for other sounds of the house. As a child, she'd loved lying in bed, listening to noises from below, and she'd have welcomed those homely sounds again. If only the house was filled with people she cared about; the shift of a chair; the stirring of a pot; plates being laid on the table; a drawer closing; a knock at the door; friendly voices.

She listened again, telling herself the sounds of barking dogs were echoes from last night and not hounds chasing her still. Annie and Betsie would be at home, safe. The dogs would be chained again, and everyone at Thorpe Hall would be proud they'd scared away suspected cutthroats. The only noises were those outside. Any noises within the cottage she was making herself; the bed creaking as she shifted; her foot on the floor; the flap of material as she dropped her skirt over her head. She wondered how Captain Pinkney had stood living alone. Maybe that was why he'd gone away all the time.

Pausing, hand on the hooks of her jacket, she waited for a cascade of women's laughter. Even a sharp word would've been a relief, but the room below remained quiet, and the adjacent room, silent.

"Don't be daft," she told herself.

Hand sliding over the wall, she descended the stairs and, turning the corner, viewed the empty room, taking in the long table, the ladder-backed chairs, the stove with the tiniest gleam of burning coal.

"Damn, damn it," she muttered, grabbing sticks from a bucket and lodging them carefully into the embers. Ash crumbled and pieces of burnt log shifted. She dropped the poker with a clang as the red glow dimmed. "No, no!" She crouched forward, blowing gently into the grate to coax heat back into the fire. Grey ash dusted a charred log. Grabbing a bundle of twigs, she placed small pieces along the wood and blew gently again. A burst of orange flared and immediately disappeared.

"Light, you bugger!"

With her fingers, she felt along the log, raising it carefully, but the entire underbelly broke off and sank its black corpse into grey-white ash. She'd have to start from scratch and waste an hour relaying the wood and pieces of coal with cold, clumsy fingers. Closing her eyes again, she listened.

A distant gull, probably wheeling over the beach, cried out. Inside the cottage, even the fire kept quiet. She willed someone to be coming up the tunnel and knocking on the secret door to be let in.

Samuel's face, as the last person who had appeared through the hidden panel, came into her mind, and she shivered.

Her hands were blackened with smut and ash, and a smudge showed she'd wiped them on her skirt. She should rebuild the structure from scratch, but instead, she pulled her shawl tighter around her shoulders and, tugging it taut across her chest, knotted it around her waist.

Before. Before Mary died, and over at Sunny Place, she'd have come downstairs to the heat of a well-built fire, with bread warm or gruel piping hot and ready to serve from the blackened pot that was always in use for some meal.

Once upon a time, Rebecca would have been there, having popped in on some errand or other. But always Mary, awake first, stoking the coals, warming broth or oats and milk, enticing Jiddy with aromas calling to her belly.

"I flaming well hate you for leaving me, Jonas Chaplow!" she shouted.

She lifted the burnt-out log and put it on the hearth. One by one, she picked out fresh sticks and piled them on the opposite side before taking the brush and jigging ash through the metal bars. Rattling a stick into crevices, she cleared more debris until, clear of detritus and the ashtray full, she drew it out and tipped it into the bucket, turning away as puffs of dust rose, no matter how careful she tried to be.

Mary would tell her to stop moping; Rebecca, dear, sharp Rebecca would have said it even more succinctly.

"Oh, for crying out loud, Jiddy, pull yourself together."

A rap on the door, short and decisive, made her jump, and she dropped the poker with a clatter.

Abe, Sandy and Big Isaac blundered in, stamping across the floor without a greeting. Scraping chairs out from under the table, they sat.

"Just because door's unlocked don't mean you can walk straight in," she said, brushing her skirt. "What do you want?"

"Ba-a-a!" Sandy bleated, and the other two laughed.

CHAPTER SEVENTEEN

J iddy placed coals in a neat cluster in the grate and ignored them.

"I'm talking about sheep!" Sandy chuckled. "You know sheep. Thick, white creatures, live off grass."

They weren't going to budge, boots crossed, legs outstretched.

"Make us a brew, there's a good lass," said Big Isaac.

Jiddy piled up a mound of twigs. "I don't want you in my home. I've told you before, this can't be your meeting place no more."

"Don't be daft. We've always used Fisherhead."

"Not anymore," she said, glancing over her shoulder. "Unless you want to join my school and learn how to stitch a pretty gown!"

Abe laughed, sinking into one of the chairs by the hearth and drawing out his pipe. "This won't do, lass. What's up with you, letting fire go?"

"Fine, stay," said Jiddy, jumping to her feet and ignoring Abe's question. "I'll get out the cottons. Lucky for you I've a fresh batch of dyed linen."

"Now listen here, missy," started Big Isaac.

"No, you listen. It's a sewing school now, and this is my property, so you'll do what I say within these walls!"

Silas, as he plodded in, closed the door with a bang. He nodded at the grate. "What's happened to the fire?"

"Sit, Silas," said Big Isaac.

"Don't you dare, Silas Biddick," Jiddy warned, brandishing the poker in his direction.

Silas, undecided, hand on the back of a chair, remained half standing, half seated.

"Captain Pinkney's letting you stay here because he thought a lot about Mary," said Big Isaac. "Don't go getting ideas you own place and can do what you want."

"I have deeds!" she declared. "Squire's got them safe! Go ask him who owns Fisherhead Cottage. Now, will you leave me in peace, or do I have to call Dragoons in? They won't be after me if I start bleating, I'm telling you!"

"You don't joke about things like that, Jiddy Vardy," said Sandy.

"I have plenty to be doing without this malarky!" She grabbed another handful of twigs and tossed it on top of the rest.

"Don't get cocky with us, lassie," warned Big Isaac, his face a mottled mix of red and purple, deepening with anger.

"Will you go?" Jiddy asked.

Groaning, Silas sank into the chair.

"No, you don't," she said, grabbing its back. "There are plenty of other places for you to meet."

"We're used to here," said Sandy. "Stop whinging and make us a brew."

"What about Mariners or Fisherman's Arms?" she suggested, picking a log and deciding whether to throw it at them or on the fire.

Big Isaac tapped his pipe on his knee, unconcerned. "We like Fisherhead."

"You can use the entrance from King's Beck for Fisherman's. You wouldn't have to walk through front door like you do here. Meetings would be completely secret," she said, clutching the log to her chest.

Abe nodded towards the pegs by the fireplace that opened the panel leading to the hidden passageway. "We can come through passage right there without anyone knowing."

"But everyone knows about passage."

"Aye, thanks to you and Jonas Chaplow beggaring about, everyone, including whole lot of bloody preventives, knows about passageway."

"That's why you can't use it," she said, recovering. "Much better to be safe at King's Beck."

Abe, having lit his pipe, puffed quietly while Sandy cracked his knuckles. Silas sucked on the few teeth he had left in his mouth, and Big Isaac's silence loomed ominously. Jiddy positioned the piece of wood onto the mound. "All right," she said.

"All right, what?" said Abe.

"All right, you can use Fisherhead, but not when I'm here."

"Where will you be?"

"Anywhere else, and I don't want to know about it."

"You might have to know if we've a job for you," chipped in Big Isaac.

"I said I'm running a school. I have another job now!"

"Sheep are important in this raid, and we need you to keep eye out. Any preventives, and you work your magic charm on 'em, right?"

"I've had enough. Charm them yourself."

Nodding to the big man, Abe rested his pipe on his knee. "There's a crew coming over from Holland with salt and tea. We've nowt to trade, and they're insisting they don't want coin on this one. Don't act silly. It's all hands on deck."

"You're telling me best you can offer is a flock of sheep?" She laughed, keeping a wary eye on Big Isaac. "I doubt they'll be chuffed when they see a load of bleating woolly bales!"

"You daft beggar. Me and Sandy spoke to newcomer, John Chaplow up at Meadow Bank. He'll be bringing fleeces, all tied, neat and easy to handle."

"You're kidding me! You've told someone you don't know about what we do?"

Big Isaac shifted his feet. "Chaplows have been here for centuries. Old William likes the odd barrel, and it's about time they pulled their weight again since Jonas left."

She couldn't believe it. "You used their cart to carry contraband inland!" she shouted. "That's not providing payment for goods!"

Abe waved his pipe. "This side of things is none of your business. Don't get above yourself, lass."

Having created a flare, Jiddy sat back on her haunches. "So why are you here planning as if it's a strategic battle against Napoleon?"

Big Isaac kicked a chair out of his way, making Jiddy jump. "We came to tell you, you're on duty. Night after next. Meet in John Chaplow's cliff meadow," he ordered.

Jiddy folded her arms. "I won't do it!"

"Oh, but you will lass," said Abe, tapping her head with his pipe. She winced, shaking her hair.

"That bloody hurt!"

"Let's be off, lads," said Big Isaac. "And have fire lit proper next time we call, Jiddy."

Before she could retaliate, the others followed him to the door with a loud stamping of their boots.

"You're a smuggler like us, Jiddy Vardy," Big Isaac said from the doorway. "Running a school don't mean you can't come out at night. Abe, Sandy and me are fishermen. Don't hear us moaning we can't carry a few barrels or shift a few sacks of the white stuff when called to, do you?"

Jiddy shook her head.

"Smuggling's in your bones now, lass. No escaping what Captain Pinkney started in you, hey?" He laughed and quietly pulled the door to, leaving Jiddy staring at the orange flames taking hold of the wood.

CHAPTER EIGHTEEN

Abe and Big Isaac surveyed the field of sheep while Sandy strolled along their flanks. The flock stood heavy in their thick fleeces.

"I thought we were shifting skins, not sodding sheep!" said Abe.

"Bleeding farmers. They have one job to do, and they can't even do that right," grumbled Sandy, kicking a tuft of grass.

"Bloody incomers, more like. Jonas would have done it right if he'd been here. John Chaplow will be wishing he'd never come to coast by time I've finished with him. Old William won't get off lightly neither."

"Steady. We'll have words tomorrow, but for now, task in hand, lads, task in hand," ordered Big Isaac. "Dutch are on their way in, and we've got to get these animals moving."

"Someone'll have to signal ship to warn them it's a no-go," said Abe, following Sandy and Big Isaac as they joined Jiddy and several lads on the cliff edge. "Ye gods, I'm going to swipe for someone in morning."

"Who's on beach?" Big Isaac demanded.

Snapped out of her reverie, Jiddy reeled off several names. She couldn't get over Big Isaac's words. *Smuggling's in your bones.* She hadn't been born a smuggler, but she'd caught the knack when she was eight years old. Is that what he meant? John Chaplow was in no way imaginable a smuggler, and she wondered what could have been going on in his head, to not do what he must have promised he'd do. He wasn't trapped the way she was. He could have declined the offer and William would surely have warned him. Now he was caught like she was because Big Isaac wouldn't listen to excuses. There'd be no holding Abe Storm back from giving him a beating. Damn it. She should have said something when she'd seen them talking. John Chaplow was nothing but a fool.

Abe towered against the navy sky, one hand tapping his thigh, the other resting on his belt. Jiddy peered over the edge. It had been a swift clamber up the cliff, all of them expecting the rolled-up fleeces would have been piled ready, with John Chaplow and a couple of farmhands ready to help carry them, and all they'd have to do was lead the way. If she could convince herself this was merely trading livestock, she'd be able to get through the night.

"Schooner's going to be a sitting duck," said Abe.

"Captain's going to be pissed off."

"Pissing off more like."

"Wouldn't have happened in Pinkney's day," muttered Sandy.

The Dutch vessel drew nearer. The water slopped flat, making barely a ripple. On such a balmy night, the air sucked in every sound and made every movement feel heavy. Tempers frayed on sticky nights such as this, and it didn't take much to set off either Abe Storm or Big Isaac.

"Sandy!" Big Isaac ordered. "Get yourself there fast and wave Dutch boat in!"

"Be a right bugger if we get caught with flock of sheep on beach," said Sandy, edging sideways down the path.

"What about goods Dutch are bringing in?" Jiddy said.

Big Isaac cursed under his breath. A sheep bleated again, and this time, other beasts took up the call.

As if it was second nature, Jiddy racked her brains what they could offer the Dutch captain instead of the expected fleeces.

"He'll have to leave his cargo on promise of payment," Big Isaac finally said. "Two of you!" He kicked the nearest backside. "Go with Sandy to help unload."

The lads scrambled to their feet, stumbling and sliding. The other three, including Jiddy, remained, watching their progress. It rarely happened and was usually dependent on the weather, but tonight, the farmers really had disappointed. No captain with a waiting boat ever took an excuse of any kind. Jiddy strolled over to Big Isaac and Abe.

"What if we give them sheep?" she said. "Fleece and mutton, they're getting two for one. A bargain by my reckoning. Might be John Chaplow's done us a favour."

Abe and Big Isaac exchanged a glance. The lads' footsteps whispered from below.

"Give 'em sheep?" said Big Isaac. "You got to be joshing me."

Abe frowned at Jiddy, but she stared back until, without warning, Big Isaac laughed.

"Give 'em sheep," Abe repeated. "Herd them onto boat as if they're wee bairns?"

"Why not?" she said. "Ships take cattle. A schooner can take a flock of sheep. Once one of ewes starts moving, rest'll follow. Easier than chickens if you ask me."

It could go either way, but Big Isaac had laughed, and that meant something. Abe spat, and Jiddy shifted her feet.

"Or we could call it off," she said. "I don't care. I never wanted to be here in first place."

They all heard the oars at the same time. Big Isaac cocked his head. Abe pointed. A crease in the water showed a large rowing boat heading to shore.

"We'll have to shift," said Big Isaac. "It's going to take a few trips with a piddling bowl of wood to carry these sheep."

Abe glanced at the lads waiting on the shore and over at the field, dotted with thick shapes.

Jiddy sighed. "If we have planks for sheep to walk onto boats, that'd help," she suggested. "Don't we have some in caves? I'm sure I've seen—"

Abe didn't need telling twice. "Get down there," he ordered. "Tell Andrew to drag some from cave. You lads!" He gestured to the three hovering at the cliff edge. "Start herding! Come on, rustle up, get round back of them!"

Hitching her skirt, Jiddy headed for the path, realising her job would not be lookout as usual. Tonight, it would be all hands on deck and hope preventives hadn't got wind of their activities.

Abe swore repeatedly, and Big Isaac wasn't far behind with his curses.

"We need a dog!" grumbled Abe before shoving one of the young lads. "Get over there!"

"Round back. Back!" shouted Big Isaac.

"Bloody animals! Get round. There! There!"

The lads puffed and slid, but eventually, they had the flock tottering down the cliff path.

If it hadn't been so serious, it would have been funny, young Storms playing shepherds and Silas cajoling sheep.

On the shore, Jiddy, Andrew and the rest of the lads worked full out, dragging planks from the cave, piling boxes and sacks on the beach from the three rowing boats bobbing in the water. All of them turned to watch the tumble of sheep, bleating and scrabbling, followed by Big Isaac, Abe and the three lads.

"Catch 'em!" shouted Abe.

Sheep hurtled onto the shingle, scrambling over the pebbles.

"Circle them," said Jiddy, gesturing to form a barricade.

They ran, arms outstretched, bending to fence in the panic of the animals. The Dutch sailors stared in bemused astonishment from their boats.

"Sandy! Andrew! Grab the planks!" shouted Big Isaac.

Confused, several of the lads stared at the scatter of sheep until Sandy yelled at them, while Andrew lifted a plank and began dragging it through the shallows.

"Give us hand!" Andrew shouted.

"Get rest to boats. Sheep need to walk up 'em!" ordered Big Isaac.

The Dutch sailors protested, but Andrew and Isaac batted them away, heaving the wood slats against the nearest boats. Jiddy glanced up at the cliff. She couldn't hear sounds of preventive horses or feet, only the wind.

"You lads, get another on!" shouted Sandy, gesturing to another of the boats.

Sheep scattered over the beach with Abe and several others stumbling to round them towards the boats.

Sandy stood thigh-deep in the water, talking to the Dutchmen until, noticing a sheep standing at the water's edge, he dragged it onto the plank. It tried to back up, but he pulled with both hands, shoulder to flank, steadying its weight. Andrew forced a second to follow.

"Halt, stop!" shouted one of the sailors.

"Start on another boat," ordered Sandy. "Four to each!"

Andrew dragged another plank into the water, and this time, the sailors in the boat helped position it while two of the Storm brothers shepherded the scuttling beasts in his direction.

To the shouts of dissent, Sandy, swiftly followed by a panting Abe, yelled they were getting a bargain. "Fleeces and meat! You're getting two for one, and all we get is tea and salt!"

"Plus, it's fresh meat," Sandy said. "Get on." He pushed a fourth animal into the boat. "Come back as soon as you've unloaded," he instructed. "Jiddy! One's escaping!"

Jiddy stumbled, falling to all fours as a determined sheep scuttled out of her reach. "Andrew, help!" she shouted, hands raw and knees painfully dimpled by stones.

Cursing, Annie's brother careered past.

A plank splashed into the water, a sheep vocal as it sank into the foam.

"No, no!" Protests. "We take back our boxes. We don't want animals. Sheep were not the bargain."

"It's mutton."

"Ba-a-a."

A couple of the lads were moving the sacks and boxes of Dutch cargo up the beach, and Big Isaac stepped to block one of the foreign soldiers from following. "Come on, lad," he said. "Fair trade and like."

"They'll be fine on ship," Jiddy called out. "Come on, we can't mess about. Fleeces are good and meat right tender. You're not going to refuse double payment, are you? You can't keep us hanging around. Every minute brings danger."

She glanced towards the causeway, hoping he'd get the message it was better to take the animals and head off the way they'd come rather than hang about and get caught by a preventive boat.

"We want fleece only," said the Dutchman.

"Oh, you daft beggar." Big Isaac ploughed through the water, shoving the man so he fell backwards into the boat.

Immediately, Jiddy and Andrew dragged the plank into position, and Joseph dragged the sheep through the water.

"No, no!"

"Yes, yes!" said Sandy, holding the man back. "Get them on." He waved his arms.

The schooner skulked in deeper water, but the two smaller boats didn't return. Gathered at the water's edge, a dozen or so sheep bleated and attempted to bolt. Noting this, the soldier pushed Sandy back, and several of the animals tumbled into the boat.

"Go, go!" shouted Big Isaac.

Silas and several others were already transferring the sacks and boxes to the cave, but it took longer than they'd intended, and everyone grew increasingly nervy.

"Tell boats to come back!" shouted Big Isaac at the disappearing vessel. They waited, darting intermittently to keep the sheep together, but one by one, the animals got away.

"Thank preacher preventives didn't get wind of this," said Abe as they stood on the beach, watching the schooner disappear into the dark.

"What we going to do with rest of ewes?" Jiddy said.

"Sod 'em," said Big Isaac, marching towards the cave. "We're calling it a night."

The sheep had begun to wander, spreading out in search of grass. One straggled up the path, a couple collapsed, woolly lumps surrounded by stones.

"We can't leave them here!" said Jiddy. "What about when tide comes in?"

Abe carried on walking. Sandy shrugged and followed. "Come on. Nowt more we can do."

"As if I give a shit about farmers like John Chaplow," muttered Big Isaac. "Let him come find his sodding flock and suffer consequences if he runs into preventives asking why there's sheep on beach."

CHAPTER NINETEEN

To confirm she, like the others from the raid were staying indoors, Jiddy tapped on the panel between her cottage and Silas's. When he tapped back, she paced, unsure if she should sneak up to Meadow Bank and warn Jonas's cousin of Big Isaac's wrath before the men went up themselves. John Chaplow had been a right pillock. Wandering sheep would no doubt attract attention, and Deputy Staincliffe would use this as another reason on top of Samuel's disappearance to have a go.

Hearing a rumpus outside, she peered out of her bedroom window. She couldn't believe the sight. The streets teemed with men, women and bairns. Bleating sheep, herded up Main Street by preventives, tottered off into side streets only to be herded back by frazzled soldiers. Women jeered, and kiddies ran after them, bleating in echo to the animals, dodging a cuffing and tripping over each other. Whistles and lewd shouts filled the air. Soldiers shoved and prodded the animals' rears with the butts of their muskets as they made their way through the crowds and the steep incline.

Head covered, Jiddy jogged down Jim Bell's Stile and, spying Dottie, joined her amongst the crowd. "What's going on?" she asked.

"They found flock on beach." Dottie laughed. "Baa-aaa!" she turned and shouted at the nearest soldier, who struggled to guide an errant ewe.

"Do they know which farm they're from?" Jiddy asked, thinking about old Mr. Chaplow.

Dottie gave her a quizzical look. "They'll find out."

Jiddy pulled her shawl closer around her face and remained quiet.

"Are these your best pick for soldiering in France?" shouted Helen Drake from across the way, making Gracie and Dottie laugh. "If so, my money's on Frenchies!"

"We're all quaking at press gangs now!" someone shouted.

Jiddy set off, but Dottie caught her arm. "Stay," she said. "Don't you want to have a jest with them?"

Jiddy shook her head. Retracing her steps, she saw a notice stuck to a door, and another further along. Below her, a commotion erupted, and someone waved a fistful of crumpled notices. As the seconds went by, she grew more anxious. She should have stayed indoors. An arrest could go unnoticed. She bounded up the path when a hand on her shoulder pulled her against a house wall.

Annie breathed into Jiddy's face. "They've arrested Andrew! There were sheep wool on his jacket and sand on his boots, they said. They're taking him, Jiddy, and Ma's distraught with Da still at sea. Come, they're in dock. Them press gangs are gonna take him, and we'll never see him again."

"Steady, Annie," said Jiddy, pulling back against Annie's grip on her arm. "Are you sure? They're fixed on getting sheep up hill, not arresting folk."

"They've got Andrew!" Annie shouted, her eyes wide with terror. "I don't care about sheep!"

Jiddy nodded. "Dottie!" she called, spying her in the crowd. "Pass on to folk that Annie's brother's been taken. They've got him in dock!"

For a second, Jiddy tossed up her options, whether to head to the farm, get inside or stay out in Bay. Annie's tear-stained face confirmed her decision. She stumbled around a straggling ewe and, shoving and pushing, trudged behind her friend.

"They've got Annie's brother in dock," Dottie cupped her hands to her mouth and shouted. "Get everyone to come back."

"What you on about?" said Helen Drake, pushing her way to reach her sister.

"It's Andrew Briggs, Helen," explained Dottie. "This is preventives' way of making arrests while we're laughing at stupid sheep."

Annie, eyes red-rimmed, broke into a run, and Jiddy followed to join the mass of neighbours as word rippled out. Fear began to rise in Jiddy's belly. As they caught sight of the sea, Deputy Staincliffe's voice cut through the babble of protest. Horses whinnied. They'd got their mounts in the dock. Clever sods. The number of soldiers outnumbered Baytowners, who, reaching a bottleneck, rammed at the bottom of Main Street.

"Let Annie through." Jiddy raised her voice. "Where's Andrew?"

People pressed sideways as the pair forced their way forward. The noise filled their ears, turning words into a mash of sounds like a farmyard of stampeding cattle, hens, pigs and goats.

Annie pulled Jiddy's arm. "There he is!"

Held on the steps for all to see, Andrew sagged between two preventive ogres while Deputy Staincliffe paraded as if he was Napoleon in front of his prisoner.

"Who was with you?" Staincliffe shouted, soldiers at his rear holding back the mob.

"He's done nowt!" cried Annie, dangerously close to one of the horses. "Let my brother go!"

Staincliffe eyed Annie before he caught sight of Jiddy and pointed an accusing finger in her direction. "Do you know anything about this?"

Jiddy's heart pounded. The threat of being arrested herself combined with the agitated mob frightened her. The mob could give her up, the preventives could chain her, or the locals could turn to save Andrew, who was one of their own. But this was Annie's brother, and Annie was her best friend.

"We're fisher-people in Bay," she shouted, despite her anxiety. "We don't know about sheep here."

The crowd roared. Preventives raised their weapons. Panic simmered. Annie struggled to stand while Jiddy stumbled forward. Soldiers brandished rifles. Locals had sticks. All hands raised, weapons ready to strike on both sides.

Without warning, fistfuls of pebbles flew overhead, and Staincliffe, eyes wild and face clenched, yelled for preventives to ready themselves.

Voices blurred with shouts. A surge of bodies threatened to knock them over, and Jiddy spun around, pushing with her hands to remain upright and not fall and be trampled. She couldn't see Annie anymore, only a mass of chests and shoulders and arms.

She pressed into the tide, shoving sideways. Buffeted, the crowd squeezed her out of their way as they seethed forward, and she fell against a wall.

Any minute now, she'd be crushed. She caught sight of Annie's petrified face and Helen Drake, never one to show fear, taut and desperate. Stone scraped her hands as she elbowed and kicked her way along the wall. Another furious roar ripped through the crowd, mingled with the clip of horses' hooves. Out of the confusion, a gun fired. Gulls rose, wings flapping from the rooftops. Hushed, the crowd cowed in a swaying throng.

Annie's scream pierced above the rumble of voices. A ripple of anger swept through the dock as row upon row strained to see. Jiddy wriggled for a better view. Higher up, on the steps of the Bay Hotel, Deputy Staincliffe held something aloft. She couldn't make it out. Annie was screaming. Some were turning their heads away; some raised their hands, fists, clutches of stones and slices of wood.

"Get back or we'll fire again!" Staincliffe shouted.

Soldiers, firearms raised, held their ground.

"Let him go!" a voice yelled.

Others took up the chant, and it rocked like an incoming tide.

"Hold him!" ordered Staincliffe.

For all to see, the two ogres raised a sagging figure. Annie cried out her brother's name.

A battleground of voices rose. Jiddy lurched for her friend. "Annie, Annie, wait, it's me!"

"I'll count to ten!" Staincliffe shouted, raising a bloodied hand. He held it high for them all to see the discoloured fingers, the dislocated thumb and the gash and trails of vessels and sinews.

Annie screamed. "They've butchered him!"

Annie was right. Staincliffe stood behind the row of armed preventives. Andrew, held up by the soldiers, could have been dead.

"Give me names or I'll cut off his other hand!" Staincliffe yelled.

The roar of outrage was deafening. Andrew's head hung limp and his legs sagged inert. Jiddy couldn't believe what they were seeing. Annie's brother was no smuggling leader. He was a pain in the buttocks, he was a tubsman on raids, Annie's cock-sure, gobby younger brother. She tried to connect the severed hand with Andrew, squinting to make out if it was really a hand, or could it be the roots of a turnip? Anything but a severed limb.

Pebbles showered through the air. Voices battered every corner of the dock. Annie lurched forward, but soldiers barred the way. "Let him go!" she yelled, her words a jumble of tears and desperation.

"He's out cold, he can't answer!" shouted Jiddy, pushing until she grasped Annie.

On the steps, clear for them to see, Staincliffe dropped his arm and the hand disappeared. He nodded to one of the ogres, who, in response, grabbed Andrew's hair and yanked up his head, revealing the lad's bruised and bloodied face. Eyes half-open, swollen lips mumbling incoherent words, Andrew proved he had regained consciousness.

"Andrew, we're here!" Annie shouted, shoving against the preventives who held her back with their weapons. "I'm here!"

Staincliffe leaned into the lad's ashen face, spitting words. "Who was with you?"

"I never..." More sounds than words tumbled from the lad's swollen mouth.

Staincliffe nodded. One of the ogres grabbed Andrew's uninjured arm and slammed it high against the inn door. Staincliffe stepped in front of the drooping figure. A knife blade flashed.

"No!!!" Jiddy yelled.

Curses and objections clouded the air. Spittle flew. Annie wailed. Others lobbed expletives along with fistfuls of stones.

"If you don't tell me who was responsible for last night's shenanigans, I promise I will cut off his other hand!" Staincliffe declared, one hand shading his face, the other brandishing the knife.

"You can't!" Annie shouted. "He's done nowt wrong!"

"They've made a mistake," Jiddy said, arm around her friend, mind racing for what they could do to stop the brutality. Big Isaac, Abe nor any of the gang were to be seen. It didn't make sense. Why weren't they protecting Andrew? The crowd surged forward again, spitting their anger.

"Bastards!"

"Knuckleheads!"

"Butchers!"

"Murderers!"

Staincliffe nodded. The preventive let Andrew's arm drop. Staincliffe took a step or two back.

Annie shoved and twisted to get through, but preventive muskets drawn, the front lines of Baytowners pushed against those crushing from behind. Jiddy held her ground.

"Deputy Staincliffe!" she shouted. He didn't hear and she raised her arms. The third time she yelled, bewildered, he scanned the crowd. "I'm here," she said, waving. "Jiddy Vardy! You've questioned me before, in Whitby. Why don't you question me again?"

He hadn't seen her. His expression hardened. "Nail up the hand," he ordered.

Annie screamed. Shouts pelted from all around. The noise swelled. Preventives inched forward, jostling, pushing. Jiddy scrabbled to stay on her feet, defiant to be taken now, daring them to arrest her.

"Let me talk to deputy," she said, grasping the barrel of one of the guns still held aloft. Straightway, the soldier, panic in his eyes, yanked the rifle free. The force of metal ripped through her palms, and she stumbled. "This is unjust!" she shouted, squaring up to the line even though her heart battered against her ribs with terror at the consequences.

CHAPTER TWENTY

The rhythmic sound of a hammer rang out as the preventives dragged an unconscious Andrew aside to reveal the door. The sight of the hand pinned to the wood hushed the crowd.

Deputy Staincliffe mounted his horse. "Let this be a warning! First to come to me with the names of men behind last night's sheep rustling will get a grand payment! And if not, I will return and cut off this young man's other hand. Believe me, I've done one, I can hack off the other!" Tugging the reins, he turned his horse.

Annie, Helen and a few others shouted. Jiddy grappled to reach the nearest preventive, but they all were retreating, and heading up King Street.

A group of Storm men were already lifting Andrew into a canvas hammock. One of the fiery family gave a command, and several of the men raised the stretcher. Annie's ma had arrived, and she, Annie and some of the younger Briggses walked silently behind. The crowd parted to let them through. Jiddy made to follow, but someone touched her arm.

"Give them their time."

Surprised by the soft tone of Helen Drake, who never spoke softly, Jiddy held back and watched the procession.

The Storms were more than a family. Everyone in the area knew their status because everyone had a spouse or a cousin, or an uncle once removed with Storm for a surname. The familiar saying had been drummed in— Storm by name, Storm by nature—but even the locals didn't expect these numbers. More Storms had appeared over the past half hour than even Helen Drake had seen before.

These Storms weren't the well-known faces Jiddy had seen during nights on a dark beach, passing packages from the sea to caves. These Storms strode with the scent of whaling ships and cold north winds. There were lads, young and middle-aged men in ganseys, frayed by rough water and arctic ice.

The sound of their boots ricocheted round the ginnels as they strode with heavy boots up Main Street, carrying Andrew as if he were a bird's skeleton. Villagers pressed against walls to let them pass, leaning from windows and ringing out cheers.

Although most of the soldiers had retreated to King Street, a couple lingered in the dock, probably wishing they had a boat ready to take them away.

"Preventives haven't done owt like this before," Helen said. "Not sure if it's better to be shipped off to Australia or locked in jail than lose a hand, if I'm honest."

Every muscle in Jiddy's body ached. Her bones ached. Her eyes ached. Andrew's hand still hung from the nail. Any moment, Annie would come running to retrieve it. Someone may try and yank it free and tear it.

"Fetch it," whispered Helen.

Jiddy mounted the steps. It hung like a creature from the sea. She took another step and looked over her shoulder. Helen and Dottie stood waiting, their faces gaunt. She turned back. The hand seemed huge. Close up, she could see blood and sinews. Bile filled her mouth and, leaning over, hands on her knees, she gagged. Sweat beaded her skin, but she shivered. Taking a deep breath, she straightened up. Helen and Dottie were watching. She took another deep breath and held it as, fingers trembling, she reached for the nail. It dug sharp into her hand. Chin up, she grasped the palm. It felt hard. Solid and cold. Grunting, she yanked out the nail and stumbled back, clutching the hand to her chest.

Helen and Dottie grabbed her elbows to steady her, and with their help, she untied her shawl and wrapped up Andrew's hand. "It's like it belongs to no-one," she said.

Helen touched Jiddy's shoulder. "Get on with you."

The crowd gobbled in on itself, hunkering into the stone, eager now to sidle indoors, away from their neighbours' prying suspicions, wishing they hadn't witnessed Deputy Staincliffe chop Andrew's hand off at the wrist and pin it to the public house door.

Lowering her head and cradling the bundle in her arms, Jiddy made her way up Main Street. Legs shaking, she stumbled along the Bolts until she reached Annie's cottage. Inside, someone was crying. She made out the swishing of skirts and clanking and clinking of pots. She smelt tobacco and a faint trace of herbs. Usually, she'd open the door and walk straight in, but right now, it seemed wrong. She listened for voices and inadvertently pressed the bundle tighter to her chest. Inside, people had begun to talk.

A woman, not Mrs. Briggs, sounded above the rest. "Thanks, lads, we'll see to him now."

"Will you send doctor to us, Abe?"

So, Abe was there. Perhaps Big Isaac, Sandy and Silas too. Jiddy readied to go in when the door opened. Stepping aside, she let a couple of the Storm men pass. Abe ambled towards her. His left cheekbone showed signs of bruising. His knuckles speckled with congealed blood. She grabbed his sleeve, but he shoved her off.

"Where've you been?" she asked, dreading the answer. "Where's others?"

"We didn't touch old man Chaplow, only his pathetic nephew, if that's what you're worried about," he muttered, narrowing his eyes as he stamped past.

Clutching the wrapped hand closer, she shouted after him, "How could you let Andrew take blame for this?"

Abe joined the other Storm men, and before Jiddy could repeat her question, a woman's voice caught her attention. "Is that what I think it is?"

Blushing at her outburst, she lowered her eyes. She couldn't worry about John Chaplow when Andrew could be dying from losing blood. She stepped into the dim interior. She wouldn't think about what went on at Meadow Bank. It wasn't her concern. One other woman stood by the fire, Annie's eldest cousin, Cassie. Already tears pooled in Jiddy's eyes.

"Should I take it up?" she asked.

Ethel shook her head. "Best wait for doctor. Andrew's not come round, but Annie and her mam are at his side."

"Where's rest of family?" Jiddy clutched the bundle, unable to maintain eye contact. If Ethel was crying, tears would set her off blubbing.

"They're at Rachel's. Young ones are better off there right now. Couldn't stop Frankie and Benjamin heading back to dock, though. Did you see them?"

She shook her head again. If she kept in the words threatening to spill, she'd send an entire ocean of tears over the floor. The creak of floorboards from above made them raise their heads.

"Why don't you go see if you can find the lads?" Ethel said. "And when you come back, I'm sure Annie will be downstairs."

Grateful for a task, Jiddy made for the door.

"Best leave that with us," said Ethel, and realising she still cradled the precious bundle, Jiddy released her hold.

Outside, she stepped straight into Betsie, who immediately flung her arms around her and buried her face in Jiddy's shoulder. Overwhelmed with relief, Jiddy hugged her in return.

CHAPTER TWENTY-ONE

Arms entwined, the two girls walked together. Groups stood around, some animated, some silent, most stopping as they passed by. Jiddy hated the tension. She avoided people's gaze in case she caught an accusation in their eyes that perhaps she'd had something to do with Andrew's arrest, being part of the gang of the previous night's escapade. You never knew. She'd been quick to blame Big Isaac and the others. The finger of reproach could just as easily turn on her. Violence erupted quickly in Baytown, nerves frayed and blame ready to bite.

"What's happening?" Betsie gabbled. "Is he dead? Is he alive? Is he speaking? Does he know about his hand?"

"Betsie," Jiddy soothed, drawing the other girl closer. "Take a breath."

They passed straggles of neighbours coming up the bank, voices subdued, faces drawn in. Jiddy's heart beat faster.

"Why don't you go home?" she suggested. "See how your mam is and if everyone's all right."

Betsie scowled. "I'm coming with you."

Jiddy pulled to a stop and faced her friend, who, finding her hands free, wiped her eyes.

"You need to tell your mam what's happened," Jiddy said. "And Helen Drake will want word. And Gracie.

They'll be wanting to know if they can come to Annie's. You should call in and let them know too."

Betsie wiped her face again. "Can't you?"

Figures lingered along the roadside. Jiddy shook her head. "I've got to find Annie's brothers and take them back."

"You'll come and get me after?" pleaded Betsie, her voice turning into a hiccup.

Jiddy took hold of Betsie's hands. "Doctor will be at Annie's. We'll give them a bit of time, hey?"

They stared at each other, neither knowing what else to say, so instead, they embraced before setting off in their different directions.

Fifteen minutes later, returning only with Frankie, Jiddy found Annie sitting on the front step.

"Young'uns are stopping at Rachel's," Annie said, her face a tear-stained map of streaks.

Frankie shoved open the door. "Helen and Dottie have brought in soup and flat cakes if you're hungry," she said.

Jiddy sat beside Annie and slid her arm around her shoulders. Annie burst into tears. Feeling her friend's body shake and seeing the tumble of damp hair twine across Annie's wet cheeks brought tears to Jiddy's eyes too. She felt so helpless, unable to find words of comfort big enough to soften the anguish.

After a few minutes, Annie's sobbing quieted. "Mam won't leave Andrew's bedside," she sniffed.

Jiddy pulled the strands of hair from Annie's face and rested her head against her friend's. "I'm sorry, Annie."

More tears trickled down Annie's face. "Doctor's taken Andrew's hand away with him." She broke down again, her voice hardly audible. "He said he'll be back in morning."

Jiddy cuddled Annie closer, hiding her own tears in the other girl's hair. She couldn't show her own misgivings. The deed was done, and doing something about it was more important than wishing she'd refused to be part of the sheep fiasco.

A breeze had got up, and the trees at the end of the Bolts rustled like the sea. A couple of rooks cawed as they took flight. The late afternoon turned chill.

Annie twisted a damp rag in her hands and sniffed. "Too wet." She forced a smile. "I didn't think anyone could have this much water in them to cry this much. Mam's not cried at all—maybe I'm crying for her as well."

"Your mam doesn't want anyone to see her weeping," Jiddy said, brushing her thumb tenderly across Annie's cheek. The poor girl's face, usually so smooth and pale, was mottled pink and bright red. "Let's go back in, and then I'll go fetch Betsie. She wants to see you."

Annie shook her head. "Not yet."

"Then snuggle up." Jiddy pulled the two of them together. "Body heat."

Annie dabbed her eyes. "What's going to happen to Andrew?"

It was the big question hanging around the house, even though no-one wanted to mention it. Mr. Briggs wouldn't be back from whaling for weeks yet, and by the time he did come back, there would have to be answers.

"Main thing is getting him better," said Jiddy.

"Better?"

She couldn't bring herself to say 'not dying', so she patted her friend's knee. "Your sisters and brothers, if they want to, can come and sew with us. Or help us out in some way. We can go crabbing, anything to help your ma, so she can be with him."

"I know our Andrew," Annie said. "I'm so worried when he wakes, and he sees bandage. Doctor has done a grand job binding it and such, but…" She began to cry again. "But when he sees…"

"Oh, Annie, I don't know what to say." Jiddy could barely contain her own anguish. "Don't loiter on it, not today."

Annie sniffed and blew her nose on the damp rag. "It's first thing Frankie said before he ran off to dock! Mam didn't hear, but I did!"

"Andrew's tough. He'll be all right."

"He's a doer, Jiddy. What's he going to do?"

They both stared straight ahead. The rustling of leaves grew louder. Jiddy shivered. "Let's go inside."

"I don't want to!" Annie shouted with atypical venom. "I mean, I can't! I know it's soft, but I can't face seeing him wake and see what's happened to his hand."

"Come on." Jiddy pulled Annie to her feet decisively. "Let's go for a walk. See if we can find some bluebells or celandine. Something pretty to put by his bed."

They headed off along the edge of the wood, vigilant for a glimpse of blue or white. Jiddy bent to gather a few lush stems, but Annie hung back, dabbing her eyes. They moved slowly, Jiddy striding into the grass to retrieve stitchwort and early cow parsley while Annie stood and watched. As they dropped towards the rear of Fisherhead, Jiddy halted. "I don't believe it!"

"What?"

Jiddy pointed. "There's Sandy Kellock heading towards my house! The cheek of him!"

"Oh! Do you want to go see?"

Jiddy definitely wanted to see. She wanted to give him what for, but the thought of Annie hearing Sandy boast about the beating he'd given Jonas's cousin, and no doubt Big Isaac and Abe making excuses or acting all bravado and discussing revenge or guilt or whatever it was they must be planning, didn't bear thinking about. "I bet your mam's wondering where you are," she said instead. "We've got a pretty bunch of flowers. You take them. They'll smell sweet in the bedroom."

Sandy, Big Isaac, Abe and Silas ignored her when she pushed open the door of her cottage.

"See you've made yourselves at home," she said, slamming the door behind.

"Sit down and stop mizzling," said Sandy. "How's Andrew?"

Jiddy dragged out a chair. Tiredness swept over her. "Where've you been? If you'd been in dock you'd know, wouldn't you?"

Big Isaac slammed his hands on the table. "Bloody preventives! They'd better not think about going back and cutting off his other hand."

"And what you going to do about it? March back up to Meadow Bank and deliver another beating to the poor sod, or are you going to march to Musgrave's and demand Deputy Staincliffe say sorry? Say we're sheep smugglers and to punish us and give Andrew back his hand? He were only helping! I feel bad and I were only supposed to be lookout! You're ones organising all raids. How did they blame Andrew for all this?"

Without realising, she'd jumped to her feet, pacing the floor, anger bursting through every sinew. She was mad, steaming, searing mad.

Sandy gestured to sit. "It were a threat," he said. "They'll not touch young Briggs again."

She whipped around, clenching her fists. "Did you hear what I said?"

"We heard," said Big Isaac. "And don't you blame me or any of lads for what's happened. Do you hear me?" He loomed over her, fists clenched, rage taut as a fishing line.

"I wondered where you were," she said more quietly.

Abe was on his feet as well. "We were doing what we always do after a raid! Sorting business then laying low! What the heck were Andrew doing parading about Bay?"

She walked to the window. A lone dog barked. "I don't know," she murmured.

"You don't know?" repeated Big Isaac. "No, well, nor do we." He sat heavily.

"Preventives will be running round like headless chickens for a day or two more," said Silas, lighting his pipe.

They contemplated the thought before Big Isaac spoke again. "Way I see it, they haven't a clue. We'll let them run about."

"How'd you mean?" said Abe.

"We're not going to give them the opportunity to have one single thread of evidence owt's going on. We're going to do what Andrew should've done and we were doing. We're not going near beach. We're not going out at night. We're not so much as saying boo to a goose."

"But what if folk start asking where we are?" said Sandy, scuffing the rug with his boots.

"Nothing! Do you hear me?" Big Isaac raised his voice, challenging each of them to say different. Silas puffed his pipe. Sandy and Abe glanced at each other. Jiddy stared out of the window at the rooftops.

"What happens when preventives realise whose sheep they were?" she asked.

The men exchanged glances. Big Isaac coughed. "Old William knows nowt about it. Sheep ran off in night. Wolf gave them a scare."

"I meant John."

"Gone," said Abe.

Jiddy glared at him. "Gone?"

"Going," corrected Sandy.

"Inland folk don't always settle by coast," said Abe, cupping his scarred knuckles.

She looked out of the window again, listening to the scuffles of their feet. "What about Andrew?" she eventually said, turning to face the room. "Do we do nothing to avenge what preventives did to him?"

"We'll take care of lad," Big Isaac said.

"And wait," added Sandy.

Abe pushed back his chair. Discussion over, Jiddy held open the door as they tramped outside.

"I don't want you walking in again," she said. "D'you hear? This is a place for young girls now, not old men."

"We're fishermen, lass," Abe said. "What would we be doing, holding secret meetings in a school?"

Silas went with them, past his house, even though he could easily have gone in, and they disappeared across the fields in the direction of Thorpe Hall. So much for staying low. Whether they would retaliate against Staincliffe's actions, Jiddy couldn't say. She couldn't decide what she was going to do, let alone the likes of Big Isaac and Abe Storm.

From the doorway, she caught the roar of waves striking shingle. It seemed fitting at least that the sea could show its anger at the day's events. Stay off the beach. Stay low. She closed the door, deciding to head to Thorpe Hall first thing in the morning. Big Isaac and the others were no doubt on their way right now, but she could wait. In the morning, when she had a clear head and a plan, she would go and see Squire Farsyde and let him know what she had in mind.

CHAPTER TWENTY-TWO

J iddy didn't expect Violet to greet her at the back door, or for her to thrust the diamond brooch Jiddy had given her into her hand.

"I can't stand it anymore!" cried Violet, raising her cap to reveal the yellowing bruise on her cheek. "If that helps get me to York, take it, because I have to go!"

"Violet, catch a breath," said Jiddy, holding up her palms. "What's happened?"

"I won't be hit anymore." Violet burst into tears. "I don't care if he don't like it. I'll not feel Da's fist again! Here, take it!"

Jiddy shook her head. "You keep it for now. We'll sort this later. I need to see squire right now. Is he in?"

Clutching the brooch, Violet nodded.

Squire Farsyde glared at Jiddy when she opened his study door after a brief knock. Taken aback, she fumbled for the words she'd planned to say.

"What do you want?" he growled, pistol in his hand yet again, cloth and bearings in disarray on the table.

She closed the door and approached slowly. Wary of the squire in this mood, she took a breath. "I take it you've heard?"

He slammed down the pistol and she winced. "I've had everybody traipsing in here from Staincliffe to Isaac!

I've got John Chaplow beaten up so bad, he says he's leaving the farm, and without Jonas anywhere to be found, how's William going to keep place going? What are you going to add to this mess? Tell me what you're going to throw at me now?" He glared at her, grey eyes bulging.

Jiddy swallowed. "I came up to ask if you could give Andrew a job here at hall," she said, "but maybe he could help out at Meadow Bank if Mr. Chaplow's on his own—"

"Where've you been?" shouted the squire. "That young man has only one hand! How's he going to be of any use on a farm?"

Jiddy clasped her hands to stop them shaking. "I thought, maybe," she began, watching the squire stride up and down. "Folk adapt? He could plant seeds, lift turnips. He can herd cattle and sheep. Rex is a grand sheep dog, he'll do all work, and Andrew's a determined beggar. You've got to give him credit."

Taking in her request, the squire sank into his chair. "Folk adapt!" he repeated. "Get out of here!" He raised his voice again. "Go see my wife! She was asking for you this morning. Go!" He waved his hand. "Go!"

Jiddy knew not to hang around when the squire lost his temper. Bounding up the stairs, she found Mrs. Farsyde in the sewing room, examining each crib sheet carefully. The tranquil scene seemed at odds with the horror of what had happened to Andrew and the squire's angry reaction.

Mrs. Farsyde, prettily dressed in pale blue, hummed to herself, oblivious there'd been shouting. She obviously knew nothing about yesterday's events. But of course,

Squire Farsyde would have forbidden anyone from mentioning it in his wife's presence, and she'd presumably not been too distressed that the officer in the window who'd looked like Samuel had turned out to be someone else. Jiddy almost envied her. Seeing her so serene made her wonder how she could possibly mention Violet's dilemma or changes at Meadow Bank, let alone the subject of Andrew, when everything centred around the coming child.

Sheets examined, Mrs. Farsyde lifted a cotton gown, scrutinising the frill around the hem and picking to find loose threads.

"You won't find fault with these," Jiddy said, deciding on her approach. "Violet hemmed them sheets, and she's a good worker. She's as good as any seamstress you'll find. If you recommend her to ladies you know, like the ones who came to your ball, they won't be disappointed."

Mrs. Farsyde raised her eyes for a moment before examining the next baby gown. "I have to be sure before I recommend anyone to the ladies I know. After all, it's my reputation."

Jiddy clasped her hands in an effort to keep calm. "Did you manage to speak to any of them?"

"Of course I did."

She stepped closer. "I meant Bay lasses. Did any of the ladies say if they'd be interested in giving any of them some work? When they're ready, of course."

The squire's wife touched her stomach. "I don't recall."

Holding in a retort, Jiddy walked to the window. Mounted on his favourite horse, the squire headed towards the gates, the clatter of hooves ringing out. What she'd give to escape so easily. He'd be off somewhere sorting out a problem, having stimulating conversations, maybe even some arguments about what had happened. Or more likely, he'd be going about his daily business, discussing the cost of grain and the machines consuming the cities. She wondered if the squires and lords talked about people like Captain Pinkney and what men like him did for the gentry's purses. Maybe they wished they were pirates sailing the seas, dodging the excise men and feeling the ocean breeze on their faces.

"Did you enjoy ball?" she asked, turning around to face the room.

Mrs. Farsyde gazed at her rounded stomach. "Was that the squire heading off?"

"Yes."

Mrs. Farsyde held a small sheet to her cheek. "I'm going to make sure I'm always around for my little one," she said. "My child won't have to ever leave me. We won't be separated for one moment. I'll guide them and nurture them. I'll smother them with love." She laughed, her face glowing.

"And take them to balls and parties and introduce them to all ladies you know and their children?" asked Jiddy, trying to keep her voice steady. The expression on her mistress's face made clear she was hardly listening to a word Jiddy said.

Walking over to the table, Jiddy stood as close to Mrs. Farsyde as she thought fitting. "I was asking about your ball," she pressed. "It was a grand gesture of squire to do for you. I know you didn't dance. I mean, I assume you didn't dance." The significant mound of belly loomed between them. "Did you see anyone you'd not seen for a while instead? I'm sure you enjoyed that."

Tears shining in her eyes, her mistress touched her cheek. "No," she said. "I knew everyone there." She patted her hair and took a few steps; the snap of silk against the floor filled the pause. "You know, Jiddy, I'd quite like to go for a walk this afternoon." She reached the window and studied the sky. "It's not going to rain. We could go to the beach like the other day."

Joining her mistress at the window, Jiddy touched the sill. "Is that wise? It's been a busy time. Maybe you'd be better off resting this afternoon. I can fetch you a tray of tea?"

Jiddy imagined the child riding on a small pony behind the squire and Mrs. Farsyde standing where she stood now, watching them.

Mrs. Farsyde continued to stare at the clouds. "The squire is out for the rest of the day. You can ask Billy to get the carriage ready. What about we take a walk at Boggle Hole this time."

"Maybe you should rest," Jiddy repeated. "Weather's not settled."

Mrs. Farsyde put one hand on her back and, closing her eyes, sighed. "This might be my last chance, and the doctor did say fresh sea air would do me good."

"We could go tomorrow."

Opening her eyes, Mrs. Farsyde smiled. "The squire will be around tomorrow, and he will no doubt want to be the one to accompany me, but I'd so like to talk to you… about Violet, wasn't it? And tomorrow, I could write a note about the girl and ask the squire to mention what a good seamstress she is, when he is next at Nunnington Hall. I believe he needs to make a visit next week."

Jiddy glanced out of the window again. "If squire's off to Nunnington Hall next week, we could set off when he does, give ourselves more time. And if you write a note for him to take to lady of house, he'll be certain to go, to please you."

Mrs. Farsyde dabbed her forehead with her handkerchief. "I want to go today."

Without stating straight out she was trying to keep off the beach at all costs and having to say why, which would mean mentioning Andrew and his hand and the uproar in Bay, Jiddy resorted to the care of the baby. "Squire will be frantic if he gets back and you're not here," she said, willing her mistress to understand. "If we go while he's at Nunnington Hall, we won't need to rush, and rushing probably isn't good for you…or baby."

Hand on her stomach again, Mrs. Farsyde watched the branches of trees lining the path sway. Jiddy kept quiet, willing her mistress to agree to stay at home. Should she reiterate the danger for the baby or leave her to mull it over? Preventives would be about in Bay; the shore was a dangerous place for everyone today. She followed Mrs. Farsyde's gaze, racking her brains for how she could be more persuasive.

"I'll have some bread and butter with my tea," Mrs. Farsyde said, "and you can tidy in here."

Jiddy glanced at the scattered baby clothes and bedding.

"I hope it rains for weeks now," she muttered when she was on the landing and rounding the stairs. She paused, one hand on the balustrade. Why wait for Mrs. Farsyde to write a note she might never write? Or the squire to visit Nunnington Hall when he might decide not to leave his wife's side? The thought of a grand house and ladies in beautiful gowns made her wonder. A certain lady might help find Violet a position. A lady who owned a large shop in York that made gowns for all the titled ladies in Yorkshire, and who would be searching for good seamstresses to employ. It needn't take weeks for Violet to be safe. Violet had said she'd give away her brooch to get to York. Jiddy could go to York herself and negotiate employment, not only for Violet but also for other girls.

At last, she had a plan, and it was one that would keep her out of the Bay and away from Staincliffe's suspicious eyes.

CHAPTER TWENTY-THREE

Mrs. Farsyde forgot about writing a note to the lady of Nunnington Hall. Jiddy didn't, but it no longer mattered. Squire Farsyde, flintlock in hand, stared in disbelief from his desk. Rising to his feet, he took in a trembling Violet.

"What's this about?" he asked.

"Show him," said Jiddy.

Violet covered her face with her hands, and the squire shot Jiddy a curious glance. "Violet?"

Jiddy gently prised the girl's hands from her face. Violet squirmed to free herself. "It's all right," soothed Jiddy. "Show Squire Farsyde. He'll help."

The young girl dipped her head. The squire frowned at Jiddy. She sighed. "Violet's da don't want her to train to be a proper seamstress, so..." She gently touched Violet's shoulder. "He's hit her bad, but Violet wants to train, don't you?"

Before the squire could speak, the younger girl found her voice. "I'd like to, sir, if you can help?"

Jiddy relaxed. "But her da has to give permission." She smiled at Violet. "I'm not going to be accused of kidnapping Violet. Will you speak to Mr. Ashner, sir?"

"Well, yes, but I'm a little confused." He eyed Violet again. "Why do you want to leave us?"

Violet burst into tears and crumpled in on herself, and the squire shrugged in confusion.

"I told you, sir, I'm preparing Violet and some of other girls for work in big houses?" He nodded and she continued. "Violet's da won't let her go and he's, well, you can see how he reacts." Jiddy gestured to Violet, who covered her cheek with her hand again.

"I want to go now," Violet said.

"She can get a skilled job in York," said Jiddy. "She can send some of her wages back here if need be."

The squire sighed and waved his hand. "Go back to the kitchen, Violet. Mrs. King will be missing you. And don't worry," he added when the girl looked horrified. "I'll sort something out with Jiddy."

Two days later, with Squire Farsyde's help, Jiddy found herself in Yorkshire's capital city. The noise struck her more than the fact there was not a face she recognised. The biggest town she'd been to prior to York was Whitby, and that place was minuscule in comparison. Buildings in York loomed larger, wider, streets longer, distances further, and without a coastline, she found it difficult to gauge direction, until she saw the river.

So much water slicked between banks and boats of various sizes bounced so close, Jiddy feared they might hit each other. Its width meant it could be called a sea. However, it smelt different. No whiff of fish or bladderwrack or brine, but rather an odour tinged by green slime and the mulch of vegetables.

The streets were different too. She had to keep her eyes on the ground for hollows and stones and scraps of unidentifiable objects. Stalls straggled everywhere along walls and buildings, a constant chivvy of offers and warnings, a skirmish of food and tools. She clutched her sack close to her chest. Whenever unsure, she asked for Vardarelli's. A few people ignored her; some shrugged; some pointed. She hated asking and having people frown at her accent.

Bustling streets, noise coming from windows above, left, right, behind, in front, eyes lingering when she asked the direction and brought attention to herself. All the colours and shapes, the smells of food and animals, coal ash and human beings—it was overwhelming.

Officers passed as if out for a stroll, soldiers in twos or threes, weapons as clean as if they'd never been used. She had to keep reminding herself this was York, not Robin Hood's Bay. These soldiers weren't preventives; she didn't have a sign with the word 'smuggler' pinned to her back or dragging along the ground behind.

She was a person going about her business like everyone else in the grand city. Business. She had a business idea to share with the owner of Vardarelli's Shopping Emporium.

She's your mam. Look her in the eyes and keeping telling yourself she's flesh and blood, not some fairy queen or remote princess. Your mam, and she combs her hair and picks apple skin out of her teeth and defecates like everyone else.

It didn't help that she didn't know the way and people talked different to what she was used to. Only one or two gave her a second glance and she held their gaze for a moment, wondering what she should say when not one of them said a word to her. *It's only a bigger version of Robin Hood's Bay. You've been to Whitby market; you know what crowds are like!*

"Excuse me, is this right way to Vardarelli's?"

A shrug. A stare. A mean glance.

If she followed the well-dressed ladies, it must be the right way, but the narrow, crowded streets made her panic. If the way led to a dead end, they'd be crushed, piling on top of one another as more and more came behind. No ways out into the woods like the Bolts. No steps leading into fields. Not one familiar helping hand.

The street had to lead somewhere if so many people walked along it. Buildings hemmed them in. She shuffled along with the crowd. She couldn't work out how some people managed to stop to enter a doorway without tripping up others, but they did. It must be a skill you learned if you were raised here, she reckoned.

Finally, the street opened out, and they spilled into a large square. A young lad carrying a tray of bread on his shoulder scowled. "Look out!"

Stepping sideways, Jiddy bumped into a woman holding two baskets of lilac. "Oy!" the woman shouted.

Jiddy stood still. Possibly, the sensible action would be to turn around and head straight back the way she had come, back to the inn, catch the first coach and head back home to Robin Hood's Bay. Doubts seeped in. What was the point of asking her mother to employ a girl from the Bay? It was a stupid idea, and the more she thought about it, the more stupid it became. Now she saw what the people of York were like, the chance of a lass from a fishing village being employed here grew increasingly remote.

A woman in front caught her attention. While others ambled, stopped, shambled, bumped and barged, this woman moved gracefully; she didn't linger but nor did she hurry. There were others, equally well-dressed, but they walked in pairs while this woman walked alone.

Don't give up. You're here for a reason. Stop getting distracted.

"Can you tell me whereabouts of Vardarelli's, please?" Jiddy asked two women.

A nod. A gloved finger pointed. Several well-to-do people strolled in the same direction. The woman remained like a beacon, and Jiddy followed. Soon, she walked several paces behind and realised how petite the woman was. She wasn't tempted by any of the stalls, clearly, like Jiddy, on a mission. Jiddy could have reached out and touched her, she came so close, when a gust of wind from an alley swept back the lady's hood and revealed the black hair of its owner. Jiddy gasped. It was her mother, Signora Vardarelli. She reached out to tap her shoulder. At the same time, her mother swept a bread roll from a pile on the adjacent baker's stall. Heart beating fast, Jiddy readied for him to shout, 'Thief!" Her mother, already a couple of paces in front, walked without haste. Confused as to what had happened, Jiddy clutched her skirt and followed.

She couldn't understand what she had seen. A well-dressed woman, not any well-dressed woman, but

Signora Vardarelli, this woman who was her birth mother, who owned diamonds, two shopping emporiums and gowns a queen would be proud to own, this woman had stolen a piece of bread. Not only that, but she'd done it so expertly, no-one had noticed. Jiddy glanced over her shoulder. The baker continued speaking to his customers. No shouts or accusations. No muskets or swords or guns were unsheathed. People kept walking. The air continued to smell of yeast, flour and warm dough. Stall holders declared their wares, skirts and capes swished past, cotton and wool muted the sound of boots.

Vardarelli's stood directly ahead with its large sign and the same lettering Jiddy had seen in London. Its windows twinkled. Treasures behind the glass drew passers-by. A bell rang every time the double doors opened, and a doorman, fine in livery, bowed his head. Signora Vardarelli reached the doors. Jiddy clasped her hands. Her mother. Madame Vardarelli. A thief. But why? She hurried forwards. Another figure. Tall. Recognisable. Lord Ryethorpe.

Signora Vardarelli nodded to the doorman. An object slid between the folds of her cloak, rolled on the ground, caught a foot and spun in another direction. The battered roll came to rest in a puddle. Close at hand, a child grabbed the morsel of food and disappeared almost as quickly into the crowd. Signora Vardarelli swept into the building. Lord Ryethorpe ignored everyone but Jiddy.

Holding his gaze, she approached the shop doors. Had she really seen the woman who owned Vardarelli's steal bread—not only steal it, but drop it so casually, right in front of the doorman and the front doors of her emporium for anyone to see? What would Lord Ryethorpe say to explain why a woman like her needed to steal a roll of bread? What would Signora Vardarelli say to explain why she would risk going to prison when she had riches other people could only dream of?

CHAPTER TWENTY-FOUR

They stood, an incongruous pair, in front of the window with its shimmering glassware on display. Jiddy's head reeled with questions. She glanced at the shop sign, the doorman and the constant stream of customers. It didn't make sense.

"I'm here as you asked me to be," she said, steadying her voice. "I've come to see Signora Vardarelli."

"Thank you, Jiddy!" he said. "I was delighted and, and I have to say, pleasantly surprised when I received the message from Squire Farsyde of Thorpe Hall. Signora Vardarelli will be happy you wish to heal the rift between you."

Jiddy took a deep breath, realising this wasn't the moment to say why she'd really come to York. "I can't believe I'm here!" she said instead.

He smiled, his eyes crinkling at the corners. "The last time your mother saw you, you told her you preferred fisher people to her, and you excused a pirate for stealing her belongings. But now, you can begin again. I am so pleased!"

Behind him, three women in their silk gowns and carefully arranged hats came out into the street. Jiddy noted their little tapestry bags with beads and neatly stitched flowers and their delicate shoes, brushed by the dirt of the road.

She held her bag tightly and stared at an array of China covered in small blue forget-me-nots. "Why would a person who owns most successful shop in York take bread and not pay for it?" she asked.

He sighed and tapped his cane on the ground. "I hoped you hadn't seen."

"She could have been arrested. Why did she do it?"

"It is a complicated matter."

"I want to understand," persisted Jiddy. "My mother owns Vardarelli's. In fact, she owns two Vardarelli shopping palaces. She's not poor, not like lad who picked it out of the puddle or the one we saw in London when I visited. She doesn't need to steal bread!"

Aware of her raised voice, Jiddy lowered her head but continued to watch Lord Ryethorpe. A wave of doubt shadowed his features. He stared at the doorman holding open the door with as much intensity as if he was going to paint the man's portrait. His face drooped in sad folds around his mouth.

After several moments, he addressed Jiddy. "Your mother came from a very poor family in Naples. She had no choice but to steal bread as a child if she didn't want to starve. Old habits die hard."

"Not true," Jiddy said. "My mother's family has money. You told me. You tried to persuade me to visit them. You said they'd feed me, that there was no shortage of food in Naples. You told me I had cousins there like me."

She raised her voice again. "You tried to get me to go to Naples! Why would you do that if people there are as poor as people here?"

She could tell by his expression what he'd told her was true, and a wave of heat swept over her skin. She shouldn't have come. These people were liars. You could never trust gentry. Jonas had told her that. Why didn't she learn? She couldn't go in now. She had failed before she'd begun, and she hated her mother for being untrustworthy as much as she'd hated her for accusing Jiddy of being a thief.

"She's a hypocrite!" Jiddy swung to face him. "She called me and Baytowners thieves. She wanted Captain Pinkney hung!" She strode in a circle, banging the sack against her leg, oblivious to people eyeing her. "How dare she! Many people in Bay are starving, and they don't steal!"

Lord Ryethorpe adjusted his hat, taking his time to reposition it. "What I said was true. You are like your cousins. You've seen for yourself how alike you and your mother are."

Jiddy screwed up her fist. "Are you accusing me of being a thief as well?"

"No, no, not at all, and I wouldn't exactly call what Signora Vardarelli has done theft either."

Jiddy clenched her jaw. "She took a roll of bread and didn't pay for it."

"She let it fall and someone else took it."

Exasperated, she threw up her hands. "Orange sun and warm stone and scented oil, you said."

Lord Ryethorpe stepped closer and spoke quietly. "When your father and I met your mother, we thought she was the old lady's granddaughter and, as such, was a lady. After Gregory died and Maria came to live with my wife, only then did I learn the truth. I never told anyone. What did it matter? She acted like a lady, and she had the old lady's jewels after all. But one day, I saw her stealing a pear in the market. I remember it clearly. She was walking ahead with Samuel, who was nine at the time. I was strolling behind, past the stalls, when I saw it. Maria, extremely casually, swept her hand through the air, cupped a pear into her palm and swept it into the folds of her cape."

"What did she say?"

Lord Ryethorpe focused his attention on the window. "Nothing, and I didn't ever mention it."

"Are you sure she took it?"

"Oh, yes. She ate it in front of me. She didn't realise there was anything wrong in what she'd done."

"I'm sorry if it seems I disbelieve you," Jiddy stammered. "I'm finding it hard to imagine Signora Vardarelli taking anything. Not only fruit." She frowned. "The jewels? Her wealth?" She shook her head when he didn't answer. "I can't believe I saw her take the bread roll, but I did, and you saw it too. She clutched her bag tightly. "I never dreamed rich people would need to steal."

"She wasn't always wealthy, but I hope you'll understand more now."

Jonas called smuggling stealing. So did the preventives and Samuel and those running the country. In their eyes, she was a thief. They would call Squire Farsyde a thief too. "It's not simple, is it?" she said.

He shook his head. "So, we don't talk about it," and neither must you."

Jiddy never spoke about smuggling to anyone who wasn't involved. Keeping secrets was as natural as breathing. "I won't say anything," she said.

Relief lightened his face. "So, you have come here implicitly to make amends with your mother. That's wonderful news."

Jiddy flushed. "It's more than that," she said. "I've come to ask if she'll give work to girls from Robin Hood's Bay. Girls who can sew."

"Ah, I see. Then you must take it slowly and not ask for too much at once."

Jiddy nodded, relieved now to be talking about the real reason she had come. "There's one lass, Violet Ashner. I want to ask about taking her on as soon as possible."

"Violet is an unusual name for a girl from Robin Hood's Bay."

Jiddy shrugged. "You could say same for me."

He smiled briefly before moving towards the door. Following, Jiddy took in his slow gait and thought how tragedy aged people. Touching his arm, she made him turn. "May I ask one last question?" He nodded. "Why didn't she stay in Naples with her family?"

Lord Ryethorpe didn't immediately reply. Stepping aside to allow people to pass, he surveyed the opening and closing of the door. "Perhaps because she wanted to see the world."

At last, a statement that made sense. Jiddy had gazed at the horizon herself and wondered what could be on the other side of the North Sea. She nodded her understanding. Lord Ryethorpe tipped his hat and stepped towards the door again. The doorman recognised him, and he didn't prevent her from following.

The room inside was an exact replica of the one she'd seen in London. A golden 'V' adorned every glass panel and chair. Marble counters bounced back sound. Clocks ticked. The scent of animal pelts, rose water and musk mingled. Ladies wore silks with colours never seen in Robin Hood's Bay, fabrics falling in folds, frills and tucks. The room exploded with dresses, ornaments, shining objects. Jiddy stood transfixed, more than ever unable to fathom why a woman who owned such splendour would steal from a market stall.

"Come along," said Lord Ryethorpe.

He strode past cabinets of gloves, fans made of lace, fretwork, gems and hand-painted scenes. Chandeliers hovered overhead, bright sparkling stars made of hard crystal. Jiddy followed.

Women studying glass cabinets filled with diamonds, rubies and emeralds paused to watch them pass. They strode between glass and wood partitions to be engulfed in rainbows of threads, spools of trimmings and buttons. The scent of wealth grew heavier. Lights shone brighter. Glass gleamed sharper. A wall of jewel-coloured silks, cottons covered in birds and flowers rose before them. Reams of fabric coloured her vision. She'd entered paradise.

"Jianna?"

Lord Ryethorpe stepped aside. Signora Vardarelli, hands clasped and with an unflinching gaze, stood in a doorway, looking at Jiddy like Mrs. King looking at a bluebottle that had landed on a gooseberry pie she'd just taken out of the oven.

CHAPTER TWENTY-FIVE

Jiddy couldn't help but stare back. The woman before her, dressed in deep-blue damask, a green pendant around her neck, green stones in her earlobes, large black eyes and glossy hair shrouded in lace, made other women pale to insignificance. Her mother's beauty dazzled. Jiddy bobbed a curtsey. "Good day, Signora Vardarelli."

"Good morning, Jianna."

Jiddy swallowed, trying to moisten her dry mouth. No-one could accuse this goddess-like woman of any bad-doing. Jiddy's body felt cold and her face hot. She couldn't find a word to say and gazed at her mother, willing her to speak.

"Jianna has come all the way from Robin Hood's Bay to see you." Lord Ryethorpe's voice brought with it a wave of relief.

Jiddy bobbed a curtsey again. "I set off before dawn," she affirmed.

Maria's eyes surveyed her daughter's figure. "You want me to dress you again?"

"No, no," Jiddy stammered. "I've not come for me."

Maria gazed past her. "You want me to dress someone else?"

Jiddy glanced at Lord Ryethorpe, who stepped forward. "I believe Jianna—"

"I prefer Jiddy!" Hot, so hot at her outburst.

"Jiddy," he corrected. "I believe Jiddy would like to speak with you."

He waited. Maria stared. It was impossible to tell from her expression what was running through her mind.

"I run a sewing school," Jiddy said, ignoring the look of surprise on Lord Ryethorpe's face that she had blurted it out without any further introduction. "One of my pupils is ready for work, and I thought of here. If you could take her as an apprentice…"

Maria continued to stare. Jiddy glanced at Lord Ryethorpe, but he looked too shocked to speak.

"Her name's Violet," she continued. "Violet Ashner."

Her mother let out a long sigh. "I employ well-mannered young ladies in York," she said, gesturing around the room at the darkly dressed girls.

Jiddy bent forward. "I meant seamstresses, not lasses selling stuff." She glanced at Lord Ryethorpe, but he had his eyes fixed on the wall above their heads. "Violet is well-trained. And mannered. She is very good with her needle. Please, try her out in your workroom and you will see how skilled she is. I know it's only my word, but I can get you a reference. Mrs. Farsyde, lady at Thorpe Hall, she'll speak for Violet. She's well pleased with her."

Maria eyed Jiddy's boots, her skirt and the bag she held. When her gaze reached Jiddy's eyes, Jiddy held her nerve. Her heart beat fast. No-one in Robin Hood's Bay made her feel inferior. Not one of the women made her embarrassed of her clothes, but here, standing before her mother, she felt ashamed. She searched for words to prove her worth, but none came.

"What will you do for me if I decide to try out this girl?" Maria asked.

"I'll be bringing a good seamstress to you," Jiddy said after a few moments' thought. "Your customers will be pleased with the fine work. They'll tell their friends. You'll get more customers. And I'll bring you more girls!"

Jiddy waited, pleased with her response. She forced a smile. "Maybe this will mean a new beginning."

Maria clasped her hands together. "I will agree to take on this girl if we first sort out your appearance. I cannot do business with a person dressed as you are dressed." Beckoning to a pair of assistants standing nearby, Maria gestured to reams of emerald cloth. "I want you to bring out the fabrics I tell you," she said.

"Oh, no," said Jiddy, "I'm not here for this."

Lord Ryethorpe stepped forward. "Is this necessary?"

"The girl is out of place," Maria said, pointing to a blue flowered fabric. "I won't do business with someone who doesn't belong in Vardarelli's."

Rolls of green and blue gleamed. Maria pointed to a skein of maroon.

"I'm not going to work here," Jiddy said. "I don't need to be dressed as you'd want me dressed. If we talk somewhere private, it won't matter, will it? I'm content as I am."

Lord Ryethorpe bowed. "Why don't we retire to your workroom, Maria?"

"I will not do business with anyone who isn't suitably dressed!" repeated Maria, fixing her gaze over Jiddy's head. The assistants remained silent. The room behind her mother glowed with a faint light. Jiddy had promised Violet. What was more important?

She dropped her bag. "Fine!" she said. "Wrap me in your silks! Dress me as you want while I'm here! You did this when I was in London. Why not do it every time we meet and let's make it a family tradition? As long as you take other girls I may bring if Violet does well."

Ignoring her daughter's outburst, Maria beckoned the assistants forward, and they came, whipping measuring tapes around Jiddy. One of them studied Jiddy's face under a glass, moving it across to peer into her eyes. Another leaned back to study her hair. Jiddy raised her arms. She'd been prodded and measured before. Assistants had studied her complexion, scrutinised her hair for the exact shade of black, examined her eyes for flecks of other colours only to find deepest coal. Exactly as they had done when Maria had taken Jiddy to the London store of Vardarelli's.

Lord Ryethorpe stood outside the office door.

"She is tall," the shorter assistant said.

"May I suggest flat pumps?" said the other.

"We need to soften her as well," said Maria, holding a lilac fabric. "But a dark shade would be better to counterbalance her wide shoulders."

Jiddy focused her eyes on a frieze of fruit and flowers around the top of the wall.

"Maybe a mid-tone so we soften and draw the eye in?" the taller assistant suggested, draping a cornflower-blue silk over Jiddy's shoulders.

The other held stone-grey folds across Jiddy's chest. Reams of dandelion yellow and dried-blood red covered the table. Lilac replaced blue. Russet replaced grey. Waves of fabric. Fields of green. They were burying her. She couldn't breathe under the shrouds of colour.

"This will complement her eyes," one of them said.

The taller one stood back. "Make her appear more petite."

"Are you happy with this shade, Signora Vardarelli? The blue transforms her."

That word. *Transform.*

"I don't like blue," Jiddy said.

The two assistants regarded her.

"When we have finished, madam, no-one will recognise her," one of them said and the other nodded.

Not recognise her? Change her so completely Jiddy would be gone forever? This was not why she had come. She gasped for air, clutched at the fabric around her throat, yanked, pulled, ripped.

"Please stop doing this! I'm not here to be transformed. It's business. It don't matter what I look like if what I'm offering you is best of best! I won't be Jianna for you! I'm not you, and I won't be dressed like you!"

"Jianna! Stop!" ordered Maria.

She couldn't see; she couldn't breathe. "This is too much to ask!" It was like the fear she'd felt when the underground tunnel grew smaller and smaller. It was like the sea squeezing her lungs. She thought she'd suffocate, and a rush of panic swept over her. Her chest pressed tight. The cloth choked her heart. She needed to be outside. In fields, on clifftops.

"No!" she shouted, thrusting the yards of blue and green and yellow away. "I came to ask about work for Violet, not be made into a copy of you!" She spotted Lord Ryethorpe coming towards them, and she faced Maria. "I've tried, now please, will you give me an answer, ma'am?" Jiddy cast off the fabric, stepping out of the folds, almost tripping. Anger flashed across her mother's face.

Lord Ryethorpe shook his head. Her mother waved her hand. The assistants stepped away.

"You are free to go," said Maria.

Jiddy took a deep breath. "I have a school in Robin Hood's Bay. I teach local girls how to cut and sew and embroider so they can work in fine houses and places like your emporium." The assistants stood, awkward and scornful. Jiddy pleaded, her eyes brimming with tears. "This has nothing to do with you and me. These lasses may not be dressed like ladies, let alone your assistants, but they're human beings." She stopped, amazed Signora Vardarelli did not interrupt but stared at her as if she'd fallen from the sky.

"Go on," was all her mother uttered.

Lord Ryethorpe's eyes shone as if he was about to cry. How could it be that tears filled her own eyes? She sniffed them back.

"These girls and their families have very little, but they need to eat like anyone here, and they need to keep warm." She laughed. "And they need treats, you know. They are people. A position here, or even an apprenticeship, would help. It would really help. It isn't a crime to want a little bit more than merely surviving, is it?"

Maria gasped, her hand touching her throat. "Why did you say that?"

Jiddy had a feeling that the wrong answer would see her being hoisted outside and maybe even arrested. "I don't know," she said. "I only know some of the girls, not all of them—some want to stay in Bay, I mean, at home, in Robin Hood's Bay—but some, like Violet, they only want, they want…" She searched for the right words to say what she meant.

Signora Vardarelli widened her arms. "They want freedom!"

CHAPTER TWENTY-SIX

Jiddy stood outside Vardarelli's, amazed people walked so close to her and couldn't hear her heart pounding. Signora Vardarelli had shaken her hand and given a promise. No-one had ever shaken her hand before. She didn't know anyone who shook anyone's hand, and it had impressed her so much, she'd made a long, low curtsey. But what mattered more than any words or reams of silk was she could go back to Robin Hood's Bay and tell Violet she had a chance of freedom. Violet now had a choice; Signora Vardarelli would give her an apprenticeship, and Violet could leave Bay and her violent father behind. Jiddy pressed her hand to her chest as her mother had done. She adored the sound of that word. *Freedom.*

She noticed people strolling in and out of the shop, those hurrying past, children gazing through the windows, and the doorman in his fancy dress of a coat. She wanted to shout she'd done it, she'd succeeded; she was a businesswoman in peasant's clothing. But she didn't. She needed space to spread her arms and open her lungs, and people in the street were too close for that. With a last glance at the golden Vardarelli sign, she set off to find open ground. She'd go back to the inn and home with good news on her tongue.

The market stalls stretched forever. If it were possible, there were even more people than before to weave between. Panic that she'd never find her way out of the streets made her head thump. *Keep walking, keep walking.*

Finally, at last, a larger patch of sky appeared. Maybe the street opened onto moorland. Maybe she'd tread on grass instead of cobbles. Bleating sheep would be better than incessant chatter, cow pats better than the stink of bodies. Quickening her pace, she headed towards the end of the row of buildings.

A chipping sound grew louder. It cut through her hurrying footsteps. Doorbells fell into background sounds. The noise became constant like tapping of sticks to warn incoming boats in a sea fret, softer than a blacksmith's hammer but harder than lobsters snapping in a barrel.

A group of figures surged towards her. It was like a high tide readying to knock a person off their feet. She dodged, nudged, pushed her way to the wall and waited, pressing close to the stone.

Go past, go away. Breathe.

They went on, jabbering and oblivious to anyone but themselves. The chipping sound continued, constant. She found her way and stood in the open, arms raised to the sky as she spun around, letting out all the relief and joy bubbling inside. It didn't matter if people stared. It didn't matter if they scorned her. Finally, she could fill her lungs, feel dirt beneath her feet, see the sky spreading overhead, walls towering higher and higher. Spires and turrets, figurines and contorted faces. Trees tickling the clouds with their leaves and birds flickering dark against the light stone.

The cliff at Ravenscar couldn't be any taller than the building facing her. Disorientated, she dropped her arms, letting passers-by move around her. It must have taken men's lifetimes to build this huge church. She gazed in awe. Voices drifted soft; the sound of footsteps eased. Only the tapping remained constant.

No woodcutter wielded an axe. On the grass at the base of the mammoth building sat a cluster of lads at trestles. An elderly man walked between them, bending over and studying a piece of stone standing in front of each one. She realised their chipping of stone was the noise she'd been hearing. Each lad held a chisel and a hammer and *chip, chip, chip* clicked at the stone. The old man said something, and the lad he was speaking to looked up. Even from that distance, Jiddy recognised him. Same hair. Eyes. Round cheeks. Jonas! Her Jonas! Tears of relief, happiness—she didn't know why she should cry, but she couldn't help it. It didn't matter. There he was. Jonas. Her lovely friend Jonas. Alive. She brushed the tears from her cheeks.

"Oh my," she whispered. "Oh, Jonas!" She took a few swift paces. Excitement gave way to nervousness. How to greet him? Hold him. Walking more slowly, she kept her eyes on him, praying he'd see her. He didn't know she came closer, closer...

She couldn't contain herself.

"Jonas!" she shrieked.

His eyes met hers, and she ran the final few steps.

"You're here!" she shouted, hands in the stone dust, face uplifted, craning towards him. "I can't believe it! What are you doing here? Stand! Let me hug you!"

Springing to his feet, eyes shining, he grinned. "Jiddy!"

The relief in his voice brought tears to her eyes again, and she beamed. "Come round and let me hold you!" She spread her arms, and he stumbled past lads turning their heads and gawping. They met at the end of the table, and the squeeze of his embrace made her gasp. His hair pressed to her cheek, and she rested her chin on his shoulder and held him tight. "My heart's going to burst!" She laughed. "I can't believe it's you!"

"Mr. Chaplow!"

The sharp voice made Jonas jump. His arms dropped, and with a sheepish smile, he strolled back toward his seat. The chief stonemason met him and, hand on his shoulder, walked Jonas along the row of now-diligent apprentices. Jiddy quickly strode in parallel until she stopped, opposite him.

"He's working, Miss," the old man said before moving further along the line.

Jiddy bent towards Jonas, taking in his dust-covered hands. "What are you doing?" she asked, and when he pointed to the lump of stone, she smiled and said, "You can tell me later."

Jonas glanced over his shoulder. The supervisor was showing a young lad with wiry hair how to hold tools against the block of stone.

"I've so much to tell you," she said.

Jonas couldn't hold her gaze, and it hit her he couldn't run off to meet her like he used to, snatching an hour away from the cows or the incessant wall repairs or milking or lambing or shearing.

She traced her fingertips in the stone dust. She'd done this before, in flour, and it helped calm her nerves. "You aren't a soldier?" He shook his head. "But you can't come and spend time with me?" The line of lads cut, chipped and smoothed their stone blocks.

"I'm training to be a stonemason," he said. "Seems I'm good at it."

He smiled a little self-consciously. Jonas was never humble or shy about anything he ever did. For a moment, her heart clenched.

"Do you like it?" she said, yearning to touch his hand. "Better than farming?"

His face set cold for a moment. "I said I'm good at this."

"Well, yes, you're good at everything you do." With an unsteady hand, she touched the dusty sheen of his knuckles. He stared at her. He appeared older with his coating of white. She reached for his face, but ever alert to the old man, he jerked back, breaking the moment.

Jiddy glanced at the lad next to Jonas, so intent on not watching them when it was obvious he wanted to. "I'm glad you didn't go to France," she said, trying to calm the tremor in her voice, "and there's no need to worry about stopping away."

In the excitement of seeing him, she'd forgotten how they'd parted. Angry. Upset. Confused. The memory of shouting her hate at his leaving flooded back. She couldn't hate him. She yearned to reach out and touch him. Reassure. Be reassured. The lads nearby were chipping at their blocks of stone, and Jonas couldn't have heard or he pretended not to hear, one or the other, because he didn't answer. He stared at his chunk of rock as if to turn it into a gargoyle or an angel or saint without having to lift his hammer.

"I've arranged an apprenticeship for Violet Ashner," she said. "That's why I'm in York. You remember Violet Ashner, don't you?"

He gave the briefest nod. The Jonas she thought she knew had disappeared again. Of course. He wasn't embarrassed that he'd not gone to France to fight, nor about being seen talking to her by the other lads. He had been well-used to the ridicule of Bay lads for that. His wavy hair, with its sheen of grey, looked sculpted in stone, his cracked hands the same. He cleared his throat, and she realised what was wrong. *She* knew they weren't siblings. Jonas still believed they were. After the first joy of seeing her, the stonemason's shout had brought him back to reality, and he'd remembered.

"Jonas," she said tentatively, "you don't need to be ashamed. We're not brother and sister. Honest, it's not true." She glanced at the master mason. "I'll let you know what happened when you finish."

His eyes flitted sideways. She couldn't wait. She opened her mouth to explain more, to make him understand, but he interrupted.

"Why are you always so blunt?"

The word stung, and she clamped her mouth closed.

"I'll get into trouble," he said, glancing at the two lads on either side. "You should go home to Bay."

She grabbed his hand this time, but he pulled back, and the half-chiselled stone rocked. Holding the trestle steady, he glared at her as if she were a rotten smell.

"When you finish, we have to talk," she said, averting her gaze so he couldn't see how hurt she was. "What time'll that be? I don't have to get straight back to Bay."

He flushed. "Six."

"Oh. Late. If you tell your master I've got things to say, I'm sure he'll let you finish early."

"No, I can't, and I won't ask."

Jiddy glanced at the old stonemason, bending to speak to another of the apprentices. She took a step in his direction.

"Don't you dare!" Jonas warned.

On his feet, his face loomed close. Anger glistened in his eyes. She could whisper words of reason, but he wouldn't hear them.

"Come back to Bay with me and see your da," she said. "He misses you."

Again, so quickly, Jonas's voice hardened. "He's not my da."

Now was not the time to touch his hand. "Please, Jonas. You were over moon to see me, and now we need to speak. I know you're scared we've done things we shouldn't…" She faltered, his angry expression and the images and feelings of what they'd done making her face hot. "Jonas, I still love you." A wave of emotion carried her words. His eyes glistened. She exhaled. "I can't talk to anyone like I can talk to you," she said, her voice breaking. "I've so much to tell you, and I'm sure you've got much to tell me. Please ask the master to let you have time off. He'll understand."

The stonemason walked in their direction, leaving behind a trail of chalky dust. They both focused on the block of stone. It was an angel, she saw that now. It was simple but beautifully carved, and Jonas had created it. She was about to say something when the old man joined them.

"Jonas?" he said. "What's going on?"

"It's not Jonas's fault," Jiddy said.

The stonemason ignored her and remained fixed on Jonas.

"My sister," Jonas said, tipping his palm. "She's visiting York."

The old man faced Jiddy. Stone dust had ingrained every line on his face, making him appear like an animated statue. He gave her a cursory glance. "She doesn't look like your sister."

Jiddy held her breath. In his quick appraisal, he'd taken in her black hair, her dark eyes and sallow skin. Jonas's copper hair, grey eyes and ruddy freckles couldn't be more different. For the first time, she saw what others must see. It was ludicrous to think they could be related. Even as cousins, it seemed unbelievable. Jonas saw what the stonemason had pointed out. He must believe now.

Jonas blushed apple-red. The stonemason nodded. "Ten minutes, and you work ten minutes after everyone has gone."

"Ten minutes," Jonas repeated as if she hadn't heard. He stalked to the end of the table, Jiddy walking opposite until they reached the end of the trestles. Jonas gestured to the corner of the building and walked ahead. They rounded the Minster. Grass covered the ground and several trees spread their branches. Jonas continued walking and stopped under a huge horse chestnut tree. They wouldn't sit, Jiddy realised as he surveyed her.

"Your boss is right," she said to fill the silence. "We aren't anything like each other."

"Of course we are," Jonas found his voice. "We are exactly alike."

She laughed. "We're like a crow and a robin."

"I don't mean how we look," he said. "You're not a crow. Blackbird, maybe." He shrugged. "I know what you meant. I hate to admit it, but we *are* alike, in that we think the same. You can say owt to me, I can say owt to you. Yes, you're all gobby and I'm calmer, but I'm not daft. I know we mesh well, but that were then. We can't mesh anymore. So. Today. Yes, I'm pleased to see you and see you're well and still caring for others, but it don't mean you and me can be as we were again. I'm glad you're all right, and you know I'm all right. Now we can let each other be."

Jiddy hated when he was like this. This was logical, calm Jonas, and it made her body freeze.

"You believe different from me right now, though," she said, keeping her words steady while her heart fluttered like a kestrel hovering over its prey. "You think we're siblings, and we're not. We're cousins, and being cousins is very different from being brother and sister! We've done nowt wrong, Jonas, so get those stupid thoughts out of your head. We've nowt to be embarrassed about."

"Embarrassed? You have no idea how I feel about what we've done! I were told different. A certain Viscount Gregory Hartshorn seduced my mam, then left her to fend for herself with me in her belly. Aren't you angry? He seduced your mam and left you in her belly! Bloody gentry, and don't tell me different."

"I won't. Bloody gentry right," she said. "But it were *Harvey* Hartshorn who seduced lasses around the county, not my da! My da were *Gregory* Hartshorn, and he loved my mother and would have married her if he'd not died, so don't put me in same basket as you!"

By Jonas's reaction, she realised she shouldn't have put it so bluntly. Jonas was right; she did call a tap on the shoulder a bash on the back. She took a step closer, but he stepped away. She took a deep breath. "Please, Jonas. We don't have same da, that's all I'm saying. I didn't mean to hurt you." A pigeon landed on the nearest tree, and the leaves fluttered. "Jonas?"

"Hold your gob," he said, folding his arms.

"Hold my gob?" she repeated. "What's happened to Jonas Chaplow who used to baffle me with his fancy words? Is that all you can come up with? 'Hold your gob'?" She smiled, anything to release the tension.

"You always try to get out of matters by making a joke."

She touched his sleeve, but he flinched. She smiled at the gesture. Jonas had made it since being a little boy. "I won't hold my gob," she said. He didn't answer. "I opened my gob to say I still love you."

198

"Do you know what?" He swung round, ignoring her admission. "Words don't prove nothing. You might resemble your mother while I take after our father."

"Oh, come on, Jonas, think about it. My da were on ship with my mother. He'd been off travelling with Lord Ryethorpe for years. They'd travelled everywhere when, on the way home, they met Maria Vardarelli. He loved her, Jonas. Loved her like I love you." While she spoke, Jonas folded his arms, and unfolded them again. She couldn't tell if he was taking it in or doing his Jonas attitude of always being the one in the right. "Come with me to farm," she said, her voice gentle. "Come and talk to your da, and he'll say same."

Jonas stepped closer. "Did you tell Da this? Did you upset him?"

"No, but he'd know, wouldn't he? That's why you must talk to him. He's a good man. He took care of your mam."

"Your Lord Ryethorpe told me we had same father," he said. "Told me he were saving me from sin. And saving you. He likes you, he said. Not sure he likes me."

"I'm not going to argue anymore," she said, watching the pigeon fly off. "All I say is, ask your da."

Jonas brushed his hands, turning them over and over. "Ten minutes, we're done," he finally said. "I've got to go back to work."

Jiddy caught his arm as he walked past. "Come with me to farm." Jonas waved her off. "Come home! It's not right. Please, come home with me!"

"This is my home now," he said, striding along the side of the building.

She hurried after him. "Last time we talked, you asked me to marry you. We can still marry. Plenty of cousins wed, farming families all over Dales, half of Ashner family are married to each other. Think of all Storms, cousins, half-cousins…" She waited. "Please, Jonas, let's go back to how we were."

"Right." He stopped and turned to face her. "It's well past ten minutes now. I'm going to be working until nightfall, thanks to you."

She flung her arms around him, but he pushed her away, and she stumbled back. This wasn't play fighting. Tears once again spiked her eyes. "What's happened? Has living in a big city made you heartless?"

He wiped his face with the back of his hand, leaving a chalky strip. His hand shook. "We're not children anymore, Jiddy. You have to face life and grow up."

"I've been holding back for so long," she said, catching her breath. "You're the one I talk to. I can be properly myself with you, so don't tell me to grow up. Don't tell me not to be me. I love you, and I can't not say it. I can't not feel it!"

"It isn't so simple," he said. "I can't come back."

"It is simple! Please come home."

He shook his head. "Even if I wanted, I couldn't. I'm apprenticed to Minster. I can't break a binding promise."

"They'll understand!"

"I've signed a legal contract."

Jonas hadn't changed. He'd been the same in their youth. Always doing the right thing. Making the right choice. But she'd learned from him. She could argue. She could find a way. "Do they need payment to let you go?"

Jonas rubbed his hair. "I like it here. I were only a farmer because I were born on a farm. But here, I have a choice. They saw something in me. I feel right here. It's honest."

She gasped. "Honest? You mean it's Bay and what goes on in Bay you want to get away from?"

He shrugged. She hurried at his side, waiting for him to explain what he meant, but all he said was, "You know what I'm talking about."

They'd reached the corner. The chipping sound of the stonecutters pierced her head. "You can tell people you're a farmer, same as a stonemason, I don't see problem," she said.

He grabbed her arms, and she took a sharp intake of breath at the strength of his grip. "I'll get sucked into smuggling again if I return," he said, so close to her face she saw the flecks of moisture in his eyes. "I'm learning to carve angels and saints here. Can't you understand? I have a choice to do something not everyone can do but I'm good at, and it's honest, Jiddy. It's honest and it's my choice."

Her chin trembled. "Robin Hood's Bay is your home, Jonas, not York."

"Meadow Bank Farm were my home, but it's not anymore." His jaw tightened. "I don't have kin there, and that makes a difference. I don't want to farm land that's not mine."

"Shouldn't my being there matter?" she asked, her voice cracking. "And it *is* your home. I know your da believes it is."

Jonas thrust his hands into his pockets. "You can make anywhere your home."

She swung her arms to appear nonchalant. "I reckon you've swallowed too much stone dust and it's addled your brain and stopped you seeing sense."

Jonas smiled, but he looked defiant. "I never thought I'd leave Bay or want to, but now I have, I'm seeing there's other ways of being and other places you can belong."

She couldn't bear it. "I've not real kin in Bay," she said, "but it's my home. It's where I belong!"

Jonas put his head on one side. His expression changed. An idea had struck him. "You could make York your home too if you wanted. You'd easily get work here as a seamstress. Come on, admit it, stop being all defensive. You always said you wanted to leave Bay. Consider it. You could get an honest job here. No temptations from Big Isaac and like." He breathed in deeply. He still found it hard to catch her eye.

"There's temptations everywhere," she said. "Besides, I bet many clandestine goods end up here."

"Robin Hood's Bay is corrupt," he said, ignoring what she'd said. "Smuggling..." He checked no-one had heard and, stepping closer, lowered his voice. "Smuggling is a dirty business, Jiddy. Get out of it while you still can."

He urged her to agree. If she was honest to herself, she'd admit he was right. She thought of the outsider, Gobbit, who had been ground by the locals into the dust for betraying them to preventives. Rebecca, shot for her honesty. James, packed onto a prison ship by preventives for his role in the smuggling gangs. How she'd dreamed of finding her real kin.

"Who says I'm not earning an honest living?" she asked.

"I'll help you," he said. "What've you to lose?"

"So, you do believe we've different fathers and we can be together and wed?"

Jonas dipped his head before holding her gaze. "I believe you. I know you don't lie. I'm angry we were lied to. It's hard to let lies go."

Agreement tingled on her tongue. As soon as she said yes, they'd be together again, on the same path, planning a life together. Slipping one hand into his, she looked at the Minster towering above them.

Jonas followed her gaze and pointed. "That one, high above the others, is you."

Jiddy's heart pounded. Tears welled again, and she couldn't explain why she felt so sad and panicked. "I don't see myself as an angel," she murmured.

He pointed with his other hand, lifting her hand with his. "Not that one, other one!" He pointed again. "It's you, telling me to shut up."

She squinted to make out the features. Hair in twisted waves, finger to lips, face contorted in an intense gaze, the creature looked more gargoyle than angel.

"Very funny," she said, not feeling it was funny at all. "That one's you."

"Oh, so you see likenesses now. Which one?"

She pointed, determined not to show how unsettled she felt. "Gap-tooth with gormless expression."

"What are we going to do?" he asked, catching her other hand and turning her to face him.

A surge of emotion swept from her belly. "I thought you were in hurry to get back to work," she said, letting tears finally flow.

Pulling her into him, he held her, and she bent her face into his shoulder. He rubbed her shoulder blades. Eyes closed, she could have leaned against him for hours. She should be happy. He wanted her to come to York. He wanted to love her again. Taking a deep breath, she stepped back. They were the same young lad and girl playing on the beach, working out why salt cost so much money, deciding how they'd run the country better than any politician in London. Deciding on their future.

She brushed her hands together. "Typical stone dust," she said. "Gets everywhere."

Jonas wiped his hands over his apron. "You're right, I have to get back to work. When will you come back?"

"Soon," she said.

He nodded again, hands loose by his sides. "I'm sorry I went away so sudden."

She sighed, words of love tingling on her lips. "It's done," she said instead. "Keep well, and I'll come and see you when I bring Violet to Vardarelli's for her apprenticeship."

Leaning in, she kissed him briefly and tasted stone dust on his dry lips and a smidgeon of salt, only to realise it was sweat, not the lingering lap of the sea beaded on his skin.

CHAPTER TWENTY-SEVEN

A week later, Jonas stepped from the coach at the Buttercross. He inhaled, filling his lungs with sea air. No stone dust. No dried sweat of bodies sleeping too many in one room. For the first time in months, he felt clean.

If he came back permanently, as Jiddy wanted, he could do this every day for the rest of his life. He breathed in again. It felt good to have seen her and have a reason to return to the coast. With a glance towards the water, he tramped over tufts of wiry grass, wondering whether Jiddy would be at Thorpe Hall or in the Bay. If he didn't go to the farm first, he'd end up spending all day with her, and he needed to find out how the situation lay at Meadow Bank so he could bring her news. He should have thought how it must be for his da instead of heading off so fast. He hoped Mr. Chaplow would still be in charge, but he doubted it. Never mind. He straightened his pack. He'd check out the farm situation; time afterwards with Jiddy would be his reward.

As he crested the tops, Jonas was met by a herd of cows nuzzling into the grass, and their intermittent bellows mingled with a cockerel's cry. Three figures stood by the top wall, and he made out his cousin and Big Isaac and Sandy. He hunched his shoulders and kept walking.

He didn't want to know what his cousin was getting himself into. The farm gate stood open, and he caught a whiff of mulch as he strode into the yard.

"Anyone about?" he called. A few hens scratched the soil, and a dull pounding came from the farmhouse. "Hello?"

His cousin's wife, wiping her hands on her pinafore, appeared in the doorway. "News travels fast. Moving back already, Jonas Chaplow?" Her face was a knot of accusation.

"Pleasure to see you too, Sarah," he said, striding towards her. "What news is this?"

"You've not heard we're returning to John's father's farm?"

Jonas laughed awkwardly. "No. Meadow Bank's yours as long as me da is all right with that. You not getting along?"

Sarah wiped her hands more vigorously. "Seems Robin Hood's Bay folk aren't as welcoming as we'd have hoped. It's not kind of place we thought."

Jonas frowned. "Takes time to settle in. Bay folk are all right once you get to know them. Has Jiddy—"

"We don't like this type!" she interrupted. "We're honest, decent folk, and we don't want no trouble." She let go of her apron. "We'll be out by end of month."

"I'm sorry," said Jonas, looking around the farmyard again. "I know Da were pleased you'd come. You'll be owners of Meadow Bank someday."

"Don't be sorry," she snapped. "Squire Farsyde has sorted matters. He's putting in some lads to help your da. Mr. Chaplow will manage until you come back."

"I'm not coming back."

She eyed him suspiciously. "Maybe you should talk to squire about it?"

Jonas shook his head. "That's for you to sort," he said. "I've come to pay Da a visit, that's all. I've an apprenticeship in York, and I want to tell him about it."

Sarah glanced over his shoulder at the gate before stepping closer. "I'm sure you won't take it wrong way if I say I'm relieved to hear that. John wouldn't want a Chaplow being caught up in goings on here. Better you're well out of anything dishonest. Can't see why they don't leave farmers alone, I really can't."

Jonas scuffed the ground with his boot. "Has anyone been getting to you?"

She shook her head, and strands of fine hair fluttered loose. She pressed her thin lips tight.

Jonas sighed. "I'm sorry you're considering leaving, but I'm not here to ruffle feathers," he said, choosing his words carefully. "Farm's yours if you want it as far as I'm concerned, and I'm sure my da will have words with any men who are taking liberties."

Sarah clasped her hands tight. "We're leaving."

Jonas nodded, taking in her drawn face and the disarray of the yard. "Is the old man about?"

Sarah's shoulders relaxed, and she jolted her head. "He's still trying to fix wall you left half-built. John says it keeps him out of harm's way, but he's making a dog's dinner of it if you ask me. If you wait, you can take him a pail of bread and cheese. Save my having to trail over the fields."

"Will you put some ale in?" Jonas asked, leaning on the door jamb. The kitchen looked the same as when he'd packed his bag. "I understand why you're leaving," he added.

Sarah cut chunks of bread and fumbled wrapping pieces of cheese. She held out the dinner pail. "Don't mention this to your da," she said.

Jonas carried the two bottles and foodstuffs in the packed bucket back along the track and veered off over the fields towards the outline of trees. John, Big Isaac and Sandy were nowhere to be seen, but Jonas spotted his da's figure and the tumble of wall. It could have been the same day as the one he'd left. The old man had made progress, but stones still littered the ground. Legs straddled, his da heaved a medium-sized rock and half threw, half angled it into a gap in the wall. He grunted. Rex, stretched on the ground, had cocked one ear. The old man cursed. Jonas scuffed a tuft of grass with his boot and the dog raised his head, barked and bounded towards him.

"I've brought your dinner," Jonas said, resting the pail on the grass.

The old man shuffled around, eyed Jonas and turned back to the wall. Crouching, Jonas cupped the dog's head and rubbed his thumbs over its jaw. William Chaplow continued to wriggle the stone into the gap.

Rex refused to quieten, and Jonas pressed the dog's head to make him sit, wondering which of them would speak first. Jonas stood again, Rex circling his legs, brushing close with frenzied movements. His dog hadn't forgotten him.

"So, what's John been up to?" he asked.

Ignored, he strolled closer, examining the stones for the right shape to bridge the next gap.

He might never have gone away for all that had changed. Rex stretched out on the grass again while his da, the old man, William Chaplow, was as dour as ever.

"Want hand?" Jonas asked.

He got a snuffle in return.

Jonas selected a stone and slotted it easily into the gap. William stood back and, taking a rag from his pocket, wiped his face. Rex sank his head onto his paws. Jonas put his hand on the wall. He'd need a couple of small stones to pin the larger ones together, and he gathered a few pieces. He worked in silence, enjoying the touch of the stones and fixing the wall solid and the weight tugging his arms and shoulders when he topped off the wall. With the fields rising to the moor and trees providing shelter from the easterly wind, time became immaterial. He lifted another stone. The wall would soon be mended.

"John's wife put in two flasks of ale," Jonas said.

That got his da's attention. "I'm surprised she spoke to you."

The old man knew nothing of John's negotiations with Big Isaac.

"Wondered if you were missing a tot of rum," Jonas said, popping the bung. "Sorry. Weren't funny." The gruff snort and turning of William's back, changed the subject. "I've worked up a thirst." Jonas lifted the flask and put back his head. The warm ale, tinged with coastal soil, eased his throat. The dog cocked an ear. "So. John and Sarah are packing up?"

William shuffled his boots, scuffling in the basket for a bottle. He gulped liquid without answering. Jonas rested his against a stone and waited for William to finish. The old man took his time.

"What's visit in aid of?" William said, fiddling with the fold of cloth wrapping the bread and cheese.

"Do I need reason?"

William tore a piece of bread. "Are you stopping?"

"No, but you can rest easy. I decided not to go to war."

William chewed the crust, ruminating over the mouthful.

Jonas folded his arms. There was no point in agitating him by asking about John and his goings on. He'd done his best, but he'd wasted precious time. If preventives came and found John had got involved in smuggling, John and Sarah were the unluckiest beggars in neighbourhood. "I remembered what you said about fact there were different ways to be brave," he said. "Do you remember?"

Nudging past Jonas, the old man bent for a stone, but he didn't immediately stand. His hair, greasily thin and stranded tawny grey, was slick to his skull. His hands showed the swellings around his knuckles and the slight twists of arthritis.

"Let me," Jonas said, the bottle of ale still in his hand as he walked to the wall.

"What did I say?" William mumbled, lifting a stone.

"You said, 'Let them in power do fighting,'" Jonas said. "You told me to let them who wants wars to stick bayonets into young lads' bellies and see what it does to a body. Let them blow lads' chests out, you said. So I did. I've left well alone."

"You didn't go to France?" repeated William, for the first time looking Jonas in the eye.

"I decided to try being brave somewhere else." Stepping aside again, Jonas sensed the tension in William's stance. "Here, give it me."

William grazed Jonas's arm as he waddled past with a stone. "John's wife's a good cook," he said, his voice rasped by pipe-smoking.

Jonas grinned. "Now you're the brave one. Wonder how we survived before she came."

"Mary's food parcels."

Jonas reached for another swig of ale. "Does Jiddy still come?" he asked, wishing she was there right at that moment to smooth the awkwardness between them.

William shuffled to the wall and ran his hands over the coping stones, putting a distance between them by following the line of the wall.

"It'll withstand winter," said Jonas, balancing the bottle on the wall before lifting another stone and laying it on the top. The old man paused, gazing into the trees as if he'd seen a movement, possibly a rabbit or a fox. "I came to tell you," Jonas continued, "I'm apprenticed to a stonemason at York Minster." He waited, but there came no acknowledgement. "I get board and lodging."

"Not well paid?"

Jonas smiled. He'd forgotten you never got praised at Meadow Bank Farm. "If I pass examinations, I hope to become a master stonemason when I'll earn a steady amount."

"How long's that going to take?"

Rex sighed and put his head back on his paws.

"Seven years and I'll be a journeyman mason."

"I'll be dead by time you're done."

Jonas cleared his throat. "After, I must complete my own build. It could be a barn, preferably a house, but with Guild's permission, after inspection, I can seek work as a proper fully qualified mason, hire others to work with me and even take on my own apprentices."

"Good job John's here," William muttered.

Jonas pursed his lips. So many responses he could make.

The trees had fallen silent, and no sound of voices travelled from the top fields. Now was the time, Jonas decided. There was nothing to lose. Rex had closed his eyes. "I came to ask you something," he said.

His da contemplated the wall as if studying it would win him a prize. After a moment, he bent down, stiff in his joints, and ran his palm over a large rock.

"Leave it a minute, would you?" Jonas said.

His da's words spat onto the grass. "Got to get this done." Shambling over to the wall, he cupped a top stone in his palm.

Jonas, bending to stroke the dog's head for a moment, strolled to join him. Now or never. "Can we be honest?"

William refused to give Jonas his attention. Instead, he ran his hands with their cracked knuckles over the wall. "Depends."

Jonas touched the sleeve of the old man's jacket. "I know I'm not your son." William didn't move, and Jonas let his hand remain. He glanced at the old man's profile. "D'you want to tell me about it? Why you married my ma?"

William hunched his shoulder to the wall, extracting a battered leather pouch from his pocket. Jonas stepped back a few paces. His da opened a paper, spread out a few brown leaves and rolled his smoke. Lighting it, he took his time to draw.

Jonas waited, hoping his da wouldn't do the usual and talk about the weather, but he was taking too long, and now Jonas had asked the question, he wanted an answer.

"You never knew her," William eventually said.

"Tell me about her."

William glanced at Jonas, drawing on his pipe again. "Not much to tell."

"One thing?"

"Hettie were a lot younger than me."

"I know, so why, when you'd been a bachelor for so long, would you marry a young lass who were…"

"Not from around here?"

"Where'd you meet her?"

"Pickering Market."

Jonas couldn't stop his heart thumping. If he asked too quickly, if he appeared too eager, Mr. Chaplow would clam up like a cornered crab. "Did…did you know her already?"

Another long drag. "She weren't strong, you know. Not like your Jiddy."

Jonas's heart clenched at the memory of them play-fighting. He missed their banter. Everything had become serious. "No-one's as strong as Jiddy," he said, swiping the bottle and chugging back the last of the ale.

Mr. Chaplow caught his breath. "Hettie had pretty eyes," he said, uncharacteristically dropping his chin and staring at his feet. "If she picked me, I weren't going to disappoint her."

"I bet you were a right catch," said Jonas.

His da eyed him, taking him in and what he'd said. He didn't smile. "She had to get away from her da. I might have seemed a good bet, with my own farm and miles from where folk knew of her."

"You put yourself down."

Throwing away the stump of his smoke, William stood astride from the wall. "I've never been what lasses wanted, but Hettie—Hettie Fletcher, that were her full name— she had to do summat and her options were slim."

Jonas had never heard his da so passionate before, and he stood, open-mouthed.

"She were with child, see." He walked along the wall, away from Jonas, but Jonas followed, keen to know more about the woman who had died when he still needed suckling.

"Did you get on?" he asked. "Were you…" He searched for the word. "Happy?"

"Were we what?" His da whipped around, the modesty gone and a hardened veneer appearing.

"I meant," Jonas struggled for words. "Why'd she agree?"

"You wouldn't ask if you'd met her father."

Mr. Chaplow set off again, scuffing past Jonas and back towards Rex. Jonas followed.

"You should wed that Jiddy lass," William said. "She knows what's what. She's not type to have her head turned by some wealthy stranger from other end of country who don't give a toss about poor lasses like your ma."

Your ma. Jonas suddenly saw her as a real person, not the frail shadow he'd imagined under the plain stone in the Bay graveyard. Before he could form another question, his da spoke again.

"Their farm were right isolated on tops, way out yonder of Pickering, place near Egton. No-one else about. Only him and a gaggle of daughters. He may have had sons, but I only remember girls. I don't care to think what her life'd been like if I hadn't taken her."

The beating in Jonas's chest gave way to a pit in his stomach. He rubbed a cold smatter of sweat from his forehead. "Who were man she fell for?"

Mr. Chaplow shot him a bitter glance. "Harvey Hartshorn were his name. Reddish-haired with a limp, and he went off back south, leaving Hettie with you in her belly and her da with a ready fist." He stared at Jonas as if willing him to contradict.

Lichen-covered stones nestled into the grass. "You've got too many," Jonas said. "I'll shift them."

"No, they're right," William said, taking out the leather case again and rolling a second smoke. "Has her at farm given you some dinner as well?"

Jonas patted his bag. "I'm covered, ta."

He didn't remember conversations being this difficult, but back then, they'd had all the jobs of the farm to talk about. Jonas towered over the shorter man. Since his teenage years, he'd been broader and taller, and now the difference stood out more pronounced as the older man had grown even thinner and shrunk smaller. They both studied the wall, Mr. Chaplow sucking in his cheeks with each draw. Yawning, Rex rose to his feet.

"Wall's pretty much done," William said.

"I'd best be off."

William squinted at the sky. "Looks like rain."

Jonas held out his hand, and William shook it. The gnarled knuckles struck Jonas, and he wondered if they'd ever shake hands again.

CHAPTER TWENTY-EIGHT

Jonas retraced his steps, shoulders bowed to the wind, and keeping a wary eye on the gathering rain clouds. He strode past the herd of cattle, but there was still no sign of the three men, only moos of farewell. Even if Jonas were free to, he couldn't come back to a secretive life. He'd said it to Jiddy all those months ago, and he'd meant it. He wanted to tell everyone he met what he did, and he could do that in York. Bay sucked you in, whether you wanted or no. John didn't want it either. He stamped his feet. He'd not brood about it.

Facing into the wind, Jonas lengthened his strides along the badly rutted road. When the chimneys of Thorpe Hall appeared out of the trees, he veered off, swishing through the long grass, jumping over the small beck and heading across a sandy track. Leaves overhead rustled. The sky, bilious now, darkened. Walking towards the house, he pondered what his next move would be if Jiddy wasn't there. He'd spent much longer than he'd planned at the farm, and there wouldn't be time to go to the village as well before he'd need to be back at the Buttercross to catch the coach.

He rapped on the kitchen door. Violet Ashner opened it. The surprise on her face made him feel even more like a stranger than he had at the farm.

"Is Jiddy here?" he asked.

Hand moving to her cheek, Violet stepped onto the threshold. "We thought you'd gone to France. Is war over?"

He stamped his boots. "We'll know it's over when they stop putting duty on tea and salt."

Violet stared. "Right," she mumbled.

The wind gusted the door, and Jonas put out his hand to prevent it from slamming. "So, Jiddy's here or not?" he asked.

Violet touched her cap. "Mrs. Farsyde's not feeling too good, and Jiddy's sitting with her." A few drops of rain blew in.

"Looks like a storm's heading this way," Jonas said.

"Are you on your way home to see your da?" she asked.

For a moment, Jonas wondered if his ma had been like the young Ashner girl. "I'm on my way back to York but I need to see Jiddy. Can you fetch her?"

Violet's face brightened. "York?"

"It's where I'm living now."

"Honest? You live in York?"

He nodded, thinking how different this wide-eyed young lass was to her elder sister. Nellie would have made a sarcastic remark, or a suggestive one. Probably both. He took off his cap. "Would you see if Jiddy can talk with me for a minute."

"Do you want a cup of tea while you're waiting?"

Violet really did have a resemblance to Nellie now she'd brightened. Larger eyes but with the same Ashner hunger.

218

"Wouldn't say no," he said, already tasting the bitter treat of hot tea. "I can't stop long, though. Need to see Jiddy then catch coach back to York."

Thunder rumbled from the east. "I'll put kettle on and fetch her while it's boiling," she said.

Violet busied herself while Jonas stood in the kitchen doorway. Jiddy would be on the other side of the door leading to the house. If Violet hadn't been there, he'd have been tempted to walk through it and find Jiddy himself. He was learning etiquette of these things, though, and he had to be patient. The young girl poured boiling water into a teapot. Jonas wondered how she'd cope if she came to the city. Strange it was so quiet. He'd only ever seen the kitchen bustling, the chief cook shouting, young girls carrying dishes and plates, someone fanning the flames, no-one standing still.

"Where is everyone?" he asked.

"Sit at table," answered Violet. "Mrs. King is resting, and there's only mistress and Jiddy at home today."

Jonas pulled out a chair, glancing at the window when a smattering of rain struck the glass.

"Bet you're glad I asked you in," she said, placing the teapot on the table.

"I'll have a word with Jiddy, and this'll see me right. Ta." How many more times would he have to say it before she jumped to action? He didn't want to appear ungrateful, but he wished she'd get on and find Jiddy. As she lifted the pot and poured the steaming liquid, he said, "We can all have a cup together once you've fetched her."

She blushed, the pink shade making her grey eyes bright. "I'll not be long."

While he slurped the tea, one eye on the dark sky through the window, he listened for Jiddy's footsteps.

***

Violet stood in the bedroom doorway. In the bed, Mrs. Farsyde snored gently. Jiddy slumped in a chair with her chin on her chest, hair tousled over the cushions.

"Jiddy?" Violet whispered.

Jiddy pulled a blanket higher to her chin. The warmth of sleep enveloped the room, and Violet glanced over her shoulder to the stairs. A clock ticked. A ruffle of Mrs. Farsyde's snore tickled the air. She crept into the room. A floorboard creaked, and she stood still. Neither of the women stirred. Reaching for Jiddy's arm, Violet tapped it but got no response. When she shook it, Jiddy jerked away.

"Leave me alone," came a dull, slightly irritated voice.

Jiddy turned on her side. She must be exhausted. The squire's wife always slept restlessly, often waking, frequently calling out. Mrs. Farsyde breathed heavily. Violet patted Jiddy's shoulder.

"Mmm-off," mumbled the sleeping figure.

"Jonas is downstairs," Violet said.

Jiddy's eyelids fluttered. After a moment, Violet tiptoed out of the room.

***

Jonas paced the floor, looking expectantly at the kitchen door when it opened. Violet had wrapped a thick shawl over her head and entered, pulling it over her shoulders and tying it around her waist. "She can't come," she said.

"What? She knows I'm here?"

Violet nodded. "She can't leave Mrs. Farsyde."

"But she understands I can't stop?"

"I tried," she said. "Mrs. Farsyde needs her there at all times now."

Jonas put down his cup. "Damn it. I have to be off."

Taking a basket, Violet strolled into the hallway. "I might as well walk with you than on my own."

"Out in this?" said Jonas, hesitating by his chair.

"It's easing off," said Violet. "And I must collect sleeping powder from doctor. Mrs. Farsyde can't settle at night without it."

"Did Jiddy say owt?"

"Jiddy has to stop with m'lady, and I must get powder before doctor goes out."

Jonas followed the Ashner girl outside, closing the door with a bang. The rain, turning to mist, created a shroud over the trees, and they headed towards the road without a word. As they mounted from the trough cradling the house, the wind dispersed the blanket of cloud and lighter patches showed through the gaps. Violet strode alongside, chattering away, though Jonas didn't take it in, debating with himself whether to return to the hall and wait until Jiddy appeared and miss the coach or catch his ride and retain his job.

"You'll tell Jiddy I called?" he reiterated.

"'Course," said Violet. "She'll be mad she's missed you."

He liked the sound of that. He'd hate her not caring. He'd wondered so often after he'd left. The loneliness of not seeing her and maybe never seeing her again had been the worst of leaving the Bay.

"Don't worry, I'll make coach," he said, catching Violet's eye, "but you're heading to Bay. You can cut off here." He nodded. "Thanks for tea and tell Jiddy I'll be over again soon."

"Jiddy's taken me under her wing," Violet said, gazing at him with her wide eyes. "For Nellie's sake. That's what Annie and Betsie said."

"That's her all over," he said, holding in his stomach when he felt it rumble. "Well, you head off to doctor. Don't hang about."

"I'll come a bit further." She continued to pick her way through the puddles so Jonas had no choice but to keep walking. Glancing at the woollen shape struggling to balance, he couldn't help but admire her determination.

"Do you miss Nellie?" he asked. She gave a brief nod. Jonas smiled. "Well, Nellie wouldn't have gone out of her way to keep me company. Are you certain you're related?"

"'Course! I'll go as far as top of bank."

"I thank you," he said, making a mock bow. "I hope you'll tell Jiddy what she's missed."

Violet nodded again. "She'll be sorry," she said.

***

Mrs. Farsyde slept all afternoon while Jiddy watched raindrops trickle down the window after she'd woken. She had the faint notion someone had disturbed her. Outside, clouds had begun to separate and reveal silver patches. The battered trees shook droplets on the grass. She listened for sounds of movement below. The glass felt cold.

"Jiddy?"

Mrs. Farsyde sat, propped by pillows in bed. "How long have I been asleep?"

"Would you like me to fetch you a cup of tea and some bread and butter?"

Mrs. Farsyde yawned. "That would be nice."

Jiddy paused at the top of the stairs and listened again. The house was never this quiet. She slid her hand over the balustrade as she descended. On each step, a sense of dread raised prickles on her neck. Why was it so quiet? She gripped the wood.

"Violet?"

No response. The portraits in the hall followed her with their unblinking eyes. The clock in Squire Farsyde's study ticked. The wooden floor creaked underfoot. She opened the door leading to the kitchen, expecting to hear noises of activity or chattering voices, but only the clock ticked here too.

"Violet?" she called again. "Mrs. King?"

Still, no-one appeared. Jiddy had never seen the kitchen unoccupied before, and she crept into the room. A lone cup with dregs of tea staining the bottom, alongside a teapot and jug, stood incongruously on the table.

Crossing to the stove, she lifted the pot and shook it to see if it held any water. It did, and she placed it onto the stove. All signs of the sky brightening had disappeared, and rain tapped intermittently on the window. She folded her arms and watched the trees smear with wet.

"Hurry up," she ordered the water. Remembering the bread, she cut and buttered a slice.

Steam began to rise, and she made up a tray, taking the jug from the table and fresh cups.

"Oooh, exactly what I need. I'm parched."

She jumped at the unexpected voice.

Mrs. King stood in the doorway, rubbing her neck. "I'll have some bread and butter with it. Is Madam having some?" The older woman bustled into the kitchen. "See you've already had a cup yourself," she said, nodding to the crockery on the table.

"Not me," Jiddy said. "Violet must have had a visitor!"

"Visitor or not," Mrs. King muttered, fussing over the butter dish, "that girl better make herself visible soon or I'll want to know what we're paying her for."

***

"I'm sorry, I'm sorry, I'm sorry," Violet reiterated shivering rain over the kitchen floor.

Mrs. King remained in her chair while Jiddy wrung out the girl's stockings and draped them by the stove to dry. "Put your shoes against stove too," she said, "and don't leave your cape on floor!"

Grasping the cape, Violet shook it. Mrs. King raised her arms. "Careful!"

"What d'you mean, you're sorry?" asked Jiddy, bustling around the soaking girl.

Violet concentrated on splaying out the cloak's folds over a chair. Mrs. King leaned over the stove to pour hot water into a large basin. "This'll warm your feet," she said.

"I tried to wake you, but you were hard on," said Violet. "Jonas couldn't wait any longer, as he had coach to catch, and I had to collect Mrs. Farsyde's medicine."

Jiddy gripped the cape tight in her fists. "Jonas were here?"

Violet nodded back at the folds of wool. "I did all but shout in your ear."

"You should have shouted!" Jiddy yelled, striding around the chair. "Why didn't you try harder to wake me?" Violet cringed.

"Now then," said Mrs. King, placing the bowl down. "Lass said she tried. Violet? Come and sit. Get your feet in this hot water."

"It were Jonas! Come to see me!" said Jiddy.

Violet closed her eyes as she dipped her feet into the hot water. "He said to tell you he'd called."

Jiddy counted. She held the back of a chair. "What else did he say?"

Violet smiled. "He said he lives in York!"

CHAPTER TWENTY-NINE

Jiddy's heart beat fast. Wagons, coaches, horses, dogs, people and overwhelming noise filled the inn's yard. Wide-eyed, Violet grasped Jiddy's arm and pushed close. "I don't like it," she whimpered.

"You'll get used to it," Jiddy said, clutching her basket and jostling against people massing around them. "Stick by me."

As they crossed the bridge over the vast river, Violet tilted her head to take in the spectacle of the Minster. It pointed into the sky, larger than any building either girl had ever seen.

"Impressive, isn't it?" said Jiddy. "If you didn't believe in God or angels or heaven, this building makes you feel they must exist." She nudged Violet. "What say you?"

The younger girl stared. "It's huge!"

"We'll come back," said Jiddy, catching the tapping sound of hammers. She didn't want to admit she was annoyed Violet had spent time with Jonas while she'd been snoozing upstairs. The feeling of jealousy took her by surprise, and she trampled it down. Maybe she was being a bit controlling not going to see Jonas straight away, but she reasoned it was wiser to secure Violet's position before any pleasure. A nugget of doubt still jagged in her brain that her mother may still turn around and say no.

They veered off into side streets before reaching the Minster and walking past market stalls and shops. Jiddy kept a firm hold on Violet's hand, who, agog at the barrage of sound and bustle, repeatedly stopped to take in the mounds of bread, sprays of herbs and tumbles of willow baskets as Jiddy had first done herself. She did her utmost not to hurry the younger girl. She yearned to see Jonas, but it was important Violet liked the city. She needed to see women like herself selling baskets they'd made and flowers they'd gathered. Jiddy pointed to windows, imagining who lived in the rooms above. "Perhaps you'll be living in a place like that soon," she said, proud of her restraint not to rush.

The narrow street finally opened out onto another square. The magnificent emporium with the gold lettering on a sign above the front doors dominated.

"It's so grand," said Violet, gaping at the shop windows.

Glassware sparkled and China plates gleamed. This was a different world to Baytown. "I'm afraid you won't be coming through front way when you work here, but I wanted you to see it. We'll go in main way this time, if doorman'll let us, and when we come out again after, you'll go round to rear entrance, which staff use."

Even in her best clothes, Jiddy felt like an imposter. She'd walked through the door with Lord Ryethorpe before, and no doorman could mistake him for a labourer. She noticed the hem of her dress had frayed from catching the ground, and spots of mud flecked the wool. Violet had done her best, having knitted a new shawl from an unravelled old one Mrs. King had donated. The bruise on her cheek had faded, but her prominent cheekbones and lardy skin still made her look like a starving wastrel.

"Let me look at you," Jiddy said, lodging her basket between her feet.

"Folk are watching," Violet pleaded.

"Pinch your cheeks," she said. "Or they'll presume you're dying of plague."

Doing as Jiddy said, Violet nipped her cheeks, creating a pink glow. "I haven't slept, I'm so scared," she said.

Jiddy smiled. "Well, it is a bit scary, but it's also exciting." She picked at the buff skirt and shawl and sighed.

"What's wrong?"

"You'll do fine," Jiddy said, straightening the shawl around Violet's shoulders. "Now, don't say a word until Signora Vardarelli asks you a question."

"What if I don't know answer?"

Jiddy smoothed her palms over Violet's bonnet. "She's employing you as a seamstress. She's not going to ask you to name kings and queens of England all way back to before people were wearing clothes."

"Don't make me more nervous."

Jiddy tucked in the knot on the younger girl's shawl. "Your name is what she'll ask you. She'll check your nails—are they clean?"

Violet nodded and spread out her hands. "Scrubbed them last night and this morning."

They walked past the doorman, who, explaining directions to an elderly couple, didn't notice the two plainly dressed figures. Once inside, both girls stared in silence. Jiddy had forgotten how it took your breath away. Chandeliers sent rainbows across the ceiling. Scents of perfume filled their nostrils. Chatter and footsteps combined to create a cacophony of sound. In that moment, she forgot about Violet and why they were there. The palace of light and colour enveloped her. A woman swept past, her dress a flurry of material.

Brought back to reality, Jiddy reached for Violet's arm. The girl had vanished. Turning around, she tried not to panic. Trust the girl to have wandered off, probably handling China and glassware or those delicate fans, and neither of their hands were clean enough. They'd be thrown out, and Signora Vardarelli would refuse to see them and the future of not only Violet but all the girls Jiddy taught would be shattered.

Customers swarmed all around, swamping the passageways. She couldn't see Violet's scrawny figure. She must keep calm. Where the heck could she be? Spinning around, Jiddy spotted the young girl's grey face, the pink tinge of earlier completely faded again. Violet stood across the room in the fabric section, gazing at the coloured silks and patterned damasks, standing out like a duckling amongst swans.

Weaving past shoppers and avoiding the alert gaze of shop assistants, Jiddy reached the awestruck girl. "So, you're keen to stay, are you?"

Violet nodded, eyes wide. Jiddy hadn't noticed how clear and bright they could be, and the urge to berate her dissipated. "If you want to stay, you don't touch anything, d'you understand?"

"I understand."

"Right," said Jiddy. "Let's go and see if you can permanently stay while we still have half a chance."

Violet gripped Jiddy's arm. "I don't know," she said. "Can we go out and come back in?"

"What? Why? No! We're here now."

Violet's chin trembled. "I'm going to be sick!"

Two minutes later, Jiddy paced while Violet leaned against the side wall of the building, wiping her mouth. Jiddy began to wonder if she'd made a mistake bringing Violet to the city before she was ready. "We'll go for a walk," she said, leading Violet away from Vardarelli's. "We'll come back when you're calmer."

The relief on the younger girl's face reappeared immediately. "I'll be all right in a bit."

They walked back through the market, but this time, Violet didn't take much notice of the stalls. Jiddy concentrated on deciding whether this was too big a step and if she should take Violet back to Robin Hood's Bay. Jonas would know. He'd know whether Violet would thrive in the city walls.

When they left the shadow of the narrow street and stood in the open space beside the Minster, Violet appeared completely herself again, and Jiddy decided they would go back to Vardarelli's in a half hour, whether Jonas agreed or not.

"What's that noise?" Violet asked.

Jiddy smiled at the tapping sound. "Let's find out," she said.

"Oh! Is this where he is?"

"Who?" Jiddy asked. Violet raised a fresh, animated face. "Violet?" A surge of heat swept through her body. She couldn't believe it. Jonas must have told Violet he worked at the Minster. Jiddy tried to see if she could spot him. She couldn't let Nellie Ashner's sister lay eyes upon him before she did. She strode towards the tables, but to her surprise, Violet ran past her towards the grand building and the source of the knocking sound as if she did know what it meant and who was making it. She hurried, cursing Jonas for visiting Thorpe Hall and talking to the gaunt kitchen maid.

The line of apprentices sat, chisels and hammers busy, a shroud of dust draped over their heads, hair all the same shade of grey, skin identically masked. Violet stood several yards from the line of trestles.

"Did Jonas tell you he works at the Minster?" Jiddy asked with a sharp tone.

Violet scanned the line of faces, and Jiddy did the same. *It's not a competition*, she assured herself while praying she spied Jonas first. Where was he? She took a step forward. Violet shrieked, making her jump.

"Jonas!" Violet shouted.

Jonas's neighbour nudged him. Jiddy reached to grab Violet's arm. "Hold on a minute," she ordered. "We can't interrupt him working. They're strict here. He can't stop because we've arrived!"

Violet couldn't contain herself. She yanked her arm free and skipped to the table. Jonas, hammer and chisel poised, looked as surprised as if he'd seen a mermaid. A couple of the lads sniggered. Jiddy didn't know whether to laugh at Jonas's face or be annoyed Violet had spotted him before she had. Recovering himself, Jonas wiped his face. The sun had brought out his freckles, visible beneath the dusting of grey.

"Awake now?" He smiled at Jiddy, but before she could answer, he gazed at Violet. "So, you've made it?"

Jiddy leaned on the table. "If you'd managed to stop longer when you called in unexpectedly at Thorpe Hall, I'd have made you dinner."

Jonas guffawed. The master builder was nowhere in sight, only the other lads, some grinning, others concentrating on their work. Violet blushed. Clearing his throat, Jonas explained, "Violet let me in, and she couldn't rouse you, not even for me. Well, I couldn't wait forever, could I? Some of us have responsibilities, you know!"

"I did try," Violet said, blushing. "I told you I tried."

"You must have been hard on," said Jonas. "Lucky for me I bumped into this one." He stood, nodding at Violet. "Can you wait until six? I finish then."

Violet looked eagerly at Jiddy.

"You know I can't stay until six," Jiddy said.

"I can!" said Violet with a beaming smile. "I'm going to be living here from now on!"

Jonas grinned. "You might as well move to York as well, you're here that often, Mistress Vardy."

"Might be better you moved back to Bay," she said, but seeing his frown, she mocked a smile. "We're here to get Violet an apprenticeship," she said, putting her arm around the younger girl's shoulders. "You're not only one who can find work for yourself in York."

"I'm sure I'm not," he said, turning again to Violet. "So, you've decided to move here for good, have you? Well done."

"I will be," said Violet, standing taller so Jiddy dropped her arm. "We're on our way to Varderyellies Emprum now, to sort it out."

Jiddy didn't correct the younger girl's mispronunciation, unable to stop herself sounding curt. "We will both be going back to Bay tonight—if this one doesn't pull herself together."

"I'm right, I'm ready," came Violet's small voice.

Jonas nodded. "Promise me you'll let me know either way how you get on?"

Violet nodded vehemently while Jiddy watched Jonas's face. For a terrible moment, she was reminded of the tenderness between Samuel and Mrs. Farsyde.

"We'll try," she said.

There was something different about Jonas when he spoke to Violet, and as for Violet, she'd never seen her this animated. Taken off guard by the sudden feeling of dislike for the wiry girl, she regretted bringing her to York. She itched to be alone with Jonas to question him about his visit to Robin Hood's Bay. *He came to see me!* she wanted to shout. *Why didn't you try harder to wake me?* And to Jonas: *Why didn't you come and find me? Why didn't you wait?!*

"Jiddy?" Jonas's voice cut into her thoughts.

"Huh?"

"See?" Jonas said to Violet. "She's always off somewhere else."

Jiddy laughed, cringing at the false sound. "Could it be possible you're saying something important, Mr. Chaplow?"

This time, he laughed. She could shake him for being so relaxed.

"I only ever say important things." He grinned at Violet, making Jiddy want to crash their heads together. "I were saying to Violet I'll keep an eye on her. She'll be safe with me."

Grasping for a suitable retort, Jiddy clenched her fists. "Sounds grand," she managed to say instead of roaring like a bull.

Jonas didn't appear to notice her anger. She'd give him safe. *When did he ever keep me safe? When did he ever take care of me?*

"It won't feel so scary in a new city when you have somewhere to stay and make friends," he told Violet.

Violet bobbed a curtsey. "Thank you, Jonas."

It could have been Jiddy's turn to be sick. She could have pushed the girl over. "He's not in charge yet. He's only an apprentice," she snapped. "It's only Jonas, former farmhand, stonemason-to-be if he stops talking long enough not to get sacked."

"She always brings me back to earth," laughed Jonas. "You curtsey all you want."

She? She? He were calling her 'she' now!

"You're an apprentice, like me," cooed Violet, all starry-eyed.

"Master Chaplow?" the head stonemason shouted as he strode towards them behind the row of apprentices.

Jonas grabbed the hammer, backside on seat, and began chipping at the stone block in front of him. Jiddy half-wished he'd be fired on the spot before her thoughts immediately flew to Violet.

"Come on." She grabbed the girl's arm. "You don't want to be cause of him losing his job, do you?"

Jiddy strode out, pulling Violet by her side, jaw clenched, mind racing. If she said anything at all, she'd regret it, but that didn't stop her planning what she would say when they were on their own. By the time they reached the far side of the square, she had her entire speech planned.

"Right," she said. "I take it you want to go straight back to Bay?"

Violet's jaw dropped. "No, I want to go to Varderyellies, I'm fine. Let's go now."

Again, Jiddy didn't correct her. "I don't want you wasting my time. I don't want to get there and you be ill again."

"I won't!" Violet protested. "I won't mess you about, I promise."

Seeing Jonas had given Violet confidence. Jiddy would have loved to return to the Bay holding his hand.

She took a deep breath. She was bigger than jealousy. She was never jealous of anyone, and she wouldn't start with being jealous of an Ashner. She'd do what she came to do, and at some point, if not today, she'd find Jonas and give him what for.

Violet had gone quiet again as they walked, but Jiddy was determined not to mull over what could be going on in the Ashner girl's head. Violet was turning out as sneaky as her elder sister, Nellie. *Get it done, leave Violet at the boarding house, and go find Jonas. It'll be all right when it's the two of us.* The tap-tapping receded as they wound their way through the market stalls, Jiddy wondering if she might move to York herself, in time, when she'd construct a system for Vardarelli's to take apprentice girls. She glanced at Violet, who walked with a much more confident air than when they'd arrived.

***

An hour later, leaving a protesting Violet with one of the more experienced seamstresses, Jiddy hurried back to the Minster. It was later than she'd hoped, and she couldn't risk missing the coach back to the Bay, but she had to talk to Jonas. The clock struck five.

He shook his head as she approached. The chief stonemason was keeping a very close eye out. It would be terrible if she lost Jonas his job, and she stood at a short distance, willing him to read her mind. *I love you.* She pleaded for him to understand. *Say it back, tell me you love me.*

He shook his head again. The frustration became unbearable. People milled around. She gripped her basket and strolled as nonchalantly as she could. As she approached Jonas, she traced her fingers along the table, pausing as she reached him. With one finger, she carved a heart in the dust.

As she walked away, she saw he'd splayed his hands over the shape. He caught her eye. Her heart swelled.

In the carriage on the way back to the coast, Jiddy reminded herself Jonas was merely being kind to Violet. He loved her, Jiddy. She had nothing to worry about. Jonas adored her. Outside the window, moorland reached to the horizon. She hoped Violet had settled in and had made a friend; she had no animosity anymore. She'd be kinder to Violet next time she visited York, and she'd be gracious and thank Jonas for encouraging Violet to stay in the city and to feel safe. If Violet hadn't stayed in York, the other girls would never have been persuaded to go. Her plan could have spectacularly fallen apart if it weren't for Jonas. Instead, it was a resounding success.

The carriage jolted over ruts in the road and knocked her out of her thoughts; she gripped the window ledge. The other passengers, three men and a woman, didn't pay her any attention. One of the men shouted to the driver, but with the rumble of wheels, Jiddy doubted he'd hear. Or care. She looked out of the window again. She wanted to think about Jonas. It was a real shame they'd had no time alone. She'd have to make sure she needed more threads and bits and bobs soon; she'd check on Violet then spend the rest of the time with Jonas. Maybe they would be able to find a quiet place somewhere, and they could talk about everything that had happened since he'd gone away. Maybe they'd kiss as well.

Dusk approached. Shadows gathered in the creases of land. Squeezing her eyes tight shut, she clutched her hands in her lap. Maybe Jonas was right after all. After her restrained behaviour today, maybe she was an angel.

CHAPTER THIRTY

R obin Hood's Bay came into view as it always did. Moorland eased back, and verdant grass opened its arms. The sea, a sparkling surprise after the peaks and troughs of the final mile or so, came with a snatch before disappearing when the land slipped downhill into shadow. A twinkle, a fluttering sparkle, and a round knoll and trees creating sanctuary, and finally, in full view, South Cliff, hunched and solid, a glorious spread of waves and a shimmering line where water met sky.

Jonas still loved her. The Bay tumbled even sweeter with the knowledge. Grouse rose out of long, waving grass. Starlings, plovers and gulls dotted the mauve sky with their white wings and distinctive call. A breeze freshened Jiddy's cheeks with the whisper of salt and shells.

She'd gazed at this view so many times, she should have been able to recall it with her eyes closed, but in the bustle of York, it had seemed a long way away. In London, she'd not given a thought to the tightly packed cottages, twisting ginnels and steep slope to the dock; the causeway, littered with lobster pots and cobles to be patched; the scaurs, scrambling out to sea; the heart stone revealed at low tide to touch with wishes and dreams of love; voices, round, warm accents cradling your ears. She heard it, saw it again as they crested the final hill. Robin Hood's Bay revealed itself. Always there. Always home.

She walked, past the Bolts, past Sunny Place, and to the sea. Brown bladderwrack bubbled over green rocks; pebbles and shells jumbled to crunch and shift underfoot. Placing down her basket, she removed her boots and stockings. Clambering over large rocks, she slipped over wet seaweed-covered stones and jumped onto shingle. It didn't matter dusk beckoned. A cloudless sky promised longer daylight hours, and she could see her way.

The cliff had crumbled a little more, cascading earthy waterfalls to reveal new fissures. She felt the cool sand moist underfoot. She and the gulls had the beach to themselves. Half a dozen or so stood in ones and twos, gazing out towards Holland. Others swooped overhead, vast wings outstretched and black eyes alert. She kept walking towards the mound of sand revealed at low tide. This was her island, where she had cartwheeled and run and danced well past her childhood. She dropped her boots, pushing the stockings inside so they didn't blow away. Kneeling, she traced her fingers to form her name.

Jiddy, each letter carefully drawn. Next to it, she wrote Jonas. Five letters each. Perfectly matched. Even so, the two names, side by side, filled her with emptiness. Jonas remained in York, miles inland. She wanted him here, needed him here, where she could taste the salt on him and smell dry grass in his hair. The sky tinged darker. Dusk crept in.

"Freedom," she said aloud, recalling her mother's words. "Freedom!" she shouted and laughed at her voice in the vast open space.

Waves trickled over the cusp of neap tide shingle, raising images of her and Jonas as bairns playing at the water's edge, learning about the taste of salt and a government in London that wanted to take all the spice from their lives.

Could she leave this place for Jonas? Violet had left Bay, but Jiddy couldn't let it go so easily. How would she survive without a sea breeze and the sound of frilling surf, even though in York she'd be with Jonas? A breath of wind lifted strands of her hair, and the memory of their conversations trickled in with the tide. She tilted her chin to feel the sun's last attempts at warmth and dug her fingers deeper into the sand.

In a few hours, her island would submerge, waves would deepen, and the beach would no longer be a haven. She'd have to leave it, scrambling up the cliff path or strolling along any remaining strip of shingle to reach the slipway. At some point in the next half hour, she'd leave it. Everyone had to eventually. Captain Pinkney in his schooner, Samuel, nibbled away to become one with the seabed, even her father, Viscount Gregory Hartshorn, had joined the skeletons disintegrating to shingle alongside broken crabs and shells, each of them either thrown overboard by sea captains like David Pinkney or drowned by greedy waves. She pictured Jonas sitting by the Minster, chipping away. Almost everyone she cared about left Robin Hoods Bay, but she remained.

Strange that she, the incomer, should be the one who stayed. She brushed her hands to rid her palms of sand.

She had a home here. Four solid walls nobody could take away. Her little sewing group stitched their way to a road to freedom ensuring any girl from the village who wanted to sew could come and join them. If they heard Violet had work in the city because she'd learned a skill to set her off, more would be knocking on the door. She'd teach them to cut a gown, to tack and paste and stitch neat and strong. They'd learn how to treat hemp different from linen. Silk from wool. How to patch and darn so you couldn't see the joins. Violet was only the start.

If she could do this, she could make the Robin Hood's Bay needle workers the best in Yorkshire, and they'd be sought after by all the grand houses. The mills would want them to use their cotton. The dressmakers and embroiderers she'd taught would be famous. London would hear about them. They could travel to Holland and France; some may even travel to India. There'd be Yorkshire accents all over the world, so no-one could pretend not to understand their northern vowels.

Lasses destined for cockle picking and mending lobster pots and lines and gutting fish would be able to escape the fate of red hands and cracked fingers. She could give those girls hope. Choice. Liberty. What was the motto Jonas had told her about? *Liberty, Equality, Fraternity?*

She breathed in the brine of seaweed, filling her lungs with the sea. She and Jonas had done this so often; swallowing air, swallowing seawater; their kisses tasting of brine. Salty lips and eager tongues. They could have babes of their own, bairns who would pop straggles of seaweed as they'd loved to do as children, their own little ones, black-haired or copper-brown, gathering mussels and whelks and splashing in the water. And their children would have proper toys made of wood and iron, not pebbles and shells and imaginations. Dolls and balls and skittles. Solid toys. She shook herself. *Stop it.*

She traced a long finger in the sand to form a letter R for Robin Hood's Bay and Y for York. She wondered if he had learned to spell so he could chisel letters into stone as well as faces of saints and angels. She pictured him, no longer an apprentice but a seasoned stonemason, stone dust sprinkled in his chestnut hair, turning it grey, dust settling into the crevices and pores of his face, making him look at least thirty. Nails and hands whitened. Would he cough dust in the night? Would all his clothes make him return home a walking statue?

The sea lapped at the edges of the island. She must have sat there longer than she'd realised. She could no longer make out the curves of coast.

Water filled the gully surrounding her sandy haven, and the idea of swimming made her dream about Jonas even more. He would be urging her to hurry as he always had, trying to hide his fear of the water as she teased him with her recklessness.

"This is for you," she said, strolling to the edge of sand and lifting her skirt. Water tickled her ankles, rising to her calves. Already it rose to her knees, wetting the hem.

Later, when it dried, salt crystals would tumble to the floor. The thought made her smile. Gulls circled. The island of sand had almost disappeared, and the sun had begun to set.

She'd not known what the sea tasted like when she was eight years old, but it had been Jonas who had shown her. She smiled at the memory of their tongues touching and how she'd recoiled in distaste. But that undeniable taste had been the beginning.

The cliff was Jonas's place, where he waited with his cart and horse for the barrels and sacks to take inland. Waited for her to clamber up the cliff and join him. It was a long time since they'd worked together at night, when she'd hidden the rope used for raising smuggled goods while he disappeared across the moors. She stared at her feet, already disappearing under the unstoppable tide. Funny how they appeared pale when they were submerged. Right now, her face and arms were tinged brown. By December, her skin would be sallow again. January, she'd look ill. Come February, she'd be desperate for spring once more and to be standing here as she was now. Years could pass like this.

She needed a plan. A strong, watertight plan. She'd be eighteen soon and an old maid, but she was a woman of property, and no other woman in Bay could say the same. That meant something. She could live here while Jonas finished his apprenticeship, and he could move back to Bay. It made sense, but seven years! Ye gods, she couldn't stand seven years apart, unless...he agreed to her offer.

She had a home where both could live. They were not brother and sister. He could return. They could be together.

Finding her boots, she swung them from one hand and, basket held in the other, strolled towards the dock. Maybe she could chip away at him as well as a new life. Maybe he'd kept her in his mind all these months, inadvertently revealing her figure in the stone block he worked upon. In the near dark, she listened to the roar of the rollers. How could he not come back to this? A shout caught her attention, and she glanced towards Main Street.

"Hey!" Jiddy shouted, waving her arm.

"I've been all over place for you! Squire Farsyde wants to see you!"

She dusted her feet and pulled on her stockings. "It's late," she said.

"He told me not to come back without you," Annie said.

Water licked black. "Can't it wait until morning?"

"No, it can't," grimaced Annie. "Mr. Ashner's pickled, and he's shouting and rollicking and wants to wring your guts in his fists for taking his daughter to York."

CHAPTER THIRTY-ONE

Jiddy held a lantern to light their way. When they reached Thorpe Hall, raised voices from the house could be heard from the bottom of the approach.

"You don't need to come any further," Jiddy said. "You get off home, see your mam."

Annie shook her head. "Mam's waiting to see squire. It's a pickle. We'd come to talk to squire about Andrew, he's finding some way to help him, but Mr. Ashner blundered in and it's all chaos now."

They exchanged a glance. "Where's your ma?" asked Jiddy.

"In kitchen with Mrs. King. It's awful, Jiddy." Annie started to cry.

"Come on." Jiddy grabbed her hand. She had worked herself into a passion as they'd marched from the village. Now, the thought of Annie's mam in the kitchen made her seethe with even greater rage at what had happened. She was exhausted and angry that her efforts with Violet Ashner weren't appreciated, and furious Mr. Ashner couldn't see the chances Violet would get at Vardarelli's.

She barged through the back door, past the kitchen entrance. "Go sit with your mam," she said, glancing into the room to her right where Mrs. King and all the kitchen staff paused, ladles raised, spoons and rolling pins suspended. Jiddy shoved open the hall door and marched into Squire Farsyde's study.

"There she is!" Mr. Ashner, Violet's da, pointed a tobacco-stained finger. Spittle framed his lips in a dry crust and glinted in his beard. Blundering over the rug, he stumbled towards Jiddy, but before he reached her, he tottered into a side table and crashed to the floor. The curses he uttered were too slurred to make out.

Taking advantage of his unsuccessful efforts to stand, Jiddy swept past him, skirt slapping his head.

"Do you still hold that Violet would want to stay here with him?" she said, glaring at the squire while pointing to the tumbled limbs of Mr. Ashner.

"That's no way to talk about your elders," said the squire, hastening to the collapsed figure and grappling to help him to his feet.

Mrs. King appeared in the doorway, wiping her hands on a kitchen cloth. "I'd like a word if I may?"

"You know how much trouble Violet has with her da," Jiddy continued. "All I'm doing is offering to help them both out."

Mr. Ashner looked as if he'd been kicked by the hind legs of a cow. Mrs. King coughed and wiped her hands more fervently. "All I know," she said, "is I'm a pair of hands short in kitchen, and I want to know what you're going to do about it, sir."

"There's plenty of lasses in village!" Jiddy said, whipping around. "I don't see what all fuss is about!"

Recovering, the cook swished her cloth against her thighs. "One good thing about all Ashner lasses," she said, "is they're hard-working, and that's not easy to find."

Jiddy flounced to the window, bubbling with impatience, while behind her back, Mr. Ashner barged his way out of the squire's support. "Let me at trollop!"

He broke loose, shoving the squire and a chair out of his way, and grabbed Jiddy's arm.

"Ger off me!" she shouted, struggling to free herself from his grasp and avoid the stink of his breath. He tumbled backwards and landed on the floor. Brushing herself down, Jiddy addressed Mrs. King. "His Kate could take Violet's place. She's as good a worker. There! Will that suit you?"

Before Mrs. King could answer, two figures appeared in the hall and caught their attention. Annie and her mother, Mrs. Briggs, tear-stained and hesitant, stood behind her.

"You said to come in," said Annie.

Mrs. King wriggled past them, patting Mrs. Briggs on the shoulder. The servants' door banged. Annie's mother's pale face crumpled. Tears rose to Jiddy's eyes at the sight, and she crossed the room.

"I'm sorry, Mrs. Briggs," she said, glancing over her shoulder at the squire. "I'll come back in morning, sir. This can wait till then, can't it?"

Annie's watery eyes filled, and Mrs. Briggs dropped her head, reddened hands clasped tightly.

Violet's da curled on his side and made a sound like a choking dog. "She's going to take all my children from me. She's gonna take them all."

"Not now, Mr. Ashner," said the squire. "Jiddy, help me."

Sighing, Jiddy reached for the man's arm while the squire heaved on Mr. Ashner's other side. Rolling on all fours, he crawled to the door, where he hauled himself up the door jamb. Annie and Mrs. Briggs stepped back, huddling together. Mr. Ashner lurched sideways before shoving past Annie and her mam. They heard him batter along the hall and swing a door too wide so it smacked the wall, then the fading kerfuffle of footsteps.

Mrs. Briggs made wretched sounds, and Annie clutched her mother's hands. The squire patted his face with a handkerchief.

"Come in, come in," he said, waving the square of fabric.

When Annie and Mrs. Briggs had collapsed into the seat opposite him, and Jiddy had repositioned the fallen table, he regained control. "What a business," he muttered. "I'm sorry, Mrs. Briggs, I'm sorry to you too, Annie."

Now the rush of adrenaline ebbed, Jiddy stacked the fallen books onto the sofa with shaking hands. Still trembling, she gathered the broken cups and plates lying scattered on the rug, feeling their eyes on her every move.

"I'm sorry about Andrew," she said after several moments. She nodded at Annie. Mrs. Briggs had her head bent and her hands resting in her lap. "I'll go." The squire cleared his throat. "I can go back to York tomorrow and ask Violet if she wants to come home," she said quietly to the squire and bobbed a curtsey. She headed to the door, eager to be in front of her own fire where she could eat and sit and take in Mr. Ashner's anger and what she should do.

Squire Farsyde raised his hands. "Not yet, Jiddy," he said. "I want this squashed before Mr. Ashner makes a bigger fool of himself."

Arms hanging loose by her sides, Jiddy thought she'd fall down herself if she didn't get out of there soon. "It's not a good idea to force Violet to come back to Bay."

"She hasn't her father's consent," said the squire.

The ticking of the clock sounded loud. All Jiddy wanted was her bed.

"I think…" Annie's voice broke through the silence. "I think Violet's sister Kate would be pleased to work with Mrs. King, and you should leave Violet in York."

"Fine, fine, I'll get Ashner's consent," the squire said, "but keep out of Mr. Ashner's sight. I mean it. You keep out of everyone's sight, Jiddy."

"It weren't only Jiddy," said Annie. "Betsie and me help her teach girls to sew."

For the first time, Mrs. Briggs took notice of the room. "What's going to happen to my lad?" she asked.

Annie and Jiddy glanced at each other.

Squire Farsyde reached out his hand. "We'll take care of him," he said. "We always take care of our own."

A noise at the door made them all turn around. Pale faced, Mrs. Farsyde trembled.

"My dear," the squire rushed over and took his wife's arm, but she thrust him aside.

"What is happening?" she asked, ambling into the centre of the room. "I heard shouting."

"Afternoon, ma'am," said Mrs. Briggs, bobbing a curtsey. "Thank you, sir. Annie and me'll bid you goodnight." She grasped Annie's hand. Jiddy stepped aside for them to pass.

"Sit, my dear," said Squire Farsyde to his wife. "Mrs. Briggs, please don't worry. We will sort something for your lad."

"Thank you, sir," said Annie, supporting her mother across the room.

The door closed. Mrs. Farsyde sank onto the settee. "Who was shouting?" she asked again. "The loud voices woke me."

Squire Farsyde waved for Jiddy to sit next to his wife. "It was nothing, was it, Jiddy? A man from the village was here. He was upset by something or other."

Jiddy nodded. "It were Violet's da. Do you want me to help you back upstairs?"

"Yes, my dear," the squire said, opening the door and walking into the hall. "Mrs. Briggs?" he shouted. "One word before you go!"

They listened to his rapid footsteps. Mrs. Farsyde, one eye on the open door, bent her head to Jiddy's. "You haven't forgotten, have you?" she whispered. "You promised if I helped you, you'd see to it we went to the seashore."

Jiddy sighed. She didn't want to traipse along the beach with her mistress. She wanted to do as little as she could. "It's not wise," she said.

Mrs. Farsyde's blue eyes shone. "Squire Farsyde is going to Scarborough to see the magistrate tomorrow. He will be away until after dark."

CHAPTER THIRTY-TWO

They walked slowly, crunching over the shingle and edging over stretches of dry sand, stopping every few paces for Mrs. Farsyde to catch her breath. The sea crept towards the shore, lapping at the far reaches of the scaurs but not yet rippling over the sand banks. They'd left Billy Hardcastle without instruction in the dock, sitting on the driver's bench, carriage empty, reins dangling through his fingers and glaring at Jiddy to tell him what to do.

"I need to find Samuel," were the only words Mrs. Farsyde repeated as they headed away from the causeway in the direction of Ravenscar. There was no-one else about. No preventives, no groups of children. It seemed eerie. Jiddy determined they wouldn't stay long. If Samuel's body was there, they'd see it, and if not, they wouldn't linger. She wanted to be with Annie and check how her friend was faring. The squire had said not to mention Andrew's disfigurement to his wife for fear it would upset her, so Jiddy tried to find a reason why she could cut short the search and get Mrs. Farsyde back to the hall well before the squire's return.

Progress was slow. Mrs. Farsyde repeatedly drew Jiddy to a halt to take a closer look at shadows in the cliff face. Every movement seemed to catch her eye. Distracted, Jiddy half-glanced at the objects Mrs. Farsyde pointed out, wondering instead what would be happening today in the Briggses' house.

Stones crackled under their feet, shells shifted, speckled and pretty, and Jiddy began to examine the objects that caught her eye. She glanced at the cliff, then behind at the empty sands. Finding herself some way ahead of her ambling companion, she stopped to wait. They'd almost reached the bulk of promontory that shielded the view of Boggle Hole, and the tide pooled around the cliff base. Jiddy sighed with relief and retraced her steps. Instead of stopping, Mrs. Farsyde ambled past, eyes to the ground, seemingly oblivious that they'd come as far as was possible.

"Mrs. Farsyde?" Jiddy called. "We can't go any further." She watched as her mistress came to a stop before slumping against a large boulder.

Slipping on pebbles, Jiddy reached her side. "Are you feeling unwell?" she asked, noting her mistress's pale face. "Will you take my arm?"

Shaking her head and holding a handkerchief to her lips, Mrs. Farsyde pointed with her other hand. There, cradled into a shallow channel of rocks lay a man's body.

With a sharp cry, Mrs. Farsyde pushed Jiddy so that she stumbled forwards. "You look, I can't," she ordered.

Steadying herself, Jiddy gazed at the body of an officer. It hunkered into the shingle, wet stones clustered in its armpits and the crook of the knees. Sand clotted in the tendrils of hair and battered coat tails, half buried, flaked dark. The feet twisted, one foot charcoal black, the other clutching the remains of a boot. Jiddy covered her mouth. The face dissolved into the beach, hiding behind its tufted skull. Jiddy swayed. She knew what the sea did to a body, but seeing it, seeing every pound and pummel, was a different matter. She closed her eyes. Gulls cried mournfully. Behind her, Mrs. Farsyde sobbed. The flaxen hair and soldier's uniform were undeniable. The sea had spat out Samuel, and they'd found him, cradled in seaweed and rock pools.

Mrs. Farsyde sobbed harder, and returning, Jiddy slipped an arm around her. Waves, further out, stampeded, frothing high and white. Jiddy felt the bile heavy in her chest and swallowed. The wind caught their skirts, which rippled like sails. They couldn't stay. They couldn't hide the fact of Samuel's body lying dead before them on the beach.

"Let's go back," Jiddy urged. Mrs. Farsyde clung closer. "We'll tell Deputy Staincliffe, and he can bring some men to carry Captain Ryethorpe. There's nothing we can do for him now."

Mrs. Farsyde glared at Jiddy with reddened eyes. "You shouldn't have brought me here," she accused, placing her free hand on her stomach.

Jiddy held back a retort. Bodies weren't supposed to be washed ashore. Nellie's hadn't been, and the two preventives had disappeared without trace, but not Samuel. Even after this amount of time, he was still recognisable. She closed her eyes. She should have been with Annie. The thought of the crowded cottage, neighbours clucking about, the smell of pies and biscuits brought, the camaraderie of women. Betsie would be there. In that moment, Jiddy hated both her mistress and Samuel for bringing her to the seashore. She took a deep breath. "I really think we should return to Thorpe Hall before the squire returns."

She'd have to dampen the salt out of the hems of their dresses and most likely help Mrs. Farsyde to bed after this shock when they got back—assuming Mrs. Farsyde could make it to the causeway and the waiting carriage. Blast her for using her position to get her own way.

Mrs. Farsyde pulled her hand free. A crab tottered from under the ripped jacket, sand trickling in its wake. Skin, torn and blubber-grey, clung to a bruised leg. The cliff cast a shadow over the beach. Gulls continued to cry, and the sea tumbled over itself. A dead body lay in the pebbles. No-one stood a chance when the sea met the land at high tide. Mrs. Farsyde began to cry, and the sound rang out as lonely as a lone ewe's bleating call.

"Why here?" she said. "How did he get swept away?"

Jiddy had seen and felt what the sea did. It had wound its tendrils around the captain's legs. When it had swept him off the causeway, it hugged him close and tossed and tumbled him, playing skittle and ball, spin penny and hump hurdle. It had played with her too, dragging her under and churning, drawing her deeper while she'd paddled to remain afloat. She couldn't tell Mrs. Farsyde any of that.

"It were high tide," she said instead. "He stood at top of causeway when sea came in, and he didn't stand a chance."

Mrs. Farsyde squeezed Jiddy's arm so tight, Jiddy flinched.

"Why didn't you tell him how dangerous the sea can be?" Her eyes shone brittle against her pinched face. "You should have saved him."

Jiddy's head crackled. She'd questioned herself so many times. It felt like he haunted her because he too blamed her for not saving him. Her heart pressed heavy. Was it guilt? What could she have done? Mrs. Farsyde's fingers hurt her skin. She pulled away her arm.

"Everyone knows high tide is dangerous," she said. The sea's belly stretched to infinity. It would take an entire regiment if it got the chance. "I couldn't," she said. Her words sounded small, dwarfed by the cliff and sea and the twisted figure at their feet. Gulls taunted with their cries that she could have tried harder to save him. Sky-bound creatures accused those on the ground. They didn't know the treachery of waves that wanted a plaything.

"I would have." Mrs. Farsyde's words bit hard.

Jiddy's eyes filled with the brine of that treacherous sea. It had flooded into her mouth, pooled in her chest, and sloshed in her belly, but Mrs. Farsyde didn't know that. For Samuel, it had crept through his sinews, surged through his arteries, replacing blood with salt water. If Mrs. Farsyde had been swept off her feet by a roaring tide, the sea wouldn't have treated her any kinder. The sea didn't know how to be kind. It grasped and it took.

Storms created undertows, and when they met the land with a body in its fists, the two fought over soft flesh and shoulder blades and cheekbones. She couldn't describe to her mistress how the weight of water smothered your lungs or how it battered your limbs. Samuel couldn't save himself, and no-one—not Jiddy, not the love of Mrs. Farsyde—could have saved him. He wasn't a soldier or a captain or her lover. He was a corpse, and he lay on the beach at their feet. *Don't be afraid.* The fragile peace between her and the lady of Thorpe Hall could fracture like ice on a duck pond, but Samuel couldn't harm her now.

"I'll ask squire to send word to Lord Ryethorpe," Jiddy said. "He will want to be here to take his son home."

"The squire mustn't touch him, nobody must!" Mrs. Farsyde cried out. Her eyes swelled like the sea. "Can't we carry him? He must be as light as a seashell."

And as pale. He might shatter if they lifted him, skin as brittle as bone ready to float like ash on the wind.

"You can't lift anything in your condition. Deputy Staincliffe's men will take care of him," Jiddy said. "He was their captain, and they'll want to do right by him."

Crouching, she studied the strands of blonde hair darkened by wet sand. Covering her mouth, she held in a scream. She wasn't afraid, but the sight of him so vulnerable and battered made her shudder. Life wasn't fair. Thomas had told her that from when she'd been very young and cried when Nellie called her cruel names. *Life isn't fair.* Lord Ryethorpe would be devastated.

The gulls laughed, circling, their curiosity piqued.

"I'm cold." Mrs. Farsyde's voice sliced through the sound of the waves. She took faltering steps towards the causeway.

Waves surged, and the shingle roared under the backwash. They'd have to find help before the tide reclaimed the body and took more bites at the flesh. It would take them at least half an hour to reach the causeway and safety of the dock with Mrs. Farsyde's uneasy steps.

Jiddy lifted her shawl over her head and pushed in her dark curls.

"Let's go," she said, guiding her mistress to take a few unsteady steps towards the village before Mrs. Farsyde stopped entirely.

The squire's wife lifted a trembling hand to her forehead. Sweat beaded her skin. Closing her eyes, she crumpled onto the sand. Jiddy leapt forwards, hands fluttering, unsure where to touch. The bluster of the sea foamed. Waves swept over the scaurs. The in-tide surged towards them.

"Mrs. Farsyde? Please, we must get back to the dock."

She glanced at the tongues of water and again to the cliff. A cave opening yawned black. Samuel had brought them here, and his body mocked from its scruff of uniform. His ghost would be laughing now. Both the women he'd kissed would be joining him if a miracle didn't happen.

She shook Mrs. Farsyde and was rewarded with a muffled whine. "Tide's coming in," she said. "We can't be cut off. Please, Mrs. Farsyde, stand. We must move."

A gravelled face lifted. Eyes watered without focus. Jiddy heaved her mistress to her feet. The path snaked up the cliff, making Jiddy wonder if she could haul the limp woman to the top of the steep incline. The sea had cut off Boggle Hole. On her own, she'd easily make it to the causeway before the tide came in, but she couldn't leave Mrs. Farsyde to fend for herself. She scooped an arm around the groaning woman's back and dragged her forward, but Mrs. Farsyde's knees buckled.

"It's coming," she screamed. "The baby is coming."

CHAPTER THIRTY-THREE

Mrs. Farsyde bellowed. The aching noise bounced off the rocks. They would never make it even halfway to the causeway now, with Mrs. Farsyde clutching her belly and hollering in pain while Jiddy struggled to keep her on her feet.

"We can make it to yonder cave," she said. "We can wait out until low tide or go through tunnels. We'll go slow. You can make it a few steps."

"No." Mrs. Farsyde groaned. "Get me to the cave and then come back for Samuel. We'll not leave him for the sea to take him from me again."

Waves roared. The sea encroached faster at this point than further along the beach. Mrs. Farsyde wasn't aware of its speed. Only those in Bay saw how the tide plotted against them. Jiddy wished she'd found a way to say no to Mrs. Farsyde. She wished Samuel's body lay at the bottom of the sea, far out, nibbled by fish and anchored by his cursed medals.

"We need to keep walking," she urged.

The loose shingle made their progress even slower than before. Crushed shells and sea-battered pebbles smudged under their feet. Mrs. Farsyde doubled over again and again, clamping her arms around belly. Jiddy tensed so she didn't shake her. It wasn't far if they kept moving.

Alone, she'd climb the cliff, grabbing tufts of grass and gorse, but Mrs. Farsyde was incapable of the climb. Even the walk to the cave seemed almost impossible the way her mistress moved.

If they could only make it and escape through the secret tunnel they used during a smuggling run, they'd be all right, but what if Mrs. Farsyde couldn't make it so far? What should Jiddy do? If only Billy had some gumption and would come and find them. Surely, he'd noticed the tide coming in. Surely, he had an inkling of what to do, but no. There was no-one coming to their aid, not even standing on the causeway to see they needed help.

"It's not far," she said. "We'll soon be back at hall, drinking a cup of tea." She wondered if she could make it and bring back a boat, fetch Mrs. Grainger to be ready for the baby coming, rouse the villagers. "Billy!" she shouted.

Water caught their shoes, and Mrs. Farsyde squealed. Jiddy stamped her feet in the cold surf frilling around her ankles. Mrs. Farsyde gripped Jiddy's arm so hard it hurt.

"Can you walk a little faster?" Jiddy said. "Please, the tide comes in right fast."

She couldn't bear to watch. Torn between helping her mistress and returning into deeper water to drag Samuel to the cave, she didn't know what to do. They were completely cut off from Boggle Hole, and the increasingly dangerous current swirled over the submerged rocks.

"The body might be all right here," said Jiddy. "If it lodges itself, it'll be here when the sea ebbs again, but we need to get to the cave."

The thought of being caught in the sea as it swept them off their feet became unbearable. "We have to move!"

She caught the fear in her voice, screeching high, but she couldn't help it. They couldn't be lifted off their feet by the water because then they'd drown. Mrs. Farsyde couldn't swim, and Jiddy wouldn't be able to hold her in her arms for long.

"Come on!" She dragged Mrs. Farsyde, one arm scooped around her back and the other supporting her elbow.

Jiddy stumbled with her mistress towards the cave entrance. Water surged around them, dragging at their hems and freezing their ankles. Mrs. Farsyde panted loudly, and Jiddy took sharp breaths. The crashing waves thundered behind them; Jiddy readied for its force.

"Please keep walking," she muttered, trying not to yelp as Mrs. Farsyde's grip on her arm tightened.

Their sodden skirts dragged. Heart racing, Jiddy kicked and pulled and heaved Mrs. Farsyde onto the rise of shingle and out of the water. Already it crept over the pebbles, giving them only a short reprieve. The cold and the smell of damp moss hit them, and Mrs. Farsyde pulled back.

"No, no, no, we need to keep moving." Jiddy pushed her mistress into the cavern.

"Won't it come in?" Mrs. Farsyde said. Her chin trembled and her face shrank paler.

"We're nearly there." The relief that they'd made it jittered Jiddy's teeth as she supported Mrs. Farsyde over the pebbles and uneven rocks to the crack in the wall leading to the passage. She felt over the rock and tucked her fingers into the hidden crevice. "You go first," she said. "I'm right behind."

She guided Mrs. Farsyde's fingers to the opening and pressed her to the gap. "Go through."

Mrs. Farsyde looked at Jiddy incredulously.

"Go on!" Jiddy again helped her mistress find the crevice.

Peering closer, Mrs. Farsyde examined the wall. "I can't get through such a narrow passage."

"Yes, you can!" Jiddy shivered. "Please try."

Mrs. Farsyde shook her head, but Jiddy pulled her to the wall. "You have to! It's the only other way off the beach. Honest, it's wider than it looks. Go sideways. You can do it."

Mrs. Farsyde shrank back. "I'll squash my stomach. I can't! It'll hurt the baby."

The sound of shifting stones made them turn around. Shining in the cave mouth, water licked towards them. Jiddy grabbed Mrs. Farsyde's wrist and pulled her to the crack in the rock. Pushing from behind, she tried to force her mistress into the opening.

"Go, go!" Jiddy urged, but Mrs. Farsyde groaned and, hands on either side of the gap, resisted. "Try the other way." Manoeuvring her around, Jiddy tried to push her backwards while Mrs. Farsyde stared, terrified, into Jiddy's face.

A sudden surge of water flooded forwards, echoing its muscle around the cave. Mrs. Farsyde screamed. "I can't, I can't!"

Water spread darkness over the cave floor. There was nothing for it. They'd have to climb onto the shelf of rock at the back of the cave where they stored contraband that couldn't be hoisted up the cliff onto carts. Grasping Mrs. Farsyde's hand, Jiddy marked out their path, praying they'd reach higher rocks before the water became too deep.

"Which way?" Mrs. Farsyde pushed her aside and stood, arms splayed for balance.

They stumbled and tripped far too slowly for Jiddy's liking towards the rear of the cave where rocks clustered at the base of a protruding stretch of wall. Here, the stone face rose at a steep angle, plateauing onto a flat area. Jiddy pointed. "We need to get there!"

Water swelled around their knees. The sound amplified and the cold mix of damp rock and drenching water multiplied Jiddy's fear. She didn't want to drown. She didn't want to die. It wasn't fair. *Life isn't fair!* "We can do it!" she shouted, hearing the tremble in her own voice. If only, if only she had reasoned against Mrs. Farsyde's pleas to find Samuel.

Silent now, Mrs. Farsyde gripped tight. Jiddy glanced at the rising water, towards the rock shelf and back again. It towered above them, higher and harder to climb than she remembered. She touched the stone, slippery with the sea's residue. Wiping her hand on her shawl, she steadied one boot on a low rock.

"Put your foot there," she said. "Hand there. Then there."

Mrs. Farsyde stood, stupefied.

"There." Jiddy dipped her hand through the water and grabbed Mrs. Farsyde's shoe and placed it on the rock. "We must get up there. Now!"

Mrs. Farsyde followed her gaze and screamed as a surge of water rose around them. Realising they needed to move fast, Jiddy clambered onto the rocks and, grabbing Mrs. Farsyde's arm, pulled her.

"Shift!" Jiddy squealed, yanking Mrs. Farsyde, who, for the first time, scrambled with Jiddy to help her climb. It became obvious to both that they had to get onto the ledge and out of the rising water and pray this wasn't a freakish tide rising higher than usual and sweeping over the plateau of rock all the way to the cave roof.

Jiddy balanced on the boulders as Mrs. Farsyde reached with her arms and held onto the shelf edge. Shaking with the strain, Jiddy once again pushed Mrs. Farsyde with her hands and shoulder. Water rose around her legs, clinging to her skirt. She could slip at any moment. They could so easily drown. She shifted her feet. *Please don't fall.* She pushed again. *Come on, come on!* Why wasn't Mrs. Farsyde helping? Jiddy's hands slipped on the folds of material. Mrs. Farsyde's shoe scraped her head. Twisting, she realised the load had lightened and Mrs. Farsyde was attempting to climb. She'd reached the ledge, leaving Jiddy with free hands to clamber higher.

Nails scratching stone, fingers raw, Jiddy caught sight of Mrs. Farsyde's eyes glinting in the dark from the wall at the rear of the flat shelf, and for a moment, anger filled her head. If she drowned, what would happen to Mrs. Farsyde? She felt with her fingers for a hold, but finding none, fumbled with her feet to garner leverage. There. Her foot lodged in a crack, and she pushed, heaving, pulling, eventually rolling onto the shelf. The cave had darkened, leaving only a shudder of grey from outside. Water settled, slick and black, inches from where they sheltered. Quiet now, it licked the rock, a freezing trap of brine. Jiddy closed her eyes.

CHAPTER THIRTY-FOUR

Jiddy squatted, her back to the wall. The sea smudged the light in the cave's entrance. Their escape route disappeared under a sludge of sea, and until it retreated, they were trapped in the dank cavern. She readjusted the shawl over her head to protect herself from the chill. Mrs. Farsyde moaned. All they could do was wait.

She couldn't help but picture Samuel's body drifting in the open water, the rocks unable to hold him, flaxen hair dark with blood and brine. Clothes ripped a little more than they had been. His beautiful face discoloured and battered further. Lips softened to mush. She shivered at the image of the smartly dressed, handsome captain floating, bruised and limp, his immaculate uniform in shreds. She pulled her shawl tighter. She'd remember him as he once was.

Mrs. Farsyde breathed heavily, groaning constantly now, and Jiddy twisted to see. "Is there owt I can do?" she asked.

Mrs. Farsyde put back her head and wailed. The noise resounded against the stone. Unnerved, Jiddy shuffled to her mistress's side. This wasn't what was supposed to happen. They were safe out of the water, and they could wait it out. Why couldn't Mrs. Farsyde wait?

She glanced at the wall. A lantern hung from a hook. If she could light the candle, that might be soothing. It might help her employer settle. Darkness was scary if you weren't used to it. She felt on the wall for the crevice where a flint would have been left for the purpose of lighting it.

"If I can give us some light—"

Mrs. Farsyde's scream drowned out Jiddy's words. "Get me out of here!"

Jiddy dropped the flint and cursed.

Mrs. Farsyde shifted her weight. "Why didn't you notice the tide coming in?" she demanded. "I thought you knew all about the sea!"

"I *did* notice. It's why we've climbed to here," Jiddy said, fumbling to find the dropped flint and not panic.

"Agh!" Mrs. Farsyde's anguish expanded.

Jiddy struck the flint and it caught. With a shaking hand, she lit the candle, and the flickering glow illuminated the shelf. In the cave entrance, waves caught the light. Grey and dense, the water formed an impenetrable barrier. The cave wall to their left bulged in a vast curve, while to their right, it made a straight inhospitable enclosure. There was no warmth to be had. Nor any escape. Mrs. Farsyde tussled with her skirt, dragging and tugging until she crouched on all fours, panting like a thirsty dog.

The baby couldn't be coming. Mrs. Farsyde wouldn't let it. Not here. Not in this place. Birth was beyond Jiddy's knowledge. She was no midwife. She didn't play with little ones, let alone babies. If she'd known Mrs. Farsyde was so close to her term, she'd have refused to come to the beach.

What could she do? That numbskull, Billy Hardcastle, should have declined to bring them in the carriage to the dock. If anything, he should have come with them along the sand, but he'd no gumption and she'd been too stubborn to ask. The squire would think Mrs. Farsyde was tucked in her bed chamber. There'd be no need to send out a search party as far as he was concerned. Surely, Mrs. Grainger must have noticed the house was too quiet and raised the alarm. Violet would have if she'd been there; maybe her sister would. Jiddy hung on to the thought. Both she and Billy Hardcastle would cop it, whatever the outcome, but at least they'd be rescued.

Jiddy mulled events over. One of the Storm boys would come out in a boat if the alarm were raised. A boat! She patted Mrs. Farsyde's hand, but the squire's wife was too busy panting to notice. The woman's face gleamed with sweat while Jiddy shivered. At least her mistress wouldn't freeze. Jiddy rubbed her arms. *Keep warm, keep warm.*

"Where are you?" gasped Mrs. Farsyde.

"It'll be all right," soothed Jiddy, crouching at her side. "I'm here. We have to wait for tide to drop, then we can make our way back to causeway."

Mrs. Farsyde leaned forward. "Fetch Mrs. Grainger!"

Sea, swollen and grasping, filled the cave. "She'll come soon."

"Fetch her now!" Mrs. Farsyde shoved Jiddy, harder than Jiddy would have expected, and she fell back, groping and grasping at the rock. Unable to catch her balance, she tumbled with a splash into the water. Holding her breath, she reached for solid rock. Already, the cold gripped her limbs and her chest tightened. There! She touched stone. Fear. The fear of disappearing, plunging too deep, crushing, drowning. The memory of the dock in Whitby and the slime flooded back. Nails scraping, fingers scratching, she resurfaced and gulped in air. Teeth chattering, heart bursting, she gripped the stone ledge.

"It's freezing!" Her voice trembled. She pressed her fingers into the rough surface and scraped her boots as she scrambled to climb out of the water only to find the weight of her skirt pulled her down. "W-w-why did you do that?"

Receiving no answer, she concentrated on hauling herself up, dragging with trembling arms until, ignoring the other woman, she rolled onto the shelf and wrung out her skirt and her shawl. Shivering, she refused to cry. When she couldn't squeeze any more, she glanced at the menacing darkness of the sea. The smell of brine and bladderwrack swelled. Oblivious, Mrs. Farsyde continued to pant, and Jiddy sat, hands cupped to her mouth as she breathed warmth into her icy palms.

As Mrs. Farsyde settled into a steady rhythm, Jiddy curled on her side, holding herself tight to keep warm. *Please, someone come*, she repeated over and over in her head until she fell asleep. A grunting sound woke her, and she unfurled, wincing at the stiffness of her limbs.

The water remained dark, the rock uncomfortable and the cave dripping damp. "Mrs. Farsyde?"

In answer, Mrs. Farsyde extended her legs, pushing Jiddy's thighs and forcing her to huddle by the wall. The older woman's guttural noises sounded painful. Jiddy reached for Mrs. Farsyde's leg, unsure what she intended, anything to offer some reassurance. She didn't know what else to do. She closed her eyes and prayed a boat would come.

"It hurts too much!" cried Mrs. Farsyde between spasms. "I need Doctor Newburn!"

"Can't you hold it in?"

"Make it stop burning!"

This was the moment she should be finding a ream of silk to rip and make a mattress to act as padding against the rock. Why was there no contraband stored in the cave when you needed it? Her skirt was too sodden, her shawl weighed down with water.

"We'll be rescued," she said. "Billy Hardcastle will have told everyone in village, and they'll be sending a boat. It's likely on its way now. We won't have long to wait, and they'll have blankets and such, and you'll be in your bed at hall before you know it."

Mrs. Farsyde strained until her eyes bulged. Untying her shawl, Jiddy prayed they'd arrive any moment and take the writhing woman home to Mrs. Grainger, who would sort everything out. She wrung the woollen material as best as she could. "Here," she said. "Let me put this under you, make you more comfortable." The noise Mrs. Farsyde made suggested it probably would not, but Jiddy persisted. "I can't reach. Here, take it. Put it under your head."

In between spasms, Mrs. Farsyde shoved it beneath her. Jiddy checked the candle. It still had hours of wick. Even in the dull light, she could see the pained woman's skin dripping with sweat. Mrs. Farsyde grabbed her hand and squeezed so hard Jiddy cried out.

"Help me," Mrs. Farsyde growled. "Something's not right, I can feel it. Don't let it die. This one mustn't die!" Mrs. Farsyde gathered her skirts, wrinkling them above her knees. "Can you see it?"

Jiddy bent her head but could only make out a mass of skirt. "I don't know what I'm looking for," she said, doing her utmost not to shy away.

"It must be there. Get closer—is it a head?"

She peered into the cavern of material, wishing the boat, with lanterns alight, would approach and put an end to this nightmare.

Mrs. Farsyde bellowed again, and Jiddy retracted. The level of water had dropped, she was sure of it. If only Mrs. Farsyde could hold the baby in for another few hours.

"I'm ripping apart!" Mrs. Farsyde screamed. "Stop the pain! Aghhh!"

Jonas should be there. He'd know what to do. He'd birthed hundreds of calves and lambs. If she saw him again, she wouldn't mock him for being a farmer. She'd respect anyone who could aid the birth of a living creature. Why the heck hadn't Jonas come back to Bay to be there when she needed him? In sodding York, playing with a lump of stone, a great bloody help he was.

"Ow!" She winced at having her hair pulled.

"Help the baby out!" whimpered Mrs. Farsyde.

Jiddy freed her hair and lowered her head. She couldn't see anything. She pulled back. The air smelt different. Strange.

"Feel with your hand!"

That was the last thing she wanted to do. "I'm not doctor!"

"Get on with it!" The words were a guttural rasp. "My stomach hurts. My chest hurts. Feel my heart. It's racing! I cannot strain any longer!"

Jiddy repositioned the candle. Holding the skirt as high as she could, she peered inside. It smelt sweet, sickly.

And there it was. Something. Matted and bloody and animal-like. It wriggled, a woolly ball with arms like a creature from the sea, slimy like seaweed and slipping into its own pool. A baby seal? A jellyfish? Mrs. Farsyde's legs collapsed, trapping Jiddy's head under the skirt, cheek against the rock. She grappled to escape, shrinking from the touch of slime and smell of blood.

Jiddy heard words, instructions, and pushing away folds, retreating, she freed herself. Mrs. Farsyde lay flat, no longer cramping and straining. "Cut the cord." She sighed.

"What cord?" Jiddy blanched hot and cold. It couldn't be happening. "What do I do? Mrs. Farsyde! Tell me what to do!"

Mrs. Farsyde didn't speak but gazed into the dark. This was worse than anything. Jiddy grasped Mrs. Farsyde's knees and shook her to get an answer. "Mrs. Farsyde, you can't go to sleep now!"

She couldn't sleep and leave Jiddy to it. She had to finish the job, cradle the baby, suckle it or whatever mothers did after giving birth. You couldn't have a baby and expect someone else to mop up. "Mrs. Farsyde!"

Knees flopped sideways, unresponsive. Muscles limp. "Oh, Mrs. Farsyde," she whispered, tears pricking her eyes. "Help me!"

She held the baby-seal-like creature in her palms. Should she lay it on the wet skirt? It would freeze, but it would suffocate under the mound of skirt. She rounded her shoulders, arched her back and, shuffling backwards, emerged from under the dress. She couldn't move any further. Something held the baby. It felt sticky. Jiddy wiped its face.

"Mrs. Farsyde?" she said, "What do I do?" No answer. Jiddy trembled. Tears pricked her eyes. The baby's limbs felt like bones. "What do I do?" she repeated, more to herself than anyone. She sniffed. Closed her eyes. Tried to remember. *Cord.* What had Mrs. Farsyde said? *You must cut the cord.*

CHAPTER THIRTY-FIVE

Jiddy cradled the newborn baby, numbed by the cold stone and what she'd had to do. It hadn't been easy holding the babe in one arm and dragging Mrs. Farsyde's shawl from under her. Her head had jolted with the final yank to free the cloth. Jiddy had waited, shocked at the movement. Gently, carefully, she'd wrapped it around the baby. At least it was only dry. Gradually, without knowing she did so, she began to rock back and forth. The tiny baby, with its eyes closed and mottled skin, frightened her, but she forced herself to examine it. Repeatedly touching its face, relieved to feel warmth, she tucked the shawl further over its cheeks and held the baby close to her chest, hoping her breath would act like a warming flame.

Shuffling to lean against the wall, she shivered. There was nothing to be done but wait. Trembling, she cuddled the baby tight, blowing intermittently into its face. "Shush, little one, shush."

When a grey streak of light seeped into the cave, she noticed the sea had receded.

"Now you go?" she accused.

The baby slept. A tear dropped onto its cheek, and she kissed it away. The candle had long since extinguished, and she kept her eyes on the cave entrance, trying to decide what she would say to Squire Farsyde. She hadn't been able to stop Mrs. Farsyde from dying. How to say that except as a fact? It wasn't fair; it was so unfair. Jiddy hadn't wanted to come, but she hadn't refused Mrs. Farsyde's request either. If only it were yesterday. She wondered what Billy Hardcastle must be doing and why a boat hadn't come searching for them. Why had no-one come?

"You'll be all right," she told the baby. "Your mammy was a lady, and she loves you very, very much." Tears dropped onto the baby's face, but it didn't wake. She leaned over to kiss them away, and the touch of its skin made her cry even more. Yesterday, the squire's wife had been well and healthy, pink and blossoming, but how quickly her health had changed. The water receded further. It was so cruel. Mrs. Farsyde had waited so long to hold her own child, and now the child would never feel its mother's arms. Tears welled. "You're tired," Jiddy told herself.

The dead began to crowd in—Nellie on the gibbet, feet and tongue black. Thomas with his halo of blood. Rebecca and wild-eyed Gobbit. Even if she'd wanted to, Jiddy couldn't drive those images from her head, and now Mrs. Farsyde. She couldn't wait here any longer. She looked at the wet rocks, wondering if she could manage the climb while holding the baby. She had to.

The rocky floor revealed puddles and pebbles as if there had never been water in the cave. A few hours. If only Mrs. Farsyde could have waited a while longer, but it seemed you couldn't stop a baby when it decided it wanted to come out into the world. No amount of crossing your legs or holding your belly could prevent it being born. It was all the squire's wife had wanted, and it had killed her. Maybe if she'd been in her bed with the doctor and Mrs. Grainger at her side, she'd be sitting, propped by pillows, cheeks glowing with joy and the baby in her arms. Instead, she lay in this dank, cheerless cave, dress reeking of blood and brine and disarray.

She touched the baby's cheek again and told herself not to mull over it. She must concentrate on getting the baby from the cave and to Thorpe Hall before it starved or froze. She shuffled to the edge of the shelf, reaching with her toes until she felt the ledge below. She mustn't make sudden movements. She mustn't drop the bundle. Twisting to hold onto the ledge, she clambered backwards, steadying herself with one hand, holding the baby close, glancing over her shoulder to see how much further. Almost there. She readied for the small jump she'd have to make onto the shingle. Readied to bend her knees to cushion the impact. Could she do it without dropping the child?

The one piece of advice she'd remembered from Mrs. Grainger. Wrap the baby tight so it feels safe. She kept it snug, wondering if it was too tight, but at least she'd reached the ground, and now all she had to do was walk out of the cave and back along the beach towards the causeway.

Her skirt dragged and her boots slipped on the wet pebbles, but she kept her hold secure, cradling the baby against her chest. She closed her eyes at the lightness of sky; a bright dawn sun fluttered between clouds.

Gulls swooped as they had before, as if nothing important had happened. Yet she held a baby, and its mother was dead. She stood still a few yards clear of the cave's entrance in disbelief they'd been in the cave so long and she hadn't noticed the sea's movement. Rocks stood exposed. The pool around the Boggle Hole headland had shrunk to puddles with gulls pecking at bladderwrack. There was no trace whatsoever of Samuel lying on the beach.

At least Mrs. Farsyde believed he had loved her. That was worth having as your last thought, wasn't it? Jiddy shivered. She was chilled right through to her aching bones. The beach wasn't beautiful today; it was rock water, and all the colder and harsher for it.

"I'm sorry, little one, but I did all I could," she whispered, kissing the bundle. "I'm sorry, Mrs. Farsyde, I'm so, so sorry."

A chill breeze tumbled over the beach, and she hunched her shoulders. The sea scratched at the land, and sand, uncovered, sucked in her footsteps. One foot at a time. One foot in front of the other, holding the baby safe. She'd never felt more exposed or alone, and she shivered again, clutching the child closer. It was not the time to think about the blame that would fall on her or the punishment proffered or what she would say in her defence. One step at a time. Baby steps.

Movement on the rocks near the causeway caught her eye. Figures. A crowd of people jogging and jiggling towards her, those in front striding out. She recognised the sturdy shape of the squire and the gangling lollop of

Billy Hardcastle. They'd come. They'd come at last, and women too, straggling young ones behind and village men slower, plodding. They were searching for Mrs. Farsyde, but they were too late. Far, far too late.

The squire arrived first and stood, red-faced and puzzled.

"Where is she?"

He didn't realise what hid in her arms. Billy Hardcastle kept walking, striding to the cliff. Annie, white-faced. Betsie, eager. Two Storm brothers. Why hadn't they brought their boat? She'd prayed so hard. She stared at them. It was as if they were strangers. All of them.

"Where is my wife?" The squire's voice cut through the rustling of skirts and boots.

She wanted to explain, but words wouldn't come. Tears rumbled under her skin, but they were useless, and she wouldn't let them fall in front of the crowd. They weren't tears anymore. Not really. Not like the tears she'd shed in the cave. Those were more like signs of panic. More like fear. She held out the baby in her arms and a cold wind snuck beneath.

CHAPTER THIRTY-SIX

Annie slumped, arms outstretched across the table. Betsie sat back in her chair while Jiddy cupped her freshly made tea and shuffled closer to the hearth. She'd hoped the built-up fire and a hot drink would warm her, but she'd felt a chill in her bones she couldn't shift ever since emerging from the cave.

"I hate funerals," Annie said.

Jiddy let the steam rise over her face. She'd not been able to talk about what had happened, though people bombarded her with questions. There'd been a crowd on the dock when she'd made her way with Annie by her side and the other women, grim in their silence. Squire Farsyde hadn't even acknowledged the bairn but trudged on towards the cave with the other men. Mrs. Grainger had taken the baby and carried it away, but Jiddy couldn't recall what she had said. She couldn't recall what anyone had said.

"Did ladies and gentlemen come from as far away as York?" asked Betsie, breaking into Jiddy's thoughts.

"They came from Scarborough," said Annie. "Magistrate and his wife were there."

The funeral had been all the more devastating with so many ladies who had been in beautiful, coloured gowns at the ball such a short time ago. It didn't seem right these same women walked around while the poor lady of Thorpe Hall lay in a black silk shroud.

"It isn't fair!" she announced, tears pricking her eyes.

Annie stifled a sob.

"Life's not fair," muttered Betsie, "especially for likes of us."

Jiddy wiped her nose. "Men should take their turn and have babes sometimes."

"D'you think they'd get on any better?" asked Annie.

"I'd like them to have a go, so we could see."

It was a blessing Lord Ryethorpe hadn't spoken to her. If he'd asked her about Samuel, she wouldn't have known what to say. She couldn't even explain what had happened in the cave to herself. It was like the sea had got her after all.

She sipped the tea and eyed her two friends. Annie sprawled across the table again, with her face hidden. Betsie had wandered to the window and idly stroked one of Captain Pinkney's hand-carved boats. Jiddy felt sorry for all of them. Most of all for the baby who would never know either of its true parents, and the squire too grief-stricken to hold the child. What she would give to be sailing far away from the grief of them all.

"People are wondering why you took Mrs. Farsyde onto beach," said Betsie.

"I didn't take her! She insisted—"

"We know," interrupted Betsie, placing the wooden boat emphatically down. "But you know some folk."

Betsie plonked into a seat, and Annie lifted her head. "I hate being a lass."

Jiddy stared into the red embers in the grate. She could fall asleep right there. Anything to distance herself from what had happened.

Annie stretched her arms above her head and yawned. "Tell us what's happening at hall," she said. "Anyone know?"

"Well, I've not been," said Betsie. "Why would I? Didn't even go to funeral, and I can't understand why you two went. Not as if you're family."

"Squire Farsyde wanted me there," said Jiddy, brushing her skirt as she stood.

"He wanted me there too," said Annie. "D'you wish you'd come now?"

"I sat with your Andrew," said Betsie. "Let everyone else watch coffin pass."

Betsie drank her tea, Annie fiddled with her hair, and Jiddy swirled the clear liquid in her cup, wishing she were alone to crawl into bed. If she could sleep for a week, she might feel better. Sleep would give her strength back. Sleep would stop her brooding about Mrs. Farsyde and the rock and the blood and Samuel's sand-clotted hair and beaten skin. She couldn't bear it. Not this silence.

"Tell us about baby," Betsie said to Annie. "You saw Katie at funeral, didn't you? Has squire given her a name?"

"He can't face looking at the poor thing," said Annie.

"Is that what Katie said?"

283

Annie sank her head into her arms again. "I feel sorry for all of them."

"Why didn't Mrs. Farsyde survive birth?" said Betsie. "Were it between her and bairn?"

"I'm not a midwife," snapped Jiddy, resting down her cup.

"You see," Betsie said, "that's what people up at house want to know. So Mrs. Grainger said to my mam."

Jiddy glared at her. "What d'you mean?"

Betsie walked around the fireside chair and leaned on its back to look at Jiddy.

"Why would you take Mrs. Farsyde in her condition all way along beach to get cut off by tide?"

Jiddy jumped to her feet. "I told you! Squire knows how determined his wife is when she wants something! Can't we leave it now?"

"But folk don't understand why Mrs. Farsyde would want to go on beach when she's never shown any interest before," said Betsie, folding her arms. "Did she tell you why? Come on, Jiddy, she must have had a reason. That's all people want to know. It's natural they're gonna ask."

A piece of wood sank into ash, spreading grey specks onto the hearth. After a few moments, Annie spoke. "Let's stop talking about it," she said. "Andrew's more important than why Mrs. Farsyde went on beach, isn't he? To us, any rate. What did he talk about when you sat with him, Betsie? Tell us about what you said."

Relieved Annie moved the conversation on, Jiddy sank into a chair while Betsie returned to the table and busied herself pouring another cup of tea. "He said he'd like me to sit with him again," she said, unable to hide a little smile of pride.

"Our Andrew said that?" exclaimed Annie in disbelief.

Jiddy tried to block out their voices.

"Why shouldn't he?" Betsie retaliated. "Me and him have always got on."

"Like a couple of adders!"

Jiddy smiled at Betsie's way of remembering their childhood. Closing her eyes, the image of the mounds of material, of grappling in the semi-dark with Mrs. Farsyde's skirt, and fear, the terrible fear of not knowing what to do and Mrs. Farsyde relying on her. The baby, so little, so helpless, depending on Jiddy. It came back to her in a rush. Fear. Heat and chill. Shivering. Teeth chattering when it was all done. The relief when the tiny creature moved. The horror because Mrs. Farsyde did not move.

She could still hear the sea and feel her panic. See Samuel's battered body lying there. It was his hair that had moved her most. To be so smart and clean one minute, then hair scrunched with sand and green trails of algae the next. His uniform, no longer bright and spotless but torn and dirty by the force of the tide, made her chest grip tight. Now that the sea had washed away his body again, and Mrs. Farsyde, the only other witness, was dead, there was no proof that he'd been washed up at all.

"Sea were coming in fast," she said. "You know cave at far end of beach?"

Annie nodded. "The big one?"

"We had to go in." She'd started to relate what had happened, but she didn't know how to describe the dark and the cold, and the effort of getting a woman about to give birth to move. For a moment, Jiddy had almost left Mrs. Farsyde, and she couldn't admit such a dreadful fact to anyone. "She wouldn't stop bleeding," she said. "I couldn't stop the bleeding and hold baby at same time, and I didn't know what to do," said Jiddy, holding in the tears.

Betsie drank her cold tea in one gulp. Jiddy leaned forward, hands outstretched to the fire.

"Do you know what they've called baby?" asked Annie.

Jiddy closed her eyes, thanking Annie for again changing the subject even if it was to repeat the question.

"Kate Ashner said them in kitchen are calling it a miracle," Betsie said. "But it's really a bastard, isn't it?" She dared Jiddy to contradict what she'd said.

"Captain Ryethorpe's dead," said Annie. "No good comes of raking up what's done. Baby's a blessing."

"Squire is one to consider now, and all he's got is his bairn. People need to be kind," said Jiddy.

Betsie coughed. "They've not found the captain's body."

"They didn't find them two preventives either," said Annie. "Are they looking?"

Betsie shook her head. "Would be another miracle."

"I hate this. I wish we were still running round without a care and didn't know about any of this stuff."

"When Jiddy thought she were queen of gypsies! D'you remember?" laughed Betsie.

Jiddy began adding wood to the embers. "I thought all sorts," she said. "I liked thinking I had a mam and da out beyond Robin Hood's Bay and they were Romany kings and queens, or noblemen and women from across German Sea, but hey, I also remember I were lucky Mary and Thomas took me in. At least they loved me, even if they weren't wealthy and high born."

"I'm glad you didn't go off to find them," said Annie. "I'm glad you stayed and we became friends."

"Well and good," Betsie said, making a show of straightening her skirt. "Jiddy's got Fisherhead, but nothing has changed for Annie and me. We don't have a chance for anything better."

"I don't want anything else," said Annie. "Jiddy, I don't want—"

"I'm just saying," continued Betsie, stopping to rest her hands on Annie's shoulders, "if Captain Pinkney hadn't left you Fisherhead, would you go live with your rich mother again or be pining for finding your fancy father's folk?"

Jiddy ran her hand along the mantel shelf, touching the various knick-knacks the captain had left behind and she couldn't bear to put away. "I belong here," she whispered.

"Yes, Betsie," said Annie. "Captain Pinkney brought Jiddy to Bay and left her with Mary and Thomas. He tried to kill her mam and did kill her da, so he owes her Fisherhead." She flushed, eyes wide.

Betsie slapped the back of the chair. "No disrespect meant," she said, "but what about families he's known all his life? One of Storms should have it, or Graingers. What about me or Annie? Our families have lived here forever. If he were going to leave it to a lass, he should have left it to Annie or me."

"Betsie, I'm too tired to argue about this," said Jiddy. "And to be honest, I don't care if I live here or have to camp on roadside, way I'm feeling."

"Well, then, yes please, I'll go get my things and move in right now," said Betsie, folding her arms.

Jiddy sighed. "I don't know why Captain Pinkney left me Fisherhead when he went away. I really don't. I only knew he said Mary wanted him to, so I had a home. You have families. Maybe this was his way of making sure I did."

"Oh, I know," said Betsie, sitting next to Annie. "I do get everything you say. I'm all in a bother, that's sum of it. What with your Andrew, Annie, seeing him so helpless, it made me want to mother him. Not like me, is it?"

Annie laughed. "No, not really, Betsie."

Betsie groaned. "I must be going soft. Help me not to go soft, please!" It was Betsie's turn to rest her head on the table.

"You've always liked babies," Jiddy said with a smile. "Not that Andrew's a baby."

Betsie shook herself. "It's all lads' fault," she said. "If James and Jonas hadn't deserted us, we'd not be moping mop heads!"

Jiddy walked over to Betsie and put her arm around her sturdy shoulders. "We're not moping mop heads," she said. "We're too busy with our own plans and ideas to mope after them!"

"But what about her?" said Betsie. "This one's moping over someone. Aren't you, Annie Briggs?"

"No, I'm not!"

"Do you mean Billy Hardcastle?" asked Jiddy.

"Who else!" Betsie struck the table with her hand.

"I don't care two hoots for him!" Annie said, flushing pink. "Jiddy, how could you? I hate Billy Hardcastle!"

"You act as if you like him. You spend enough hours talking to him in the stable when he's rubbing down squire's horse."

Tears brimmed in Annie's eyes. "It's only because there's no-one else to talk to when you're busy, and I feel out of place at hall. He makes me feel as if I'm not odd one out."

Jiddy reacted straight away. "Of course," she said. "I'm sorry, Annie. I were getting carried away, pairing us all. It were silly. D'you know what, Betsie? Forget James. You and Andrew are much better suited, and if you and he could wed and have a house full of young ones, and Andrew got himself a job, say, at a farm not a million miles from here, I think you'd, dare I say it, be happy?"

Betsie scowled. "Very funny. And what about you, clever-clogs matchmaker?"

"I could maybe wed a certain someone and find a job not a million miles away either."

"You can't up and leave us and your home here!" said Annie.

"Why not? I could go and live in York and wed Jonas and settle there. Nothing to stop me from leaving Bay when I can always come back and visit my best friends from time to time, is there?"

CHAPTER THIRTY-SEVEN

Within a week, Jiddy returned to the city, dressed in her least-worn skirt, bodice and cape, and headed directly for the Minster. Walking with a spring in her step, oblivious to everyone she passed, she envisioned Jonas's face when she told him she would move to York for him. She might not work at Vardarelli's, but she would find work easily enough. They'd wed, set up house; they'd have perhaps two bairns of their own. Jonas would be thrilled.

Betsie and Andrew could live with Jonas's da and help take care of Meadow Bank. Squire would make sure Andrew had all help he needed, there'd be no worries about that, even if it were Big Isaac and the gang doing shifts. Least they could do. Annie could run school at Fisherhead. And Jiddy would visit when she could. It was all coming together perfectly. She'd visit the churchyard to tend the grave, spend time with Annie, perhaps visit the hall and see how the squire's daughter had grown. She hurried her step, eager to tell Jonas her decision.

Stopping for a moment, she caught her breath. There towered the Minster, the wonderful sound of the sculptors' hammers and chisels ringing out. The excitement of telling Jonas her news built in her belly. She strode towards the line of tables, only slowing when she saw Jonas standing with a slender young lass at the corner of the building. Approaching, unseen by either, she stared in disbelief.

She couldn't see Jonas's face, but she could see the girl's expression. Rosy, pink cheeks, wide shining eyes, every sinew focused on Jonas. If it wasn't for the tilt of Violet's chin and the gaze of devotion, Jiddy would have yanked the besotted girl from Jonas's arms and forced her to return to Bay whether she wanted to go or not.

When Jonas made the gesture she thought he only made with her, Jiddy clasped her hands over her stomach. She'd never been kicked in the belly by a horse, but that's what it felt like.

Jonas gently moved his palm over Violet's hair while Violet stared into his face. A tidal wave of fury swept through Jiddy's body.

Had he ever let her stare so long at him? Or run his hand so gently through her hair? The gentlest they'd been with each other had been the kiss she'd instigated in his da's barn before he'd run away from her like a hare across the fields.

She held her stomach tighter, jerking in breaths. Was she a wounded animal? Or a feral bull? If she went over to them, bent by the pain in her belly but powered by burning anger, what would happen? Taking several steps, her body shaking, she rounded her fists.

No lass had ever made her worry as far as Jonas was concerned. Not even Nellie, even though the elder girl had tried to turn Jonas against her by pointing out her different skin colour and fact she wasn't from Bay and how none of the girls wanted to be her friend. Jonas had never thought of being anything but a mate with Nellie same as he was with other Baytown children. Jiddy was the one he'd spent hours on the beach with, who he'd tumbled with, who he'd kissed and wanted to marry. No-one else. Yet here he was, looking like he cared for Nellie's little sister as if she was his sweetheart.

No, she wouldn't have it. Violet may have moved to York first, but now Jiddy Vardy was coming. She and Jonas were sweethearts. Not Jonas and an Ashner. Tatty-haired, scrawny-faced, sly Violet Ashner. Jonas knew she and Nellie had hated each other. How could he do this to her?

She took a few more paces, but they still didn't notice her. A wave of hatred swept over her. How could anyone run their hand over scratty, mousey hair like Violet Ashner's? She should never have taken pity on her. Never given her that diamond in the first place to give her airs and graces and make her believe she was good enough for Jonas. Violet had tempted him with riches. She and Jonas would be able to wed straight away. Rent a pleasant room. Have babies! No! That couldn't happen. She should never have taught Violet any skills or gone out of her way to help her get away from her drunken da. And it was all her fault; she'd brought the conniving little beast to York.

She couldn't watch any longer. She strode towards them, swept in a mist of jealousy, anger and betrayal.

She was almost upon them, and still they didn't turn. His hand lingered on Violet's shoulder. Violet stared enraptured. Jiddy clenched her fists. Jonas never touched her in public like he was touching Violet, and as far as she could recall, she'd never let him. Why hadn't they? They'd always acted as mates when around others, never kissed or held hands or stared into each other's eyes. Not like this. Not like this!

Half a dozen paces. What should she say?

How do?

What are you playing at?

I hate pair of you?

Three steps. Two.

They heard her approach. Their faces turned, innocent. Open.

"Good day to you," she said. She turned to Violet. "Shouldn't you be at Vardarelli's?"

Turning deep pink, Violet studied her feet.

"Violet brought me a pie for my dinner," interjected Jonas. "What are you doing here?"

"Bit early for stopping to eat, isn't it?" Jiddy said, anger flowing over.

Jonas studied her. She readied to shake the pudding head.

"I didn't stop to eat anything yesterday," he said, keeping his voice steady, "so Violet wanted to make sure I had something when I did stop."

He gave Violet a tender look, like the look Samuel gave Mrs. Farsyde, and it drew a smile out of the girl.

"So, you came here yesterday as well, did you?" Jiddy asked, readying to grasp the simpering girl's arm.

Violet nodded, scratty hair wavering.

"You know Violet doesn't know anybody but me yet in York," said Jonas, as if that made it all right. He gestured to the Minster. "It's not a job you can do in a day." He laughed. "I'm going to need lots of pies!"

That did it. She didn't care she'd come to break good news to him. She could barely look at him, never mind plan on spending the rest of her life with the cheating toad. White-hot, alum-mine rage ripped through her brain. "Well, someone else will have to bring them as Violet's da wants her home," she said and, turning to Violet, cocked her head on one side. "I've come to take you back."

"What? No! I don't want to go." Violet stared in confused horror at Jonas, as if he could step in and wave his chisel and save the day.

"He thinks I made you come, and I won't have it said I forced anyone to do anything they didn't want to do," Jiddy declared.

"But you didn't force me! Tell him I wanted to come."

"Squire wants me to bring you back as well," she said, taking the girl's hand. "We've got to fetch your belongings, so we'd best go now. I said we'd be on one o'clock coach back."

"Are you serious?" said Jonas.

Jiddy nodded. "I'm not having people say I bullied Violet into coming to York."

Violet wrenched herself free and grasped Jonas's arm. "But she didn't!" Turning to Jiddy, she repeated, "Tell them you didn't!"

"I told them, but they didn't believe me, so you'll have to tell them yourself. Come on, let's be going." Jiddy shot Jonas an angry glance.

Taut with anguish, Violet's face appeared bonier than it had ever seemed in Bay.

"Jiddy, you can fix this," said Jonas. "You can convince a fish to come on land. It's all right, Violet, Jiddy will sort it out without you having to go back."

Sort it out? She'd give Jonas sort it out! "They need her word," she said. "From her own *mouth*!" She spat out the word.

Violet dodged behind Jonas, and Jonas, half-laughing, held her there. "This isn't like you, Jiddy. What if Violet writes a note and signs it?"

Violet's face appeared. "I can't write good, but I can try."

Jiddy couldn't help but snap again. "Why aren't you at Vardarelli's? I put myself to great trouble getting you in there, and you should be working right now." In her head, she saw a block of red and she wanted to shout, *"Get away from my Jonas! He loves me! Get away!"*

"I had an errand," Violet said, recovering her confidence.

She stood next to Jonas as if Jiddy was the intruder.

"I've a message from your da as well." Jiddy ignored the younger girl and squared up to Jonas.

Jonas held her gaze. "Is he well?"

She clenched her jaw, glaring with all her might. Jonas got the hint. "Thanks, Violet," he said, "I'd best not be keeping you and getting you into trouble. Jiddy's right, you should get back, but I appreciate the pie!" He glanced at Jiddy. "That will sort it, won't it?"

Violet's expression changed too. "You will tell Da I want to stay here, won't you?" she said, hesitating, unwilling to leave.

"I'll try." Jiddy sighed.

"Go on," encouraged Jonas. "I'll see you later or tomorrow."

Reluctantly, Violet left, repeatedly looking over her shoulder until she disappeared into the crowd.

"I'd best be getting back too. My half hour's nearly done," said Jonas before Jiddy could say what she wanted to say. "You will put Violet's da straight, won't you?"

She jabbed his shoulder with her fist. "Pie? You do know she's besotted with you? You do know she's Nellie Ashner's little sister?"

"Hey, hey!" Jonas held up his palms in surrender. "She's a child!"

"She's all bobble-headed over you! And she's Nellie Ashner's sister!"

Jonas tapped his fingertips into her sides, making her crease over. "Jealous, are we? Worried I'll love someone else rather than you?"

Slapping his hands away, she struggled to remain calm. "Don't tease me, Jonas. Not today." Her eyes filled with tears, and his smile dropped.

"What's happened? Has Violet's da gone violent on you too?" She shook her head. "What is it?"

She stared at him. "It's too much to tell you here," she said. "A lot's happened, and it's dreadful, but I came here…I came with good news." Jonas touched her arm, eyes trained on her. "All right," she said, resigned. "I came here to tell you I will come to York, and I will wed you, but I don't know now. I don't know if you deserve me."

He smiled, relief softening his face. "I'll have you even if you have a green face and a devil on your shoulder," he said. "I've seen you in a worse state than this."

She hit his sleeve. "I can't believe she brought you pie."

"Delicious too," he said, licking his fingers.

She hit him again. "You're going to have to get back to work or you'll be in trouble, aren't you?"

"What did you want to tell me about Da?"

"Oh." Jiddy sagged. "It's farm, really. Squire's got lads going up to do most of work, but with John and Sarah gone, he's on his own in farmhouse at night."

"What about Rex?"

"Yes, he's got Rex, but I wouldn't want to be up there on my own on a night, would you?"

Jonas looked over his shoulder. The other lads already sat at the tables.

"I suppose Violet's lonely," she said when he didn't answer. "It were thoughtful of her to bring you a pie."

Jonas put his hand on her shoulder. "Can you come back later when I finish and catch a late coach back?"

It wasn't Violet's or his fault there was no time left. They weren't expecting her, and she'd arrived without warning, but the thought of them having tomorrow together and the next day and the next made her skin prickle despite herself.

"I can do that," she said. "As long as it's only me and you and there's no food pixie."

He gave her a quizzical look again, and like a sudden wild wave, a jealous fury swept through her body, only this time, it didn't recede.

CHAPTER THIRTY-EIGHT

Jiddy couldn't reignite the excitement she'd felt on her arrival in York. The unsettling thought of Jonas spending time with Violet wouldn't go away. *Busy, busy, keep busy.* She bought reels of cotton to take back to Bay and wandered around the market stalls. Knives and spoons caught her attention. The knives became weapons. The spoons morphed into hammers. Willow baskets and leather satchels became ways for Violet to carry masses of pies and picnics and ale to Jonas. She couldn't cope with the noise. She couldn't stay in the market. She wandered into the narrow side streets. Having eaten early and not expecting to remain in York for the entire day, the temptation of meaty pie smells and fresh bread forced her to roam further afield. She'd never eat a pie again. Never. She walked past Vardarelli's what felt like a hundred times. She hated the place. She hated everyone who worked there, from its owner to the latest addition to its staff. She hated all the people, the streets, the shops. Especially the pie shops.

By the time Jonas finished work, her belly was rumbling, and she decided she could never live in York and Jonas must move back to Robin Hood's Bay. Leave Violet Ashner in York to make cow eyes at some other gullible fool.

Jonas covered his partly finished sculpture with a cloth and gathered his tools. Tapping her foot, Jiddy urged him to make haste. "I still don't understand why you can't carve stone in Bay," she snapped when, unable to wait any longer, she'd marched to his table. "Or Whitby. There's an abbey in Whitby. They must have apprenticeships. Or you could go back to farm, you know. Why don't you move back? There's plenty to do on farm, plenty of stone walls to fix, and your da needs you!" He didn't answer at first but brushed the table with the flat of his hand. "Jonas?"

"You've asked me this, and you know I can't," he said. "What's got into you?"

"I know," she said, drumming the table with her fingers, "but if you don't come back, what's going to happen? Meadow Bank has been in Chaplow hands forever, folk say. You know your da would have you back in a snap."

"I carve stone now, Jiddy. It's a specialist trade that takes years to be any good at, and I want to be good at it. I don't want to shovel cattle shit, fix walls and cut grass my whole life."

"All right, no need to be uppity, but I'm sure they have apprentices in Whitby and Scarborough."

"Not sure it's me being the uppity one," he said, and when she didn't answer, he continued. "I am assigned to York Minster," he said. "Do you know how many lads want to work here?"

She shrugged. "A few?"

"I were picked out of a hundred. Could have been more. Violet understands…"

Folding her arms, she stared at the rows of stone saints on the Minster wall. "When did you start confiding in Violet Ashner?" she asked, trying to sound as if she didn't care what he answered.

He rolled his work tools in a cloth, tying the thread carefully and tugging the ends to make them neat. "I don't confide," he said. "I talk. She listens. She talks. I listen. It's called having a gab. Give over, will you? You're not your best when you're like this."

Her head flared hot. "You said you've seen me worse!" she said, watching him ignore her. "I wanted to point out you have options." She sensed him smirk, so she set off, listening for the thud of his boots following behind. He nudged her arm, and she glanced sideways at him.

"I hate you," she said.

"I know. You told me that before."

"Well, I'm reminding you."

He knocked her elbow again. "You know as well as I do Ashners don't let on they've a weakness," he said. "Violet's not going to tell anyone she's lonely. She'll stop hanging around me when she settles in and other lasses at store befriend her."

"I know," Jiddy snapped again, before sighing. "I'm tired, I'm hungry, and it's getting late. And I've not long before I have to catch coach back, as you well know."

"That's my grumpy lass," he said, rounding his arm around her shoulders.

And there he was, the Jonas she knew, annoying and lovable at the same time. She elbowed him in the ribs. "I don't miss you, either," she said.

They fell into an easy stride and cut towards the bridge straddling the River Ouse, and as they walked, her anger and jealousy dissipated.

"Have I told you I have a house?" she said.

He stopped, jerking her to a halt. "You what?"

"I know!" She laughed. "I have to pinch myself every morning when I wake, but it's mine and no-one can take it off me. It's all legal, and I've got my little school, which I run there. I teach Bay lasses to stitch and mend and cut out. It's not only Violet. I teach many of the young lasses."

Arms hanging loose at his sides, Jonas gaped. "A real school, in your own house?"

"Yes!" Jiddy laughed again, feeling a little uneasy at his reaction. "It means Violet's got a job here, and other lasses will be able to get jobs too."

"Nice one," said Jonas, continuing to stroll. "Violet's a determined lass. She'll do well."

The excitement of her plans growing, she spoke rapidly. "Annie's sisters and Betsie's are learning as well. They're coming on grand, and they'll be wanting to come to York when they hear how well Violet's doing."

"And they all want to leave Bay, do they? You're not stealing them away from their mas and das?"

It was Jiddy's turn to gawp at him. "Why are you finding fault?"

"I'm not. I'm joshing. Where's your sense of humour? Left it cooking on your very own stove, have you?"

She frowned. "You're scoffing at me wanting lasses to have a choice in what they do."

He lifted his hands in surrender. "No, no, I'm not. It's picture of you being a school ma'am." He grinned.

Heat rose, all enveloping. "I'm a very good teacher!"

His eyes crinkled. "I'm sure you are, but you have to admit, you were never one for patience, and I thought a teacher had to be patient above everything else."

Grabbing his arm, she yanked him to a halt. "Ask Annie! Ask Betsie! Ask any of them. Ask Violet! She's around you so much, I'm sure you can ask her."

"Hey, hey." He held her shoulders, his face so close she felt the stone dust in his hair on her skin. "What's rattling you today?"

Tears sparked her eyes. "I didn't expect to see you again," she said. "And now I have, I can't bear not being with you, and I can't stand Violet is. I hate it! Come back to Bay. Come back with me!"

"To your house?"

"Is that's what's wrong? I have my own house? We can share it. It's legal. It were given to me by—"

"Stop."

Taking her arm, he led her to the side of the bridge. He wiped her cheeks with his hands, cupping her wet chin and shaking his head. "I don't care. Don't tell me. It's whatever has happened." He looked away. "You shouted you hated me when I left Bay," he said. "Is there a small part of you that still hates me?"

"I don't hate you!" Her voice cracked, and she wiped her face with her sleeve. "But you shouldn't have gone away."

He took her hands. "I didn't know what else to do. I couldn't stay, believing we'd broken rules and might do even worse if I'd stayed. I loved you. I wanted you so bad. I still love you."

She touched his face. "Why didn't you talk to me?"

"Because I couldn't talk to you without wanting to hold you. Still can't."

Jiddy leaned forward and kissed his lips. "I've never really hated you."

He kept hold of her hand, but more gently now, and they set off again towards the Station Inn.

The horses were being harnessed to the coach when they arrived, and they stood watching. Jonas couldn't come back with her, but she didn't want to leave him either.

The horses fidgeted in their harnesses. People started to board the wagon.

"So, this is goodbye?" she said.

He grabbed her arm and, without a word, pulled her into an embrace. Resting her forehead on his shoulder, she held tight. She hadn't expected them to embrace, and certainly not to feel as if her heart was pouring out of her body. She wouldn't let go. She'd hold on until…she didn't know what she'd have to wait for. He moved his head, pushing her face so she had to lift it, and unexpectedly, wonderfully, they were kissing.

She tasted stone dust and dry skin. Jonas gave in first, gripping her hand and pulling her around the corner and out of sight. She dropped her bag, and he pushed the sack of tools around his back. The taste, the feel, everything about him was different but also familiar.

His lips, parched by stone dust, so different from the moist sea kisses she remembered, made her want to douse him in the waves, freshen him, make him of the coast again and not the city. Someone shouted.

"All on board!"

The horses' harnesses rattled; boots clattered on wood. Voices, shifting of skirts and coats. Dogs barking, the landlord shouting, a bell ringing.

"Last call!"

Jiddy held Jonas tight. If she kept hold, maybe the coach wouldn't leave. She wanted more time. Needed more time with him.

"Ready for off!"

"I don't want to go."

They stared at each other before Jonas led her around the corner and into the yard. The coach driver repositioned a couple of bags while a passenger climbed inside. "Wait! One more here!" Jonas shouted, waving her bundle.

"Hurry up, lass," said the driver.

Jonas lifted Jiddy's sack, and a woman took it. "On you go," he said, stepping aside to let her climb, but she hesitated, panicked she'd never see him again.

"You could come?" she said, holding his sleeve.

He shook his head. "I'll try for Saturday, when I've finished."

"I've not got all day," said the driver.

"I'll stay. Please." She held out her hand for her bag.

Jonas shook his head at the woman.

The driver jerked the reins. "We're off."

"Promise you'll come on Saturday," she said, holding his lapels.

"I promise," said Jonas.

The driver clambered into position, and she hauled herself onto the wagon.

"I'll meet you!" she shouted from her perch. "See you on Saturday at Buttercross!"

The driver clicked his tongue. The horses set off, wheels rolling and the passengers on top of the wagon lurching. Jiddy twisted to wave as they passed out of the inn yard, and Jonas followed behind, standing in the archway as the coach wagon headed east.

CHAPTER THIRTY-NINE

It didn't take long before Jiddy swore she'd never catch the late coach again. Although the carriage lanterns lit the track, the driver slowed the horses and the journey took well over the usual time. She shivered, even though they were allowed to sit inside the carriage after Pickering where most of the passengers had disembarked. The sight of the pitch-black space where the moors should have been would have frightened a ghost. Finally, exhausted, she climbed from the coach, stiff-limbed and famished.

While the other three passengers headed in the opposite direction, Jiddy hurried past the Buttercross, pulling her shawl around her face, anxious to be home. Nobody waited around the crossing of paths at night. Too many people had been hung from the gibbet in the lonely spot. It had taken all of Annie's, Betsie's and her nerve to free Nellie's body from the noose that dark, windy night, months ago. Now, the thought of Nellie and her greening bones haunted the vicinity, and she broke into a run to reach Baytown's cottages and the presence of living human beings.

The relief of closing her front door at Fisherhead and finding it quiet and without anyone else there overwhelmed her. She dropped her bag and, finding a cold potato cake, gobbled it down before ladling water from the pan by the stove into her mouth. She crawled up the stairs, dragged off her shawl, prised off her boots and fell into bed.

The next morning came too soon, and she woke bleary-eyed to the sound of the gulls outside and voices below. She didn't want to think about how she'd felt and how she'd behaved yesterday. Jonas was coming to Bay on Saturday, which was all that mattered. It didn't matter Annie and Betsie had come round already. Nothing mattered but Jonas's promise.

The sight of Andrew sitting by the hearth, a skein of wool around his raised arms and Betsie, seated on a low stool near his feet, winding the wool into a ball, caught her by surprise. Even though Betsie had grown soft on Andrew and was a frequent visitor at the Briggses' house, Jiddy did not expect to find him domesticated at Fisherhead. She kept questions about him helping out at the farm and Squire Farsyde to herself.

Annie sat at the table, head bent over a sock and a darning needle.

Amber flames flickered in Andrew's eyes. For a moment, Jiddy tried to make out what must be going through his mind, sat there with Betsie and Annie when he'd have scoffed at such a scenario before losing his hand. Jiddy saw his embarrassment and devastation. She jumped the last stair, landing with a thump. Annie caught the sound, and Andrew twitched to stand but unable to gain leverage merely shuffled in his chair.

"Betsie." He nodded his head in Jiddy's direction.

Betsie twisted around. Annie scraped back her chair.

"You don't mind, do you?" Annie said. "Mam's tormenting Andrew with fussing and Da's in a right foul mood and littluns don't notice Andrew can't always mind himself and they get in his way."

"You don't need to make excuses for me," said Andrew, letting slip the loop of wool over the stump of his arm.

"No, stay," said Jiddy, stepping towards the fire.

"Are you tired?" asked Annie. "You look tired. There's gruel in pan."

"I'm right," said Jiddy, hoisting her skirt and stepping over the tangle of wool. "See Betsie's got you working hard."

Betsie stiffened, and Andrew's cheeks glowed red. Usually, he'd have given her a right mouthful.

"Betsie and me were wondering," said Annie, "if Andrew could help us."

"Can we talk later? I've just woken."

Andrew, on his feet, the skein of wool on the floor, nudged past Jiddy. "Sod off, lot of you!" he shouted, slamming the door behind him before anyone could call him back.

Betsie reached for the dropped wool. "He's sensitive," she muttered. "You could have said yes."

"Andrew's not doing well, he's going to take time to recover," added Annie, bustling to help Betsie, who pushed her away, leaving Annie to stand at a loss.

"Hasn't squire had a word with him?" asked Jiddy, plonking into the chair he'd abandoned.

Gathering the wool, Betsie threw it on the table and, drawing her shawl around her shoulders, banged the door behind her as Andrew had done.

Annie sat in the chair Betsie had vacated and poked at the fire. "Andrew's not talking much," she said.

After a moment, Jiddy sighed. "I didn't mean it as it sounded." She glanced at Annie. "I wouldn't worry too much. Squire will make sure he's taken care of, and between you and me, I wouldn't rule out a certain farm."

Annie bowed her head. "I know. Mam's been up to see Mr. Chaplow. I'm not worried really." Pink-cheeked, as Andrew had been, she glanced at the bag on the table. "Did you get to tell Jonas you'll wed him and you're happy to live in York?"

"Does Andrew know Betsie's soft on him?"

"Fine, don't answer. You know he wouldn't have been sat here if he wasn't soft on her," Annie said, deftly rewinding the wool.

Jiddy smiled. "Peas in a pod."

"I want them to wed, but what's he to do?"

"If your mam's been to see Mr. Chaplow and squire has a say in it, I say they'll be getting wed before long."

Annie sighed. "You know Andrew. He's a fisherman. It's going to take some persuading to get him to set foot on a farm."

Jiddy glanced at Annie, who shrugged. "Well, he can always pound nettles and make dye for us," Jiddy said. "But I'm not sure it's enough for them to set up home."

"I suppose you'd charge them rent if you let them live here," Annie said.

"My! You're being quick to get rid of me." Jiddy smiled ruefully.

Annie's face dropped. "No, never. I meant with you. If you let them live here with you!"

"Not sure that would work."

"It were just a daft thought." Annie pushed the ball of wool into the sewing bag. "Betsie's good for our Andrew, and the odd job for us is all well and good. I hope he'll not be stubborn and he'll take place at Meadow Bank."

"It's best option all round," Jiddy agreed, watching Annie grasp the sock she'd been darning.

Annie waved it towards the door. "I hope she caught him up."

Jiddy concentrated on the sound of the wind outside and the breath of it whirling in the chimney. The normality of the sounds, coupled with the muted crackle of flames, made her feel as if bad things like Mrs Farsyde's passing couldn't have happened.

"I had a dream last night everyone left," she said after a few minutes. "I were wandering round empty streets, banging on doors and shouting for you and for Mary and Thomas and Jonas. I were even shouting for Nellie and that hoddy-doddy James Linskill, though how he'd have heard me all way from Australia…"

Annie dropped on her knees in front of Jiddy. "What's wrong?"

Jiddy wiped away the tears with the back of her hand. "I don't know," she said, her voice barely audible. She caught her breath as tears again filled her eyes. "I don't know, Annie," she repeated. "I only know with Mrs. Farsyde gone, I'm not needed at Thorpe Hall no more, and out of sight means I'll not be getting help for trips to York from Squire Farsyde and, well... Feels like luck can change on a coin's edge." She wiped away the tears. "I'm being daft," she said. "Take no mind of me."

Annie smoothed out her friend's skirt. "You're not going to move to York and leave Bay, are you?"

CHAPTER FORTY

Jiddy watched the gibbet creaking above her head. It wasn't yet dark, but it made her as uneasy as if it had been. She walked a couple of paces and faced the moor road, willing the coach bringing Jonas to appear. A wind blew. A lapwing's pure call pierced the whispering of long grass. *Nothing to be frightened about. Nothing to feel sad about. All will be well.* Andrew would find work of sorts, and Betsie and he would wed, and the school would flourish. She'd move to York. She could do it. All would be well.

She shivered. Buttercross was merely a place, nothing more sinister than a hanging spot, and a place where farmers sold their milk and butter. No such thing as ghosts coming back to haunt the living. She drew in her shawl and took a few more steps along the York Road.

She smelt woodsmoke drifting from the village and felt the dry ground shift underfoot, but night creatures hadn't stirred yet. The coach should be arriving any time now. She only had to be patient and hold her nerve, but doubt crept in with the dusk. What if he'd seen Violet again and he liked how Violet brought him a pie and listened to him and didn't stop and give him a hard time.

The question niggled. Should she tell Jonas about Mrs. Farsyde and the baby? Would it seem odd she'd not told him straight away? And how could she tell him about

Andrew and that neither she nor Sandy nor Abe nor any of them had been able to save him from being mutilated? What would he say when he found out she'd continued being part of the smuggling ring? Someone else might blurt these things out—Betsie would for certain if she saw Jonas—but Jiddy couldn't bear the thought of telling him she hadn't been able to save Mrs. Farsyde or Andrew. She wanted him to remember the fun they had; she wanted him to think of her as someone who helped people. Not how she failed them.

The rumble of wheels came as a relief. She strolled back to the Buttercross, standing away from the gibbet on the road tipping to the bay. The rumbling grew louder, and the solid shape of the coach appeared with two lanterns glowing. Laden, it rocked, the rapid movement of horses disturbing the bird's song.

Two people climbed down, and for a moment, Jiddy panicked he hadn't come. When Jonas walked around the coach, her heart leapt at the sight of him.

"I didn't expect you'd be waiting here on your own," he said, ambling towards her, arms outstretched.

She snuggled against him. "I told you I would."

He nodded. "I'll walk you, then head to the farm. Cousin John won't begrudge me sleeping in the hay loft."

She felt a pang of jealousy again. "I thought you'd come to see me."

"I'll see you tomorrow. Don't worry, I'll come early."

She hated they were talking practicalities, but on the other hand, it meant the words she wanted to say were

314

held in, and tomorrow, well, tomorrow, she'd be calm, and she'd speak about Andrew and Mrs. Farsyde without tears or fear Jonas would judge her.

"Should we get moving?" he said, slipping an arm over her shoulder. "It'll be late by time I get to Meadow Bank."

They walked in silence, the sound of their footsteps and whisper of her skirt circling their progress down the hill. Her mind raced. Violet's name caught in her throat. If she talked about Andrew, she'd have to mention they were smuggling, and he might get angry, and they'd argue, and he might go to the farm and return to York without seeing her again. If she mentioned Mrs. Farsyde, he'd question what she'd been doing on the beach, and she couldn't mention Samuel because his name might set Jonas off, and he'd be jealous and again they'd be arguing.

"Does it feel strange being back after so long?" she said, feeling the gush of emotion rise in her belly.

"No, it's as if I've never been away. Nothing changes here."

She glanced sideways at him, striding out as if he owned the place. He walked as if he were a lord's son. York had changed Jonas.

"Place may not change, but people do," she said.

"Bay folk?" He laughed. The sea made muffled ripples, and the road tipped. "Are you going to tell me who's changed?"

She shrugged. "That's not why you're here."

They continued without speaking, seeing no-one, the only sound their footsteps.

"You're not usually so quiet," he said as they rounded the corner before they reached Sunny Place. "Is there a raid on tonight and I've spoilt your fun?" She laughed overloud to cover her shock at his openness, and he stopped her with his hand. "If there is, I'm going back."

She swallowed. Of course he'd ask. He knew Bay. He knew her.

"There's no raid tonight," she said, setting off again.

"Jiddy?" He dodged to catch her eyeline until she couldn't avoid him any longer. "What's wrong?"

What's wrong? Me! And I can't tell you! "I suppose I'm worried about you getting to farm so late," she said. "They'll be asleep as it is, and they might have locked up. Maybe you should head there now, and I'll see you in morning."

"Look at me."

"You must be tired as well, after day's work and journey," she said, glancing at the path to Fisherhead.

"Jiddy, talk to me. What's wrong?"

"Nothing."

"Are you angry with me?"

She shook her head again.

"Still angry at Violet?"

"No. 'Course not."

"Has something else happened since Wednesday?"

She pursed her lips, on the brink of telling him. "We'll see each other in the morning," she said instead. "Go on, get off with you or you'll lose all sense of direction and walk off cliff in dark."

Taking her hand, he led her up Jim Stiles, but she tripped and stumbled.

"It's easier single file," she said.

"You're one more likely to lose your way and walk off cliff, way you're going," he said with a smile. He stopped outside the cottage. "Odd this place is now yours. You sure Captain Pinkney's not waiting behind door?"

Rubbing his arm, she stood beside him. "You can leave me here."

"I'm not leaving you like this," he said. "You're hiding something, and I want to know what it is."

He walked inside and took off his hat and satchel. A fire glowed low in the grate, and the familiar smell of coal dust tickled her nostrils. Lighting a candle, she crossed to the fire and added a few sticks of wood, prodding them into the centre and giving herself time to decide what she was going to say. When she felt his hands on her shoulders, she jumped.

"That's not the usual effect I have," he joked.

Folding her arms, she crossed to the other side of the fireplace, and they faced each other. The wood caught, and a sudden flame made Jiddy jump again.

"I hope it's not me making you so edgy," he said. "Have I to guess what's matter?"

"I don't want someone else to tell you, and I don't want to talk about it once I tell you, but it's Mrs. Farsyde." Her words tumbled out.

"Mrs. Farsyde?"

"She died." *And it was my fault. It was my fault!*

The teasing smile dropped from his face. "Did she have the child?"

"Yes. Her baby's alive, and it's a miracle." Tears welled, and she put her hands over her face. "And Betsie and Andrew will be wedded soon!"

"Jiddy, you can't tell me something so serious and then josh me with nonsense about Andrew and Betsie. Annie's brother, Andrew? No way. Stop taking me for a nicky-ninny."

"I wanted you to remember Bay as best place in world!" She burst into tears. "Some bad things have come about, and I don't know how to tell you! And I'm useless and you'll hate me when I tell you how it all happened!"

"Hey," he said, his voice turning gentle.

"And I thought I'd grown out of being a mardy child, but I haven't! At turn of a coin, I'm having a tantrum because you gave your attention to Violet Ashner!" She twisted the edge of her shawl. "How can you want to wed me when I'm such a strop head." Sniffing, she wiped the tears away.

"D'you know what?" he said, unbuttoning his jacket. "Is it all right if I stay night? Don't shake your head." He took hold of her chin and studied her eyes. "I'm not leaving until you've told me all you need to tell me, and I will never hate you. It'd be like hating myself, and I'm not going to set about hating myself, am I?"

CHAPTER FORTY-ONE

Jiddy could tell it was early by the absence of the gulls' cries. She stared at the wall, not wanting to move. Cradled against Jonas's torso, his breath tickled her neck where her hair, fallen on one side, left bare skin. If Annie and Betsie came in and saw his boots, coat, hat and satchel, they'd assume straight away what had happened. They'd be wrong; she and Jonas had spent the hours talking and crying until, finally, they'd fallen asleep like children. And now it was morning. She kissed his hand, balled into a loose fist across her chest, but he didn't stir.

If it wasn't for the numb sensation of her arm beneath her, she'd never have moved, but resigned, she drew away, rolling onto her back and letting his hand splay on the mattress. Soon, the gulls would start, and he'd wake, and they would break their precious cocoon. Darkness lifted into a pale dawn. His arm was riddled with tiny freckles and fine, copper-tinged hair. She loved the brightness of him.

If no-one disturbed them, they could stay in bed all day, sleeping and waking and sleeping again. Secure. Cradled. Safe. Did anyone ever do that, she wondered, and not go to chapel?

His breath changed and she met his gaze. "Good morning," she whispered.

Sleepy-breathed, he pressed his lips to hers. Dreamy, warm, quiet. He moved his hand over her cheek. They didn't need to speak or ask. It was so quiet and snug and, stars sprinkling into the corners of her brain, she pressed into him. Easily, calmly, without a word, quietly, so quietly. She didn't expect the quick, sharp pain drawing in her breath. His concerned face. The sensation her body would never be the same again. Jonas's eyes hazed over. She didn't want to let go of him. She felt she'd never be angry or stroppy again. Their breath filled the room. This would be early Sunday mornings from now on. Their bed. Their private time. They were grown-ups now.

Their tousled nest smelt sweet and heavy and, lying side by side, staring at the ceiling, they heard the first gull alight on the roof and scratch its feet. The signal set off the morning cawing, and they listened to the Bay waken.

"You have to come to York now," he said, smoothing her hair.

"Right now, this minute?"

"We can wed here in Bay," he said. "We should wed here, but good God, Jiddy," he kissed her, "as soon as we can."

Sunlight fixed a square of window on the bed, and the morning cacophony of gulls clambering and cawing and clattering outside made her laugh.

"We can wed this month if we see Reverend today!" he said. "So we can do this every morning."

"Are you glad we know what it's like now?"

He frowned. "You can't be with child out of wedlock," he said. "I'd not do that to you, Jiddy. I want us as a family. I'll not have it thought I've used you."

"No-one'll think you've used me," she smiled, "or I've used you if it comes to it."

He reached across the bed, pulling her into his arms.

"What if Annie and Betsie come round?" She laughed. "They know you're in Bay."

He pressed his lips to the soft rise of her chest. "They can make us tea and bring us a feast."

She laughed again at his hair tickling her skin as much as the thought of Betsie bringing a tray of tea and buttered bread.

His hand on her neck, lips on her mouth, if she closed her eyes, touch and sound and smell guided her. She opened her mouth, and their tongues tasted not of salt but of nighttime and each other.

They heard voices as they dressed. Jonas flushed rosy, loose-limbed, sleepy. Jiddy, quicker, felt the urgency of the hour.

"It's them coming to see why we weren't at chapel," she said. "Quick."

"Why? What's it matter?"

"When they arrive, the spell will be broken, and I told you. I'm not ready for real world yet."

He held her gaze before nodding.

Sitting by the fire, he pulled on his boots and grabbed his coat. Jiddy gripped his satchel, and he took his hat.

They jostled to the door only to be met by Betsie's and Annie's voices.

"I'm not ready!" she said, panicking, and she grabbed his hand. "Follow me!"

CHAPTER FORTY-TWO

The cold and smell of the dank passageway hit them when Jiddy opened the panel next to the fireplace. Undeterred, she checked Jonas was following. His expression showed his reluctance, and she took his hand.

"Pull door shut behind you," she whispered. Sounds from beyond the front door were already muffled as the density of stone enveloped them.

Jonas closed the door, and light vanished. No raid meant no lamps illuminated the passage. She hadn't prepared for the pitch-darkness swallowing them, and for a moment, she thought they could be better to remain still until Annie and Betsie left.

"We can't wait," she said as the cold began to bite. "Put your hands on the rock on either side of you and take small steps."

"Isn't this one of them passages?" Jonas's voice had a hard edge to it.

"Lasses have used it for centuries, so they didn't get cut off on beach by tide when they were crabbing or collecting whelks, didn't you know that?" Jiddy answered, quick as a flash.

They shuffled a few paces. She waited for him to say what he really meant about it being a smugglers' tunnel, but her answer seemed to have been enough. She ran one hand along the wall, listening to his footsteps. The chilly air made her shiver.

As they progressed, she said, "You all right?" too many times, and sometimes Jonas answered; more times he didn't. His stumbling boots echoed instead.

When the wall on her right gave way to a gaping hole and a breath of air, she stopped. She knew firsthand what could happen if you strayed off the main tunnel, and she fumbled to touch stone again. "Ignore tunnel on right," she said, leaning against the rock to wait.

"Bloody hell," he muttered, and she caught the edge of fear in his voice.

Usually, she grew hot, skin dampening, cheeks burning, but today, she shivered the entire way. Excitement, not fear or fatigue, propelled her steps and her fingers gliding over the dimples and edges and the dense black, and she shouldn't have noticed the cold, but she did. His breath, an ever-present noise, told her he followed.

"You all right?" she repeated.

"Bloody great idea, this were," came his response.

"Not far now."

"As if you can tell. Ow!" He swore again as he stumbled.

She laughed, a strange sound of relief and amusement, murdered by stone. At least Betsie and Annie would never dream of following.

Odd. She noticed so much more in the dark than if she could see. At every step, she could tell if the ground sloped up or down or level. Down to the cave, to the beach, to sand and sea and sky.

The air fluttered.

"Almost there."

No response.

The wall rounded in front of her, and she explored for an opening in the rock. There. Almost sharp, surprisingly narrow, she traced the crack. "Follow me," she ordered, wriggling into the pinched opening.

Straight away, light made her squint. Her feet crunched on stones, and the rustle of the sea with its fresh breeze lifted. She took a few paces forward, determined not to look to her right at the high ledge where Mrs. Farsyde had died.

Jonas shuffled behind. "So, this is where it leads?" He walked past her before turning around. His skin paled in the dull light, his hair and eyes dark.

She took his hand again as she had when they first entered the tunnel. "We made it," she said.

He took in the high ceiling, the darkness at the back of the cave and the draw of the lighter entrance, like a picture frame, showing the grey of water and sky.

"Let's escape further," she said, shaken that the cavern made her so emotional. Grasping his hand tightly, they wobbled across the pebbles towards the light.

Jiddy focused on the touch of breeze. As they stepped out of the cave's shadows and onto the sand, Jonas slid his hand across her back.

"I'd forgotten the smell of the sea," he said.

Dim sunshine created a copper sheen on the water, and the delicate sky spread high and wide.

"I forgot too," she said, staring at the pond-like sea. The only sign of the tide ebbing and flowing was the usual straggles of seaweed left behind. No bodies, no footprints in the sand. The innocent beach of their childhood stretched before them.

"If we lived at Fisherhead, we could come here every day," she said.

He squeezed her shoulder and tipped back his head. A gull wheeled over the cliff.

Not so long ago, she'd have grabbed him, or he'd have grabbed her, rock against rump, shoulder blades, skull. She wasn't even sure if she wanted to grab or be grabbed ever again when the softness and quiet of the bed had cushioned them.

"What are you thinking?" she asked.

"It feels like a long time since I've been here," he said. The water rippled. Peach and grey and white. Morning colours. "We're not children anymore, turning sea water into salt. Remember you with those dishes of sludge?"

"I remember you and Silas being right scathing of my efforts."

"You liked experimenting."

"What about you making us touch tongues to see what salt tasted like! Now, that was odd."

Jonas laughed. "You hated it."

"Not something we'll ever forget, though."

"Let's walk," he suggested.

Hand in hand, they strolled along the beach, feet sinking into the mixture of shingle and sand, the noise of disturbed pebbles mingling with the frilling of the water's edge. Jiddy couldn't fathom how peaceful she felt in her body and her head. What they'd done earlier hadn't been like she'd imagined it would be. They hadn't hurried, and it had been even sweeter because of the time they'd taken. She glanced at Jonas, wondering what was going on in his brain.

Three gulls wheeled high, high as the clifftop. A rivulet of dry soil whispered to the cliff.

"Feels different here today," she said.

He squeezed her hand. "I'm here."

"No, it's something else. We've been here plenty of times together. It's because of last night." She smiled. "This morning."

He raised her hand to his mouth and licked her knuckles. "Mmm. Salty."

"Ha-ha!" She pulled her hand free. "Better than touching tongues!"

"Better than trying to make salt from sea water."

She laughed, relief and amusement bursting out.

She could see them, at eight and eleven years of age, sitting in the surf, rough, tousled, wet, faces scrunched at the touch of pimpled tongues. She liked the taste of salty sea-dipped skin and the sound made by a skirt, bone-dry, sprinkling white grains on the floorboards at home.

"Let's head onto tops," she said.

They headed along the familiar path, single file, she in front, grasping tufts and hauling herself, balancing, aware

Jonas stopped when she did, panting gently and content to follow.

Reaching the top, the wind dragged her skirt and whipped strands of hair across her face. Jonas stood beside her, face flushed. Taking off his hat, he breathed in the blustery air. "Why've you brought me here?" he asked.

She gaped at him. "I thought you'd want to," she said. "You've always said it's your favourite place in Bay."

CHAPTER FORTY-THREE

S he had to admit something she'd never admitted before; height gave a beauty to the sea that differed from the shore. From here, she could see further and wider, as he'd always said you could. Mary used to say Jiddy only wanted a certain shell or pebble because it was out of reach, or wanted to take a journey in a boat or feel hot foreign sun on her skin because she couldn't find it or touch it in Robin Hood's Bay. Here, on the tops, with the vista of sea, sky and horizon, it felt like anything was possible and any place reachable.

She shook her hair from her face and held out her arms. "Ta-da!" she proclaimed. "Do you want me to say out loud this is the best view and you were right? I will, you know! Jonas, you're right. This is a better view of the sea than the one from the shore."

"You don't need to worry. You've not grown up," he said, that loved-up glaze to his eyes she knew so well. "You're complete, and you're not stroppy, you're passionate. And look how you admit you're wrong. You've never done that before." He smiled with the familiar wink, and she smiled back. "So, we're straight, are we? We can be children and we can be grown-ups too? And view is better here than on shore?"

She nodded. "I can admit I've grown up," she said. "And that I can be both Jiddys."

"Good. Now, more importantly, shouldn't we have brought some food with us?"

"Oh, you!" She laughed. "Do you remember me trickling ale into your mouth?

"I remember you burping and catching a piece of meat pie with your nose."

"Your bare chest put me off!"

In one stride, he embraced her, and she wrapped her arms around his shoulders. They didn't need the sweetness of hops to kiss and bubble up the passion of hot summer days. Hat discarded, satchel on the ground, flinging themselves in the long grass, they were their old selves. His skin flushed pink. She breathed in the smell of sawdust and stone embedded into his coat and, raising her head, smiled at his expression.

"I can't wait for you to have the name Chaplow," he said.

She froze. Change her name. By rights, if they admitted it, both their names should be that of their fathers, but Jonas would never use that name. As if he read her mind, he said it aloud. "I may not be a true Chaplow, but I will never use the name Hartshorn."

"Neither of our mams took it," she said. "I don't want it." They slipped apart and sat, facing the sea again. "If I take name of Chaplow, it'll mean I'll no longer be Jiddy Vardy."

"You'll be Jiddy Chaplow."

"I'm not sure I want to lose my name."

He laughed. "If anything, it should be Jiddy Vardarelli."

"Jianna, if you're being so particular." Her voice hardened. She blinked. The clifftop was his place, not hers, and she regretted climbing up to the tops. The ground was unstable here. It collapsed. It wasn't safe.

Leaning around, he kissed the tip of her nose. "You'll always be Jiddy to me."

"Jiddy Vardy?"

"Yes, but you want to be Mrs. Jonas Chaplow, don't you? For us to have same name?"

She used to love his quizzical expression, which he had so often when they were younger.

"It's a grand name," she said, smoothing the wrinkle from between his eyes.

The tide had ebbed further, exposing gnarled scaurs and abandoned bladderwrack, islands of sand and rock outbreaks. Gulls strutted, stick-legged, pot-bellied. The movement of the tides would go on forever. The sea played with everyone, rich or poor. Nellie, scrambling, desperate to get of the Bay. Nellie, rotted away, nibbled and pecked at, while Samuel, who didn't belong at all in Bay, rotted in the same sea, devoured by the same waves and tides and time. Driftwood bones. Bladderwrack hair. Salt pools like blood pits. That was all those lost in the sea could ever be. And her and Jonas? You could be as lost on land as much as in sea, it seemed.

"I'd give you a coin for your thoughts if I had one to spare," said Jonas.

His voice brought her back, and she grabbed his hand. "Let's go," she said.

They headed towards the rooftops cradled in the ravine, drawing nearer to the sounds of voices and barking dogs. As they entered the lanes, the call of Jonas's name rang out from women gossiping on their front steps, from men leaning against walls and, as they walked downhill, even from bairns coming to see what the fuss was about.

"Where've you been, lad?" The same question was reiterated over and over.

"We were told you'd gone to France."

"So, you're back at farm?"

"Your da'll be pleased."

"Will your cousin be stopping on?"

The constant refrains.

Jonas avoided answers until, finally, caught on Chapel Street, they stood outside the Preaching House.

"What do you want with Minister?" asked Dottie.

Helen Drake would be announcing news Jiddy and Jonas were to be married before the first banns had been read!

"He's not in," Dorothy Storm said, nodding at the door. "You should have been at service."

Jonas stepped inside anyway, and Jiddy followed, if only to escape their questions. Once the door closed, the quiet of the building enveloped them. He walked directly to the vestry while she waited by the pews. The wood made its own noises underneath the thud of Jonas's boots, the whisper of sawdust, of petals dropping and the lingering shuffle of Sunday's congregation edging from the long seats.

"Reverend?" Jonas's voice echoed.

He reappeared in the vestry doorway. Not stone-dust Jonas or fresh-air, bright-eyed and alert Jonas. This Jonas stood anxious, uncomfortable, as if embarrassed and sad. As if he remembered something unpleasant.

This was where he'd found her kissing Samuel, but he would never mention it.

"He's not here," he said.

She reached out her hand. "Let's go."

Miraculously, most people had disappeared and those in doorways, on front steps and wending their way, had seen them or heard the news. Questions became greetings.

"How do, Jonas."

"Now then, lad."

"I have to be heading back," Jonas said. "We'll walk slowly."

She threw him a smile. "Don't want to miss coach."

At the Buttercross, they faced the Scarborough Road and listened for the rumble of wheels and clop of horses. He stood quietly while she strolled along the road, scuffing her boots over the ruts before returning to join him.

"I thought I'd be babbling away, but I've lost ability to talk," she said.

He squeezed her shoulder. "Where's my lass gone, huh? What have you done with her?"

Turning to face him, she took hold of his lapels and smoothed them. "Is this what marriage is, do you think? Does it mean we will stop talking?"

He laughed. "Can't see anything stopping you talking!"

"No, be serious," she said, resting her palms on his jacket. "It's suddenly hit me, and I don't know why because I have loads to tell you, I do. So much has happened, questions I have as well...but I don't know. After last night, I can't find words. I don't even mind not talking. What about you? You're terrible quiet."

He kissed the tip of her nose again. "You're not giving me much chance."

"I am still Jiddy. She's still here."

"We'll figure it out," he said, looking over her head at the road. "We'll see Reverend next time I'm over."

They listened for the coach. He rubbed locks of her hair between his fingers, distracted.

"Do you feel different?" she asked.

"I feel calm. Like after a big meal, only I haven't had one."

He kissed her. Slipping her hands around his waist, she closed her eyes, so easy to fall into the familiar pattern of his lips. The warmth of the early morning came back and the sheets and soft mattress and pillows and the sky through the square of skylight and the quiet of being undisturbed.

"I wish you didn't have to go," she said.

"Soon," he said. "I'll have to come back so we can set banns and you'll move to York and see your mam about work, and I'll get a second job if I can, maybe something on Saturday afternoons, so we can set up home proper, and we'll have to find lodgings too. We're going to be busy."

"You can't take a second job, you bumpkin, and you've signed a contract you can't get out of. You said so. Besides, you want to be a stonemason, so you mustn't jeopardise that. It'll be well paid in end."

"If you worked at Vardarelli's, maybe your mam would make you a partner?"

She stiffened. "Can't see me taking ladies' measurements and being polite all day, can you?"

He leaned back, brushing the hair from her face. "You did that for Mrs. Farsyde, didn't you?"

Her voice came out strained. "Not all day every day, and anyway, look how it worked out. If I upset a York lady, I'd be thrown into dungeons."

He smiled. "Yeah, probably. We'll have to think of something else. Maybe Violet will keep us?" Hearing the approaching wheels, he glanced at her. "I'll be back next week, and we'll go see Reverend Cook."

She held his arm as they waited for the sight of the horses and the shape of the carriage.

"Can you come to York during week?" he asked, readying to greet the coach. "Not sure I can wait until next Saturday evening."

"I need to see squire first," she said. "He's helping me with my fares and buying stock, but well, if I can."

"Good," he said, embracing her. "I feel for squire and bairn. Pass on my condolences?"

The stampede of hooves made them stand back from the roadside.

"You'll send me word?" he said.

"Of course."

"I'll tell Violet. She'll be pleased to see you again. I can't keep her company as often as she'd like."

The noise of the carriage's wheels made their words difficult to hear.

"How often?" she shouted.

Snatching a kiss, he let go and approached the slowing vehicle. "How often what?" He threw the words over his shoulder. Heaving himself onto the roof, he tipped his hat and said something to the old man already seated. "Goodbye, Mrs. Chaplow-to-be!" he shouted.

The driver cracked his whip and the horses stepped forward, the carriage turning towards the moors. She waved until the tapping of hooves, grinding of wheels and cloud of dry earth disappeared. The gibbet, nooseless, with its triangular support silhouetted against the sky, creaked. She stared at the now-empty track mounting the hill leading inland before she turned around and gazed at the sea. She'd done this more times than she could count, and she never grew tired of it. The thought of living in York made her heart sink like one of the massive stones from the Minster.

CHAPTER FORTY-FOUR

Jiddy glanced along Bloomswell and afterwards the Bolts, wondering if Annie was home with her family, chattering and bickering, the youngest feeding, her ma fussing over Andrew and her da smoking his pipe. Glancing towards Sunny Place as she always did when passing, she couldn't resist and headed up the slope. She'd have given anything to be little Jiddy again, nagging Mary if she could go to the farm or down on the beach to play with Jonas. If only she'd appreciated it more, really taken notice of Thomas coming in and hanging his coat on the back of the door, stayed every hour with Mary instead of yearning to be outside.

Voices brought her into the present. Other noises joined in. Cracks of wood, a dog and a cacophony of gulls. She turned around and set off in the opposite direction. As always, she was aware of the entire village, from the beck, splicing the village in two, the Fisherman's Arms, no doubt smoky and ale-drenched, to cottage fires and front steps, broken lobster pots and cobles.

Jiddy soon reached her own front door. Voices there as well. Placing her palm on the wood, she leaned in, listening. Annie's voice rang out. Relieved she'd have an evening chattering with her two closest friends, Jiddy pressed the snatch. An array of faces met her.

Eight girls sat around the table, three along each side and one at either end, all of them concentrating on piercing a square of material with their needle and thread. Kate Ashner coughed, fidgeting as she glanced at the others, but seeing them all fixated on the task, bent her head again.

Jiddy remained in the doorway, reluctant to interrupt. A breeze ruffled her skirt.

Annie and Betsie stood side by side, watching the girls at work, Annie with a gentle smile on her lips, Betsie with forehead furrowed.

The fire crackled. Jiddy's skirt ruffled again.

"You don't mind, do you?" asked Annie. "We couldn't find you to ask. Where've you been?"

Jiddy fondled an embroidered square. The blue and yellow flowers blurred, and she replaced it. "You're all doing so well," she said.

Betsie hovered at her elbow. "We came round first thing, but you weren't here, so we got on with things ourselves."

"I'm sorry. I didn't expect you or others to be here seeing as it's Sunday."

"Only day lasses are free from chores and their mams will let them come," muttered Betsie.

Annie's face lit up. "There's so much to show you, even in a few hours. It's like you said. When it clicks, a new world opens. Honestly, you'll be taking five or six girls to York next time and finding them all work! So, how is Violet? You didn't get chance to tell us when you got back.

We want details! Kate wants to know all about her sister, don't you, Kate?"

Kate glanced at Jiddy, showing the resemblance to her sister.

"How is she? What did she say?" persisted Annie. "Is she eating right and behaving? She hasn't upset anyone, has she? Oh! How'd you get on with your mother?"

"I told you, and Kate, she's getting on grand." Jiddy stood at a loss, the visit to York no longer in the forefront of her mind after everything that had happened since.

Kate Ashner scowled. "Suppose she's forgotten about us already."

Annie laughed and patted the girl's shoulder. "I'm sure she hasn't!"

"I'll make some tea," said Betsie. "Why don't you tell us how Jonas is doing, since you've hidden him from us? He did come yesterday, didn't he?"

"Maybe later," said Jiddy, shaking out her shawl and hanging it on the back of the door.

"'Course," said Annie. "I'll tell you about the girls." She glanced at Betsie as she went on. "Kate's as good as Violet at tiny stitches, and Maggie's brilliant with the white work, and I'm showing Sarah chain stitch."

Annie leaned over Sarah Grainger. Their two faces, close together, both concentrating, reminded Jiddy of how Mary had taken so much interest in them all.

She crossed to the fireplace and, taking her time, straightened the pans hanging over the secret passageway. Her hands shook with agitation, and she didn't want anyone to see. Luckily, Annie had turned her attention to the pillowcase in Maggie's hands while Betsie rattled a spoon in a pot. Jiddy surveyed the table where each girl sat engrossed.

"Annie?" Eliza Cooper raised a hand for attention.

Annie glanced at Jiddy instead of answering the girl.

"Annie?" the girl repeated. "Will you help me?"

For a moment, Annie and Jiddy held each other's gaze before Annie broke eye contact and went to Eliza's aid. Taking the opportunity, Jiddy mounted the stairs. At the top, she let out a long breath and headed into her bedroom.

Though sunlight from the little window still cast a bright square on the floor, a strengthening breeze rattled the glass. She closed the door and sat on the unmade bed. If the girls hadn't been downstairs, she'd have snuggled under the blanket and remembered her hours with Jonas, his deep-auburn hair on the pillow, his skin—the smell of him lingering on the sheets. She listened to exterior sounds of the gulls and the sea, but persistent voices crackled through the gaps in the door. If she concentrated on her direct surroundings, blocking out what went on below, she could pretend Jonas still lay in the bed, warm and sleepy and smelling of love.

She would wake every day with Jonas once they wed. In York, she'd start a new life, the life of a wife and, soon after, a mother. What could be better? A life with Jonas would be more important than helping Bay lasses learn a skill. More important than aiding Abe, Sandy and Silas and the rest of Bay to smuggle in goods. Someone else could do it; she wasn't indispensable. But York. What would she do of any good in York other than take Jonas his dinner and give him children?

"Jiddy?" A shout from below.

Brushing down her skirt and smoothing her hands over her hair, she stood. "I'm coming!"

She wiped her eyes with her fingertips. Life went on. The wind beat sea salt against the glass, the tide swept in debris. In an hour or so, she'd have Fisherhead to herself. She could face Annie and Betsie and the girls for an hour or so.

One of the girls' voices filtered up the stairs.

"We don't have to leave Bay just because we can sew proper, do we?" Eliza asked. "Can't we go work at Thorpe Hall like Jiddy?"

Their voices stilled as she appeared. She saw a couple of girls had already gone. Kate shifted her needle as if her life depended on her finishing the design.

Jiddy pulled up a chair. "Violet's settled," she told her. "She's building a life for herself, and she's canny. You don't need to worry. You never know, one day you may be joining her in York."

A taller girl interrupted before Kate Ashner could answer. "It's only Nellie and Violet who wanted to leave Bay," Maggie said. "Rest of us girls…" She looked around the table at the others, needles poised, listening. "Rest of us only want to learn stitching because it gets us out of mending nets, but we don't want to leave Bay. Are you joshing? This is our home."

Jiddy looked from one face to the next. "Is this true?"

A couple of the others nodded.

Kate pushed back her chair. "I've got to go. No offence," she added. "Sewing's useful but it don't feel right on a Sunday after all." She pushed her needle into the cushion pad and nodded to Annie. "Ta," she said and headed for the door.

"She don't love God, she just hates her sister," said Martha, rubbing her nose with the back of her sleeve.

"All of Kate's sisters are jealous of each other," said Maggie. "But it don't mean they all want to follow each other like puppy dogs."

Betsie clapped her hands, making Jiddy jump. "Get yourselves off home," she said. "Roll up your work, and tidy away. Needles in box and chairs in. Quick as you like, but before nightfall, hey?"

The scramble of hands gave Jiddy time to stand outside and take a moment for herself. Chattering out of sight, the girls left. Jiddy didn't know what to believe after what Maggie and Kate had said. She rubbed her forehead. She could do with heading to the beach for some quiet thinking time, but dusk was drawing in, and Annie and Betsie wanted news of Jonas. They deserved to hear about him.

She watched her two friends clearing the table and neatening chairs. They moved comfortably around each other; they'd established a routine.

"Seems like it were a productive day," Jiddy said, as she closed the door behind her.

Frowning, Betsie continued to sweep stray strands of discarded cotton from the tabletop into her palm whilst Annie swept the floor.

"Seems like you can manage without me." Jiddy forced a laugh.

"It's all in hand," said Betsie, throwing the scraps of thread onto the fire.

"They don't mean what they said," Annie added with a smile. "Take no notice."

"Oh, I don't." Jiddy waved her hand dismissively. "I know some will stay and some will go. I'll prepare for next time. All will be well."

"Good," said Annie. "And there's no need. We got the girls to do it today when they arrived, and they did it fine. They know where everything's kept, and it's good for them to help each other. Maggie supervised. She likes bossing the others about." She gently nudged Jiddy as she swept the flags near the door and, reopening it, brushed dust outside.

"Never seen it cleaner," said Jiddy, moving towards the stairs. "I'll get out of your way. Pull door too when you go, and I'll see you tomorrow."

"Oh, no, you don't, lady." Annie blocked her exit with the broom. "We want news, don't we, Betsie?"

Betsie sank into a chair by the fire and yawned. "I don't mind. Violet's fine, but Kate wants to do opposite of her sisters. What else have you to tell us?" She stared at Jiddy.

"If you don't want to tell us about Jonas, fair enough, but does that mean he didn't come after all? Typical of lads to promise one thing and not do it."

She wanted to correct Betsie, tell them everything she and Jonas had spoken about. Instead, she sat and played with a stray thread of cotton left on the table.

Annie plonked herself in a chair, resting the broom against the edge of the table. "I'm relieved to see you, Jiddy. I were right worried where you were, if I'm honest. I'm sorry Jonas didn't come. Did you spend day at Thorpe Hall visiting baby instead?"

Before Jiddy could answer, Annie continued. "You seem tired. Don't let girls upset you. They're a bit nervous of big city. They'll come round."

Betsie stretched out her legs. "Don't seem right leaving Violet on her own, not knowing anyone, but if as you say, she's all right..."

"Of course she's all right!" Jiddy raised her voice. "Jonas has taken her under his wing, so stop mithering."

She hadn't meant to tell them about that either, and now it was out and it was obvious she was cross, they'd ask more about it. She studied the fire as if it was the most interesting sight she'd ever seen, sensing Annie and Betsie were exchanging glances.

"How's Jonas?" Annie asked. "Did he really not come?"

Now was her chance. *We're going to wed! I'm moving to York!* The words were on the tip of her tongue. She shook her head. "Jonas did come," she said.

"And is he coming back for good?" asked Betsie.

Jiddy covered her face.

"You mean, not until after his apprenticeship," corrected Annie. "How long does an apprenticeship last?" She gently lowered Jiddy's hands. "How long did he say?"

Seven years. If she lived in York for seven years, it would be her home too.

"He's asked me to marry him."

"He hasn't!" said Betsie.

Annie clapped her hands. "I knew it, and you've kept it from us since Wednesday?"

"He asked me today. It's where I've been all day. Talking. We went to see Reverend Cook."

Betsie shifted in her seat. "He went back without seeing us?"

Annie bent over and hugged Jiddy. "News indeed! So, you put in banns?"

"Not yet. Reverend weren't about."

Betsie folded her arms. "So, you'll be moving to York." Jiddy nodded.

Annie glanced at Betsie. "Won't he come back to Bay?"

"He can't until he's made a master mason." Jiddy forced another laugh. "And besides, he's in love with the Minster's angels!"

"Told you," said Betsie.

"What do you mean?" asked Annie.

"It's obvious. His da is an old man. Andrew's been offered a place up there. With help, grant you, but who knows? He may want to settle down and have a family at farm."

"Betsie!" said Annie, "You are thinking ahead!"

"Oh, shut up," said Betsie, although a smile hovered on her face. "I'm only thinking where's Jonas to go if he does want to come back. Where'll he live, and what'll he do here?"

"He can live with Jiddy, right here at Fisherhead!" Annie squealed. "He'll leap at chance. You've got to ask him, Jiddy."

"What'll he do?" said Betsie. "He's not a fisherman, and there's no place for him at farm anymore. Can't see him wanting to run school with Annie-bobs here."

Jiddy traced a finger over her knee. "There's nothing to fret over," she said. "I'm going to York. We'll live there."

A gust of wind whispered around the chimney.

"But…" began Annie, "Do you want to live in York?"

Jiddy clasped her hands together. "'Course I do. Jonas is training to be a stonemason at the Minster, and then he'll get an important job. It's not like building a wall at farm. He carves angels and saints out of stone. You can't learn to carve a person's face so easy." She clicked her fingers, recalling the ancient figures that had stood looking down for hundreds of years. "I'm right proud of him. We'll all have to go to York together and you can see what he does. It's beautiful!"

Betsie and Annie stared as if they didn't understand her words.

"It's not any apprenticeship," she reiterated, "it's York Minster. They don't take on any old body to work there.

You have to be really gifted and clever, and it takes years to learn."

"He's really never coming back, is he?" said Betsie. "Which means you'll never come back."

"I don't know about that." Jiddy pressed her lips together. None of them spoke, taking in the finality of her words.

Betsie prised herself to her feet. "You know what?" she said as she pulled her shawl over her head. "Jonas is right to stop in York, and Violet's right clever to have got a job at the Vardarelli shop, and you should wed Jonas if he's asked you and go there too and not give us in Robin Hood's Bay another thought."

Jiddy rose from her chair. "Betsie, you said it were all right, and you've got Andrew and—"

"As I was saying," Betsie cut in, "Violet and Jonas are both clever to have got themselves jobs. Andrew, Annie and me are stupid ones for stopping here." She marched to the door, pausing on the step. "You coming, Annie? I want to say night to your Andrew before I head on home. Some of us have to get on with our lives right here. Some of us don't have opportunities others have dropped in their lap."

The door banged. Jiddy prodded the fire, sending up sparks.

"Is that what you feel?" she asked.

Annie shrugged. "Betsie's just upset Andrew's taking so long, but she is impatient, as we know!" She smiled, eyes sparkling with tears. "None of us want to leave Bay. We don't really understand why anyone would."

The fire glowed orange and gold, throwing out a gentle heat. Jiddy closed her eyes, still seeing the bright colour through her eyelids.

CHAPTER FORTY-FIVE

S quire Farsyde stood in his late wife's dressing room. After a few moments, his attention wandered to the window before he eyed the cupboards again. Jiddy waited, listening to Kate Ashner's footsteps descend the stairs. The squire still didn't acknowledge her, although she'd been standing there for several minutes. He walked to the window as if expecting the arrival of a visitor.

Jiddy wasn't sure what she'd expected, but it wasn't the rush of emotion at seeing the squire in this particular room. The room had been tidied, leaving no visible sign of dressmaking or femininity on show, and the adjoining door to his wife's bedchamber remained closed. It didn't stop the flood of memories. A few jewellery cases stood on the table, and the closet door had swung ajar. She clasped her hands, readying for the squire to tell her that her services were no longer required. She'd expected it, but not so soon. Not here, where she'd spent so much time.

It didn't feel right to mention Violet or Mr. Ashner, as she had come to the hall to do, or to ask the squire for the assistance he'd always been so ready to offer.

Crows from the high trees cawed. As if that was the sign he'd been waiting for, the squire finally turned around. His face appeared puffy and pale. He ambled to the closet, grasped the open door and stared inside. Moments later, he strolled to the large chest in the centre of the room and lifted its lid, heaving it open as if it weighed more than he could manage. Jiddy glimpsed a blue gown inside, the one Mrs. Farsyde had worn at the ball Squire Farsyde had given in her honour. She readied to hear an instruction, a dismissal, or some words to help her understand.

Instead, the squire dropped his head. The sight of his slumped figure brought a desire to speak. If only she could find the right words. Crows alighted on the treetops, and the discordant flurry of sound became unbearable.

"Sir?"

Her voice roused him, and for the first time, he registered her presence. His eyes held a mixture of a child who'd lost a beloved pet and the bemused expression he'd shown when she'd handed him the baby. And another too—the confusion he'd aired at the ball when surrounded by men of the county. Ambushed by pity for him, Jiddy took a deep breath.

"I came to let you know Violet Ashner has settled in York," she said. His confusion deepened, and she took a step backwards, towards the door. She shouldn't be witnessing such grief. "D'you want me to leave you? I can come back later."

Her question stirred him. "I want you to have what's in here," he said, gesturing to the chest, "and what's in the closet."

It was Jiddy's turn to be bemused.

"Billy is bringing another chest to carry everything to Fisherhead," he said, "but I wanted you to check through them here first."

She stared at the gowns with their folds of rich fabric. "These are Mrs. Farsyde's."

"They can't stay here," he snapped, faltering as he tried to hold back sobs. "Who else should have them?"

"Keep them here! I mean," she lowered her voice, "your daughter, when she is grown."

He shook his head and, hands behind his back, returned to the window.

She closed the closet doors. "They are safe here. There's no rush to make any decisions about them."

Turning swiftly, he marched back to the closet and swung open the doors again. "I want you to empty it when Billy brings the crate," he shouted, his voice harsh and unexpected. "He'll be along soon, and you can do it straight away. I want the chest and whatever is in here gone!"

"But they are the family's. Wouldn't it be better to take some time?"

"If they are here, I will think she is coming back!" He glared at Jiddy until, unable to maintain eye contact, he strode to the table beside the window.

She looked at the gowns again, unsure what to do or say. She'd never have reason to wear gowns such as these, but she couldn't contradict him. A thought sparked. She could unpick them and make new gowns.

351

"I will make sure they are packed," she said. "Should I go and see if Billy's arrived?"

The squire's face had taken on the confused expression again, and he fingered small boxes stacked on the table. "Do you know what these are?" he asked.

The sight of the velvet and leather cases filled Jiddy with dread.

He opened a casket. "You must take this as well." Jiddy stepped back. He held out a small wooden box. "Here."

The sight of Mrs. Farsyde, pale and lying dead on the rock in the cave flashed in her head, and she retreated further, until the chest blocked her path.

He walked towards her, holding out the box Jiddy had given to Violet.

He held it out. "This is yours, I believe?"

She flattened her palms. "But I gave it to Violet Ashner."

The squire thrust it at her. "She left it with me before you took her to York." He opened the box. The diamond brooch Mary had buried for years under the white stone at Thomas's grave sparkled. "Take it," he said. "Captain Pinkney gave it to Mary for you, and you should have kept it. He wasn't such a scoundrel, after all, and Mary saved it for you."

She shook her head in disbelief that Violet had given it back. Closing the box, she held it to her chest. "I thought Violet would need it," she said.

He cleared his throat. "Good, that's settled."

Jiddy thought of all the times she'd visited the grave with Mary and never guessed what treasure was hidden there. Captain Pinkney had tried to look out for her, her entire life, and she'd repaid them by giving the diamond away. But it had come back. Violet had given it back.

Standing at the table once more, the squire picked up several boxes and placed them on the top of the gowns in the chest. He glanced at Jiddy. "I bought these from Captain Pinkney for a pittance. He paid nothing for them. They're yours as well."

Her hands trembled. No-one would believe his actions, not even if he relayed them himself.

"I'm sorry, sir, but I can't take those," she said. "Your daughter must have them when she's grown. A mother's belongings always pass to her daughter, not to an outsider. Not to me. And gowns too, if I'm to speak truth. There is a fortune in them. They can easily be altered if fashion changes."

"Hang the gowns. I will not gaze on those again!" said the squire, his voice cracking. "The jewels do belong to you. They were your mother's. I merely bought them. Your mother…" he cleared his throat. "Mother to daughter, you said so yourself. Some matters don't change." Easing her away from the chest, he closed the lid and strode from the room shouting, "Billy!"

Jiddy stared at the window, focusing on the black iron holding the panes of glass. The squire's footsteps resounded on the wooden floorboards. Noises filtered up the stairs. Now wasn't the time to mention Violet again and ask him to let Mr. Ashner know his daughter was content to remain far away from him in York.

She jumped. The squire leaned on the doorframe. "Billy is on his way," he said. "Now, the jewels in particular." He rubbed his hands, a flush of pink on his cheeks. "You'll need to hide them and not tell anyone. This is particularly important. I know secrets aren't easy to keep in Bay, but for your safety, you must. At least Captain Pinkney's place must have plenty of hiding places no-one knows about. Don't tell me, but find one and put these away."

She startled at his practical instructions. It wasn't right; it was far from right.

"It's true," she said. "Secrets in Bay are impossible to keep, so please store it all here. Everyone will see Billy with these chests, not only here but in Bay, and do you imagine kitchen maids and stable hands and everyone who works here will be able to keep it a secret? No-one carries chests into Bay, and everyone here at hall has family in Bay! It'll be like pointing a big sign at Fisherhead and shouting, 'Come and see treasure!' I'm sorry, sir, but I can't. Don't you see? I can't do it!"

She waited for him to see the sense in what she said and the absurdity of carrying not one, but two trunks full of treasure to Fisherhead. There would be no hope of keeping that a secret, not even if Billy carried them in the middle of the night.

"What I can do is take one gown at a time," she suggested. "I can use it to teach girls how to make alterations, and it can be sold or passed on, but they will be useful for lasses to learn."

She waited while the squire walked to the window. "One at a time," he said, raising a hand. "If you take one jewellery box at a time as well, it will work."

She joined him.. "I will put them away carefully here," she said. "You don't need to see them, but they need to be safe."

The sound of Billy dragging a chest, banging and scraping and muttering curses made them turn around.

"Take it away!" Squire Farsyde shouted, marching to the door before pointing to the chest. "Choose one," he said. "Then get it out of my sight!"

***

On returning to Fisherhead and climbing the stairs, Jiddy closed the panel in the upstairs room and held her hands against the wood. The line of slats ran evenly along the wall, without a sign of a hidden chamber.

Captain Pinkney had been as expert in creating secret hiding places as he had at finding them on ships. The gowns along with all the other jewellery boxes remained at Thorpe Hall, and the little box she had secreted under her skirt had been out of sight. Kate Ashner had seen the chests opened again and would tell the cook and midwife and all the maids and anyone she saw that the squire wanted all trace of Mrs. Farsyde out of his sight in rooms he would never enter again.

The squire may keep away, but Jiddy would enter as she always had. She would transform some of the gowns, use the fabric for her students to learn how to re-paste into a new design. It would all make sense, and the squire's baby daughter would not be cheated out of her inheritance. It was enough that Jiddy had her own gown, given to her by her birth mother and kept safe in her own closet.

But the diamond brooch burning in the dark behind the wooden panelling would remain hidden until it was needed. Captain Pinkney had wanted her to have it, and Mary had kept it for her. She owed them to use it wisely. The red and ochre gown from her mother lay on the bed. It needed a little work, but it would suit as a wedding gown. The gown and the diamond brooch would ensure she and Jonas could wed straight away. It was time. She touched her belly. Was that excitement she felt?

CHAPTER FORTY-SIX

She didn't expect to be shown York's underbelly so brutally now she'd decided to live there. It wasn't about the noise; she'd heard filthy words, guttural insults, gobs of rage plenty of times in Bay. She'd seen beatings, battering; the sight of Gobbit or rather the flattened, unrecognisable pulp of his body, beggared into the ground, but never the extent of the scene that erupted. How could a grand city with a towering Minster and glittering opulence like Vardarelli's also be so savage? Whitby had its stocks, Pickering and Helmsley too, but York stocks had to be witnessed to be given credit. Jiddy stared at the faces of the people nearby, ugly with anger, or rather some form of twisted superiority. She shrank from the cruelty in the throng.

It all centred around one person. A woman drooped in the wooden clasp of the marketplace stocks, cap trampled on the cobbles revealing greasy, greying straggles of hair and glimpses of cloud-like face, cut and smeared with brown, red and green. An accordion emanated cheerfulness and fairground flavour, at odds with the menacing glee of the crowd.

A sludge of colour flew at the woman's head, followed by a battery of shapes. Tomatoes, rotten spuds, stinking cabbage and sods of earth. The entire area around the stocks stank with greening eggs and vegetables. A dog cocked its leg against the wooden structure.

Excrement splattered into the woman's face as it landed on the ground directly in front, but she didn't flinch. A shriek of laughter. A rigid cat, long dead, hit hard. This time, the woman shuddered. Jiddy yelled out in protest, but her voice merged with yells of encouragement. The ground, already littered with missiles, steamed, while the woman, suspended between the cuffs and neck brace, hung her head.

"She's only been here an hour," someone said. "Not going to give us much of a show."

The crowd raised their arms, a barricade of shoulders closing in. Jiddy's heart pounded. She didn't usually walk away when a mob attacked a person, but the number of people here held her back. She'd seen the same look on the faces of Nellie, James and Betsie when they'd flung fistfuls of stones at Gobbit from their high position on the bank. Baytowners could be brutal with pans and ladles. They could wound. They could kill. But to trap a woman in the stocks so she couldn't defend herself or even run, that was a city punishment. And what could you do when held by the weight of those planks and locks you couldn't pick?

She could still hear the accordion from streets away; the Minster's pinnacles pierced the sky. Angels and saints, stony-faced, gazed with blank eyes, high above the crowds and the stocks. Unmoved. Jonas created statues like that. Curls and chiselled roses, windows without glass. Gargoyles protruding ugly with laughing mouths.

Without emotion, these stone effigies surveyed the scene in the square below.

Clogs, boots and shoes clattered noisily as the crowd nudged back to normal lives, to their stalls and errands and their everyday business. Dropping back her head, she gazed at the white sky. Voices and the chipping of stone grew louder. She smelt damp straw and horses. This was no place to remain. She meandered slowly, distancing herself from the scene of the stocks, but it was difficult to avoid the masses. The market stalls smelt of fresh bread. Daily needs met. Trade. Normality. She side-stepped a couple of women and wove around three gentlemen. Pleased with herself for navigating more expertly, she jumped suddenly at the sound of a blacksmith's hammer. For several minutes, she enjoyed the regular rhythm and the smell of the fire. There was work here and ordinary people going about their business. And Jonas. They could still visit Bay and she'd smell the sea and feel its breeze from time to time. She took a deep breath. She could hear Betsie's voice. "If you love him, you'll do owt."

She watched the flounce of her skirt and the appearance and disappearance of her boot caps as she walked. The thought that the woman in the stocks could have been wearing similar boots and a similar skirt and could have walked through the marketplace smelling bread and hearing the blacksmith's hammer struck her. Women behind the stalls, bare hands grabbing apples, bread, bags of dried fruit, open palms taking coins, busy, busy; women passing quickly, slowly, loitering, standing still.

The woman in the stocks could have been any of them. Could be any of them. All it would take was the wrong word spoken to the wrong person, a mistake, a moment of forgetfulness, absentmindedly taking a piece of fruit or a roll of bread, being in the wrong place at the wrong time or looking at the wrong person in the wrong way.

She turned a corner into a narrow street. What was the matter with her, thinking in this way? She shook herself. Too much time on her hands. She needed to concentrate on work. Vardarelli's could be the starting point for her as well as Violet. *Violet.* The squire had said she didn't want thanking for returning the brooch, but Jiddy had to thank her.

She breathed in the scent of rosemary, thyme and other herbs as she entered another market square. The bright stripes of a canvas tent caught her eye and a scratching voice cut through the babble. Laughter caught her attention. Of course, York had many faces, and she needed to see them all, the fun and good as well as the bad.

Amidst the rumble of noises, another voice rang out, discordant, harsh. "Where's the baby?"

"Excuse me?" She leaned towards a girl standing against a wall, selling sprigs of lavender from a tray suspended around her neck. "What's happening?"

The girl, eyes sharp and small, flickered for possible customers. "It's fair day," she said.

"But who's shouting?"

The screeching voice cut in before the girl could answer. "Sausages!"

The voice, if it could be described as a voice, seared across the yard, followed by laughter and a smatter of applause.

"What's funny about sausages?" she asked the girl.

A loud thwacking of wood hitting wood rang out, followed by more laughter. This time, the girl looked at Jiddy. "It's Punch," she said. "He's always here on fair days."

"Who's Punch?"

The girl eyed her as if she were stupid. "It's a penny to watch show," she said.

Jiddy didn't have a penny, not for a show or a few sprigs of lavender, but she strolled to the edge of the crowd anyway. A striped canvas booth with puppets bobbing in a picture frame held the crowd's attention.

"Who's a naughty boy?!"

A garish figure with brightly painted cheeks, a huge beaked nose, frilled collar and triangular hat burst into animation. Jiddy squealed, and a gentleman nearby, his attention caught, made his way to her side.

"No need for alarm," he said. "Mr. Punch can't leave the booth."

She eyed the smart hat and jacket and boots and stepped sideways. Tapping his cane on the ground, he sidled beside her, dropping coins into a hat a small boy held out. Punch waved a long stick, cracking it on the counter until another figure appeared, a woman, equally garish and beaked.

"Mistress Punch," the man explained.

Before Jiddy could respond, the stick came down on the female puppet's head, not once but several times, the sound of wood on wood echoing out.

"Ow, ow, ow!" cried Mrs. Punch.

"That's the way to do it!" declared her husband.

Thwack, thwack, thwack. Laughter. Shouts. The man too close at her side.

"He's hitting the woman," she said. "What's funny about that?"

The man leaned closer. "It's funny," he said, "because it's his wife."

CHAPTER FORTY-SEVEN

S weat pricked Jiddy's neck.

"It's only a joke," reassured the man. "Punch is outrageous. He turns the world on its head, and you can't possibly take him seriously."

Rows of children, heads tipped back, stared at the battering of Mrs. Punch. "Young bairns shouldn't see this," she said.

One little one, facing the crowd, had tears brimming his eyes. An elder sibling, noticing, scooped him up, jigging him on her hip. Adult laughter ricocheted when a dog appeared, and Punch swapped hitting the wife for hitting the animal.

"I don't understand," Jiddy addressed the man at her side, who guffawed at the antics. "If he keeps hitting the dog, it'll either bite him or he'll kill it."

"He's hitting the dog because it's stolen the sausages," the man explained.

"But dogs will steal meat if they smell it. Why have puppets make a fuss about it?"

"I suppose it is odd if you've not seen the show before," he said, and after a quick glance in her direction, "Punch and his friends have perhaps not reached the provinces yet...which is where you reside, I presume?"

Jiddy walked away, but the gentleman followed. "I don't want to watch a man hitting his wife and his dog," she said, "even if they are puppets and not real. City folk are strange, and yes, I'm from provinces, as you call them, and proud to be."

"I thought you weren't from York." He touched her elbow, and she jerked it away, eyeing him suspiciously.

"Good day, sir. Thank you for explaining show to me."

"I feel I should put your mind at ease," he said, still keeping pace. "Everyone knows they themselves can't act with so much violence, and no-one we know is painted so vivid or is so wildly dressed, which is what makes it so entertaining. Some may secretly wish to hit their wives over the head with a wooden baton, but they'd never go to such extremes as Punch. It's a parody, designed to poke fun and make people laugh at the absurdity."

She rushed on, her skirt flapping, determined not to ask what parody meant, though from the rest of his words, she could tell he was trying to justify the violence.

"Thank you. I understand people in York have an odd sense of humour," she said. "*Good day*, sir."

He laughed and for a moment, she gave him her attention. "You're funnier than Punch!" he declared. "May I introduce myself?"

Something about the man made her uneasy, and Jiddy bobbed a curtsey. "Thank you, but if you'll excuse me, sir, I must be on my way."

"He's merely a naughty Punch, but I think you are—"

"I don't reckon you may say who I am," she interrupted, glancing about. She didn't recognise the street, and there were few people around. Distant laughter told her they couldn't be far from the marketplace, but she wanted to return to the familiarity of the Minster square and find Jonas.

He raised his hat. "I am at your service if you would allow?"

She hated to admit she needed help. "I need to get back to the grand church, the Minster," she said. "Can you direct me, please?"

He raised his cane, giving it some thought, before lowering it again. "It so happens, that is where I am headed."

He waited. The street stood deserted but for them. Jonas was expecting her. She nodded.

They walked the length of a narrow street. The noise of Punch faded, and in the quiet, with only their footsteps, she began to wish she could still hear the screeching voice and wood hitting wood.

He strutted now, tapping his cane with each step, but it wasn't a comforting sound as of the stonemasons. This tapped with menace. "Did you know the very first Punch came from Europe?" he said. "It was Bologna or Pisa or maybe Naples, somewhere a long way from England."

Questions tingled on her tongue at the name Naples, the place of her mother's birth.

"It's this way." He pointed to his left. "A Signor Gimonde, his name was, anyway. A puppeteer.

He invented the character," he continued as if they were out for an afternoon stroll. "Punchinello, he called him, and we have shortened the name to Punch! I think we've given him a more memorable name, don't you?"

Jiddy couldn't believe it. The gentleman wouldn't stop talking; not only talking but lecturing her.

"On second thoughts," she said, stopping abruptly. "I'd like to head back to the square and give him a second chance."

"Certainly, this is one foreign entertainment that has caught on, for the masses of course, hence appearing at the marketplace fair. If you want to see him again..." he paused, the cane held to his mouth.

She waited. "Why were you watching if it was for the masses?" she asked.

He laughed. "I was watching you."

Unsettled, she stiffened. "Why?"

"I was intrigued." Lowering the cane, he tapped her shoulder. "You're a little different from most of the young women who come to the fair."

She stepped back, feeling the wall strike her shoulder blades. Still no-one appeared, and voices remained distant. "Thank you for your time, sir," she said, "but I can find my way now."

The cane shot across her chest, barring her path, and she gasped.

"May I suggest you find your way to showing a little respect? A country girl or, if I'm not mistaken, a foreign girl, should offer a gentleman some gratitude when he has shown her kindness."

Jiddy could tell immediately her stare unsettled him, but it also incited his cruelty. She'd been rash, stupid. She'd never have acted like this in Bay. Even in Whitby, she knew to be canny, but here, where she should be most vigilant, she'd trusted a stranger. No Baytowner trusted a stranger. If she ran, what if she cornered herself? *Don't show fear, Jiddy. Whatever you do, don't show you're afraid.* She didn't doubt the cane, like Punch's baton, could give him the upper hand.

She smiled. "You're right," she said, "I am from the country, and if you'd tell me more about this Punchinello, I can take something of the city back with me."

She hoped he didn't see the nervous flutter on her mouth or her eyelashes twitching with apprehension. He studied her, and she had no clue which way he'd choose. A battering and an assault or what she hoped he'd presume would be a better choice.

He lowered his cane. "The Feathers has a good reputation. I can tell you more about Punch while we dine. A much more pleasant approach, wouldn't you say?"

She nodded. The Feathers stood off the marketplace, a coaching inn she had heard of, and she'd find her way from there. At least there would be other people at hand.

They didn't speak as they walked. He didn't need to charm her now, and she didn't need directions. Voices grew louder, the smell of people and food grew stronger.

She sensed the pressure of bodies ahead and the excitement of people gathered. She sensed his confidence too.

If she held her nerve, she would soon be in the throng; she'd use people as shields, be able to ask for directions, and find the way to the Minster and Jonas. Not long now. A few more turns.

"What time does your coach leave?" he asked.

His question took her by surprise. "Not for a few hours."

It pleased him. The barrage of noise drew them both to a halt. They must have retraced their route. Punch screeched. People guffawed. She made in the direction of the voices, but he shunted her sideways, and she stumbled. His hand gripped her wrist, guiding her towards another street leading off the marketplace. Away from the crowd. She had to act quickly. His grip tightened. Too soon, they stepped away from the throng and into an alley.

"Help!" she shouted.

"No need," he said, gripping her arm tighter. "I am merely making sure you don't stumble again, my dear. Ah! Here we are!"

Gentlemen and tradesmen stood in the inn's doorway, and they passed between them. Faces leered, mouths flabby and wet. The smell of ale and meat enveloped them. Voices loud, guffawing and men's backs, a solid wall. Inside, the dim light cloaked figures hunched at tables and standing along the bar. He guided her to a table by a window in a corner and gestured for her to take a seat. A couple sitting at the next table shifted, hats disguising their faces, to another table, raucous with too much beer. A row of backs blocked the doorway.

He raised his hand and a serving girl approached. "Beef," he said, "and wine."

Jiddy placed her hands on the table. No charm touched his lips or eyes. He saw her only as a country girl. A foreigner. An item to be taken.

The girl put down the wine and two cups. He took a large swig before filling her a cup. The serving girl retreated. She must only have been thirteen at most.

Furtively, Jiddy scanned the overcrowded room. Voices loud, people bent in on each other. Screaming wouldn't be enough. He'd hush her before anyone worked out the direction of her cry. And why would she scream? They were dining on beef and wine. People in places like this took no notice, and he was dressed like a gentleman and she like a country lass.

"I'm beginning to understand about Punch," she said as he took a second drink. "Or Punchinello, if that's his real name? It doesn't really matter he were from Naples or Bolly, Boligna, does it? But that it were a man who invented him?"

He leered, making her recoil. "Only a man could have invented Punch or any of the characters we see in plays," he said.

She bowed her head. Make him think he were right. Make him believe he ruled the room, the marketplace, the whole of Yorkshire.

"Yes," she agreed. "Only men can invent a puppet like Punch."

He frowned, his hand on the bottle, unsure whether she was complimenting or insulting him. She smiled to reassure him she thought he was in control. Jonas wouldn't have fallen for her flattery, but this man was no Jonas.

The sight of the girl carrying the plates across the room distracted him. Jiddy followed his gaze. The girl wove past tables filled with other diners, all intent on their food and not noticing anyone else or what others did. Closer, closer, she came. This was her chance. Perhaps her only chance.

"I understand now," she said. "Gentlemen like watching another man, even if it is a puppet, hitting his puppet wife. Must be what all gentlemen secretly wish to do." She smiled and raised her glass, clinking it against his. "Should we toast to humour of great men?"

He smiled back and took another swig.

The girl presented his plate first before leaning across the table to set down the second plate. Blocked from his view, Jiddy took her chance. She slid from her seat, behind the girl. Squeezing past tables, she rushed, and tripping on a chair leg, she saw him waving his napkin like a flag of surrender, his face contorted as he yelled. The young girl froze. Jiddy grabbed the chair back, levered herself along, past tables, past diners, a row of impenetrable backs blocking her escape.

"Stop her!"

Three men, big farmers, red-cheeked and beer-swilled, leered. She shoved through, determined not to be stopped, shoulders and elbows sharp. Someone grasped her arm. She jabbed the man in the ribs. Grumbles. A discordant shout. Raised voices. Finally, an open door and fresh air. She ran into the crowded street. Free.

CHAPTER FORTY-EIGHT

By the time she found the Minster yard, Jonas had packed his work tools and stood tapping his feet. "Where've you been?" he asked, swiping up his bag.

Jiddy spread her arms. "I hate York!"

"All right, tell it as it is," he said. "Fill me in."

"City people!"

Straggles of figures meandered around the yard. Jonas slung his tool sack over his head, the strap crossing his chest. "Didn't any of these kind people give you a job? You might have to go see your mother after all."

"I didn't get there," Jiddy stamped over the ground. "Got waylaid, didn't I?"

Jonas hurried behind. "What d'you mean?"

What was there to say? She shrugged. "I got a bit lost in maze of streets."

He laughed. "Bay lanes are worse," he said. "Many a visitor gets lost there."

She smiled. Nodded. Yes. That's what the higgledy-piggledy lanes were all about. "It don't matter," she said. "You know me. I get a tad stroppy when I'm tired."

"Come on," he said. "Can't have you missing your ride back to Bay and risk you causing a riot here. It's good to see you, thanks for making trip, but it's a long way and costly if you've not done what you planned to do."

She forced a smile. "I planned to come and see you, didn't I?"

They fell into an easy walk, bumping shoulders every now and again. The river could have been a sea it stretched so wide between banks. Boats of all sizes sailed past, weighted by cargo and teeming with grimy boatmen.

With each step, she tried to still the panic fluttering in her belly. The entire day had unsettled her, and she didn't know how to put it back in order. She glanced sideways at Jonas. He looked as tired as she felt.

"Can we stop and talk for a minute?" she asked. "I saw a show in marketplace. I didn't like it. Have you seen it?"

He followed her gaze and caught Punch's shrill voice. They listened for a minute until Jonas shook his head. "I'm not keen."

It all poured out. "A gentleman started talking to me," she said, "and he told me the man who invented Punch might have been from Naples." She let out a sigh of relief to have begun. "I hate what he said."

"Because someone dared speak to you, or because Naples is where you're from?"

She pulled a face. "I can only hope women from Naples are more pleasant than men."

He smiled and wagged his finger. "Well, I've only seen show once, but even so, I can tell you're better-looking than Punch. I give you that."

"I meant..."

Punch's voice sliced to the river. Jiddy thought about the baby and the dog and the sausages, and their hard wooden shapes hitting the wooden frame of the striped marquee.

"Do you ever wonder how certain men can behave like they do?" she asked. A long boat sailed past, its deck almost at water level. The river was crammed with vessels, darkening the water and sludging the banks. "It made me think about Napoleon. He's a monster, isn't he? That's what folks say, and he's from near Naples as well, isn't he? Both him and Punch do what they want and batter people into submission, don't they?"

"I'd hate to be in your brain," smiled Jonas. "Let's get you to inn and we can hang around there before you turn York into a battlefield as well."

She sighed. "Show were dreadful, and gentleman that told me about Punch were an odd fish as well. I'm not keen on York folk."

"Punch is a puppet to make people laugh," said Jonas. "He can't hurt anyone. And this chap, he's probably an outsider if he's at fair watching a show like Punch. Napoleon is real, though, and he's no-one's puppet."

"I don't like any of them."

"What's this about?" Jonas said, touching her hair. "What's going on in this bottomless cavern of a head of yours?"

She pulled away, smiling ruefully at him. "It's where it all began, isn't it?"

"In your head?"

"With falling out! Hurting each other! War! Our government putting tax on salt and stuff to pay for fighting

Napoleon. If they hadn't done that, we'd not be standing here, would we?"

"I can't keep up!" Jonas laughed. "But taxes started before Napoleon. I know we're always fighting France, but we fought America as well."

"But it affects us," she said, pushing back the desire to shout. "Shows like Punch. War and duties on goods. They make folk desperate. They make us do things we might not otherwise. I know it's against law, but can't law be wrong sometimes? You know what I'm talking about. I'm talking about smuggling!"

"Hey, shh." Jonas took her arm. They descended worn steps towards the riverbank. "You've got to be careful," he said, staring at her in disbelief. "You can't bandy such words around anywhere. What's wrong with you?"

Jiddy let out a long, slow breath to stop herself shaking. "I've not eaten all day. I get jitters when I'm hungry."

Jonas shook his head. "Let's get you to the coach. Didn't you bring owt with you?" He rummaged in his bag and pulled out a small hunk of cheese. "Here," he said. "Eat this." She munched slowly, struggling to swallow. "Better?" She nodded. "Right, no more talk of war and government and rest."

She grabbed his arm. "I want to say I'm sorry. It's my fault you're here, and I'm sorry. So, so sorry."

He laughed, fastening his bag. "I'm happy here. Don't worry about it. You've nothing to be sorry for."

She held his arm again, forcing him to take her seriously. "It is my fault," she said. "If Captain Pinkney hadn't given me my first bag of salt, I wouldn't have gone in cave and found skein of silk, and you wouldn't have hidden it at farm and wouldn't have been arrested. Unfairly. And you having to leave Bay."

Jonas scuffed the ground with his boots. "I'm not sure what you're trying to say."

Jiddy didn't know if it was fear or fatigue or excitement fuelling her, but she couldn't hold back her train of thought. "You left Bay!" she announced, her face lighting up as the idea struck her.

"Always said you were the brains."

"You left Bay," she continued. "Both Punch and Napoleon crossed seas and explored other places. And you're all men." He smiled. "No!" she said, feeling her heart race. "Why don't we hear of women who've left Bay or crossed seas?"

"I'm sure some have." Jonas hitched his bag over his shoulder. "You're coming to York. Your mam left France and before that Naples."

"But you don't hear about it! There are no shows about them! You don't hear about them leading armies, do you?"

Jonas frowned, and a trickle of dust sprinkled his face. "I don't think so," he said, wiping it away.

"Makes you wonder what we could do if we dared to, doesn't it?" She brushed her hand over his face, powdering more dust. He tapped it away.

"What's point you're making?" he asked.

She strolled to the water's edge. Two men on the nearest boat threw a bucket full of peelings into the water.

Jonas was the most intelligent person she'd met. He'd talk to her about whatever caught their interest, about why there were wars, about how wars were paid for. He had ideas, and he wasn't afraid to share them. The thought of all their talks made her chest hurt.

"I miss our times together," she said.

He touched her shoulder, and she faced him. "Then stay in York."

"What, now?"

He nodded, and she closed her eyes, not wanting him to see how much she wanted to stay with him.

"I can't," she whispered. "My work is in Bay. I can't come."

"Open your eyes." The softness of his voice made tears well, but she opened them. She loved his face, every expression and imperfection. He cupped her cheek in one hand. "What's wrong?" he asked. "What are you worrying about?"

Confusion filled her head, cramming out words, jamming her heart and head with a glut of emotion.

"I'm thirsty," she said.

He squeezed her hands as if he saw through her bravado. Tears swam in her eyes, and the knot in her stomach tightened. *Stand still. Don't move. Ever.* Water splashed the bank as a boat ploughed past, voices distant, their calls from the boats slapping the river. Punch had stopped shouting.

"Why are you going on about Naples?" he asked.

Hot sunshine and the bright colours of orange and gold and a sea bluer and warmer than any she'd seen in Robin Hood's Bay. It was part of her, maybe a small part, but an important part. It made her a foreigner. It meant she came from somewhere other than Yorkshire. It lived on her skin and in her eyes. The master stonemason and the gentleman in the marketplace had seen it. Samuel had found it out. Lord Ryethorpe had seen it in her mother, and he saw it in Jiddy. And she felt it.

She touched his cheek, soft with its shiver of hair. "I'm the best I ever can be with you. You make me wittier and funnier and more the me I want to be than anyone else can ever do."

He swallowed hard. His eyes begged her to keep talking, and she did.

"It's not like you want to change me. I'm not saying you do that. You bring out what is there but make it brighter and shinier." She paused, picking at the mottled weave of his jacket. "Am I making sense?"

He nodded, his eyes now a sea of liquid, and he leaned his forehead on her shoulder. She stroked his hair, twining the thick locks between her fingers and then stroking gently and holding his head in her palm. "I love you more than Mary, Jonas, and it's dreadful of me to say, but it's only way to describe it. I loved Mary completely, but you—you're in jelly under my skin. You're in my bones and my nails, up my nose, under my armpits!" She laughed tearfully.

Squeezing her close, he rocked his head against hers. "What do you want me to do?"

She couldn't stop the tears. A boatman threw slops into the water. The sounds of the carts and hooves and people shouting continued as if there was nothing momentous going on by the river.

She pulled his arms around her waist so they stood close together, and she smelt the powdery scent on him and the suggestion of other things she couldn't explain. "I wish we were still young bairns playing at water's edge," she said.

"We've changed, Jiddy. We've both changed. We're not children on beach anymore, turning sea water into salt."

"Or tasting salt on each other's tongues."

"Which you hated."

She studied his face. "I got lost in back streets," she said. "That's what's wrong. I couldn't find my way, and I got frightened."

"When we wed, you'll change again." Uncertainty cracked his voice.

When we wed. The words seeped into her brain. When. If. *If* they wed, she'd have to give away her independence, whether Jonas wanted her to or not. Move where he went. Betsie would. Annie would. Nellie would have leapt at the chance. She loved Jonas, but it meant she'd have to give up all the choices she'd made to be who she was now. All her dreams. That was the law.

As it stood, she owned Fisherhead. If she married Jonas, or any man, they would own her property. They'd own her and any bairns they may have. She hated the Government more than ever for making such a law. She'd seen firsthand the women of Baytown, how they changed when they wed. And when bairns came, mothers didn't have time to raise their eyes above the doorstep. There would be no horizon, even if they lived in Bay. She and Jonas wouldn't have time to linger in their kisses, but oh, as he opened his lips against hers, she realised why other lasses surrendered their freedom.

She felt his deep intake of breath. *Love me*, it said. She kissed his cheek, feeling the soft hair against her lips. All trace of salt had gone.

CHAPTER FORTY-NINE

Jiddy stepped down from the coach and listened to the faint hush of waves. She'd thought about Jonas for the entire journey across the moors, seeing his face in every tinge of undergrowth shrouding the land. She hadn't mentioned the diamond brooch that would mean they could wed. She hadn't mentioned the red-and-gold dress she could wear. And he hadn't said anything when they left the riverside. His face, so solemn as the coach pulled away, had spoken volumes.

"I love you," he'd whispered.

Walking towards Baytown from the Buttercross, she stared at the lowering sun over Ravenscar. A haloed orb hung between heaven and earth.

Jonas was right. The view of the Bay never changed. The same rooftops tottered towards the sea and South Cliff towered into the sky. She caught smells of fish and brine. After the city odour of densely populated streets, of people's crowded living, of bread and markets and women's perfume, the air smelt like home. She inhaled again. In moments like this, there was nowhere she'd rather be.

But she couldn't stand and admire the scene forever. Descending the hill, she reached the first cottages and cut left along a narrow row.

"Kate! Alfie! Home before dark!" Mrs. Fletcher stood on her doorstep, looking sideways along Bloomswell.

"How do, Mrs. Fletcher," Jiddy said as she strolled past.

"Oh, Jiddy, love," the woman called her back. "We were chewing over what you said about our Sarah. We don't mind, I suppose, if she comes to learn a bit of stitching with you of a Saturday afternoon, or if needs must, a Sunday after Chapel."

The woman yelled for her two youngest again.

"All right," Jiddy said. "I'll tell Annie and Betsie."

Shouts for children to come inside rang out in all the ginnels. Children didn't readily respond. Mary had stood on the step at Sunny Place, beady-eyed while Jiddy had always hated leaving Jonas and the beach and playing in hidden corners. It had become Jonas's job to march her to her door at sundown.

"Ta, Jonas," Mary had always said.

At the time, Jiddy thought she was the one who should have been thanked for acquiescing to return. When she'd finished her tirade, for which Jonas stood there, patiently waiting, Mary always smiled and, taking Jiddy by her scrawny shoulders, manoeuvred her through the doorway.

"Ta, Jonas!" Mary had always repeated.

Jiddy merely grumbled, but Jonas grinned. *Funny what you remember*, she thought.

It showed nothing changed in Bay. A couple of other women stood together on Silver Street.

"Gilly!" shouted Mrs. Baxter, all frizzy hair and rolled-up sleeves. "Get yourself in!"

The women ceased their gossip. "How do, Jiddy?" said Dolly. "How's Violet Ashner settling in big city?"

"She's doing grand," Jiddy said without stopping.

"Can I have a word?" One of the women had followed and touched Jiddy's arm. "As Violet Ashner's doing so well, I thought..."

Jiddy waited while Mrs. Baxter glanced at the gaggle of women huddled in on themselves but listening to every word.

"It's been a long day," Jiddy said when she could wait no longer. "Is there anything I can do for you?"

"There is." Mrs. Baxter leaned in. "Our Gilly is desperate to join your...school? I can't say no to her, can I?"

"Gilly wants to learn to sew now?"

Mrs. Baxter nodded.

Jiddy trudged to Sunny Place and reached the corner of the Openings, where she stopped to take in what the women were asking. Sarah and Gilly would be learning to embroider ladies' purses and cut out dress patterns after all. The tumultuous effort of installing Violet at her mam's emporium had been worth it. A large gull landed on a rooftop and preened its feathers. More girls would be taking jobs. They would have opportunities. She let out a long sigh and her shoulders relaxed. She'd have to tell Annie and Betsie they'd be welcoming a few more keen stitchers.

"Evening," she said to the woman who sat cradling her baby on the top step of Sunny Place. The woman's shining eyes struck Jiddy. Curling a straggle of hair behind her ear, the woman raised the baby to her shoulder and kissed its forehead. It gurgled.

"I've got to feed this one," she said. "Would you mind seeing if you can fetch my young'uns from beach? You're familiar with them, aren't you?"

Jiddy still wanted to call on Annie, so she hesitated for a moment.

"'Course I know them," she said and instead of heading across to the Bolts, she continued towards the dock. Molly's and Jane's mams were out on the roadside.

"Back from York?" asked Molly's mam. Jiddy nodded. Whole of Baytown knew where she'd been.

Standing on the slipway, she stared out to sea. A silvery line hung over the horizon, and the sea glowed pink and gold with the dipping sun. Bay women trusted her with their daughters, and their trust made her feel as bright as the evening sky. Big Isaac, Abe, Sandy and many others trusted her to find out information they couldn't get from preventives and officers, and they trusted her not to blab about it. She, Annie and Betsie had their own secrets binding them. She looked along the dusky beach. There were little ones playing catch and chase and messing about all along the shore.

As she'd done. As Nellie and Annie and Betsie and Jonas had done. As Andrew and his mates had done. She hugged herself. The children's voices and flurry of moving figures jolted so many memories. She'd forgotten. "Take it in," she told herself.

She'd grown so used to the quiet of a deserted beach, searching for driftwood to burn, or later, for bodies, first for Nellie's greening corpse, then the sea-battered preventives, and finally, barely recognisable, Samuel. She couldn't bear the sight of the cave where Mrs. Farsyde had died and had spent less time since, gazing across the water, but now, hearing young voices, she remembered how she loved the shoreline. Crunching over the pebbles, glancing at the sloping land and at the placid waves, she spotted Sarah, Gilly, Molly and the older girls, shawls loosened and caps dangling. The neap tide served them well in the evening for their strolls while keeping an eye on their siblings.

Spying a small group gathered along the shadow of the cliff, Jiddy headed towards them to see if any of them were from Sunny Place.

Like them, she'd spent half her life on the beach, most of that time with Jonas. The little group were a mix of Graingers and Storms, and she passed them by. They ignored her, and she smiled. She'd ignored her elders as a child. She caught sight of the cave where Captain Pinkney had handed her salt and where Mrs. Farsyde had given birth. She shook her head. She was growing soft, crying at the slightest thing as old women did. She had children to find. They played in twos and threes, not one on their own. She wondered if Captain Pinkney happened to chance on them, would he pick any of them to initiate into smuggling as he'd picked her. She'd learned the power of salt and of a pistol thanks to him. Who amongst these young ones could say that? He'd left her Fisherhead Cottage when she could have been homeless.

The sun, now a golden ball balancing on the cusp of the clifftop, created a silhouette of Ravenscar. Jonas loved sitting on the tops rather than the beach at this time of day.

"You get better view from here," he'd say.

She had never agreed, preferring to see the colour of pebbles, the wet sheen of seaweed and the intricacies of crabs up close. On the beach, she could study the light making shadows in the shallows for hours. They'd fought about what gave the best view, but she'd admitted he had been right when you wanted to see into the distance. When you wanted to believe other shores existed. She squinted at the waving grass against the sky. You really could see further and wider and dream bigger on the tops.

A trickle of soil cascaded down the cliff, and she turned her back on the cave. Not only had it been the scene of her initiation into smuggling and both birth and death, but it was also where she'd found the ream of silk that had started the whole turn of events for Jonas leaving Robin Hood's Bay. If only she'd left the contraband material be, Jonas would still be at the farm with his da. But finding the silk had also meant Jonas now lived doing what he loved doing. Would he have felt the same staying at the farm? If anywhere could convince her that Jonas had made the right decision to leave Baytown, it had to be that cave. She'd thought it a bad thing, now she saw the possibilities it revealed.

It was time to fetch the Sunny Place youngsters, and then she'd go home to Fisherhead and a fire and her supper. It would be too late to call on Annie and explain to her why she was leaving the ochre-and-red gown she'd been given in London to Betsie.

Following small footsteps in the sand, she walked towards a boy and girl sitting at the water's edge.

The girl pointed. "How long does it take to reach over there?"

The boy cupped water in his hands. "Two weeks," he said.

"How long would it take if you were on that ship?"

Jiddy raised a hand to shade her eyes. A full-sailed schooner sat on the water as if waiting for its crew. She smiled at the boy's confident answer of two weeks. Two weeks on a ship would be an adventure.

"Do you think there's two Frenchies sitting on a beach over there, wondering about us?" the girl asked.

The young lass couldn't have been more than six or seven, wild, unkempt flaxen hair, skinny arms and legs and a brown skirt, dark with wet, clinging to her thighs. The boy, older and angular, had rolled up his trousers and squatted rather than sat. He let water trickle through his fingers.

"Doubt it. There's a war on over there," he said. "And my da says we shouldn't be giving our money for soldiers to fight when nobody's asked us if we want them to."

"Why do they need money?" the girl asked. "Is fighting a job? Their master should pay if it is. Who's their boss? Is it Squire Farsyde?"

The boy splayed his hands in the shallows, watching his palms sink into the sand. "I think it's King George."

Jiddy stood near enough to see the freckles on the girl's nose. Facing the water, they wouldn't bother about a grown-up strolling past them. To them, she'd be of no consequence. The boy squished his palms further into the sand, and the girl stood, skirt sticking to her legs. She raised a hand to shade her eyes, as Jiddy had done. She wondered if she should explain war to them, as Jonas had explained it to her, but instead, she watched them; she liked they were working it out for themselves.

"You wouldn't catch me fighting people I don't know," said the boy as he stood up. Side by side, they both squinted into the darkening sky.

"How much money do we give King George for letting us fight?" the girl asked.

The boy examined a shell. "Da says we pay him by not having things we need." He turned the mollusc over. "It's his treasury, I reckon. They call it duty, or some such word."

"How do we know we need things if we don't have them?"

Jiddy smiled. The girl was clever.

"It's something to do with taxes," the boy said, "but you wouldn't understand."

"I would."

"It's tricky."

He sounded exactly like Jonas.

"Tell me!" the little lass insisted.

He sighed, making a show of it. "Tax makes goods cost a lot, so only rich people can buy them," the boy said, nodding his chin in emphasis.

"Like what?"

The boy threw the shell back into the water. "Da says it's not as bad as it was, but them who make laws are daft. He says they've finally worked out making things cost more makes folk so desperate they'll do owt not to starve, so king's going to...what's word?" He paused, biting his lip. "Lower! That's it. He's going to lower them duties."

She looked again at the schooner anchoring in the distance. An unlikely sight, to be resting near the shore. Brazen, if it was carrying salt or brandy, right under king's men's gaze. These little ones weren't stupid. They listened. Even if they didn't call it smuggling, Bay folk had found ways to get what they needed.

"You don't talk sense," the girl said. "Do we have what we need or don't we?"

"They used to burn fish on beach because fishermen didn't have enough salt to preserve it. You don't see that no more."

The lad also understood what Government had failed to grasp for years. These two really could be little Jonas and Jiddy. She touched the mound of her woollen scarf and knotted it across her stomach. Clouds hung in deepening bundles and gulls created wheeling specks. The sound of splashing water caught her attention. The boy kicked his legs. Spray sparkled into the air.

"Mam says it's flour costing too much," the girl said, following him.

"That's different. Da says it's greedy landowners copying King George, only instead of salt, they don't want us to have bread."

The two walked further, brushing against each other, talking continually. Friends. Jiddy liked they were friends. They meandered on the shoreline, deep in their childhood world of shell collecting and problem solving. She glanced again at the horizon. The ship rocked peacefully between sea and sky. A lone figure stood on the ship's deck, and Jiddy squinted to make it out. A tricorn hat and a long black cloak. She gasped. The cape wafted on a gust of wind like a sail. The hat turned. The ship's captain stared directly at her. And she knew.

That night, she'd open the hidden panel in her bedroom and take out the small wooden box holding the diamond brooch. She'd lay out the red-and-ochre dress on the table for Betsie with a note wishing her wedded bliss. Annie would know. Annie, like Jonas, already knew. By the next morning, before anyone woke, Jiddy would be standing by the sea skipper's side, on the deck of the schooner, and sailing towards the horizon, heading for a new adventure. She'd be the only lass in Robin Hood's Bay to sail off for new shores. Songs would be written about Jiddy Vardy and sung at dusk and around the lanes when tramping home from a fishing trip or by children wending their way homeward to bed. It was what she'd always wanted since carrying her first bag of contraband along the ginnels. She took a deep breath. Whatever happened, good or bad, it would be her choice.

At dawn, she'd walk towards the causeway, the rising sun setting the horizon aglow. It was as if she'd been waiting for Captain Pinkney to return, and she'd only realised this when she'd seen his ship.

She strode quickly until she noticed three small figures huddled together. Recognising them as the young ones from Sunny Place reminded of her mission, and she hurried towards them, readying to persuade them to leave the attractions of the beach for home. They had made a house in the sand and were decorating it with shells and sticks.

"Hello," she said. "Can I see?" The sand structure, decorated with seaweed flags and curved-shell windows stood solid above a dry moat. "What a grand castle you've made, but your mam sent me to fetch you. You know who I am, don't you?"

They stared at her wide-eyed. "You're Jiddy Vardy," said the eldest.

Taken aback by the girl's reverence, she smiled. "Correct! And you're Bertha!" The girl nodded, her eyes wide. Jiddy turned to the younger two. "Time to go, Will and Maggie! I'll gamble your mam's got your supper ready. Are you hungry?"

The three children nodded, and one by one, they stood. A group of older boys and girls ran past them towards the water.

"Jimmy!" one of the lads called to the boy and girl further along the beach.

"Jessie!" shouted another.

The gaggle of youngsters ran towards the little pair, leaving their footprints in the wet sand. Jiddy felt a punch of sadness in her belly. She held out her hands. "Come on, let's be getting you back safe to Sunny Place."

They took her hands without a word of resistance, making a line heading towards the causeway. Their palms, grained with sand, clung tight. She took a last look. Jessie and Jimmy stood watching Captain Pinkney's ship as the crowd congregated at the water's edge. Some splashed and shrieked in the surf, spraying droplets that sparkled like diamonds.

Jessie scooped a handful of water. After a moment, she squealed, and her voice pealed crystal clear. Jiddy heard every word. "Sea tastes of salt, Jimmy!" the little girl shouted, "It tastes of salt!"

The End

ABOUT THE AUTHOR

Ruth Estevez is the author of six novels, a semi-finalist in the BBNYA Awards and the Guest Speaker in the Cheshire Prize for Literature 2023.

Ruth has previously worked as a scriptwriter on the children's TV series *Bob the Builder* and worked in theatre and TV from Opera North, Harrogate Theatre-in-Education Company, Pitlochry Festival Theatre to ITV's *Emmerdale*. She has taught scriptwriting on the Contemporary BA Film and Television degree course at Manchester Metropolitan University.

Ruth is also Project Coordinator for the Portico Sadie Massey awards for Young Readers and Writers, based at The Portico Library in Manchester.

You can contact Ruth on...

Instagram: @ruthestevezwriter
X: @RuthEstevez2
Facebook: @RuthEstevezM
Website: www.artgoesglobal.wordpress.com

BY THE AUTHOR

Erosion

The Monster Belt

Meeting Coty

The Jiddy Vardy Trilogy
Jiddy Vardy
Jiddy Vardy – High Tide
Jiddy Vardy – Full Sail

BEATEN TRACK PUBLISHING

For more titles from Beaten Track Publishing,
please visit our website:

https://www.beatentrackpublishing.com

Thanks for reading!

PLOT SUMMARY SO FAR ...

Ruthless smuggler, Captain Pinkney, boards the England-bound ship carrying Jiddy's mother, Maria Vardarelli. Also on board are Harvey Hartshorn, Maria's lover, along with their friend, Lord Ryethorpe.

Sixteen-year-old Maria has just given birth to a baby girl when the violent Pinkney shoots Harvey and tosses Maria and Ryethorpe into the wild North Sea.

Fighting for their lives, the two finally reach the Yorkshire shore. Maria wears Harvey's coat, its pockets filled with treasure; Ryethorpe is keen to return to his wife and young son, Samuel.

Meanwhile, on board the ship, Pinkney discovers the infant hidden in the cabin. When he sets foot in the insular fishing village of Robin Hood's Bay, where he bases his clandestine raids, he finds the child a home with an elderly couple. And so Jiddy's life unfolds.

Always the outsider in this close-knit community, black-haired Jiddy grows up defiant of the other children's wariness and curious about who her real family may be. A Romany king and queen? Royalty from distant lands?

A local farmer's boy, Jonas Chaplow, is her closest ally, and an unlikely friendship eventually turns to love, while local lass, Nellie Ashner quickly becomes Jiddy's nemesis.

Years later, a new preventive, Captain Samuel Ryethorpe, ordered to root out smugglers robbing the Government of its levies, turns Jiddy's head with his charm and gentility. Nellie, too, looks beyond the Bay for a new life, but her actions end in tragedy for herself and exile for Jiddy. It seems Samuel is on Jiddy's side, and he accompanies her to London where she is finally reunited with her birth mother, now the wealthy owner of a department-style store. But it is Robin Hood's Bay and Jonas that hold Jiddy's heart, and she cannot stay away for long.

In book two, with Nellie dead, Jiddy's friendship with shy Annie Briggs blossoms. However, the complications of finding out the truth of Jonas's real father send Jonas away, far from Jiddy's love. Angry at his sudden departure, Jiddy throws herself into the Bay's violent and dangerous smuggling activities. It is not an easy route, with preventives ready to raise a fist to women as well as men. Even Samuel, whom she thought she might love but has rejected, turns to another's arms and punishes her at every turn. When Mary, the woman who took her in, dies, Jiddy is left destitute and at her lowest ebb. At this point, Captain Pinkney returns from his travels. At Mary's bequest, and driven by his own guilt, he offers Jiddy his home.

Spring is a time of high tides, and the sea does not care whose life it takes, rich or poor, man or woman. This time, it is the life of Samuel Ryethorpe it has taken, and Jiddy is the last person to see him alive...

Printed in Great Britain
by Amazon

32796610R00233